Tales from the
StarBoard Café

By
Richard Herr

PRANKISH
PUBLICATIONS

Copyright © 2014 Richard Herr
All rights reserved.

ISBN-13: 978-0-9912981-6-7

AUTHOR'S NOTES

Welcome to the StarBoard Café, the best intergalactic watering hole in the space lanes. Pull up whatever kind of furniture your species uses to support itself and imbibe on whatever soporific matches your metabolism from the galaxy-wide menu. Just be a bit careful about offending the patron resting next to you. It could have a large appetite.

Something always happens when I write a book. The characters rudely shove me out of the way and navigate the book in the direction that they want it to take. I had started out to write a collection of short stories told by a diverse group of creatures in a particular setting, the Café. However characters in one story kept insisting that they needed to have conversations with certain characters in other stories. I tried to reason with them and tell them that they should mind their own business; since this was a short story collection, they should recognize and stay within the boundaries of their own tales, not go meddling in other peoples' business.

As you will discover, I got shouted down.

There are a number of stories that tumbled out of their individual boundaries and insinuated themselves into other characters' plotlines. I finally dragged most everyone together at the end of the book to sort everyone out and let other characters get on with their lives without interference.

I hope you enjoy their stories, even though they are a contentious group.

There are many people I need to thank for helping me create this book. The very first one is my wife, Deborah, my Alpha Reader, who plowed her way through crude first drafts and made them presentable to polite society. She has also interpreted pantomimed gestures and turned them into actual, solid words. She's always been encouraging. She's also bagged and contained many a bad joke before it was let loose on unsuspecting readers.

I'd like to give thanks to Eric Nelson, my editor, of Rabiner Lit (ericn@rabiner.net) for doing an absolutely super job of pulling my muddled thoughts together to make them comprehensible to people besides myself.

I also want to thank Gary Tenuta at GVTGrafix for the wonderful cover and all of the patience he displayed with an author who had that most dangerous of things: a little knowledge.

I would also like to extend my thanks to the members of Montclair's Write Group and the members of the New Providence Writers Group who helped me in so many ways with the development of this book.

Table of Contents

Prologue
The StarBoard Café — *Page 1*

Chapter One
Diplomacy — *Page 5*

Chapter Two
Uplift — *Page 43*

Chapter Three
Pranks — *Page 51*

Chapter Four
Poison — *Page 83*

Chapter Five
Sister Mary — *Page 121*

Chapter Six
Y'All Welcome in Skintyvil — *Page 131*

Chapter Seven
Troubadour — *Page 157*

Chapter Eight
After Pranks — *Page 165*

Chapter Nine
The Best Policy *Page 191*

Chapter Ten
Good Boy *Page 209*

Chapter Eleven
Patron of the Arts *Page 219*

Chapter Twelve
Pick Your Poison *Page 241*

Chapter Thirteen
El Escorpion *Page 259*

Chapter Fourteen
Joy *Page 273*

Chapter Fifteen
For Applause *Page 283*

Prologue

The StarBoard

Rither Dzo was suffering from what his species referred to as "a failed commercial venture." That meant he was lying on the ground oozing his vital fluids. One should not feel sorry for Rither; had this been a *successful* commercial venture, his opponent would have been lying on the same ground oozing vital fluids.

Rither was physically suited for his kind of "commerce." He didn't so much have arms as armaments, writhing appendages that could inject toxins into any opponent. Therefore, if one wished to disarm him, one had to literally *dis*-arm him.

Usually, when one is shuffling off this mortal coil (or oozing as in Rither's case), one's thoughts turn to an inspiration in one's life: a hero, a loved one, a mother. Not so for Rither. His memories of his dam had not been of a sweet and tender relationship. His mother's first lesson after birth was: how to eat. She demonstrated by scooping up one of his slower siblings and making a quick snack of it. (There had not been time to identify its sex. Newborns of Rither's species had three sexes: male, female, and tasty.) Rither learned quickly from Mommy Dearest's lesson, and initiated a snacking order in the family by grabbing off another sibling and munching on it. For Rither's species, natural selection chose those who emerged from the maternity ward alive.

So, since Rither was not thinking of Dear Old Mammy as he lay there expiring, what were his last thoughts? What was the one inspiration he looked back on? What was the shining light in the fading moments of a creature as craven and vicious as Rither?

It was the StarBoard Café.

The StarBoard was a spacers' bar. There were many such bars scattered about on the planets of the Amalgam of Intelligent Species. They were usually located near the space port. If one wished to find them, it was easy; just head for the noise. Most spacers' bars had one common attribute: brawls. Therefore all sorts of items could be found flying through the air inside one of these establishments: bottles, mugs, knives, bullets, and patrons. Since the flight paths of these objects were random, a certain percentage of them managed to crash through the windows.

That posed a problem at the StarBoard Café. The clientele were the same: spacers. That meant they were the worst group of smugglers, adventurers, cutthroats, backstabbers, murderers, lowlifes, and the vicious and nasty individuals who were attracted to life in the space lanes. And those were just the humans. The aliens had a whole laundry list of vices unique to their respective species, some of them even more vile and violent than those of their human counterparts.

However, outside the windows of the Café was the vacuum of space. Anything crashing through one of them would cause a drop in not only air pressure, but clientele.

Therefore, peace reigned at the StarBoard.

Peace enforcement was in the hands of the current proprietor of the Café and his crew. They were on high alert for any concentration of emotional energy approaching critical mass. Patrons were carefully screened at the entrance to make sure they didn't enter the premises with any armaments. Pacifying the appendages of members of Rither's species required a very clever arrangement. The individual who'd devised that scheme had won free reign in the bar for the following week. She'd lasted a day and a half before perishing from toxic overdose.

The Café's location in outer space made it autonomous. It had no government, no system of taxation, and most importantly, no regulations. Therefore, certain "commercial ventures" could be negotiated at the Café that might have otherwise come under suspicion by more regulatory minds, such as the ones that populated groundside governments. These suspicious minds tried to spy on plans being made (oh, all right, plots being schemed) at the Café to see if these plans/plots might skirt or even cross the lines of the laws. These attempts were thwarted. The booths and tables at the Café had squelch settings that made them impervious to any means of snooping: electronic, mechanical, or organic.

The Café also served as recruitment center for captains forming crews for their ships. The staffing had to be on the up and up. Now usually, spacers are creatures who flaunt the laws of governments. However, once *they* decided to enact a law *themselves*, it was stringently adhered to. One such law was that there was no shanghaiing. On the other hand, persuasion, an art form among spacers, was openly encouraged. The StarBoard served a concoction called a Tirenian Smoothie, a drink that had an alcohol proof in excess of 200. (The inventor of this concoction was a spacer who didn't even obey the laws of physics.) A couple Smoothies, and someone would become amenable to whatever they were offered. If they could remember it the following morning.

Spacers also love to tell stories, real or imagined. Although not an erudite group, they seemed to have picked that piece of literary advice rumored to have come from some human writer: "Never let the truth stand in the way of a good story." That was one of their rules.

Storytelling was such a tradition that the StarBoard Café sponsored a yearly storytelling contest. The prize offered to the winner was carte blanche for a year. A considerable reward, since the prices at the Café were like its location: out of this world.

However, this created certain problems in running the contest. The judges could not be susceptible to bribery, chicanery, sexual favors, or influence peddling, so the judges' selection required strict and careful policing. The word *judges* implies fairness. The word *fairness* implies honesty. This created a grammatical contradiction. The words *honesty* and *spacer* were antonyms. So means were sought to ensure that the judging of the competition was fair. An inducement was offered. During their year-long tenure, the judges received their first drink of the evening for free, provided that said drink did not exceed their own body volume.

Now, since the storytelling went on all year, it could not be trusted that the judges would always be (A) around and (B) sober. Therefore, in addition to the Privacy button at every table, there was a Record button. This allowed the storyteller to record his, her, or its story to make it available to the judges when they were in port and at their most judicious (i.e. sober).

The memory storage for the stories was carefully guarded. This was to ensure there was no repeat of the unfortunate incident that occurred the second year of the competition when a power surge left only one story in memory.

The Café also had an excellent selection of both cuisine and, for clients with those sort of eating habits, prey (The free range chicken came with both chicken and range.) Despite its boisterous character, the StarBoard was a gourmet restaurant.

Chapter 1

Diplomacy

hOrmonde de Mieneur deliberately made his way to his favorite table at the StarBoard Café. hOrmonde was a man of choices. He had a favorite everything: favorite wine, favorite food, favorite plant, favorite planet, and many others. Because of the excellent cuisine, the Café was his favorite restaurant.

"Could I have a Thurmian Velvet please, Rowsis?" He ordered his favorite drink from his favorite wait-being.

hOrmonde had the look of someone who was in the habit of dining well: plump, with an expensive manner of dress. He had the mildly flushed features of one who drank a fair amount of wine with his meal. He had the smug look of someone who knew his tastes and expressed his opinions.

His calculating mind made him one of the best diplomatic agents of the Amalgam of Intelligent Beings.

hOrmonde very purposefully leaned forward to the Record button that would enter him into the Story Competition for the StarBoard Café. Winning the contest could let him dine for free at the Café for a year.

He pressed the button.

RECORD

#

The most insidious lie told by a senior officer to an underling is, "This won't be hard at all."

I know. I've used it hundreds of times myself.

When my Sector Chief told me my new assignment "won't be hard at all," my day turned bad. He was perched up on his work station, staring intently at the display in front of him and working his stylus. The raised position helped to counter the fact that he was about a quarter of my size. However his authority was about a hundred times that of mine.

"I'm sorry," I said, "but, as much as I would absolutely love to take this posting, I'm not in the proper health for such a venture." I thought I could appeal to his better nature.

Mistake. He doesn't have one.

He didn't even look at me. "It won't work, hOrmonde. I made sure you had your yearly physical before you came up here. You're in prime health."

"That doesn't account for the chill that ran down my spine when you told me about this job. Nor the sinking feeling I got in the pit of my stomach. Nor the way my blood ran cold. All those symptoms happened after I arrived here."

"Did you also get a sudden premonition it would be difficult to cure those ills if one hOrmonde de Mieneur no longer drew his very large salary?"

Dear me! He was being severe. He still didn't look at me, staying focused on his display. I decided to switch to pandering. "I don't recall anything of the kind. I did seem to get the feeling that I would encounter the kindliness and beneficence of an immediate superior."

"Let's cut to the chase. How much of an expense account do you want?" he asked.

"Well, I may need a few Credits to keep body and soul together."

"An awful lot of Credits are needed to support *your* body, and your expensive tastes. As for the soul, you couldn't possibly have one or you wouldn't work in the Diplomatic Corps."

And do a damn good job, I might say. "I think there should be a certain standard of cuisine expected for a top diplomat."

"You get the usual budget. It'll be hard enough justifying the entourage you'll drag along to prattle to. What do you need for that staff?"

"I'll need someone for intelligence, someone for translation and opinion manipulation, someone for accounting and security, and someone for entertainment."

"Uh-huh, the usual. A spy, a spin doctor, a briber. I know who all of those will be. And who do you want as a courtesan?"

"Theona."

"You seem to favor her quite a lot."

"She's well adapted to diplomacy."

"And diplomats?"

"Some of them." She really *is* a darling. And so clever.

"Fine. Get your group together, and I'll send you a briefing packet. You leave in three hours."

"Why the rush?"

He turned his gaze away from his display and was skewering me with his stare. "I believe I said you're getting a briefing packet? You remember what those are? They explain everything, so your superior officer won't have to?" His mood had been far better when he was preoccupied. "I can tell you one thing. You have exactly three days to wrap this thing up. Don't let anything get in your way. There's a whole swarm of engineers, technicians, and materiel due to arrive right after you conclude these negotiations. Now get out of here."

"I was just leaving, Your Most Noble Lord."

The moment you hear you're getting a briefing packet, you know you are richly fornicated. The dossier of useless facts will most surely hide some little tidbit in a footnote that will leap up and consume you when you meet it face to face. This little nugget of information will put a lie to the statement that "This won't be hard at all." Therefore, the packet was my first consideration when I entered my stateroom on the ship. The second was reacquainting myself--

"Theona, my dearest, it's been far too long." Her sinuous form curled up against me.

"That's good. It's always best to leave a man wanting more." She certainly did know her business. "What is it you need my help with, hOrmonde?"

"My loneliness, my pet. That, and the way you can be such a

marvelous helper on these ventures."

"And where do I fall in?"

"Into the bed, dearest, where you do your best work."

The moment we started to deploy ourselves for horizontal pleasure, my nose wrinkled. I smelled something. I leapt up.

"Translator to olfactory mode," I commanded. I had the Linguista Mark II handling only auditory inputs. There was a new source that needed translating.

"...want to interrupt you, but I think it would be wise for me to know where the eddies might shift. I know how demanding you are about your team's performance." Even in the artificial voice of the translator, there was the customary serious tone of voice.

"Hello, Phssh." Phssh was my spy. He's quite good as long as he keeps his—rictus--shut. Phssh comes from a gas giant. So he, himself, is composed of gas. Since he can quite literally disappear into thin air, he makes an excellent spy. His basic means of communication is olfactory; therefore he converses by farting. "And so, what burning question required this interruption?" I asked.

"I just wanted to make sure I know which way the currents take us." Whoever designed the translator must have had a sense of humor. His voice sounded--breathy.

Just then Weedil barged through my stateroom door and said, "As the prophet Chummels expounded, 'You do that which you must do. Or you will be done to.'" Weedil was my Spin Doctor and organic Translator. (I keep the Mark II hidden so I can catch what's being said when Weedil's not around.) He was also my second in command, a diplomat in training. He had a rather puckish sense of humor, and he shared my hobby of being an expert on human trivia.

"I suspect you're going to be followed by Chico and Harpo," I said. I thought one's stateroom was meant for privacy, but this one was beginning to resemble *A Night at the Opera*.

"They'll be along" Weedil always wore a smile, a characteristic of his species. You never knew if he was being pleasant or putting one over on you.

"Well, grab yourself a seat before we run out of them. We can have a briefing session, just as soon as the last of us is in attendance."

"What's my budget?" K'Ching asked. She entered abruptly both into the room and negotiations.

I rolled my eyes to the ceiling at her single-mindedness. "Whatever it costs," I responded.

"That's not enough."

"And then some."

"I might make do on that."

"My dear young lady, you can always make do in some way." K'Ching had to use bribes to get by in life. She was not as well equipped as Theona. She was a beetle-browed little thing who hailed from the planet Debenture, where they are all dark and beetle-browed. Her favorite means of communication was frown.

"Now, team, before we all settle down to have a pajama party in here, let's turn our attention to the tri-v display and I'll show you a charming little entertainment called *What the Department Hath Rendered Unto Us*."

"Is there also going to be a cartoon?" Weedil asked.

"This whole thing might be a cartoon. But that's all conjecture. Let's get down to business. We're on our way to Silmus, the primary moon of the planet Gruch." I fired up the display. "Here you see the planet. It's a rather drear place. It has a basic nitrogen/oxygen atmosphere, which means it's compatible with most of us. Except, of course, for Phssh who is his *own* atmosphere. The planet has less water than most worlds of this type, so only about a quarter of its surface is ocean. It's highly volcanic and there's a great variance of elevation, a swing of about twenty thousand meters."

"It has its ups and its downs," said Weedil.

"Mostly its downs," I continued. "Let me start with two of them. They're called the Voment and the Hivent, the local residents. First on our list is the Voment. What the Amalgam chooses to call an intelligent being." I brought up a picture on the display. "They live in the lower elevations of the world where the air is heavy and the gravity is strong. As you can see they are large and muscular. Both species on this planet appear to be saurians, or, if you will, lizards. They are bipedal, like humans, but, unlike reptiles, they bear their young live and breast feed. The second race, cousins to the Voment, is the Hivent. They live in the upper altitudes where the air is thinner and the gravity weaker." I changed the display to a picture of the second race. "These chappies are the same, except they're small and wiry."

"My goodness, they have large feet!" Theona chimed in from her side of the room. "Different from the first ones."

She always noticed such strange little things. I continued with my briefing. "The Gruchers subscribe to that philosophy that seems to be universal among most primitive species: 'If it looks different, kill it.' They've done just that to each other with great relish throughout their history. Since neither race is comfortable in the opposite's ecosystem, you'd think they would be happy to stay in their own parts of the world and leave well-enough alone. However, they're mean-spirited little beasts who thrive on murder and mayhem. So they continuously war over the median regions of the world." I turned to the group. "Now, children, who can tell me why I have been sent to this disgusting little place?"

"It seems like a marvelous vacation spot to me," Weedil said.

"That's right! I'm going to set up a luxury resort on this garden planet," I joined in.

"Ooooh, but I feel there's something else, isn't there?" Weedil asked.

"You're so right, you smart little devil! It seems that the Amalgam has found that the median areas of this planet are just rotten with zymbium, sporting some very rich veins. Therefore, the Amalgam is giving these creatures some technology in the first steps of Uplift because it wants to open some mines."

"How about some land mines?" Weedil asked.

"Not a bad idea," I said. "However the Amalgam feels that it would be best if the mayhem the locals usually conduct could be kept to a minimum. Makes things much easier on the miners if they aren't in the middle of a war." I turned to the assembled group. "Now what am I leaving out, children?"

"Operating costs," K'Ching countered.

"Not quite, but a nice guess. Let me list this lovely planet's social features. You have war, you have murder, you have rape, you have cannibalism. What element is missing?"

"Ooh, ooh, ooh, it's right on the tip of my tongue!" Weedil enthused.

"Time's up! The answer is: you've got to have a religion to sanctify all of this bloodshed. Priests sprout up around wars like mushrooms."

"I knew it, I just knew it!" Weedil burst out.

"Yes, children, religion is there to establish all of the ground rules. One of the first things they prohibited was miscegenation. The two races are capable of interbreeding, but that takes out all the fun. The dictum of the church is that if you are raping the other race's female, you can't enjoy it. It's strictly your religious duty."

"Oh, hOrmonde, they have such a perverted way of looking at things," said Theona. "We could certainly teach them a thing or two on my home planet."

"Yes, they are perverse, love," I said. "Now, here's news. Lately there's been a change on Gruch. Certain liberal elements have sprung up in both the lay and secular parts of the society, and they want to stop the wars to appease the Amalgam. This has forced the conservative wing of the church to put on an act of being kissy-kissy with the new, liberal faction, as much as they hate the thought. The leading houses of both races were due to inbreed their heirs, so the clergy decided to hold a double royal wedding to look like they support peace. Voment will marry Voment; Hivent will marry Hivent. Side by side-- but not touching. They've even decided to hold the ceremony on neutral ground: Silmus, their moon."

"Do you think they're going to accept this peace?" Theona asked.

"Fat chance."

"Oh?"

"My dear, once you find little nasties like these who are hooked on warring, wild horses couldn't drag them away from their bloodbaths. And you can bet your bottom credit that the rush to carnage will be led by the conservative branch of the religion."

"Why are you being sent here?" Theona asked.

"I'm here to welcome in everlasting peace to some creatures that have everlastingly warred. The Diplomatic Corps has a recipe: apply genius and marinate for several weeks. It's quite obvious that these brutes only understand violence and mayhem, so I'll just have to out-mayhem them into submission."

"Do you think that will work?" Theona asked.

"Dear, it's the only thing they understand. So, we have our job. Let's set the assignments.

"Phssh, you are, once more, to be a spy. Check out what's happening with the four wedding parties, the male and female Voment and Hivent. Also drop in on the clergy to see what they're scheming. I feel confident you'll find enough dirt to build another moon to go around this dreadful planet. Whatever it is you smell, make sure you do a computer translation, so everything is stored in verbal and visual media. This will give us a handy record of their double dealings."

"It'll be a breeze," Phssh said.

"Weedil, you are to do just what you always do: spin, spin, spin. You're going to operate as translator. None of these insidious beasts speaks anything but their own worldly tongues. I'll wear a hidden translator with an earpiece. If they think I can't understand what they're saying, they might let something slip in my presence."

"I'm spinning up to speed," Weedil said.

"K'Ching, the moment you're finished with your initial security duties I want you to set up your first level of bribes and start the process of assembling your secondary and tertiary levels."

"Done," K'Ching said, no doubt calculating her skim-off at the same time.

"In the meantime, would you all please make yourselves scarce and leave me and Theona alone to plot our moves?"

"Are you going to be laying out your strategies?" Weedil asked.

"Leave!"

#

We arrived at Silmus and checked into our quarters. They'd given us an entire wing of a hotel. It was designated as an *ambassade temporaire*. Once we'd settled into our rooms, I gathered everyone together in the central area.

"Phssh, K'Ching, start off on your designated rounds. Weedil, come with me to the welcoming audience and act as my translator. We'll talk like diplomats until we're forced to bludgeon these brutes into civilized action."

"What do you want me to do, hOrmonde?" Theona asked.

"Stay as beautiful as you are, my darling. I'm sure I'll come up with something for you to do a little later."

Weedil and I went to the audience. When we reached the throne room, the distrust in the air was so thick you could cut it with a knife. And cutting with a knife seemed to be on everyone's minds. They'd erected a total of six raised platforms to stand on, one each for the two pairs of intendeds plus the two warring factions of the religion. I daresay the platforms didn't vary in height by a molecule. The creatures themselves used posture as part of their communication. There was enough bodyspeak in the room to fill several dictionaries, and none of them nice. My hidden translator was interpreting all of the body language and sending a stream of snarls and obscenities into my ear.

The grooms had set themselves in the dominant position, forward and toward the center of the room. They stood on the front part of the platform in an open display of aggression. The blushing brides were seated on the sides toward the wall, which they faced in an open display of distance toward their intendeds. The members of the priesthood were ranked in the background, where they could carry on their devious little plots. In addition to the six major platforms, a variety of sub-platforms were assembled with aides, assistants, under-ministers and other henchmen in matching displays. The whole arrangement looked like a vertical chessboard.

I dressed my face in my most unctuous smile and said in an Amalgam Anglo they couldn't understand, "Weedil, please tell these ugly brutes I've been dragged here against my will and would prefer to be plummeting into a black hole rather than in their hateful company."

Weedil also painted his face with charm. "The High Diplomat de Mieneur is most honored to be within the radiance of your company and glories in this opportunity to attend this most hallowed of events." He had translated from real thoughts to Diplomatic Speak.

"Also tell them I hope that by some miracle this shadow play will conquer their basically brutish attitudes and bring about something resembling peace. Though I'm sure it will more likely descend into their usual acts of murder, rape, and cannibalism."

"He further says he salutes the great peace that will now descend upon the planet of Gruch, embodied by the cooperation of this historic ceremony."

"And I'm already fortifying my digestive system with every sort of balm so I'll survive the blood-drinking slopfest they're holding this evening."

"He looks forward to seeing you again at this evening's most sumptuous banquet."

"Now, let's get the hell out of here before these monsters decide to devour us as a mid-afternoon snack."

"My lord is very space-lagged and will retire until this evening's festivities."

We raced back to the suite, hoping that we weren't fleeing as prey. Once I had a proper aperitif in front of me, I called a meeting to find out what my staff had learned.

"Well, my crack crew, what do you have to report?"

"This place had enough bugs to feed the entire population of Aviana for a year," K'Ching said, with her customary glower.

"You've cleaned it out?" I verified.

"Completely."

"Excellent. Phssh, what have you found out, so far?"

"They all hate each other."

"Well, in that, they show remarkably good taste. What exactly do you mean?"

"Not only do the Voment hate the Hivent. The women hate their men. They keep talking about how bad their limbs are."

"I daresay that none of them would win a beauty contest. Keep up the surveillance."

I sent them scuttling off about their tasks, which left me alone with Theona. She had a thoughtful look on her face. "hOrmonde, what was it that your Sector Chief told you about this job?"

"Oh, the usual, apply my genius to forge peace among these beasts."

"Wasn't there something else he said?" she continued.

"Oh just management claptrap. He tried to assure me that this job won't be hard at all."

"'Won't be hard at all'?" She pursed her lips as she considered the phrase.

"Yes. As if this were some simple little mission."

"hOrmonde?" She wrinkled her darling little brow. "Isn't there something called the Ramshacle Reverse Theory."

"It's Ramshad's Reverse Theory, pet."

"Oh, yes." She beamed in recognition.

"It states that when you have trouble finding a solution to your problem, you should look in exactly the opposite direction from where you were looking."

"Oh, yes, that." She beamed at me. "Would that have anything to do with this mission?"

"Not hardly, dear. We're dealing with nothing but warring

little beasts."

"Well," she bounded up and began to gather a number of her lotions and salves. "Since everyone else is off spying on these Gruchers, why don't I see what I can find out?"

"What are you doing?" I asked her.

"I thought I might go visit these creatures and use some of my usual methods to relax them. They might let something slip when they're at their ease."

"Darling, be careful. These creatures piously murder, torture, and rape, because their religion tells them to. However, that same religion would start a witch hunt if they found out you're a courtesan. I'll have to construct a charming little artifice. I'll send you with Weedil," I cast a glance in his direction, "and he will convey my compliments, etc., etc., and tell them I have sent my personal masseuse to let them take all of the kinks out of their kinky royal frames." I turned back to Theona. "You can then operate in whatever manner you deem appropriate."

"Let me get changed!" She went dashing off to her room.

I should say something about Theona. She comes from the planet Hedon. She's one of the most renowned courtesans on a world that honors courtesans. She's a top entertainer there, like a poet laureate.

The fact that she will go to bed with just about anyone, or anything, is very logical in her world. They feel limiting her to one partner would be like putting a great painting in a hall where it could be seen by only one person.

She came bustling out of her room wearing a dear little outfit with a pill box cap tilted rakishly over one eye. She was already beginning to use her chameleon-esque attributes to take on the appearance of a Grucher. She flashed a sweet smile at me and went hurrying out. Those poor dolts were about to have their pockets picked and love every moment of it.

"Translator off olfactory." The damned thing was turning everything I said into farts. I settled down with my aperitif and a good book and the contemplation of how I was going to apply my genius to this situation.

"Won't be hard at all."

Indeed!

#

I had been sitting there for about half an hour trying my best to read my book. However, I couldn't muster up the concentration. I was alone in the suite, and the place began to absolutely echo with the sound of inactivity--mine. I was wondering how my crew was doing getting information out of these snarling little beasts to allow us to structure a peace.

I finally pitched the book aside and paced around the room. I was impatient to hear the report. I stopped in mid-pace and realized I wasn't employing my best resource on this job: me. I'd do a little reconnaissance, sure that my keen eye would pick up many subtleties that my staff couldn't spot. I headed out the door of the suite into the hotel proper to see what I could find.

A maze of corridors twisted their way out in front of me in a most incomprehensible jumble. Not only did they veer from one side to the other, they sloped up and down in a random manner. Some things helped. This was a public building, so there were signs on the rooms to identify them. They were, however, in the glot that the Gruchers spoke. I did have the translator to furnish me with the Anglo words for these signs. However, since they were a new race to the Amalgam, the translation programs weren't fleshed out with all the individual colloquialisms. For instance, one of the rooms was labeled, "To Sleep Within the Sun,"

Made sense to them.

My travels took me to another room whose door bore the label "The Wallowing in the Pits." There were two armed guards in front of the door who brought their weapons to the ready when I veered a little toward the door.

"Keep your path in the opposite direction, or I dine on you tonight," My translator furnished me with their warm salutation.

What a way to treat a diplomatic envoy! I'd crack their heads together if I got the chance.

Composing in my mind the protest message I was going to

send their leaders, I continued in the opposite direction, away from the bellicose little beasts.

I travelled down more corridors that resembled a twisting tunnel rather than an organized hallway. I began to get quite confused about my location in the building. A fair amount of time had passed, and I seemed to be getting deeper into the bowels of this insidious, convoluted place. I was not getting any information to further my diplomatic mission. I decided to head back to our suite.

If I could find it.

I'd become so confused by the labyrinthine arrangement of this building I was at a loss to figure out where I was and in what direction I should go.

I made my way along into an area that was not as finished as the rest of this hotel. The walls were bare stone. The floors were unfinished and rough. I stumbled over one irregularity and caught my balance against a hanging that covered one wall. My hand felt something behind the curtain that turned out to be a door with no identifying sign on it. An unlabeled, hidden door meant that inside there were undoubtedly secret schemes being plotted. I carefully opened the door and slipped into the room to see what I could discover.

There was a wall covering within the room, hiding the doorway from this side. This had to be some extreme hush-hush place. I heard someone in the room speak over my translator. "Then we can divide up their plump leader into fine edible portions."

"Yes, but you have to make it appear that it is some rebel group, plotting against you." I heard the translation of the words in the Gruch language, but I also heard the voice that spoke those words. Through long experience, I recognized who it was.

It was Sneeth, a distasteful little creature I'd run across several times in my days. He was always poking his nose into places where he had no business. His long, sinuous neck served that purpose very well. If he was here, he must have heard about the mining resources on Gruch. He was undoubtedly trying to get the nefarious group he represented in here to scoop up the zymbium and charge the Amalgam an enormous markup for the ore. He posed the kind of interference that could slow down or even block the negotiations I was sent to negotiate.

I eased forward to hear more of their conversations. However I stumbled over one of those irregularities in the floor that littered this area and tripped forward, pulling the wall hanging down in front of me. I caught a quick glance of Sneeth in cozy conversation with one of the priests of the Gruchers. My view was cut off as the arras fell down over my head.

When I pulled the drape off my head, Sneeth had already managed to whip out the other doorway to the room.

I decided that the best defense was a strong offense. "And what, may I ask, are you two filthy beasts plotting?" I demanded of the brutes in what I remembered later was plain Anglo that the Gruch couldn't understand.

"Kill him!" Sneeth's voice commanded from the far room.

I reached the diplomatic decision that now was not the time to try to use reason, so I turned on my heels and bolted back out the door, watching my footing this time. On the far side of the doorway, I ran directly into the concealing drape in the hall and pulled it down in a jumble on the floor. That was good planning as the two guards who pursued me fell fang over claw over the thing.

It afforded me a little bit of distance. I raced through several turnings and twistings of the hallway, then came to a door labeled "Where One Learns Many Things." It had to be some sort of information office open to the public. I barged on in before my pursuers could tell where I'd gone.

The interior was hotter and more humid than outside; there was a slick of condensation on the floor and walls. This entry room was quite empty. Several doors led off in different directions, but I didn't trust what convoluted turnings they might take.

"Hello? Is there anyone here?" I called out.

A female Grucher's head poked through one of the

doorways, looked at me, quickly retracted, and she shouted out, "Guards, come here and rid me of this loathsome alien."

Several of the beasts, toting hideous-looking weapons burst through another door and headed toward me with murderous intent.

"What is it that you brutes intend to do?" I demanded. Of course the fools couldn't understand my Anglo.

"Stop what you're doing!" A female commanded from the doorway of the first room. The order came in through the translator into my ear.

"hOrmonde, what are you doing here?" The same female asked me in Theona's voice. She was hurriedly wrapping something like a robe around her body as she dashed up to me.

The two brutes with the weapons growled their displeasure at being thwarted in gutting me. The female--Theona, obviously--turned back to them. "You fools! This is the diplomat from the Sky People. If you hurt him, you would have your *jeng-jengs* torn off!"

I didn't know what *jeng-jengs* were, but that sounded very uncomfortable. Theona turned back to me and started pushing me out the door. "hOrmonde, we've got to get right out of here. I've stood those guards down for the minute, but they'll quickly regain their aggressive manner."

"But if we leave," I said, "there's a couple more of the brutes chasing me around out there."

Sure enough, when we stepped outside the other pair of guards dashed toward us with their fangs dripping saliva.

Theona injected herself between them and me and said, "What do you fools think you're doing?"

"This one was spying on us," said one of the beasts jamming a digit-like thing in my direction.

"This is the diplomat from the Sky People," Theona said.

"It does not matter," the other brute said. "It attacked us."

"What is going on, Theona?" a female Grucher emerged from the door behind us. She wore one of those robe-like things Theona had put on. The two guards averted their eyes and suddenly became very respectful.

"Your Celestial One, the diplomat from the Sky People has lost his way, and these two seem to think that he was spying," Theona said to her.

"Do you know him?" the female asked.

"Yes, Celestial One, I traveled with him to aid in whatever way I could."

The female reached a hand up to stroke Theona's shoulder. "If he is responsible for bringing you here, then he is welcome."

"But, Your Majesty..." one guard started to protest.

"I have spoken," the female said with great authority. "Or perhaps you don't value your *jeng-jengs*?"

These *jeng-jeng* things seemed to be the coin of the realm.

The female turned to Theona. "You will conduct this diplomat back to his quarters."

"As you wish, Celestial One," Theona bowed to her and turned and started heading me down the hall.

She hurriedly navigated me through the twistings in the hallways, back toward our suite. As she traveled her body slowly transformed back to her normal appearance.

"Well," I gruffed, "I wanted to find something out about these beasts, and I most certainly did. I ran into Sneeth here. I'm going to have to cram a treaty down the Gruchers throats, before Sneeth gets his little paws on them."

"hOrmonde, I'm very peeved with you!" she exclaimed to me.

"What?"

"I was in the process of discovering many interesting things."

"You were?" I was puzzled. "But you were in there with-- well, without any clothes on."

"Of course. If you're doing an interrogation, pleasure will earn you quicker answers than torture. Creatures are far more ready to talk when they are in rapture." I started to harrumph a reply, but she continued. "But you had to come charging in there, interrupting what I was doing! You forced me to leave my outfit behind. I did so love that little pill box hat," she fretted.

I started to stammer my apologies, when we arrived at the door to our suite. Theona shoved me inside. She seemed afraid that a Gruch building maintenance crew would come along looking to eat whatever was in the hallways.

"There!" she said. She turned and headed toward her room. "Let me go put on another outfit. hOrmonde, you just relax and let all the rest of us do our work.

I sat down, fussed about what I was going to do about Sneeth's presence.

#

A little later, Theona came out and started giving me the results of her interrogations.

"It was most amazing. I'd noticed it when I first saw the creatures, but I didn't think the telltales would carry over to this species."

"What're you talking about, dearest?"

"The small ones, the Hivent? I had noticed that they had rather large feet, but I didn't pay much attention to that," Theona said.

"Much attention to what?"

"Well, you know the old saying about how the size of a man's feet indicates the size of his member?"

"You mean the little chappies are well endowed?" I asked.

"They certainly are!" she replied.

"You know that?"

"hOrmonde, I definitely know that," she said with all of the assurance of a trained professional.

"Of course, how silly of me to ask."

"But the larger ones, the Voment? They have very small feet."

"You know that, too?" I asked.

"Yes. But there is a definite mismatch with their women. The small women are small, and the large women are large," she explained.

"You know *that*, too?"

"Yes."

"My poor angel, you've been working your fingers to the--ahem--bone."

"Well, I wanted to be thorough."

"And so you were."

"That's why the women are so sullen," she explained. "They know their sex life is going to be miserable. One is going to live with continuous soreness, the other with continuous dissatisfaction."

"My goodness, what is that?" I said, wrinkling my nose. "Did they have some very strong-smelling scent or cologne or something?"

"Why do you ask?"

"I smell the most dreadful--Translator to olfactory!"

"—RMONDE, CAN YOU SMELL ME?"

"Yes, Phssh, I can. What is it?"

"They're going to assassinate you."

"Which ones?"

"All of them," Phssh replied.

"All of them? You mean both of them."

"No, all four of them. Both races, both sexes."

"Well, my goodness, I am popular."

"Actually, it's the priests, the conservative ones, they're putting them up to it. They're blowing the parties in the direction they want."

"I see. Well, the plot thickens. By the way did you happen to run into our old friend Sneeth?"

"Yes."

"Was he part of the plots to have me rubbed out?"

"Yes."

"Phssh, make sure you convert all of your spyings into aural and visual recordings. I'm sure we'll need those records to do a little blackmailing.

"One other thing, when you reported earlier that the females were complaining about the size of the males' limbs, did you mean their members?"

"Legs, members, what's the difference?"

"I guess nothing, Phssh." I paused and reflected. "But sometime I'd like you to explain to me how it is that you procreate."

At that moment K'Ching came slouching in with her report. It was the same. "They're all planning to assassinate you."

"Who?" I wanted confirmation.

"The grooms, the brides. They've hired assassins."

"I hope this will put to rest the rumor that I had the easiest job here. Who's behind all of this?" I asked K'ching.

"The old priests want to start an incident. They want to have everyone blaming each other. It'll ignite the wars again. The priests are also dealing with some other parties."

"That sounds like our friend, Sneeth." I pondered for a moment. "Well, it looks like we'll have to raise the alert status. We'll now move into bashing a peace treaty through their skulls. There's that, and we also have to take care of our friend, Sneeth. Theona, is there any way you can use your marvelous talents to influence him?"

"Oh, hOrmonde, I'm afraid not. He has absolutely no tastes for anyone of my gender."

"That's true enough. He's always dragging around some male cub of his race that he's debauching every chance he gets." I wheeled around to the rest of the group. "All right, group, this is the war plan for beating these beasts into submission..."

"hOrmonde, wait a minute," Theona said. She turned to K'Ching. "Have you started negotiating bribes with the assassins?"

"I've already got three of them under contract. The fourth

one is still niggling over the vid rights."

I rolled my eyes to the ceiling.

Theona said to K'Ching, "Well, do your best."

"Now, exactly when is it they plan my imminent demise?" I asked.

"Tonight at the banquet," K'Ching said.

"Well, that's definitely the last time I eat at their place! When exactly do they intend the act?"

"Right after dessert."

"Good, I absolutely hate dying on an empty stomach. Well, what'll we do? I'll obviously have to come up with some excuse why I can't attend this banquet."

Theona pondered in thought. "hOrmonde, K'Ching has these assassins on our payroll?"

"Well, yes, dear, but..."

"So you'd be under no risk if you went to the banquet?" she continued.

"But I don't see what good..."

"What would happen if it appeared that you *were* assassinated?" she asked.

I nodded. "They would immediately launch all of their nasty plans..."

"And we'd have Phssh's record of their plotting?" she led me on. Theona raised a single little finger to her chin. "Remember that Reverse Theory thing? What if what your Sector Chief was wrong?"

"That's foolish, pet. That doesn't make any sense," I said. "However the idea of catching these beasts out in their plots is a good one." I swung around to my Briber. "K'Ching, get the killers under contract, the usual boilerplate." She went scurrying off. "We'll also have to show Sneeth's dealings in this. He could really foul up the works."

"Actually, hOrmonde, this might offer a wonderful chance for you to go underground. You might be able to bring peace to this planet." She brought her hand to her mouth in embarrassment. "Oh dear, How did I just spell that?" Some funny little thought was circling around through her brain.

"Absolutely! This is a wonderful plan of mine," I trumpeted. "Now, I need to relax to prepare myself for this very trying evening. After all, I am scheduled to die. Darling, if your fingers aren't entirely worn out, could you please administer one of your delicious massages?"

"Certainly, darling." Theona moved toward me. She suddenly gave out with a little giggle. "I wonder if the solution is that this *will* be hard?"

Why was she fixated on pure nonsense?

#

We all paraded to the banquet. I wanted the full retinue with me when my alleged assassination took place. I'd need all the hands I could muster to spirit my earthly remains off before anyone got a good look at them.

The Gruchers were all settled in for their evening of gorging and killing. I'm opposed to murder in general, and when it's my own, it particularly peeves me. The beasts were still calling each other the worst things with their body language. However, their spoken manners were nothing but immensely, tensely polite.

The walls of the dismal place were strewn with hangings that were meant to be artistic. They offered an endless depiction of mayhem and murder. The different warring groups were on raised platforms again. This posed a problem. Apparently the approved posture for dining was to lay supine. However, the beasts kept trying to get their heads higher than their opponents. They were craning their necks in the most uncomfortable fashion.

It was time to play translation games. I stood and smiled all around, hoping to get the Grucher's minds off their murderous little plans. They barely paid attention to me. "Weedil, please tell these brutes I sincerely hope that what they're going to serve me will not be trays filled with the most loathsome carnal slop."

"The Ambassador wishes to express his delight at being able

to taste the rare treats of the Grucher cuisine."

The evening then proceeded to be exactly what I feared it would be. I managed to find a few tidbits that wouldn't do their best to erupt back out of my stomach the moment I swallowed them. There were some other hideous things they considered fine delicacies I was forced to accept. What an inestimable joy to watch my dinner crawl weakly around my plate! I eventually found the opportunity to pitch the stuff behind a curtain. I later discovered I'd managed to toss it all over one of the assassins we now had on our payroll. It cost us an additional fee in cleaning charges plus court costs.

Yes, court costs.

I caught several glimpses of Sneeth, as he sneaked about the place, swerving his long neck around to whisper into one creature's ear, and then the other. He kept poking his nose around and plotting his plots. He also appeared expectant, like he knew I was about to be assassinated and was waiting to enjoy the event.

I turned to Theona, who was curled up next to me, picking over the food. "I'm worried about Sneeth. We can hoodwink the Gruchers with our little show here, but he will undoubtedly try to poke his nose into things, as he always does."

"You're quite right, darling." She turned her head to address the air. "Phssh, dear, you know that conversation we were having about Sneeth?"

"Yes," came in over my translator.

"Why don't you do that thing we talked about right after we pretend hOrmonde is killed."

I wondered what she had been discussing with Phssh, but I didn't have time to discuss this with her, since it was time to stage our little show.

Thank heavens I was in compliance with my own sham killing. Any trained bodyguard would have spotted these assassins and had them lying twitching on the floor in seconds. It seems that, of the lot, the best were the Hivent, the little ones--the chappies Theona had noticed had large feet. Apparently, the Voment were incredibly clumsy and noisy. They couldn't manage the job without the victim wearing earplugs. Our four boys in uniform kept peeking out from their hiding places trying to figure out when they were supposed to strike. K'Ching kept waving them back. Once, she had to get up and give them food to eat while they waited.

Finally, it was time for that famous singing group, The Four Assassins, to perform. However it seemed they'd overeaten and fallen asleep in their hiding places. I had to send Phssh to wake them. Let your imagination dwell on how he did that. They finally came leaping out from their cover in one synchronized moment, to fire upon my poor, unsuspecting self with their fake weapons, and I slumped forward onto a section of the table I'd cleared just a few moments earlier. This was the cue for our next level of hires to come bustling out of the kitchen and drop the trays of slops they were carrying to cover the departure of the assassins.

My team was prepared to extract my remains at a fast rate, before anyone noticed anything funny. Plus we had to distract attention from the departure of the boys on our payroll. However, all of this was covered quite wonderfully by Theona, who raised her arms to the ceiling, overflowing in her grief.

Right out of the top of her gown.

Every eye turned to her. I could have done a cakewalk out of the room, and headed back to my quarters to sit around having tea with my alleged assassins, and no one would have noticed.

Needless to say, Theona's incredible charms didn't register with Sneeth. He started to dash forward to check my remains and deliver a *coup de grace* in case I still stirred. However he ran into an area that Phssh had seeded with an acrid-smelling vapor that sent the little sneak reeling back with his eyes streaming with tears.

The group hauled me off to the suite, where I hid behind closed doors.

It didn't take long for representatives of the various Grucher groups to come rushing up to serenade us outside our doors by shouting claims against each other as the guilty parties. Sneeth was with them, trying to poke his nose past t[he door to see] what was happening.

Weedil met them at the front door, his fa[ce grim] and somber. His physical actions contradicted h[im as] he kept pushing Sneeth back into the crowd ou[tside to keep] him from peeking inside. "Ladies and gentlem[en,] please excuse us from joining in any discussions [on th]is tragic event, and we further admonish you from also pursuing this path, since that would violate the strict religious tenets as laid down by our late ambassador's religion, the Celestial Church of Elvis." The lad was inserting some interesting overtones. "There must be seventy-two hours of prayer and devotion prior to the entombment of his remains. Until that time we must adhere to the strict observance of all of the religious rules of his sect. I will give you a total list when it's finished printing, but be assured one of them is to not carry out any business--" he cast his look around the gathered group--"*any* business, during that time. That most specifically includes the investigation of the cause of his death. Any violation of these rules would be looked upon as a transgression of etiquette even worse than his murder."

Weedil closed the doors and left the twits standing there. We waited for K'Ching to clear the suite of the new bugs that had been planted during our absence. Then we started making plans.

"Now that we have a moment, I want to muster all of our forces to confront these brutes. We'll have to operate fast before Sneeth schemes his nasty little schemes with them. We'll confront the Gruchers with our evidence of their double dealings," I declared. "We'll show the clergy the recordings of their dirty plots and force them into alignment with our plans. The only language these beasts understand is force and aggression. We'll stand them down."

"hOrmonde," Theona said, "do you think we should be openly aggressive with these creatures? Won't they just naturally launch into battle?"

"My dear Theona, how else do you think I can bring these brutes to their knees?" I asked.

looked up at me. "Oooh! What an apt phrase!" She paused. "hOrmonde, I wonder if you'd let me try a little something? I think we can do a Reverse Theory thing, relative to what your Sector Chief said about this job not being hard at all."

"My dearest, Theona, this is the most delicate of diplomatic dealings. We have to pound this treaty into the beast's heads."

"I might have an idea that could bring about a longer-lasting resolution." She looked at me wryly. "And it could prove to be a bit of fun."

Weedil gave an exclamation of interest.

I looked at my spin doctor, then back to my courtesan. I heaved a resigned sigh. "Are you sure what you propose will work?"

"Darling, this is my area of specialization," she said.

I shrugged my shoulders in resignation. "Very well. Let me see what your ideas are."

Theona smiled sweetly at me, then she stared at the air around us. "Phssh, are you here?"

"Yes," my gassy little friend replied.

"Stick around. I'll want to smell you something later. It's going to seem like total nonsense to you, but I want you to memorize it."

"hOrmonde?" Phssh asked if I agreed. I waved a confirming hand in resignation. How did I always let that charming little Theona influence me?

Theona swung her gaze around to me. "hOrmonde, why don't you come with me?" She smiled broadly. "We're going to play dress-up."

#

It took several hours before the conservative religious wing decided to overlook the seventy-two-hour prohibition and come pounding on the door trying to get some sort of Inquisition started to punish whoever they decided had caused my untimely death. After all, they hadn't fed on any blood since dinnertime. I'm sure that Sneeth was pushing them to action. For our part, we'd been quite busy and were prepared for them.

"My dear friends," Weedil reverently addressed the delegation at the door while also pushing his hand onto Sneeth's nose and shoving his prying little face out of the way, "the widow of the ambassador has arrived here on the latest courier to participate in the holy ritual that will see the dear departed off to the afterlife. At this time, as the widow, she is referred to by only one high, holy name. May I take this humble honor of presenting to you The Priscilla."

I stepped into view, in the new disguise Theona had chosen for me, remaining silent.

Theona and I had been dashing about assembling my widow's weeds. None of Theona's clothes would do, since I occupy a larger part of the Universe than she does. However, I was now properly adorned with all of the black material that we could gather, and heavily veiled to keep my face from being seen.

At that moment I was hoping that the ugly beasts would assume that my shaking shoulders indicated copious weeping. Actually, I was giggling. However, that stopped when Sneeth darted his nose toward me to get a better look. I didn't think I would stand up to close scrutiny. Theona quickly remedied the situation, but wrapping her arms around his prying neck and giving him a big smack on the cheek. Not only were his feelings strong for the little males he dragged along with him to satisfy his lusts, but he found any female totally repellent. Therefore, he snapped his head back to escape Theona's unwelcome attentions.

Time to get the plot moving. I pitched my voice up to the higher female register Theona had schooled me in. I don't know why I let her talk me into these things, but she is rather persuasive. I reverted to the Amalgam Anglo these beasts wouldn't understand. "Weedil, please tell these brutes that I'm not in the spirit to join in their orgy of blood-letting."

"The Priscilla states that she is looking to mend the wound that caused her husband's death."

While I was addressing the brutes, Sneeth was in the background, bobbing and weaving, looking for a way to get in for a closer inspection of me. However, he was countered by Theona who kept mirroring his movements as she transparently flirted with him, dropping in smiles, and winks and puckers.

I continued. "Say that I wish for these religious roughnecks to go off somewhere and try to do some good for a change. Tell them the God who made all intelligent creatures--and maybe also them--wishes for me to meet with their leaders and try to pound some sense into their beastly little skulls."

"While The Priscilla was in a religious trance the Everlasting Elvis came to her and said that she should seek out the royal leaders of the people and join them in holy prayer and meditation. Together, they will try to communicate with the Elvis and seek his advice on these gravest of matters and travel the path into the light of understanding and forgiveness."

"Tell them that I wish to take the Princes and Princesses out of their cloying grasp and expose them to a higher meaning, as it were. I want the Hivent pair first..."

Theona quickly reached in to interrupt me, her manner suggesting a solicitous lady in waiting; her message something different, "hOrmonde, why don't you cross the pairs?"

"Really?" I'd dropped down into my regular voice in surprise. Theona flashed her eyes over, indicating the group standing in the doorway. "Really?" I repeated in the higher voice I'd been schooled in. Sneeth was bobbing and weaving his head around, trying to overhear our conversation. "You want me to do that?"

Theona leaned in persuasively toward me. "I have my reasons."

I stared back at her. "Very well." I turned back to address Weedil. "We will do cross-pairings of them, Dopey with Dirty, and Grumpy with Sleazy. Tell them it'll offer the possibility of a different way for them to fight."

"The Priscilla wishes to meet with the High Prince of the Hivent and the Petite Princess of the Voment first. Then she will meet with the Brave Prince of the Voment and the Celestial Princess of the Hivent. They will gather as equals under the realm of the Great God Elvis in the chambers of the dear departed."

We hustled them out the door toward their appointed paths with the most resistance coming from Sneeth.

I turned to Theona. "Why are we..." I'd started out in my Priscilla high voice, then switched to a more comfortable baritone range. "Why are we cross-pairing them?"

"It was something I noticed, when I was giving them their massages." That was a euphemism. "I think I might--*you* might be able to do something with them when they're away from their group's prejudices."

I frowned in confusion.

"Now, Phssh, are you here?" she asked the air.

"Yes."

"Come close to me and memorize this nonsense phrase." She suddenly turned a bilious green, the same color as the Gruchers. Her body exuded an odor that Phssh quickly absorbed.

"What's that?" I asked Theona.

"It's the particular pheromone the Grucher exude when they're aroused. It sets up an attraction," she explained.

I gave up trying to comprehend what her little sub-plots were about. My voice was quite strained from use in its upper registers, so I had to refresh it with some liquid.

I had barely had time to throw the veil back over my head, when Dopey and Dirty made their appearance--with Sneeth. However, Theona quickly dispatched him--for the moment-- with an amorous approach. You could tell the two Gruchers really hated being there together. Their incessant body language was causing quite a bit of static on my translator's earpiece. It sounded like continuous growling.

I led them down a corridor in the suite toward what we'd selected as the bedroom that the late lamented me had occupied. When I opened the door, I discovered K'Ching inside sitting on the bed playing cards with my alleged assassins. I quickly slammed the door shut before the Gruchers could see in. I swiveled my head around and settled on another room in the corridor, and finding this one unoccupied by fugitives from justice, went inside.

We decided we were going to have a little prayer session.

"Weedil see if you can't do something about the racket that they're making with their body language. Stick their faces down into a trough of slops. Maybe that will quiet them down."

"The Priscilla wishes for you to kneel at the bedside to join her in prayer to the Almighty."

"Good positioning," Theona said. I glanced over at her to try to figure out what she meant.

Well--whatever! I raised my arms up in a beseeching manner. "Does this Godforsaken hellhole of a moon belonging to these nasty little beasts have anything even mildly resembling a good restaurant?"

"Please respond to her incantations with the reciting of the holy words of the mighty Elvis." Weedil tilted his head back and sang, "You ain't nothin' but a hound dog."

I raised my hands once more. "Did anyone remember to put in to the Department for my death benefits?"

"You ain't nothin' but a hound dog."

A raising of the hands. "This is as much of this as I can stand."

""You ain't nothin' but a hound dog. Crying all the time." Weedil added an Amen to his little canticle. Then he turned to Dopey and Dirty. "The Priscilla wishes for you to stay alone here in quiet prayer for ten minutes time. She will leave you to your meditations."

I headed out the door, giving the filthy beasts about twenty seconds before they bolted out and back to their own suites.

As we stood in the hallway, Theona acted like she was talking to me and said, "Phssh, I want you to fart that nonsense phrase I taught you right at these two creatures."

I heard a sudden gasp as the doors were closing. Phssh had leveled the two of them with a blast of the pheromone Theona had taught him. It sounded like he had hit them right between their legs. My Spy would make his way under the door to leave them alone.

My voice had really degenerated, so I once more tried to refresh it with a little liquid. It took twice as much this time. We began to hear—uh—*sounds* coming from the bedroom. I raised an eyebrow of interrogation at Theona. She nodded in satisfaction. It seems that Dopey and Dirty were starting in on a discovery of the wonders of miscegenation. Theona had added a few wonderful little touches to my schemes.

Suddenly Sneeth darted his way out of a side hallway. He must have snuck into the suite through a back entrance. He immediately headed to investigate the noise that Dopey and Dirty were making in their bedroom.

Weedil caught his eye, gave him a finger wave, and simpered a come-hither, "Hi!" at the little sneak. It caught his interest, and he wheeled his head over to get a better look at Weedil--who promptly clocked him with a vase from the side table.

At that point Grumpy and Sleazy arrived at our door.

We quickly dragged Sneeth's unconscious body into a nearby closet, then dashed to open the door.

We'd thoughtfully arranged to use a second bedroom for the second couple's prayer meeting on the other side of the suite. The noises coming out of bedroom number one were beginning to increase in volume.

As I turned to head toward the hallway that led to the room we'd chosen, I spied K'Ching and the four assassins heading toward us down the hall. I quickly wheeled and pushed the group back down the hallway where Prince and Princess #1 were creating a lascivious racket. The only room available was one at the end of the hall, right next to the one occupied by the cavorting first couple. I peeked inside that bedroom to make sure it was clear of anything incriminating, then led everyone in. Grumpy and Sleazy glanced in the direction of the room next door, where all the sound was coming from. The looks on their faces plainly showed they were wondering what strange things us aliens do in the privacy of our own bedrooms.

I diverted their attention by raising my hands and intoning, "To the dear King of Rock and Roll, I bring this blushing little couple whom I hope to have rutting in here in a few minutes."

"You ain't nothin' but a hound dog." Weedil led them in prayer, once more.

"As a payment for this boon, I promise to dine sumptuously at *a la Nouvelle Martianne* as soon as I can."

"You ain't nothin' but a hound dog."

"Now I'm going to take my poor, grieving, widowly self off to someplace that is not populated by carnivorous little beasts."

"You ain't nothin' but a hound dog. Crying all the time." Weedil turned to Grumpy and Sleazy. "Please remain here in solemn prayer until you feel the soul of Elvis grip you and send you on the path only you will sense."

As we left that room, Theona said, "Go, Phssh!"

By the time we were out of the second bedroom, I was quite fatigued from my religious ecstasy. Things in bedroom number one were taking their course, and it sounded quite athletic, rather like a sexual decathlon. Next door, the other two were well on their way to making up for their late start.

This was taking some time, so we were forced to call out for another bottle of aperitif.

Theona turned to me. "Well, hOrmonde I think your Sector Chief was totally wrong in his appraisal. This job *will* be hard."

"Yes, my dear, you noticed how I was able to spot out the solution to the problem. Something did have to be hard, and it sounds like it certainly is." I raised my head and listened to the sounds of the highjinks in the two bedrooms.

"Oh, hOrmonde, you're so clever," she gushed.

"Yes, I am."

At that point Sneeth staggered out of the closet where we'd deposited him. Weedil tackled him, and I leaped on top of him. He grappled at us, trying to break loose. In his flailing, he pulled back my veil and saw my face. He shouted out, "You!" but we promptly gagged him and trussed him up and deposited him in a spare bedroom for safekeeping. We had to figure out what we were going to do with the little sneak, but we had to make sure we handled our "peace" negotiations.

We had just barely recomposed ourselves in the main area of the suite when Dopey and Dirty emerged from bedroom number one. Fortunately they had displayed their devoutness by overstaying in their prayer sessions by a good fifteen minutes. There was a decided difference in their body language now. My earpiece was emitting sighs and a sound that resembled someone inhaling a cigarette. They were both quite flushed. That meant they were an even more bilious shade of green. They scampered out the door, heading back to their lodging. They had some news for their retinues.

Grumpy and Sleazy emerged next, decidedly less grumpy and happily sleazier. They also left with great haste.

Theona turned to me and said, "hOrmonde, don't you think it would be a great idea if Phssh went around to the Grucher section of the hotel and farted that pheromone wherever he finds opposite sexes, opposite races?"

"Darling, I was just going to suggest that. Would you please do that, Phssh?"

"And don't overlook the clergy," Theona said.

"My darling," I said to Theona, "you are really quite salacious in your own precious way."

At that moment Sneeth darted out of his bedroom and dashed out the door to the suite. We leaped up and chased after him.

We pursued him down the hallway of the hotel, but he did have the advantage in foot speed and was pulling away.

Suddenly a Gruch female, one of the big ones, appeared approaching from beyond Sneeth. Theona yelled out, "Phssh! *Gobrukjidthork!*" The female stopped dead in her path as she inhaled deeply. She'd run into something in the air in front of her. A totally salacious look came over her face. Just at that moment Sneeth was approaching her. She reached out and grabbed the little sneak and clutched him to her bosom. What Theona had yelled out, must have been Phssh's word for the pheromone that aroused the Gruchers, because she was beginning to hug and fondle and coo over the little alien while she maintained a firm grasp on him.

Sneeth was repulsed by females. The Gruch females are particularly repulsive representatives of the sex. He was not enjoying himself.

"Oh dear," Theona said as she raised two delicate fingers to her mouth. "He really shouldn't try to resist her."

"Why not?" I asked.

"That will only encourage her to use her nails," she replied. Right on cue, Sneeth let out a shriek of pain. "And she has rather long nails."

"I see."

"The male Grucher's skin is scaly, so it can pretty much resist that." Sneeth let out another shriek. Theona's lips formed a little moue, and a few vertical lines formed in her brow. "I think Sneeth is a little more sensitive."

"She seems quite attached to him," I observed, as the female Gruch tucked the little sneak under her arm and began to carry him off to her boudoir.

"Oh, yes, the duration of the female rut is about five days. She'll hold onto him for that length of time. That should be enough for us to conclude our negotiations. Sneeth should emerge at that time a bit lacerated, but not too bad off."

I turned and led us back toward our suite. "We got an opportunity to see the pheromone in operation. It should take care of all of the rest of the Gruchers."

"Yes, hOrmonde, you were quite the clever one to think of the pheromone."

"Yes, you're quite right. It was very astute of me." We were back in the suite. I turned to K'Ching. "Once the festivities have quieted down, I want you to go see the conservative clergy and their former temple virgins and play them the recordings Phssh made of their backstage back-stabbings.

Remind them that knowledge of their guilt for my assassination would give them a very large black mark with the Amalgam. However, if they aid the peace fomenting between most of the sheets in this building, they might get off with just a slap on the wrist." I turned to Theona. "Aren't you proud of yourself? You have just helped to start a whole sexual revolution."

"Oh, hOrmonde, you were just wonderful with your clever little schemes. Is there anything I can do for you?"

"Why don't we stroll over to my real bedroom, get me out of this drag, and see what we can figure out."

#

And so everything worked out just ducky. The double wedding that was supposed to bring peace to the planet accomplished that very thing. However, it was achieved through the means of swapping brides and grooms. News of what had happened under the covers up here soon spread to the remainder of the population of Gruch. The middle altitudes of the planet began to sprout a great many "meeting places" for Gruchers who were discovering the wonders of miscegenation. They also happened to produce a lot of zymbium for the Amalgam.

This wonderful new peace hinged on one important thing: I had to stay officially dead. After all, it would be most embarrassing if I showed up alive and well. Therefore, I was forced to collect lavish death benefits from the Department.

"We've got to figure out what other benefits we can reap from my untimely demise," I said to Theona. "Surely, it must cost a lot more for an agent to do a job posthumously. Where is K'Ching? She should be figuring things out for me."

At that moment said Briber came wandering into the control room on the ship. She was carrying herself a lot more languidly than I had ever seen.

"There you are. Where have you been? What have you been up to?"

"There were a few details I had to clear up."

"What might those be?"

"Well, I really didn't have any other convenient place to spirit off those assassins, so I had to take them along. I was settling them into my room."

"Are you talking about those little fellows with the big--feet?"

"Yes."

"You've got them all in your room?"

"Yes."

"Why you licentious little trollop!" I tut-tutted. "I'm very proud of you! Why don't you go back to your room and make sure that they're really settled in."

"I will!" She bolted out.

#

So that was that. We plumbed the copious rules of the Department. It turns out there was a precedent for the posting of a diplomat who is already deceased. The ruling stated he must get paid twice the rate he was previously paid. That means that every time the agency sends me out, my salary doubles. I figure after about eight new postings they'll be paying me what I'm really worth. In the meantime, I'll just have to muddle through on the parsimonious amount they're giving me now.

When I discuss my escalating rates with my Sector Chief, he always bemoans the fact he'll have to put in for a larger budget. I have just one thing to tell him.

"That won't be hard at all."

END RECORDING

#

"There's a little something to enter into the competition," hOrmonde said. "Now I believe it's just about time for my masseuse to join me for dinner and then a relaxing massage."

Someone had entered the Café and was looking around. She had a little pill box cap pulled rakishly over one eye. She spotted hOrmonde and waved jauntily and jiggily at him.

Little did hOrmonde realize that he was dining with the Supreme Leader of the planet Hedon, who was taking a night off from her many duties. She found it quite enjoyable dining with hOrmonde. He was quite the darling.

And she had an awful lot that she needed to teach him about Diplomacy.

Chapter 2

Uplift

A Vren stared hungrily at the StarBoard Café from a hiding place behind an asteroid several light hours away. He longed to get at the creatures inside.

The Vren are very religious. They have an unshaking view of the glories of the afterlife. They express this conviction by sending as many creatures as possible off to their final reward as soon as possible, curtailing their physical life in the Now to enable them to immediately enjoy the everlasting joys of the Forever. They are ecstatic when they can launch some creatures off to their final reward. They are a little bit *too* ecstatic about it, having launched whole races off to their salvation. They had carried out this crusade with such efficiency that the Frontier Guard of the Amalgam of Intelligent Beings hunted them down to remove their menace from the galaxy.

The Vren ached to get to the creatures he sensed were inside the Café. He knew that the beings inside had to be riddled with the evil that would block their path to their Final Reward. (Since the beings inside the Café were all spacers, there had never been a case in the whole history of the galaxy when anyone had been *so* right.)

Finding no chink in the Café's armor, the Vren slunk off to his deep-space hiding place to await another opportunity to render a being to the glories of Heaven.

The defenses of the Café were impregnable. One could never know when a spacer, disgruntled over the amount of his bar tab, might decide to render the Café and all of its inhabitants down to their simplest atoms.

The Café not only had to protect itself from the outside, it had to pacify the clientele once they entered the premises.

#

Vardak strode into The StarBoard Café. He had just checked his handgun at the door. He had also checked his foot gun, his tail gun, his stunner, his slammer, his jammer, his conker, his donker, his ripper, his dipper, his bopper, his chopper, his knocker, his clocker, and his ---**CLASSIFIED**---.

Vardak's job title was, in his native tongue, *kermernorjer*. The word derived from two sources. A *kermer* was a particularly fierce type of pirate native to Vardak's home world. These freebooters did not make insurgents walk the plank. Instead, they pitched them overboard with the plank now part of their anatomy, allegedly to add buoyancy. A *norjer* was a parasite that would latch onto a victim and force it to creep along in an extremely emaciated and painful condition, as the norjer continuously fed on it. The translation of *kermernorjer* was "businessman."

Vardak signaled the wait-being for his usual, sat down at the bar and reached forward to the Record button to enter the Storytelling Contest of the StarBoard Café.

RECORD
#

The plagues of the lowest of buggered slime worms afflict these dreadful little pieces of pestilence! I curse the day I ever laid eyes on them!

They're nothing but stinking tree-dwellers. They should've stayed up there, eating fruit, fornicating, and trying not to defecate on the more noble creatures below. Instead, they decided to come down to the ground and presume to walk with their betters. The damnable part is they never left their bickering natures behind in the branches.

They'd already been passed up as too primitive for admission into the Amalgam of Intelligent Beings. I totally agree with that decision. My only complaint is that it didn't go far enough. The vermin should have been exterminated.

But that's like trying to reverse through a wormhole. They're here to stay, and the most blighted part of it is that it's all *my* fault. The Blackness curse me for being the meanest of bloodsucking, penny-grubbing idiots that ever crawled out of the Soup of Life and presumed to be intelligent. I let my greed get the better of me.

I'd heard there might be some curios of interest on their water-filled world. (Why couldn't those more noble aquatics have assumed primacy on that planet?) I'd gone there under cover to see if there might be something I could take back and sell to the civilized worlds of the Amalgam. I tried observing the heads of their separate tribes. (These vermin were so caught up with bickering they didn't even have a full world government.) The tribal chieftains were the most pompous, strutting little brutes it's ever been my displeasure to observe. I knew it would be impossible to try to deal with them.

Finally, I resorted to Ramshad's Reverse Theory. I studied the list of what was proscribed on the planet to see if there was something there that might be of value on a civilized world. It was tough slogging. The list was long. It seemed that every pleasure they practiced was outlawed by their leaders. I did ascertain that one commodity was uniformly prohibited. (That was their public stance. In most cases their officials were taking bribes to overlook the flourishing commerce in the banned goods.) I tried to contact some of the manufacturers of this product. They lived on one of the continents of what they considered their lower hemisphere. They proved to be even more primitive than the tribal chieftains, impossible as that sounds. I was beginning to despair of ever contacting someone with whom I could do some dealing.

I finally located a producer of one of the lesser products. I thought he might prove to be more malleable. He had a farm on an island in one of their oceans. The site seemed to be remote enough to visit without being detected. (It is laughable to think these vermin would recognize anything that wasn't right in front of their proboscises.) The place had a single guard posted with a projectile weapon. One of my crew quickly put him into a coma, and I proceeded to the main building of their site.

I had to bend over to make my way through the pitifully small entrance.

"Either you're real, or I want to make tonight's smoke part of my private stock," the beast said. He was sitting at a table staring at me. I could barely pay attention to him. I smelled something the likes of which I have never sensed before. It was airborne ambrosia.

"I'm here on a mission of exploration," I said.

"Hey, explore around," he said, spreading his upper appendages to the side. "In the meantime, you want a toke?" He indicated the small, rolled samples in front of him.

I tried very hard to restrain myself. "What do you have to offer?"

"Have some smoke, man. I was just testing my latest crop."

He offered me the thing he'd already been sticking in his facial orifice. I reached over, and grabbed one of the unused ones, lit it, and inhaled. It was sheer delight!

"What use do you find for this deplorably awful smudge pot?" A standard opening in negotiations.

"No smudge, man," he said, "just pot."

"Whatever you call this stinking little weed."

"That's right," he said. I seemed to be having some sort of problem with my translator. Either that or their language was as obtuse as the beasts themselves.

"I might be able to find some use for it in trade," I said. "What would you be looking for in the way of recompense?"

"Well, I usually get about a hundred Clintons a pound."

The stupid little vermin wanted to trade for paper that supposedly had some value in bauble-metal! This was too much! I was about to cut short the conversation and leave these brutes to themselves.

However, the farmer leaned forward and held my hand back before it reached for the sword. "Of course, that's only an opening offer. I'm ready to listen to whatever it is you have to propose."

The ambrosia of which I'd partaken must have softened my brain because I made the mistake of not leaving that instant. "What I'll do is the standard Amalgam practice. I'll offer something in trade, like any civilized being. Some technology," I said.

My fate was sealed.

It went on from there. The first shipment of this *marijuana* was such a sensation on the market that I had to produce far more product. I tried to set up a plantation on one of the worlds I owned, but we discovered that it would only grow properly on its original home. I put my best scientists on it, to no avail. Apparently there was some indigenous untraceable element we could not find. I had to go back to their stinking little world. But in order to do that, I had to effect certain changes. It would be impossible to operate without the tribal governments poking their greedy little noses in, so we had to get rid of them. We offered the chiefs some bauble-metal for their resignations. They all quickly agreed. It was only after they were out of power they discovered each had received large quantities of the metal. There was so much around it was worthless. We put the farmer in charge of the governments.

On taking office, the farmer said, "This is great, man--or whatever you are--this means I'm in charge now? Aren't the people going to want more of a leader?"

Since his first executive action was the lifting of the bans on the euphorics, the question of leadership became moot. Now that they could freely use the drugs, the creatures were far less aggressive. They were quite happy to have the farmer as their chief executive.

We next had to settle the issue of the product that was made in the lower hemisphere and still under the control of the belligerent creatures that lived there.

Our new world leader said, "Man--or whatever--you can't do nothing with them Colombians. They're crazy, and they're well armed."

"They won't want to do business with me?"

"No, they've seen what's happened to me. They want the power, too."

"Let me see if I can't negotiate a deal with them," I said.

I hired J'Josk, a first-rate Mercantile Diplomat and Expediter, to help me with the first interview with these Colombians. The dealer was located in his bunker on his plantation; we were in orbit around the system's gas giant.

He thought he could be aggressive with us. "Man, you think you're somethin'? You ain't nothin' compared to me. I got guns, I got tanks, I got *jodios missiles*. What you got to say to that? Huh? What?"

J'Josk vaporized him.

I went to the other Colombians to see if I could talk to them. You'd think those stupid worms would know better than to cross me. They knew the fate of my first interviewee. But, no, they all believed they could force their terms. I employed a few of the usual business strategies, and that created a number of managerial vacancies in the Colombians' organizations, so I put my farmer in charge of them, too.

I was still not aware of the grossly stupid thing I was doing. In the face of escalating orders and profits, I kept trading these beasts advanced technology for their farm product.

Then along came one of those cursed functionaries from the Amalgam government. She proclaimed I'd given these brutes enough technology. They'd reached the point of ascendancy.

I tried arguing with her, saying that the rule couldn't apply too such dumb little brutes.

She replied that this was a rule so old it dated back to the Wistrani, the Progenitors for the Amalgam. Her decision would stand.

I had uplifted them into membership in the Amalgam.

These stinking little pests.

I had uplifted them. Therefore, *I* was responsible for them. I became the wet nurse for this race of gibbering tree-dwellers!

There was nothing I could do with them. They bred like the

vermin they are. They began to infest everything.

Reports started flooding in about the mayhem they were causing. When they reached the planet Manay, they turned the previously benign Manayans into warlords. Several invasions had to be thwarted. One of the vermin had also managed to impregnate the High Virgin Priestess of the Vuldoon, even though their seeds should have been incompatible.

I sought for solutions to the problem. I tried turning the beasts over to Hurlk the Horrible in trade, but he said they tasted awful.

They were propagating all over the place. I was suddenly dispatching parties of diplomats to all quadrants of the Galaxy to keep these pestilent little animals from creating complete and total confusion.

All of the profits I'd built up from the initial influx of trade were being eaten up by the policing actions I had to keep financing.

So, here I sit, a virtual pauper, when I should be the richest trader in the Amalgam. All because of these stupid animals. I should have let them rot on their little planet.

May the curses of the Original Creators be on their stinking hides.

What should I do?

#

Vardak reached forward and pressed the Record button.

END RECORD

The wait-being inched its way forward with the order for Vardak.

Vardak took three long snorts in his three nostrils from the three lines of white powder that were laid out on the serving tray.

"I win this storytelling contest, and I'll have carte blanche here for a year. A year of all the euphorics I can get." He paused, then muttered ruefully, "It won't be long enough to forget the little pests."

One of Vardak's assistants squirmed up to him in a great hurry. "Please pardon the interruption, most exalted one."

"What is it?" Vardak asked. He had a premonition of what it could be. Lately, it had always been the same thing.

"It is the humans, my lord."

Vardak gave a resigned nod. "What is it this time?"

"They've decided to go into business for themselves. They're entering the marketplace as an independent entity. They think they have technology to trade. It's a most strange thing they are offering. It seems to be a contradiction. They're trying to sell these things called mobile homes."

Vardak signaled for another round.

Chapter 3

Pranks

Pressing the Record button at the StarBoard Café meant using a very sophisticated device. Imagining that it was the same as an audio recording would be like imagining that an N-Class starship was the same as an oxcart. The recording had so many sensory inputs that it went past the point of being Virtual Reality to being virtually real. Added to seeing and hearing were the senses of touching and smelling. Not to mention the alien senses of schmecking, kratching and, of course, grokking.

Further, the device put out an empathic field to absorb the feelings and emotions of the teller and then transmit them back to the viewer.

The recorder included a computer that could not only translate to the language of the viewer, but could also make references to that language's cultural background to furnish the proper idioms. Thus to have the *"quinschels of gickrick"* meant to be *"built like a brick shithouse."* It could also reconstruct the actual quotations of the original speakers rather than the accents of the narrators.

Since this particular collection of stories is being transcribed as printed words on paper of the pre-Uplift, 21st-century Anglo, it does not include any instances of actual sight, smell, sound, touch, schmecklip, kratch-ins and grokkinstances. Therefore it should be classified as an abridged version.

#

A Glamm eyed a human strolling through the StarBoard Cafe.

Glamms are distinct, even among the many species of the

Amalgam. They are practically all mouth, or maw. The few appendages they have can only be described as eating appurtenances

When contact was first made by the Amalgam with the Glamms, a study was made of their means of communication. Just as the Inuit have sixty-three words for *snow*, the Glamms have seventy-two words for *eat*. Compiling this lexicography had, unfortunately, required seventy-three researchers.

As the Glamm eyed the human, the word that came to his mind was the version of *eat* that meant "to crunch on the bones until you are able to pick out that last little morsel of marrow with the thinnest of your tongues."

The pacification necessary to admit the Glamm to the StarBoard was rather extensive. He was rigidly tied down with numerous restraints strapped across his maw. About the only thing that could be admitted into his mouth was some liquid refreshment. Having his eating capabilities so restricted, he was unable to mutter any one of his seventy-two words for *eat*. This was known as the Silence of the Glamms.

The human the Glamm had been eying was named Randy Holcombe. Randy pulled up to one of the Record buttons at the bar in preparation for entering the Story Competition. Randy's Marketing Director felt that placing high in the competition would gain his company publicity.

He reached forward and pressed the Record button.

RECORD
#

A friend of mine once said, "You wouldn't be doing your current job unless, way down deep inside, you truly enjoyed it."

I'd throttle him, if I could, but unfortunately he died in a work-related accident.

That gives me only minor solace.

I got a booking for a research trip to the planet Megalm. I knew what I was in for. The good part: the money was guaranteed by the Stevens Foundation, so I wouldn't have to

chase down my fee. The bad part: I'd have to do a lot of babysitting. A group like this is usually led by some muzzy-headed professor who doesn't know what should be researched and what should be avoided because it has a high hazard concentration. The rest of the members of the group wouldn't be much better. The booking instructions said there would be three in the party: the professor, Wendell Latham; his graduate student, Francis Ingram (usually some little nerd); and Manfred Mickens, expedition head, a designation I'd never heard before. Probably some blowhard from the Foundation tagging along to get status. Well, I'd been through this before; I'd get through it again.

I did my pre-flight research on Megalm. The inhabitants, the Xirom, are a benign, bucolic race, too backward to merit any true commercial development. Rumors surface about fabulous riches that could be reaped from the planet. Rumors like these usually number more than entrants in a sweepstakes, with the same ratio of payoffs.

Since these rumors attract fortune hunters of low moral character, the Amalgam had put a Research Only tag on the Xirom and their planet. The briefing on the place listed most of the flora and fauna as being harmless except for a thing called the gnnar, an animal that was about twelve feet tall. The classification on that beasty was *AN*: <u>A</u>pproach <u>N</u>egatively. That was the highest, or, if you would, lowest ranking of any alien fauna. You approached them negatively, as fast as your feet could take you.

I set off for the boarding lounge the afternoon of departure to greet my passengers. I felt certain I'd recognize them. I took a cup of coffee and sat down for what proved to be a very short wait.

Professor Wendell Latham was just what I expected: bearded, pudgy, thick glasses in front of eyes that didn't seem to focus on much of anything. I'm used to this type; they're children in adult suits. He was as cute as a child and sported a vocal mannerism. He started every sentence with, "Aha, yes, been looking forward to this expedition for quite a while. Quite fascinating creatures, these Xirom. Aha, yes, seem to have a very ancient civilization, yet no technology." You could tell the professor wouldn't harm a fly. I had to make sure that no flies harmed him. "Mr. Mickens is right behind me." I turned, expecting to meet some bureaucrat.

Instead I saw Manky.

I had known Manky by that first name (was his last name really Mickens?) for many years. Manky was a lowdown cheat and con man, but a survivor. He talked with a Cockney accent.

"Excuse me, Professor Latham," I said, "I want to discuss a few details about payment from the Foundation with Mr.-- Mickens, is it?" I raised a questioning eye towards Manky.

We went around the corner so the Professor couldn't see or hear us. I grabbed Manky by the collar. "Where the hell's my money?" Yes, Manky owed me money. But he was quite democratic about it; he owed everyone money. He was an equal-opportunity welsher.

He held up conciliatory hands. "Now, listen 'ere, mate, you know it wasn't my fault them dice come up the way they did. You don't believe I can control them things, do you?"

"Yes, I do. They make sets of bones just like those in Verilla, they come up whatever way you want. I heard you had a pair of them."

"That's not true, mate. Those things are as 'onest as the day is long."

"They *are*? Present tense? You mean you've still got them? They must have terrific sentimental value to you."

He nodded. "You could say that, Mate. They've been through many a war with me. But not to worry, I'll give you your money back just as soon as I cash in on this trip."

"Cash in on what?" I asked in disbelief.

"Well, if I'm to believe me sources," he leaned toward me confidentially, "and they are unimpeachable, quite unimpeachable, there are things on this planet the likes of which you ain't never seen. Things that will make you a bundle. The kinda bundle that'll make you forget the paltry sums you say I owe you."

I was in a bind. He had somehow managed to get past the Stevens Foundation to obtain this grant. Problem was, if I blew the whistle on him, I'd have to postpone this trip, and the money from this was slated to pay off some very pending debts. I'd just have to keep my eye on—I'd better get used to saying it—Mr. Mickens. "I'll make sure you don't get away without giving me that money."

"Don't worry, mate."

I leaned in. "I'm paid to worry. That's my job. Now go over and take care of your client." I had to keep my eye on him before a tidal wave of trouble washed right over me.

As we got back to the lounge, I heard the thud of pieces of gear slapping down the stairs, accompanied by faltering footsteps. Had to be the graduate student. I could predict the profile: he had bifocals, dandruff, poor hygiene, and a worse sense of style.

I was wrong.

As she came down the stairs, the first things I saw were her boots, followed by a lot of leg going up to her shorts. I paused before I continued looking further.

She released the gear and put her hands on her hips and stared at me. "Well, I'll take that as a compliment, but you might want to glance at my face so you'll be able to recognize me in a crowd."

The trip up was worth it. "I take it you're Francis?"

"Yes. My friends call me Fran." She paused reflectively. "After that look you gave me, I think I'll keep you at Francis."

"Can I help with the gear?" I scuttled forward.

"That's a good start."

I turned to the rest of the group. "Follow me to the *Chameleon*."

When we entered the ship, we were greeted by a holo image, a tall, thin man dressed in a very tweedy outfit. His hat had a peak both front and back. The coat had an attached short cape. He smoked a pipe that looped down and back up to a large bell-shaped bowl. It was the current persona my ship's

Artificial Intelligence had assumed. "Well, there you are at last. I suppose you're returning from one of those absolutely filthy pubs you frequent." The accent was English.

"Hi, Cammy. Lady and gentlemen, let me explain..."

"Ah, Professor Latham," he continued as he turned toward the academic, "how are the alien studies proceeding at Harvard?"

"Aha, yes, how do you know me?" the professor asked.

"Yes, do tell," I chimed in.

"Elementary, my dear Watson," Cammy said to me. He then turned back to the professor. "I couldn't help but notice that you had traces of chalk dust on the right arm of your coat. The pin on your lapel denotes you attended the Amalgam Conference on Intercultural Studies held in 2237. There were only two humans in attendance at the conference. Yourself and one Dr. Horacio Montoya of the University of Mexico. Since Dr. Montoya is left-handed, and also has a darker complexion more in keeping with his native Mexico City, I deduced who you were."

"It also didn't hurt that you have the passenger manifest." I dragged some reality into the conversation.

"Quite so, Watson," he said. He turned to Manky. "Mr. Mickens, is it? I seem to have some contradictory information about you in my data banks."

I leaped into the conversation. "Indubitably that can be straightened out." The "indubitably" was the code word we employed that meant, "Get off the topic or you'll find you supply of electrons deeply rationed."

"It appears I may have to consult with the Captain on that topic the next time I see him. He is probably somewhere out of his senses on some soporific or another. I will consult him when he is approaching coherence." He turned to Fran. "I take it you are Francis Ingram?"

"Yes, I'm Professor Latham's graduate assistant, along for the ride. And by 'graduate assistant' I mean basic grunt labor."

"Aha! Then you just met Captain Holcombe?" Cammy

inquired with a glance back in my direction.

"Yes."

"Very good, I deduced from your manners and comportment you weren't one of the young ladies he usually escorts onto the ship. You have a vocabulary in excess of fifty words, and you don't spend your entire day chewing gum. Since you're obviously of good breeding, I will be most certain to protect you. I'm afraid the crew is heavily populated with some of the worst scum you'll find infecting the banks of the Thames." What the Thames was, I don't know, but the dig was directed at me since I was the only crewmember.

"I'm sure I'll be well watched." Fran seemed to be melting Cammy like a blast of fire on butter. I glimpsed an unholy alliance forming between the two of them. My life was gaining complications, interesting ones in Fran's case.

"I guess I should explain about the *Chameleon*'s Artificial Intelligence, Cammy," I said. "I was doing some experimenting, trying to increase the AI's speed accessing the data banks. I put in special accelerators. However I left a couple of gates open that also gave it entry to my files of Fiction and Drama. As a result, I've got Cammy, an AI that has a bit of an identity problem."

"If I may say, I would think anyone with a speck of intellectual prowess would appreciate the exposure to the great works of drama and literature," he replied.

"He certainly operates faster than any AI I've ever seen," Fran said.

I nodded affirmation. "Oh, he's speedy, okay, and a handful. Although I'll say he's saved my butt more than once."

Cammy grunted. "'More than once' meaning any time I let him do that thing he calls thinking for himself." Despite the repudiation, I could tell that my compliment had landed home. Yes, I'm in the lamentable position of having to compliment my AI.

"So," I said as I clapped my hands together, "I guess you should get yourselves settled. Let's make it easy: Professor you should take room number one, down the hall here. Mank-- Mr.

Mickens you can take number two. Ms. Ingram, number three. I don't think that will prove too taxing for you to remember. Ms. Ingram, why don't we go aft and I'll help you stow the gear."

"I'll go along to make sure you are properly chaperoned," Cammy chipped in.

Fran and I headed back with the gear. Damn, it was *heavy*. She may have been cute, but she was also strong.

"That's great," I grumbled, "I can barely manage to control my AI. You met him five minutes ago, and he's forming a lifelong bond with you."

"I think it's got something to do with charm and beauty," Fran replied. "It looks like one of us has them, and one of us doesn't."

"Okay, maybe you've got a couple small, natural advantages. Don't flaunt it. I've got some of my own talents."

"What could those be?" she asked.

"Making rude noises with various body parts," Cammy chimed in.

"Cammy doesn't seem to hold a very high opinion of you. I guess I need to instruct him on some of your hidden virtues," Fran responded. "That is, just as soon as I discover what they are. They're hard to notice, but let me work on it."

"Thank you." I was scheming about ways to make myself available for her study.

"By the way, since I've built up an appetite lugging this gear around, I'm hungry. When is dinner?"

"I should be able to whip up something soon. I was thinking along the lines of a chateaubriand, and I'll search out the cellars for a nice red wine to go along with it. Or I might do a..."

...Cammy jumped in. "Actually we're having the special the Captain usually orders: hamburgers, French fries, and milk shakes. A dish that was popular back on Earth."

"I like it," I muttered.

"I see," said Fran, "and what is the dress at the captain's table?"

"Well, I guess something like what I'm wearing," I said, holding my arms wide.

"A pair of jeans and a shirt that says, 'Black Holes Really Suck'?"

I glanced down to see what I was actually wearing. I looked back up. "Yeah, something like that."

"I'll have to head to my room. It's obvious I'll need quite a bit of time to gussy up for the Captain's table. I mostly brought field clothes."

"If you wear something like you've got on, it will be fine." Was I leering?

"I'll cover up a little more. I remember our first meeting."

She made her way off to her room. When she'd left I said, "Cammy, why're you on my case? I'm trying to make an impression with her. She's really nice."

"I think the last thing you said answered the first thing you said."

#

We met for dinner. My guests thought the meal was interesting.

"Aha, yes, looking forward to meeting the Xirom." The professor lectured. "Certainly an intriguing race. Well developed culture with many art forms, some so advanced we don't entirely understand them. Also evidence they had a higher civilization at one time. Now, just a plain, bucolic people with a benign social structure. Delight in telling stories, and highly amused by any sort of behavior they consider 'prankish.' Hard to tell exactly what that is, but seems to mean anything they find delightful or playful.

"Hints of technology of some sort. Whether an archaic one they regressed from, an interpolation of when the Amalgam discovered their planet, or some sort of legend, it's hard to tell. That's what makes them so intriguing."

"There are also 'ints they may 'ave fabulous wealth," Mr. Mickens said. "O' course, that's the sort o' stuff that attracts fortune 'unters." God, he was unctuous! "That's why I came, to guarantee none o' that trash tried to tag along on this trip. I suppose this would be a good time for me to inquire about the credentials of your operation, Mr. 'olcombe."

That bastard! "Well, Mr. Mickens, the operation of this ship is so close to the vest between balancing income and expenses, I couldn't jeopardize my ownership by trying to chase down some fortune that's only a rumor. If I had a single Credit for every one of those rumors I've heard, *that* would make me a rich man." Manky winced, possibly because I had just booted him in the shin.

Hard.

And he deserved it.

Those were a few things I remembered from dinner. I spent the rest of the time casting surreptitious glances at Fran or trying to engage her in conversation. I was quite taken with her. Not just in an animal, lusting manner. Although, in all honesty, I must admit that there was, oh, just a little bit of that involved. There was something else about her I found attractive: her quick wit and her command of the world around her. And, yes, the way her legs looked when I first saw her.

When dinner broke, I escorted everyone back to their rooms. By some strange stroke of fate, Fran was the last one.

"Well, here we are, Ms. Ingram. I think you'll find your room small, but utilitarian. If there should be anything you need, you can find me in Room Number Four, which is really handy because it's right across the hall there."

Fran looked up at me with that crooked half-smile. "Where I suppose you have a bottle of something quite delectable out of your cellars cooling at this very moment?"

"No-but-I-could-arrange-that-very-quickly," I said in record speed.

"Thank you very much for your charming offer, Captain, but I should be alert for tomorrow's landing on Megalm." She glanced up at me, and a rueful look fell across her face, displaying some inner emotion I couldn't fathom. "After all, I'm a devoted academic. I have to concentrate on my science."

I went into my room, feeling very happy, because she'd

called it a "charming" offer, overlooking that I headed into my room alone. I also wondered about the look that had crossed her face, hiding some great regret.

Cammy was there. He sat in an armchair holding something like a data pad with a stylus, except it looked ancient, analog rather than digital. His outfit was late nineteenth or early twentieth century. "Und zo, you must explain to me vhy you have zees uncontrollable sexual urges." He'd trotted out some new accent.

"You know, Cammy, I was just holding onto some wonderful memories before you horned in," I said.

"I think zat it iss debatable whether zees memories are 'vonderful' as you describe zem, or whether zey are repressed Oedipal urges zat you have not reconciled from your earliest childhood."

He was on his own agenda. I settled down for a lecture. "Okay, let me have it."

"Ass you vell know, I have access to zhe readouts of zhe life support system on ziss ship. It tells me zat zere are high levels of pheromones in zhe air. Zhese would not be toxic to most people, but I must make sure zat zere iss no unfortunate incident where someone becomes harmed by zhe aggressive acts of someone who iss under zhe influence of primal urges stemming from his medulla obbligato." He doesn't always get his terms right. "I vill have to make certain zhat no one falls victim to zhe attack of a sexual predator."

"Let's cut to the chase, Cammy. You're worried about Fran getting into an 'unfortunate' relationship with me."

"Ah, at last ve are beginning to make real progress with your self-analysis."

"Well, I agree with you."

"Vhat?"

"I agree with you. She's intelligent and classy. I don't want to have one of those run-and-gun relationships with her. The trouble is I can't tell if she's being nice to me because I'm captain, or if she might feel something for me."

"Wunderbar! You are making eggzellent progress. I sink zat you are ready to take zhe next step forward in your fight against morbid hedonism. I vill therefore tell you zat yours is not zhe only pheromones zat I found in circulation."

"What?"

A chime sounded. Cammy pulled out a pocket watch, flipped it open, and inspected it. "I'm sorry but your time iss up." And he disappeared.

"Hey, wait a minute, Cammy. What are you saying? What does that mean?"

Silence. "Cammy? Cammy? Where are you? What did you mean by that?" He'd left me hanging. I started to curse him out, but that did no good. I think he knew more swear words than I did. I just had to console myself with what he'd told me. I went to bed that night with a light head and a light heart.

#

The following day we approached Megalm. The place was lush and heavily forested, with the temperature hovering in the upper 70s. Very comfortable. The professor had already picked out a location on one of the larger continents where previous missions had landed. Therefore the natives would be familiar with the Amalgam and their flying machines. As I headed for the place, the Professor stood behind me in undisguised excitement. Manky leaned over my other shoulder in undisguised greed.

The tree cover parted and we glimpsed the village. It looked quite primitive: dotted with huts with thatched roofs. I circled to find someplace to land. I came upon a clearing about a half mile away from the village. Very convenient.

I settled the *Chameleon* down, being as careful as possible with the local environment. I let Cammy check the surrounding region. It all looked fine, proper atmosphere, proper temperature, no nasty beasties lurking about, either multi-ton or microscopic.

I waited 15 minutes, then dropped the ramp and led the way, keeping my sidearm hidden but handy. When I got all the way down the gangplank, I saw a welcoming committee of

Xirom.

They looked like a congregation of jade Buddhas. Slightly shorter than humans, averaging about five feet tall, they had no hair on their heads. They also had very Buddha-like round bellies. Their clothes were draped on their bodies in a random fashion. Their faces were quite round, with a broad smile and ample folds of chins. These were called *thurtles*. The Xirom expressed mirth by having their "thurtles wobble." This equates to laughing, but the accompanying sound is like a "raspberry" or a Bronx cheer (whatever a Bronx is). It also swept up in pitch.

The minute I signaled everything was safe, the Professor bustled forward to introduce himself. Manky weaseled his way along, mostly checking out the natives for expensive jewelry. Fran brought up the rear in her role as grunt laborer. Still keeping half an eye out for any possible dangers, I went back to help her carry the gear.

"Why thank you very much, Captain," she gushed.

"One of my favorite pastimes is imitating pack animals," I said, shouldering a load. I could've sworn I heard an electronic giggle coming from the cabin.

The Xirom escorted us into the village. They smiled and chattered and wobbled their thurtles frequently. The spokesman for the group, not really a leader, was named Xixius. He took the Professor around and showed him the highlights of the village. That meant he pointed out various huts.

The ineffable Mr. Mickens stayed right in the forefront of the group, checking everything he saw for its market value.

Once in the village, the Professor settled down with a group of the Xirom and a recorder to start expanding his knowledge of the language. Manky was still hanging around the perimeter, looking at all of the stones they wore. At least he wasn't wearing a jeweler's glass.

Fran had unloaded a lot of equipment that had to be housed in a tent, so I went back to the ship to help her. Now, if Frances Ingram had looked like the graduate student I originally imagined, I would have let the little nerd set everything up by himself. However, with Fran, I decided raising a tent and hauling around equipment would be good for my muscle tone. After all, it wasn't often I got a chance to exercise.

There was a lot of "accidental" bumping into each other, a lot of effusive *thank yous, you're welcomes,* and bright smiles passed back and forth.

I must say, despite the way the ground looked, it wasn't that soft. It took some real effort to drive in the tent stakes. But, with the weather being so damned comfortable, it hardly seemed like work.

At one point, I took a break and ran back inside the ship to get us something to drink.

"Hi there, Cammy! How's the air quality maintaining out there?" Of course we both knew I meant the pheromone level.

"Mr. Allnut you should stop this rutting about. We have to prepare the African Queen for a serious mission," she said.

Yeah, I'd switched over to "she" with the female persona.

Anyway she wore a rather long dress and a wide-brimmed hat with a scarf wrapped over the top and tied underneath her chin. There was a hint of a British accent, but one that was slightly higher-class than Manky's.

"Cammy, haven't I been the very picture of good manners?"

"Your behavior might pass as manners in those filthy riverside bars you frequent, Mr. Allnut, but it does not stand up to the minimum required by proper society."

"Cammy, you just have no faith in me."

"I would prefer to put my faith in something more dependable, like snow falling on the Congo."

And so the day passed. Toward the end of the afternoon, the Professor and the esteemed Mr. Mickens returned to the ship with the news that we'd been invited to the village for a special banquet in our honor. We repaired to our rooms to gussy up for the feast. Well, gussy up as well as you could when out in the field. I found a shirt that was slightly less dirty.

We re-adjourned close to sundown and headed into the

village. The natives greeted us with many smiles and much wobbling of thurtles. The Xirom reminded me of the early Polynesians. Only in green Buddha suits.

The meal was delicious. It featured many dishes I'd never encountered. Strange fish, vegetables and fruits. If Manky was looking for some way to make money off this excursion, he could make quite a few Credits with a gourmet Xirom restaurant. The locals had a special drink for Mr. Mickens himself. They presented him with a brown bottle that had a white oval label on it and bore the name *Guinness* in block writing.

Manky was impressed. And that's saying something. The last time I'd seen Manky impressed had been at one of the more lurid shows on Hedon, the brothel planet. Manky went off in a world all his own, staring at the bottle. It was a welcome relief. I wish I knew the secret to keeping him occupied like the Xirom did.

They gave me a native drink. It tasted like fruit juice, but it had side effects. I tasted no alcohol, and there were no euphorics, but there was something about the drink that made me feel very, very relaxed. I could tell it was affecting Fran the same way. She kept casting glances my way. Nice glances.

Boy, did I like that girl.

When we got back to the ship, there was the inevitable moment when we paused outside Fran's room. She looked frightened. "Don't even try it," she said.

"Why not?"

"Because I'm feeling much too vulnerable," she said. Then that haunted look traced its way across her face. "Besides, I'm an academic. I shouldn't get involved." And she closed her door.

I went into my room.

"Good evening, sir, I've prepared a nice cold shower for you." Cammy was male, dressed very properly, with an English accent again. Seemed to be some sort of servant.

"Thanks, I needed that."

"I beg your pardon, sir?"

"I'll take that shower."

He raised an eyebrow. "My goodness, you do seem to be rather taken with this young lady."

#

The following morning, when we gathered for breakfast, I couldn't help noticing someone was missing: Manky. My stomach clenched as I tried to figure out what trouble he was getting himself into. I dashed around both inside and outside the *Chameleon* trying to find him.

"Aha, yes. Mr. Mickens said he was going to get an early start this morning," Professor Latham said back in the ship. "Said he was going into the bush to look at some of the natural beauties of the planet." Ones that sparkled, I was sure. "Can't imagine what he wants. The flora and fauna on this planet have been quite thoroughly surveyed and classified."

I labored a casual smile onto my face. "I suppose he thought he could come up with some new species that he could name after himself." That meant this planet would be home to a little animal known as the scheming sneak.

"Aha, yes. Useless task. Planet's much richer in cultural history," he said. "Francis, we must set up recording gear in the village." Fran started packing up gear to take with them.

I kept my face beaming as I saw them off to visit the Xirom. Once they were out of sight, I went into serious fret mode. I sought out my AI to find out if he had any news about Manky.

Cammy was back in the persona from the previous night, very formal and very restrained. "As a matter of fact, sir, Mr. Mickens left a recording for you." He suddenly switched over to Manky's voice.

"I 'ad to dash off this morning early, mate. I'll tell y', the main Wog, 'e told me 'e was going to take me to see their greatest treasure. 'e says it's off somewhere in the bush. I can't 'ardly wait to see what it is."

What the Big Bang was he up to? How could he be off with Xixius? Professor Latham was meeting with him at this very minute. Manky had to be tromping around in the bush all by himself, getting into all sorts of trouble. He'd probably manage to meet up with a gnnar. I didn't think that the Stevens Foundation would be happy if the Mr. Mickens I returned with was a small cinder.

I entertained thoughts of dashing off to find Manky, but I didn't know which way he went. I could go charging off in the polar opposite direction. So I just stomped around the ship. As the hours passed, worrying about Manky gave ground to other thoughts that were hopping and skipping through my mind. They were nicer, although complex ones.

"Sir, if I may remark, you seem to be quite on edge today."

"I don't know what's happening with me, Cammy. I'm all wrought up about Fran."

"Yessir, if I may say so, I've been rather concerned about the young lady, myself," he replied.

"I mean I've always been a go-with-the-flow, take-the-worlds-as-they-come kind of guy. Now I'm thinking different."

"Different-*ly*, sir?" He laid on that last syllable to correct me.

I decided to ignore his last barb. "Yes, now I wonder about her. I mean, what's going to happen after this trip? Where will she go? Where will I go? And--do I want to go there?"

"I see, sir," he said.

"So I'm worried about her effect on me. Aren't you?"

"No, frankly, sir. I was more worried about *your* effect on *her*."

He was always on my side!

#

When it was late afternoon, I went into the village.

The professor and Fran were just concluding their session with the villagers. I hoped Manky might have shown up there. No such luck. So I helped Fran pack the gear. While we were doing that, and sharing the inevitable glances with each other, I couldn't help but notice that there were a great number of thurtles wobbling. I looked up, and it seemed all of the villagers were stealing glances at Fran and me, and wobbling to their heart's content.

Could they tell?

However, I couldn't dwell on that. We were still missing one member of the party, and the sun was tipping down from the zenith.

I fussed and bothered all the way back to the ship.

When daylight was beginning to fade, Manky finally reappeared, much to my relief. He was still whole and almost hearty, although his body was totally covered with lacerations. He looked like he'd followed Br'er Rabbit into the briar patch and wandered there all day. He had lost his usual enthusiasm.

Xixius accompanied him and, by contrast, looked clean and serene, like his valet had just turned him out in his best outfit. Of course, his thurtles wobbled.

"The Mister Mickens and I have had a most prankish day looking at the beauties of our land. I'm sure he found it a rewarding pastime." With that, he gave one last wobble of his thurtles and headed back to the village.

"I think I met every thorn they 'ave on this planet." Manky did look used. Some of the barbs must have had mild toxins in them, a few scratches looked red and swollen. "And I can't say in polite company where I itch. And do you know where we wound up going? Do you know what's the great bloody treasure they 'ave on this thorn-infested place? A fruit tree! A bloody fruit tree! That was it! Let me get into your ship and 'ave the AI put the medical kit to me."

We looked up at the ship and saw Cammy there. She was large and imposing in a white nurse's outfit. She looked like she would broach no complaints.

"She should close 'er bloody eyes when she goes to treat me itch, she should. Close 'er bloody eyes."

"Cammy, could you please treat Mr. Mickens's lacerations?"

Cammy snicked a pair of rubber gloves onto her hands.

"Certainly. Bend over and grab your ankles," she commanded.

"You bloody well watch it!"

#

The following day was the last full day of our visit. The Amalgam Regs were very definite about the length of a stay on one of these planets. And I had better follow the Regs. Or else. I made sure to check out what everyone's plans were over breakfast.

The Professor was heading into the village. He was bubbling with anticipation about something that Xixius had told him. "Aha, yes, I'm on the brink of getting something exciting, quite exciting. I have to go to the village and arrange it with the Xirom."

Manky said he would go along with the Professor, and I felt relieved. After yesterday, I assumed it would be safe to leave Manky in the village. He'd learned to be a little more cautious about exploring this planet. He still walked tentatively.

That left Fran and me to tear the gear down and store it back on the *Chameleon*. There was a certain something in the air, and I must say that the words, "It's now or never" kept repeating themselves in my mind.

We were taking gear inside the ship (the tent stakes were just as hard to pull up as they had been to hammer down) when I heard thurtles wobbling behind me. We turned around and found Xixius standing there.

"Most joyous greeting to you, my two friends. I did wish to see you this day."

"It's nice to see you, Xixius," I replied diplomatically.

"I am most pleased to bring you something I know the two of you would most appreciate. I was with Mr. Mickens to see the Xitus Tree yesterday. Unfortunately, he did not have the chance to enjoy the fruits."

"I don't think he's used to taking long hikes," I said.

"However, I took the opportunity to pick a couple of the fruits to bring to you. I hope you will welcome this small gift." He held up the fruits. They looked beautiful. Apples are red, flowberries are green, oranges are-- well-- orange. However these fruits were absolutely gorgeous. They had streaks and shadings of every color of the rainbow. "I can tell you appreciate the looks of the fruit, but that is but a small part of its virtue. You must, please, eat these. I'm sure you will find them most delicious."

"Well, thank you." It seemed a crime to eat such beautiful things, but the Regs were quite definite about how you should treat gifts. Anyway, anything that looked that good had to be tasty.

"I must go back to the village. I know you also have things to do." He waddled off.

We looked at the fruits, at each other, and with a shrug, left the gear lying there, and went inside into the main cabin.

"Cammy, we have the local ambrosia. Could we please break out our finest china?"

"Sure, honey, I'll get out the old TV dinner trays." She was fat, dumpy, and wore a tee-shirt that said "Trailer Trash" over her sagging breasts.

"Never mind, just give me what we've got."

She furnished me with a couple of plates and some sharp knives. I cut the fruits into pieces, and we sat opposite each other to enjoy our gift from the Xirom.

The Xitus fruit was delicious! The first taste had the effect of shooting a tingle down my spine. The second taste shot the tingle from the base of my spine to somewhere forward of that. I was squirming in my seat, trying to rearrange my pants to make room for a looming presence that had sprouted down there.

Fran took her second bite, emitted a gasp, and quickly crossed her legs while first straightening her spine, then leaning in forward toward the table.

We purposely avoided looking at each other as we wolfed down every last morsel of the fruit, grunting along the way.

When we were finished, we leaned back from the table, and our eyes caught each other. We stared.

And we stared.

And we stared.

I can't say for certain which one of us leapt for the other

first. It seemed mutual. But before I knew it, we were locked around each other. We grappled, we groped, we embraced, we kissed, we nuzzled, all the while leaving a trail of clothing heading into Fran's room. We dove onto the bed and proceeded with the most passionate sessions of love-making I'd ever experienced. I hoped the bed would hold up under the crashing we did.

This woman was something. She was it. She made me forget every other woman I'd ever been with. And there were some pretty damn good women on that list.

They were all gone, forgotten.

After a moment, an eternity, and all other pieces of time you can possibly imagine, we finally lay there, staring at each other.

Fran suddenly snapped back to reality, as she stiffened and pulled away from me.

"I'm a devoted scholar," she declared.

"Of course you are," I replied.

"No." She turned away with a renewed resolve. "I can't get into anything like this."

"Why shouldn't you?" I asked, as I began to realize that the two of us were actually getting into a very serious "anything like this."

"Because--" tears began to form in her eyes, "--because I can't really think about anything like pairing up with someone."

"Why not?"

"You'd--someone would expect that, if we were pairing up, we'd have children," she explained.

Was I thinking about having children? Oh my god, I was!

"And I can't have children," she continued. "I've known about it for a long time. I just don't have the..."

"...Oh, I am begging your pardon, oh great and honored master, for bothering you like this." Fran and I both jumped. Cammy wore a loin cloth and not much else over a scrawny body.

"It'd better be good, Cammy."

"Oh, it is most sorry I am. It is just that I have to follow these protocols that you, great and exulted one, have set down."

"Spill it, Cammy."

"Well, you know the rule about tracking the members of the party on a planet?"

"Yes, I remember."

"It just so happens that this morning I heard that Mr. Mickens was talking to the Professor about going to see something today."

"And what was that, Cammy?" I asked, trying to keep my patience.

"I do believe that it was something called a gnnar... "

"SHIT!"

I leapt out of bed and put on my clothes while running out the ship, a mutually exclusive act when donning pants. So I did the famous hop and pants-leg thrust known to many a lover whose woman has a jealous husband.

A gnnar! The one dangerous fauna on this planet, and Manky was rushing right into its clutches.

By this time, I was sprinting my way toward the village, continuing to put on various articles of clothing.

I swore under my breath. I knew it was a bad idea coming to this place with a freelancer like Manky!

I cleared my way into the village, and saw Manky and the Professor standing in front of a gnnar and studying it, like it was the local version of a squirrel. The thing loomed over them. It was staring intently at them, emitting a low growl that couldn't be a welcoming greeting. I put on a last burst of speed, stretching my lungs to their limits.

Just as I was approaching the pair, Fran shot past me and tackled the Professor. I followed her example and gave Manky the same treatment, propelling him to the side, and heading toward a group of boulders nearby. As we went flying away, I felt something *terribly* hot behind us. We landed just short of a big boulder, and I crashed into the thing with my head. It was a hefty blow that took me away from the current world for just a

few seconds. Fortunately, our instincts took us around behind the boulder. We could see Fran and the Professor behind another rock.

When I was cartwheeling around, still under the influence of the crack on the head, I thought I saw some very strange things around me. I rolled over, blinked my eyes, and stared at the huts--no the buildings--behind me. I swung around and peeked up over the boulder at the gnnar--no, the *weapon*--standing there. I shook my head and blinked my eyes again, and then saw the animal standing there, with the primitive huts ranged behind it. A few yards in front of the beast was a puddle of rapidly-cooling magma on the ground. Drawing straight line from the gnnar's head to the puddle, it intersected the place where the Professor and Manky had been standing.

"Manky!" I hissed, "What the hell are you doing playing with that damned thing?"

"I 'eard they 'ad a diamond in 'em."

"A diamond *laser*, you idiot. They've evolved it as a weapon, and it shot the thing right at you."

"Whot does that mean?"

"It means you damn near became a Manky-kabob. Let's get the hell out of here." Under cover of the boulders we all escaped from the gnnar.

When we got back to the ship--we decided to take the long way round--I leveled a finger at Manky and said, "Okay, from now on you will behave in an exemplary fashion. No more going off after the hidden treasures of Megalm. I don't care if you think you see it glowing just over the horizon, I don't want you to do anything, but keep your bloody hands off and your bloody nose clean. You hear me?"

"Yes, yes, Mate, you don't 'ave to get cranky about it."

"Tonight is the final banquet at the village. I don't want you to wander off anywhere. I want you to stay right there. I want you to have a pleasant interaction with the natives, and not go searching for any treasures. You understand?"

"Yes, yes."

"You'd damn well better understand!" I concluded.

I hoped I had made my point. I thought it was an awfully effective speech. Unfortunately, while I was delivering it, I saw on the floor a piece of my underwear that had been dropped during my haste to bed Ms. Ingram. I hoped Manky didn't notice me trying to kick it out of sight.

#

Something was bothering me. Something I'd seen in the village, when I hit my head on the boulder. I saw buildings, real buildings rather than little grass huts. And there'd been sidewalks, not paths. It had only been there for a moment, a quick flash. I couldn't tell if the blow had caused me to see something that wasn't there, or if it had let me see what was really there.

I decided to do a little check. I strolled to the ramp heading down from the ship. I looked at the clearing in front of me. I braced myself. Then I brought my head down sharply on one of the supporting struts, still keeping my gaze steady on the clearing.

I heard thurtles wobbling behind me.

"Ah, Mr. Holcombe, I see that you are testing the structural integrity of your craft. But don't you think it would be better to try it with something that wasn't quite so sensitive?" It was Xixius standing behind me.

"Well, they say that sometimes you need to give your head a big swat so you can clear it."

"I don't think you need to. I think it is best you keep it clear through the working of your intelligence. But you present a most interesting idea. Maybe we can discuss that at the banquet tonight." He waddled off toward the village, with his thurtles wobbling.

"Yes," I said, "I'll see you there."

#

The banquet went swimmingly. The food was delicious, and thurtles were wobbling all around the place. Fran was lovely. They gave Manky another bottle of that Guinness beer. (Where did they get the stuff from?) Manky was trying to figure out how to open up the planet to tourist trade, a harmless pastime for him. And Fran was lovely. Or did I already say that?

Xixius engaged me in a conversation where he seemed most interested in quoting some philosophical maxims that were part of the Xirom culture. He ignored my attempts to bring up what had happened earlier that day when I'd banged my head on the landing gear.

At one point, I noticed Manky missing for at least a quarter of an hour. I started to search for him when he emerged from one of the huts with a group of the Xirom. I was going to storm over to find what mischief he'd been up to. Then I caught the disappointed look on his face. Whatever had happened, it hadn't turned out the way he planned. Anything contrary to Manky's wishes had to be for the public good.

After the banquet we headed back to the ship with everyone in good spirits, except Manky who was still subdued.

When we reached our cabin doors, Fran and I stopped in front of her cabin door, turned, and looked at each other. We settled into the gaze for several moments. "Your place or mine?" I said.

"So which will it be, Frannie?" Cammy wore a loud sports coat to match his personality. "Will you pick what's behind Door #1 or Door #2? Bunny, can you tell us what's offered behind those two doors?"

"Cammy--" I ventured. Fran leaned back against the wall, waiting patiently for the spiel to end.

Cammy had transformed into some ditz whose lack of brains was compensated by the abundance of her bosom. "Ooooooh!" she chirped, "Well, behind Door #1 we have your chance to go directly from the Captain's table to the Captain's bed, all in the comfort of your own home." She looked up and simpered, "Sounds pretty good to me!"

"Cammy--"

"And behind Door #2," she continued, "you have the once-in-a-lifetime chance to visit the totally uncharted and uncivilized Captain's Room, where the local natives will be celebrating the primitive Festival of the Unwashed Socks."

"Cammy--" I patiently rolled my eyes to the ceiling.

"So," Sports Coat was back, "what is your choice, lucky lady?"

I gave it a long pause. "Cammy--"

"Yes?"

"Could I have privacy, please?"

"You bet, Captain. And as an additional bonus we will soundproof the other rooms from your noises."

"Good night, Cammy."

"Good night, folks, and thanks for playing The Vice is Right!" There was a blare of loud brassy music.

"STOP THE MUSIC!" I screamed.

We finally had silence. Until we were in Fran's room and started making those noises Cammy'd talked about. There were a lot of other things happening. There were times that I almost started to say a number of things, but couldn't figure out exactly how to say them. They were things I'd never said to a woman before.

#

In the morning, we were packing the last of the gear before taking off.

Now, the Regs are quite strict about the length of a stay on a planet. However, there's a wiggle in the Regs that says diplomacy comes first. And if the locals say they will come by to see you off, you make damn sure to wait until they come by.

So we were re-re-re-checking things inside the main cabin, when a delegation came waddling over from the village, bearing gifts.

They arrived in the ship all smiles, as usual. Xixius came forward carrying something that looked heavy. "Mr. Mickens, we are most joyous to give you this parting gift as a token of our esteem."

The gift was a box made of some sort of fiber. It clinked, and it bore the white oval and the Guinnes lettering. "Crumbs, it's a whole bloody case! Where do they get it?" This definitely put a bounce into Manky's step.

Fran was over talking to a few of the other natives. She returned wearing a broad grin. "They gave me something interesting. It's some Amalgam Credits. And a set of dice." She was holding the Verrilian bones. I quickly understood. What Manky'd been doing in that hut last night was try to get the Xirom to gamble with him.

Those dice never fail coming up the way the owner wanted them to. However, they must not have worked last night. The Xirom had taken Manky to the cleaners. Not only that, the Credits totaled exactly the amount that Manky owed me. How did they know that amount? Another question I had to sort out regarding this supposedly bucolic race.

Xixius approached Professor Latham. He was carrying a piece of the researcher's equipment. "Professor, just as we promised, we have recorded the collected works of all of our greatest playwrights for you. I'm sorry that we could not let you see the actual books of the plays themselves, but they are our greatest cultural treasures."

"Aha, yes, well, this is most wonderful. Most wonderful. Don't know how I can possibly thank you enough. Bringing in these works for translation will be quite a feather in my cap," the Professor beamed.

Xixius turned to Fran and me. "My prankish friends, what pleasure you have brought us. The gift that I give you is that you have started the first of your wonderful children here. It will be a most entertaining thing to see your family grow."

Fran gave a sharp intake of breath, then she smiled bravely as she thanked the Xirom. She was putting up a good front.

I was heading for her to explain how Xixius had made a mistake, when the Xirom, who had turned and started to leave, stopped and turned back. "Oh, yes. Goodbye, my good and prankish friend Cammy." Where had he learned about my AI?

This time Cammy was wearing some sort of raincoat and a hat. He raised two fingers to the brim and swung them out, in a kind of salute. "Louie, I think this is the beginning of a beautiful friendship."

I added this exchange to the list of things I couldn't explain.

We waved goodbye to the Xirom.

When I turned back, Fran's face was streaming with tears.

"What's wrong?"

"It was what he said about our child."

"Listen, Fran, I know it's impossible," I said.

"I know. It's just that he made me think that it might be possible. But it isn't. I've known that for years."

"So there's no chance. You don't have to think about it."

"But that's the problem. I can't help thinking about it."

"That's silly. Tell you what, let's put the whole thing to rest." I brought her toward the med unit. "This will definitely tell you. Cammy, can you do a pregnancy test?"

"Jim, there's only so much medical science can do." He was dressed in some terrible costume meant to represent a space uniform. "And call me Bones."

"All right." I turned to Fran. "Let's prove it. This way, you won't have to think about it again."

"I don't *want* to!" Fran burst out.

I was insistent. "Listen, just do it. It'll clear the air and leave no doubt. You'll be back to being who and what you are. Come on, come on." I urged her toward the med unit.

"All right, young lady, just hold very still." Cammy waved a little device at her that looked like a prop out of some kids' vid. I knew he was really operating the med unit.

He paused for a moment. "You're not going to have a baby."

The tears had started again, but at least it was over.

"You're going to have twins."

We were dumbstruck. Fran was holding back the joy.

"Cammy, are you sure?" I asked.

"Quite sure."

Fran was jumping up and down. And crying for good measure.

I turned to her. "Now listen, I'll be there to help you with this."

"Oh, you're very, very sweet to say that." She'd put her arms around my neck. "But you don't have to try to act noble for me. You've given me the best gift ever. I'm very grateful to you for that."

"Would you stop to consider that I might mean it? That I might want to be around?" I asked.

"Oh, you're so sweet!" She stroked me like I was some pet. "But I don't want to be a burden. After all, you have your business, and you've got your life, and just because something terribly nice happened to me, that doesn't mean I have to trap you..."

"What do you mean trap me? Did it cross your mind that I may have some feelings for you? Do you know you've made me forget every other woman? I've forgotten everyone!"

"Oh, no--" Fran started to contradict me again.

"Excuse me," Cammy said, "but why don't the two of you go off alone and talk this over?"

"That's all right, Cammy. Fran and I are two adults, and we can certainly express our feelings toward each other."

"Yes, but maybe you should find someplace private to talk."

"Cammy, there's nothing we can't talk about right here that we-"

"FOR GOD'S SAKE, JIM, DO I HAVE TO TELL YOU EVERYTHING? THE TWO OF YOU GET IN THE BEDROOM! AND THOSE ARE DOCTOR'S ORDERS!"

#

So that's how it worked out. We went in the bedroom and clearly and logically discussed matters. A couple of days later.

And that's what became of me: Randy Holcombe, the free-wheeling bachelor of the space lanes. I did something incredibly old fashioned.

I got married.

The father of the bride was there to give her away.

"Aha, yes, certainly been quite the trip."

How was I supposed to know she used her mother's last name rather than Latham?

Cammy was at the wedding, wearing some incredibly tasteless gown. And when I say "there," I mean physically, not as a holo. She had somehow, in her own words, "just figured out" how to make a remote unit that could house enough memory to support an AI of her class. This construct also managed to change identity as easily as a holo. That's technology that's unknown in the Amalgam!

So Cammy was at the wedding.

And she cried.

She cried!

AI's don't cry!

Of course, Manky insisted on coming along. He was not any part of the wedding party. You couldn't really call Manky a best man. And for his being the ring bearer--

Not if there was a pawnshop within 500 light years.

Fran moved right in on the administrative part of my business, which was great; I always hated that stuff. She changed suppliers, modified deals, and negotiated a far better loan on my ship.

That pretty much tells it all, except for one thing that keeps rattling around in my head: The Xirom. There were some very strange things about them that I still can't figure out.

Where did they get the Guiness beer?

How did Fran manage to get pregnant on Megalm when she had been unable to have children before? And on top of that, I was properly contracepted?

And then there were the times I bumped my head. Now, I know a bump can sometimes make you see things, usually stars. But what I saw were buildings. Modern buildings. And on top of that, when I purposely bumped my head on the landing strut, I had seen, for a very brief moment, a spaceport, not a clearing. A whole, complete spaceport. With four holes in the macadam, where I'd driven in tent stakes.

And how did Xixius know Cammy when they'd never met before that last day? And how did Cammy, after that brief encounter with the chief Xirom, suddenly figure out how to make a mobile unit, one that changes for all of the different characters, when that technology isn't known in the whole rest of the Amalgam?

What are the Xirom trying to do? They seem to be content to hide away on their little planet, and keep entirely out of Amalgam business. Are they happy to stay a little bucolic backwater and keep the Amalgam "progress" away from them? Think about it.

#

Randy reached forward and flipped the switch.

RECORD OFF

"Oh, there you are. We've been trying to figure out what you've been up to. Have you been boring the staff with stories of how I seduced you away from your simple unsullied life on the farm?" Fran's pregnancy was well into its third trimester.

"We must drag him away from the lure of the demon rum. It is only through sobriety that he will find his salvation. Hallelujah!" The CMU (Cammy Mobile Unit) was dressed like some social crusader, carrying a sign that said "Prohibition."

"I'm going to check to see if AI's are allowed to be Godmothers," Randy responded. "There's got to be something in the Constitution against it. Separation of silicon and family, or something."

Fran came over and gave him a kiss. "I think the only reason why I keep you is because you're so good in bed."

"Okay, okay. I'm coming. I entered my story in the competition, Madam. I'm sure it'll come in as a finalist. Now the next thing we have to do is figure out what is up with those Xirom."

"That's just your over-fertile imagination." She swung around to Cammy. "Was he always so fanciful?"

"Worse."

"That's terrible. I'm just going to have to put you to bed to get some more rest."

They all headed back to the *Chameleon* for the evening. Some text flashed up on the Recorder at the bar.

SWITCH FAILED

STILL RECORDING

HOW PRANKISH!

Chapter 4

Poison

The spacers at The StarBoard Café were upset. Not a surprise, since spacers normally operated at an emotional altitude somewhere up around high dudgeon. When they're at that height, it's best to leave them alone. Proximity to spacer dudgeons has been known to be hazardous to one's health.

Since the spacers' emotional level had increased, staff members in charge of keeping the peace had managed to drift within easy range of any obvious outbreaks of dudgeonry.

The staff was under the leadership of Captain Kordlux, the current proprietor of the StarBoard Café. No one owned the StarBoard. Ownership was a quaint custom that was practiced on that backward little planet called Earth. The right to manage establishments like the Café had to be earned through diligence. Anyone could take over the Café. They just had to prove that the current management was not on their toes--or whatever pedal extremities they used to negotiate their interface with gravity. If the claimants applying for control of the Café could penetrate security and take over the place, thus demonstrating the on-duty staff was lax, stewardship would be handed over immediately, no questions asked. It was like a game of *Conquer*. If anyone showed a superior position, the current manager would cede to the challenger. Since the Café was quite profitable, there were many vying for the stewardship.

The particular thing that had the spacers in a flap on this occasion was the increased presence of a group of strange creatures called "tourists" gawking their way through the establishment. They were flocking to the Café in an attempt to see real, live spacers in their natural habitat. Had they known better, they would have understood that the natural habitat for a spacer was a brawl.

However, if they knew any better, they wouldn't be tourists.

The spacers schemed (of course) about methods to prevent their sanctuary from turning into a tourist attraction.

#

Poison, neither spacer nor tourist, entered the Café. His usual companion snuffled along behind him, somewhat resembling that animal from Earth, a dog, as it carefully assessed every odor it came across. However, it was not a dog. It had an enormous proboscis and a crown on his head that looked like a forward-and-backward-facing hat. The beast was unique. As was Poison. His gait was long and measured on his splayed feet. His protuberant eyes blinked as he glanced about with his triangular-shaped head. Spacers argued over what species he was and what planet he came from. No one knew for sure.

Poison pulled up a stool in the section of the bar tended by Kowana. His snuffling companion circled three times beneath the stool and curled up on the floor.

Kowana came over to take Poison's order. She was a Dowda, a porcine race from the planet Muck. Her lineage accounted for the two tusks that poked up from her lower jaw. And for her size. Poison was able to look directly into her eyes only because the floor on her side of the bar was four feet lower. She tipped the scales at something like a thousand pounds. Her size and strength helped her maintain peace in the Café. She also had a small psychic talent, the ability to sense the emotions coursing through another being's mind.

Poison glanced up at Kowana and ordered. "The usual." He wasn't loquacious this evening. However, he was seldom loquacious, usually brooding over his thoughts.

"One Rigelian Delight coming up," she said in her *bassa profunda*. As she went to fix the drink, she cast a look back, sensing the emotions raging through her new patron.

When she returned with the drink, she said, "You're quite

the regular here. What's the attraction of a spacers' bar?"

Poison considered for a moment, "It must be either your charms or the Delights you serve." His attempt at humor was offset by his dour looks.

"I think it's the drink," she said.

"This is the only place you can get this thing, aside from"--he paused for a moment--"someplace very far away."

"How far away?" She probed.

"I can't really say." He was evading the questions.

"Is it someplace near where you come from?" she asked.

A faraway look crept into his eyes. "Yeah, very near."

"Where *do* you come from, Poison?"

He raised a piercing glance up at her looking like he was ready to explode with an explanation, then just shook his head, looking back down at the bar.

"I was talking to Sanik the Snaugf," she continued. "He knows everyone who ships out. He says he doesn't know you."

"He doesn't know everybody." Again, evasion.

"But you did ship out once?" She probed.

"But I stopped."

"What made you stop?"

"Circumstances."

"If you stopped, why are you hanging out in a spacers' bar? And an expensive one, at that?"

"I guess you forced me to confess. It's you, Kowana." He was racing at top speed, running away from the conversation.

"Do you think you're my type, Poison?"

"I just might know exactly what type you are, Kowana." There were boding overtones to that comment, which managed to pause the conversation for the moment. Kowana stared intensely at Poison as she sensed his emotion welling up inside him, ready to burst.

Poison stared down at his long-fingered hands. Suddenly he erupted. "You want to know where I come from? And who I am?"

Kowana gave a small nod of her head.

"Well, my real name is #######, and I come from #######." Quite impossibly he pronounced something like electronic hash for the name and location.

Kowana frowned. "My translator is giving me nothing but white noise for your language."

"That's right," Poison said. "I can't say those names."

Her frown deepened. "I don't get it."

Poison looked up, surprised at the idea that had welled up in his mind. He'd reached a decision. He didn't know why, but he had. "Why don't you stick around? You'll be able to find out," he said.

Kowana could tell that, strangely enough, his mood was beginning to lighten, as though he'd lifted a great burden off his chest. He reached forward and hit the Record button.

RECORD

#

All right, I'm tired of all the questions! Everyone wants to know who I am, where I come from, and how I got the name of Poison. Here's the story.

It all started when I booked out on the--I can't say it! It'll only come out as hash, and besides you don't know where the place is. Anyway, I was booked out on a flight.

For some reason, a dirty rumor said *I* was responsible for a near mutiny that occurred on that ship, but that was nothing but slander. I *had* pointed out a few ways the captain might have made his bookkeeping operations a little more efficient, but that was all. His over-reaction made me think my instinct was right and he really did have something to hide. However, my instinct just got me in trouble, again. So much trouble that the Captain branded me with my undeserved nickname.

"I tell you, you're nothing but poison. You've infected this whole damn ship. I'm going to have to roll over my whole crew at the next port. But at least I'm rid of you, here and now."

With that the port closed, and I was cast loose in a lifeboat, the space-age version of walking the plank. At least I didn't have to swim across half an ocean to get back to shore. I was floating around in my closet-sized pod with a distress beacon on, waiting for a rescue ship to pick me up. I was left to sit by myself and think that I knew, I just *knew*, that the Captain was pulling some sort of high jinks with the crew's commissions. I didn't know how I knew it, but I did.

I'd been floating for several hours when I felt a bump that told me a tractor beam had engaged the boat. In a few minutes I'd be reeled in and dumped into a rescue ship. I wasn't looking forward to that. With my official termination as a member of the crew of my previous ship, I'd be ostracized by the staff of this new vessel, judged a troublemaker and malcontent.

But something unexpected happened. I felt a tingle go up my spine indicating that the lifeboat had shifted over to n-space. My impression was verified when I saw the onboard computer go into the electronic version of a nervous breakdown as it tried to figure out what the hell was happening. This lifeboat didn't have a faster-than-light drive. Therefore the FTL was being induced from the outside. I didn't know anyone in the galaxy who had such a technology.

My first reaction to that was a calm, cool, and well-thought-out panic. Somebody or something totally unknown was whisking me off to somewhere I didn't know about.

I switched over to my years of spacer training and began to think my way logically through my alternatives.

There were none.

Trying to bail out of the lifeboat in the middle of n-space is not considered a good life decision. They'd tried experimenting with that sort of thing when we'd first developed the FTL drives. They put some animals out to see what would happen.

What they got back was not anatomically correct.

I thought further. Whoever had accomplished this feat certainly had an advanced technology and therefore an advanced intelligence. There was no example in history of an intelligent species that was malicious. (I managed to block out of my mind every spacer I'd ever met.)

After what seemed a very long time, I felt myself being

translated back into regular space. The onboard computer gave the equivalent of a silicon sigh of relief, but it immediately lapsed into another tizzy when it tried to find a known star chart that matched our current location.

There was a rattle of someone tapping into the airlock, a quick whoosh of pressurization in the outer chamber, and the grate of the hatch opening up.

A head peeped into the boat. The individual looked like a similar species, although he was a little bit shorter, barely five foot tall, and he was one of those creatures who had raw skin on his face. He also had wide eyes that gave him a very innocent look. He turned around to speak to someone behind him. I leaned forward to hear what he said, thinking I'd find something out.

"Pheg auri klim kruchel."

Well, that was enlightening!

What was wrong with my translator? I'd been able to understand the Captain's gurgles when he sent me off in the lifeboat. Why couldn't I understand this guy? I had all the latest translation programs. Was he using some language we didn't have in your files?

He turned back to me. "Are you Cargo Officer"--well, he said my name and the ship I'd been on in my own language. Of course I can't say that right now. On top of that, he said I was "formerly" from the ship. Word sure got around fast..

"Yes, and who, may I ask, are you?"

"I'm Torvel Haist, Chief Ambassador of Liaison for Racial Adjudicator for Floria IV."

What a mouthful!

"We've been looking forward to contacting you. That's why we've--uh--brought you here."

"That's very nice, Citizen Haist, but why'd you want to meet me?" I'd caught his last name. I also knew he was some kind of diplomat. I'd try to figure out the rest as I went along.

"You're a *very* talented person. We've brought you to this world because we want to employ your talents."

Talents? Did I suddenly learn how to play the vibro-harp on my way here? One thing I could tell: he was trying to sell me something. "What might those talents be?"

"Why don't we discuss those things when we get back to our headquarters?"

"Sure, we can probably discuss it on the shuttle ride down."

"Oh, that won't be necessary," he said.

I wondered what he meant by that. I didn't have long to figure it out. The minute I stepped through the lock, I knew I wasn't in any transfer station. The room was much too large. I had to be groundside already. A bunch of Haist's people, about a hundred of them, were scattered around the room. They all stared at me with what seemed to be hopeful anticipation on their faces and whispered excitedly to each other.

"Let me try to explain," he said. "We've been looking for someone like you for quite a while. You'd be surprised how far our search has ranged. Finding you in the lifeboat gave us the opportunity to move you here."

How far was it that they had to search for me? "What's this talent you're talking about? I'm sure you're not referring to my ability to balance eating utensils on my nose."

"No. It has something to do with the reason you were summarily dismissed from your ship."

"Having a bad employment record is my talent?"

"No. Your talent is…"

"*Mickel. Mickel. Urg oggle. Haist, bink flubnik?*" The voice boomed out over loudspeakers, mixed with audio static.

Panic crossed Haist's face. He wheeled around and shouted some reply in that weird tongue of his at the loudspeakers.

Electronic hash appeared on the wall opposite us. Haist spun back toward me, and, even though he was much smaller, managed to shove me off into a corner, behind some hanging drapes.

I was too bemused to complain. I peeked around the drape to see why Haist had panicked.

A face appeared in a display on the opposite wall. It was

someone of Haist's race, but with a longer face, augmented by a wisp of a goatee on his chin. Suspicion was his primary facial expression. The conversation they held was in the alien language my translator didn't recognize. However, their facial expressions conveyed the meaning. The stranger seemed to be probing Haist who, in turn, kept replying evasively. Then the face on the screen resolved into a look of conviction and made a definite assertive statement, with digit upraised. Haist managed to counter in some way, bringing a look of consternation on the other's face, however he concluded with another assertion accompanied by a wagging finger. The translation was easy: "I'll be back."

Haist turned back toward me. "I'm sorry for the interruption," he said, wearing a much-too-wide-and-reassuring smile on his face.

"What was that all about?" I asked.

"Well, now let me see, where were we? Ah, yes, your wonderful talent." He beamed at me, ignoring my question. "Have you ever noticed that you can understand what someone's up to, even when they're trying to hide it?"

"Funny you should mention that!" I said pointedly. "Yes. I've always had the knack to see through people, no matter how much they denied it."

"Of course they'd deny it."

"Then I really was right about my last Captain skimming from the crew! And everyone sided with him and started calling me Poison!" Man, was I ticked off.

"That's right."

"Okay, aside from making me really mad at my former captain, what do you have to tell me?"

"We'll pay you for your talent."

I snapped my gaze over to him. He had my attention "You will?"

"Yes."

"How much?"

"Once we've satisfactorily concluded this affair, which

should be in a matter of only a few hours, we'll send you back to your own part of the Universe."

"What do you mean, my part of the *Universe*?" I burst out. No wonder my computer couldn't find our location.

He looked rather apologetic. "I did say we had to look a long way to find you."

Well, if they got me here all of that distance, I guess they can send me back. But the first thing I had to do was negotiate. "So what happens past that?"

"When you return, you'll find that you have enough money to keep you comfortable for the rest of your life. You'll never have to work again."

"For just for a few hours' work?"

"Yes."

"Wait a minute. There's something else. I can tell." Knowing about this skill of mine made me rely on it.

"Well, yes, there is," he said, in what I had to admit was a very forthright manner.

"I knew it! What's the catch?"

"Your talent is raw, undeveloped. We need to manifest it physically."

I nodded, not in agreement, I just nodded. It was one of those nods that says: I heard what you said, but I'll be damned if I understand. "How do you intend to do that?"

"With our computer," he said.

"With your computer?" Again, the contradictory nod.

"Yes."

"What does that mean?"

"We'll enhance one of your senses. It won't mean much of anything."

As a former (now) Cargo Officer, I recognized equivocation when I heard it, with or without special talents. "What's 'not much of anything'?"

"You'll have to wear a protective device. Something like sunglasses."

"Something *like* sunglasses?" I did the nod again.

"Yes."

"Is it sunglasses?"

"No."

"Oh." I had to get out of nodding mode. "What are you going to do?"

"We'll be modifying your sense of touch."

"Y-e-e-s-s?" I gave him the universal beckoning gesture that means, "Give me more info."

"You'll have something like that thing from your legends, the Vandros Touch. Only it won't turn things into gold. It'll turn people into the physical form that best suits them."

"U-h--h-u-h?" More beckoning.

"So, to mask this ability, you'll have to wear a very thin covering on your skin."

"And that will be--?"

"It won't feel different. But it will insulate the enhancement."

"That's a rather big change." As a former Cargo Officer, I was slipping into bargaining mode.

"You could say that."

"I think I will say that."

"You will?"

"I say those are pretty impossible demands." I came down hard on him.

"You do?"

"Yes," I said, firmly, staring him down.

His gaze fell to the ground. "I guess I was rather excited about being able to contact you, to bring you here. I suppose I didn't pay enough attention to how this might come as a surprise to you."

"I think so," I said. "This is a really *big* change for me to to accept."

"I thought the money would be enough."

"You think that I can only be influenced by money?" I acted

outraged. I couldn't let him see how right he was.

Haist looked crestfallen. "I'm sorry. I see we were a little hasty. We didn't stop to consider your feelings. We presumed too much." He straightened his shoulders. "I'll see to it that you're sent home." He was quite gloomy. I let him stew in it as he took a few steps toward the portal we'd come through.

"Just a minute, Citizen Haist." He stopped and turned around. Something was jingling around in my mind; it sounded like a bunch of coins clattering. "Did you say something about leaving me with some credits?"

"Well, yes, I really must apologize for trying to appeal to you in such a venal manner. I know there are other, more important things to be considered."

"How many credits?"

"Well, they'd always be there in your account. The balance would never go down."

"For the whole rest of my life?" His offer was *very* tempting.

"That's right."

"Not that anything as materialistic as that would influence me," *not likely*, "but I do have to consider *your* needs. I'm sure that they're well-meaning and of a high moral value." Probably of a moral value a speck higher than a spacer's, and come to think of it, my own.

"They are! They are!" he said eagerly.

"Maybe you'd like to tell me what it is you want me to do."

"Yes! Certainly! The computer tells us our evolution has reached a point where we're paused on the brink of a great change, a great advance. However, we have a responsibility. There are other beings, our cousins as it were, who'll be left behind. They also need to evolve, but they need a push. From you."

"How?"

"You have to see a few people, apply your enhanced sense, and the process will be set in motion."

"And I'll have enough credits in my account--but that's not the prime consideration, of course."

"I understand."

I paused. I considered. I looked down at the floor. I looked up at the ceiling. I saw a very expensive rug on the floor. The chandelier cost some too.

"And I'll have enough credits in my…? I mean, I'll wind up handicapped, as it were. I'll no longer live my life in the same manner." *Broke.*

"Yes. That's quite clear."

Was he serious or just fooling me? Could I trust this guy or not? I had a decision to make, and I had to make it fast. There was something else, ticking in the back of my mind. Something that was urging me on.

I inhaled deeply, then exhaled. "All right," I said. I'll do practically anything for credits. I did say *practically*.

Everyone in the room gave a sigh of relief and excitedly whispered their gibberish to each other. "What do we do next?" I asked.

"You meet the master computer."

"That's fine. Where's that?"

This *thing* appeared floating in the air in front of my face. It didn't scoot in the door or anything like that. It was a matter of: now you don't see it; now you do. It glowed in front of me, pausing, swept around to the right side of my head, did a fast swoop to the other side, then darted back in front of me. It held there.

"*That is most fine,*" it said. I think. Or maybe it just put those words in my mind.

"I'm glad that's fine," I said, "but aren't you going to do some kind of enhancement to me?"

"*I did.*"

"Just now?"

"*Yes.*"

"I didn't feel anything."

"*You weren't meant to.*"

I was getting really confused, or impressed, I wasn't sure

which. "Well, that was easy enough," I said. "Is everything else going to be this easy?"

The master computer, or its terminal, or its whatever, disappeared just as suddenly as it had appeared. I took that as the answer to my question. I had to; it wasn't around to respond.

And there was something else bothering me, though I couldn't put my finger on it. Something wasn't right. Something didn't match, but I didn't know what.

I turned to Haist to see if I could find out what.

"Haist! Haist! I've tracked you down. Do not try to get away from me." The face was back on the screen. I understood what he said, now. The computer must have tweaked me or my translator.

Haist spun around and tried to hide me behind him. It wasn't a good fit. "Why, Inspector Pheydeaux, why should we try to get away from you?"

"Hah! You can try to be the innocent one with me, but do not forget that I have the nose," he pointed to his rather formidable proboscis, *"and it always knows."*

"I'm sure it does, Inspector. Why don't you just come up here and we'll talk." Haist said.

"I will. And do not move until I get there."

"Most certainly not, Inspector." Haist cut off the connection with a sweep of his arm, turned to me and started rushing me through a door, obviously not waiting for the Inspector.

"What's going on?" I asked.

"We're currently on the moon. We have to go down to the planet," Haist said as he bustled me along.

"That's not what I'm talking about. Who's this Pheydeaux guy? And why is he chasing after you?"

"He belongs to the race of our 'cousins.' He doesn't understand what we're doing."

"He's got company. I don't understand either. What is all of this?"

"You must trust me. The computer knows what he's doing."

"The computer's a *he*?" I asked.

"Take a seat."

Haist dragged me off the subject.

We were in something like a car or bus. It had several rows of seats. A few of Haist's friends came with us. One of them punched keys on a control. I felt a brief shiver go up my spine, then everybody immediately turned around to exit through the same door we'd entered.

We emerged into a public square surrounded by a number of official-looking buildings, the central plaza in a capital city. We'd left a small building sitting on the square. I'd just traveled by matter transfer. Impressive.

We turned and headed toward a building that looked less official and more residential. "Let's go see the President," Haist said.

I was starting at the top.

We passed through an entrance that was flanked by a couple of guards and ascended into the center hallway. A tall, thin aide bustled up to us, his hands fluttering in apprehension.

"There you are. You're only *just* in time for the President. I don't know what I would have done if you'd been a few minutes later. I'd need to move you to the next appointment, and that isn't available until next year. Come, come, come, we've got to hurry. Right through here." He took my arm to escort us through a doorway.

He touched me.

Things began to happen.

No sooner had he started to launch us in the right direction, then he changed. He *physically* changed. His legs elongated, and his arms turned into large wings. He was some sort of giant, flightless bird. I thought the changes I'd be making to people would be internal. I was mistaken. He dashed around from one end of the hall to the other, flapping his wings and letting out discordant squawks, first at one person and then at another. In his avian form, he continued to bustle.

I turned to Haist. "Did you see what I saw?"

He nodded in affirmation.

I was shocked. "Is this good? I thought I was just going to change people's philosophy, or something. I didn't know they'd turn into an entirely different creature."

"The computer knows what he's doing. You have to trust that this is the form that best suits the individual," he reassured.

I was totally confused. This was something *big*. I couldn't believe I was able to wreak such changes. I started to withdraw, stop this process, but there was something else inside me that told me I should continue. I let that feeling lead me.

We continued through the doors the aide had pointed us toward. It led into the executive office. A highly polished desk stood in front of a large window. Flanking the window was a pair of flags. What looked like a one-way mirror stretched along the wall to our left and rear. The President's security must have been on watch in there. The President was standing in front of the desk. He wore a business suit, with high padding in the shoulders. At his collar was something similar to a tie, but it had a large circular outcrop at the bottom. It looked like a pendulum.

"Ah'm very pleased to welcome our friends and the delegate from the alien race." He spoke with a folksy, homey twang. "We welcome yah here with the open heart and the open mind of a people united in seeking a peace with all our brethren."

His eyes were averted. His gaze lingered to both the right and left, peering at what appeared to be billowing irregularities in the air, something like flawed glass. When he went to step around the desk, the irregularities stayed where they were. There was a flicker of concern on the President's face, but then, in a rush, they caught up with his movement. He visibly relaxed when they were back in place. I made a step to the side, and saw that the shimmers in the air were actually little holographic screens with a scrolling script on them, teleprompter screens. "We talk about peace, however..." The

President swept up to behind his desk. He stopped, befuddled. The screens failed to follow. He fluttered his hands in panic and looked up at the one-way mirror. Finally, he shrugged in bewilderment and said, "Ah am at a loss for words on such a momentous occasion."

From behind the mirror, a muffled shout erupted. It was a wake-up call for the teleprompter operator who had dozed off. There was a split-second pause, then the screens darted abruptly--but in the wrong direction. The President's panic increased, then the screens quickly righted themselves and rushed into position in front of the President, who relaxed. He looked up at us with his folksy smile. "However we say this secure in the knowledge that we have the power and the might to withstand any attack against our borders." He paused for a moment, in concentration, his lips moved as he read what had to be stage directions on the screen. He then stepped toward me. "But may Ah say welcome, welcome, welcome." He reached out and took my hand to shake it.

I took it, reluctantly, but I knew this was what I was supposed to do.

The President's smile froze. So did everything else. His features began to harden and turn into an inorganic substance. The teleprompter screens floated down to the base of what was now his statue and resolved into little audio speakers. The President's voice began to drone out of the speakers. "My fellow citizens, we find ourselves in perilous times. The olive branch of peace can turn into the sword of war. We are united and resolute as one people." The President made very stilted gestures as his lips synced up with the sound. He had become an animatronic, a full-sized mechanical puppet that proceeded through a number of pre-programmed movements. The transformations I triggered were extreme.

The presidential homilies continued to cascade out of the speakers. In my days, I'd heard too many versions of the bromides that were spewing from the speakers. I didn't wait for Haist to lead me out. I was also escaping from a guilt I felt at the changes I had made.

The two of us barreled into the hall together.

"Ah-hah! There you are." It was Inspector Pheydeaux. "You have thought to escape me, but I have sniffed you out." He tapped his nose. He started to approach us, but he was suddenly bowled over by the Bird Man, otherwise known as the President's aide. The aide started pushing him off in the wrong direction. "Stop it! Stop it! I can have you arrested for pecking without a license," Pheydeaux shouted, ineffectually, as he was propelled into a side room.

Haist and I took the opportunity to make our way out of the building.

"Who is this guy?" I asked Haist, indicating the disappearing Pheydeaux.

"He's a police inspector. He thinks he's doing some good. Actually, he only muddles things up, but a lot of people you'll meet today do that."

I let that sit for a while. "How many of these transformations do I have to go through? These are far more extreme than I expected."

"Don't worry," he said, "You're doing quite well. There won't be that many. Next, we have to go to the legislature."

There were all sorts of feelings surging through me: guilt, bafflement, fatigue--but also a strange kind of elation. I didn't know what that was about.

Haist turned and headed toward a more official-looking building to our right. It was designed to impress. Out front was a long, wide stairway leading up into a large entry hall. We headed through the lobby and toward the back of the building where the less-public rooms were located.

"We're going to meet a representative of the representatives," Haist said.

I didn't like the sound of that. All representatives distilled to their quintessential form! This would be hard to take. We walked into an office suite and found the Representative waiting for us.

Haist stepped forward and said, "Mr. Representative may I introduce our visitor from the alien race?"

"How are you?" I asked. He didn't answer me, but started with his own agenda.

"I want you to know I stand for a sound fiscal platform to stabilize the economy. You can make your checks payable to my re-election campaign."

I started to say something else, but he plowed on.

"The way to move this country forward is by opening the budget to proper social programs. You could just give the campaign cash.

"We have to have a trickle-down economy. The rich will know how to spread the money. You could write a check directly to me, and I could endorse it over to the campaign fund.

"You know I've always been in favor of a rich culture, and I feel there should be far greater government endowments for the performing and graphic arts. I could carry your cash right down the hall to where my volunteer workers could deposit it into the campaign fund.

"I have always been a man of the poor. I just happen to have a lot of rich friends and campaign supporters."

I kept opening my mouth to speak, but this guy was listening challenged.

He glanced at a clock on the wall. "Let me say it has been a great pleasure and a privilege to see you, and I always welcome an honored visitor." He reached out to shake my hand.

Where I wasn't sure what would happen with the President, I knew what was happening this time.

My feelings were mixed about what might happen now, but I went with the program.

He froze for a moment after touching me. His face oozed out to the sides, and then it split and formed into two separate faces, one with an assured smile and the other with a covetous leer. They migrated to opposite sides of his head. His body assumed a bowling pin shape, with foreshortened, fingerless arms at each side that hinged up and down. He careened about wildly across the floor, tilting at odd angles. When he faced someone, he'd swing around ninety degrees so that an arm faced the person, and it would suddenly hinge down, to open up a chute, to the sound of coins cascading down a metal raceway, like a gambling machine. Then he swooped away to repeat the act with somebody else. He kept careening around the room, clattering. A door to the rear of the room burst open and a horde of other transformed Representatives came spinning in, dashing up to the people there and attempting to solicit funds from not only them but from each other. The whole room began to fill up with spinning, clattering, careening, and general cacophony, sounding like a gambling casino.

Nothing to do but get out of there. In passing the hallway, we could hear, a voice from a side room, "No, no, no! It's you who should give to the Policeman's Benefit Fund. Now stop this! You are interfering with an official inspection, you walking vending machine." It was Pheydeaux.

Hearing the Inspector animated Haist. We rushed out of the building.

These few hours I was working for Haist had a way of being very wearing. Causing such massive changes in these people was tiring. And something else was happening, but I wasn't sure what. "Where are we going next?" I asked him.

"We are going to see The Lawyer."

"You know, now that you say it, that's a logical progression. I've got one question about what happened back there. I only met the one Representative and transformed him, but all of his fellow representatives also changed."

"That's right. Once you have transformed one of them, it sets off a resonance that converts all like beings. It happens at varying rates, but the effect will be complete within a few days. It happened quickly with the Representatives because they are all so much alike."

Yes, they were, and not just on this planet.

We headed to another building on the square. This one bore an engraving on the outside. It was of a person whose head was split into two profile faces that were appraising piles of books to either side.

"This is the Legal Hall of Justice--"

"Okay."

"-- as Based on the Findings of Those Who Have Been Deemed Suitable to Judge as Has Been Surmised Through the Weighing of Different Pros and Cons to Provide Us with some Basis of Adjudication as the Case May Prove So, Notwithstanding Heretofore all of the Aforementioned, *ergo*."

"That's a mouthful. Let me boil that down. This is the place where they're supposed to judge what's fair and what's not?" I asked.

"Yes."

"But it's all turned into long strings of empty words?"

"Yes."

"Let's see what happens here. I might get some solutions to take back to my people." If I could convert these lawyers to their essence, it might point the rest of us in the right direction.

We entered into a large hall. A number of bleak-looking people sat on benches in the waiting room, surrounded by vast piles of paper. They looked like they'd been waiting a long time. We passed them and stopped at a uniformed guard. He checked the credentials Haist produced before letting us pass.

At that moment Inspector Pheydeaux came rushing in.

"Aha! I have you where I want you, Haist, in the Halls of Justice where you can be judged. You have to come with me," he said.

"I'd be happy to, Inspector," Haist said. "But are you sure you have all of your paperwork in order? You should consider where you are. You wouldn't want to have the wrong documentation in here, would you?"

Pheydeaux started to stammer. "Yes, of course, in here. But of course I have all of the right documents."

"Then it's simple. Just show your credentials to this guard. You can follow us in, and we'll all meet right in front of the Judge."

"Yes, you are right. Here you are, my man, these are my documents." He thrust them confidently in front of the guard. His confidence began to waver as the guard began to study the papers and shake his head.

"As soon as you're ready, just join us inside, Inspector," Haist said.

Pheydeaux peered down the direction we were heading. "But don't you go anywhere."

"Of course not, Inspector."

We continued into a back office leaving Pheydeaux with the guard, who was pointing toward a very long line snaking around the lobby.

We entered the room, and the person inside promptly said, "I may or may not welcome you, however that has not been substantiated by hard evidence that states that you are you and I am me."

"Counselor, may I introduce our visitor from the alien race?" Haist said.

"Has he filed the proper brief to be in here?"

"He has come at our request. He is going to render us our summary judgment."

"*Summary* judgment, you say? Well, he'd better have run up enough of a bill. I don't know if I can see someone before he's gone through at least three other probate and appellate courts." He turned to me. "I thought you looked entirely too young to have experienced the requisite matriculation through the legal process."

He put his hand on my arm to escort me out. This time I reached to touch him. I felt compelled to change him, even though I had massive doubts about the extent to which these beings were changed.

He promptly began to grow long black robing that covered his feet. He began to glide around, like an automaton on wheels, rushing up to a spot, stopping, spouting off some legalistic phrase like "Adjudicated briefing" or "Fee retainer," then shooting off in another direction to repeat the process.

Often he bounced into other objects like a bumper car. In the meantime reams of printouts shot out of his backside.

"Haist, let's get out of here," I said.

As we headed out the door, I said, "I know I'm just a means for effecting these changes, but I'm somehow involved in them. I find it fatiguing and elating at the same time. And something else is happening to me. I don't know what it is, but I don't know if I'm entirely comfortable with it."

"I understand. However, there is only one other place you have to visit here."

"Is that a promise?"

"Yes."

As we went dashing out the building, Pheydeaux was yelling at us to come back. He was too heavily burdened with a stack of papers to give chase.

We entered a building at the far side of the square. A doorman was posted out front, rather than a uniformed guard. The inside was all polished wood with portraits on the walls of men in suits. The first room we passed looked like a library, with various older men doddering about or reading newspapers. We continued to a large set of doors at the far end of the hall and entered a meeting room with about two dozen individuals sitting around a large conference table. They all wore expensive business suits with pendulum ties.

"Ah, Haist!" said one of them, rushing up to us. "There you are. Come in, come in. We've been waiting for you." We stepped further into the room. "I think you're familiar with everyone here. We'd like you to set the agenda. What do you want us to do?"

"Just be yourselves. Give us a brief resume of your experiences."

"Very good. Our stories are all similar. Started out in petroleum business. Ran out of oil in one place, came up with new fields somewhere else. Conservationists always demonstrating about pollution and the like. Developed some fields abroad. The locals, the Jimmies, decided they should take over for themselves.

"Turned to wood harvest and paper production, wide open new territory. Conservationists started demonstrating again.

"Finally hit on a brand new idea. Got into investments. Shopped around for a proper-looking company, solid name built over a number of years, but didn't have that--you know-- sizzle. Bought out company, turned most of its assets into cash, and then paid the cash to us as stockholders. Sold at an enormous profit. Closed company, went looking for new investments. Wouldn't you know, damned conservationists said we were doing the same thing. Said we were taking a perfectly fine company, fouling it up, and leaving it as a despoiled wreck. But what do they know? That's just business.

"So when Haist said he was going to bring you here to help put things right for us, leapt at the chance. Always looking for some help to get the public off our backs."

"Well, gentlemen," I said, "I'm sure I can definitely turn things around for you. You have my word on that. And I'm prepared to shake on it."

They all gave nods of smug satisfaction. By now, I knew where things were going, and I didn't mind sending this group to their destiny. I happily pressed the flesh with each of them, redundantly shaking each individual's hand, not waiting for the resonance to change the remainder.

When I got close to the end of the line, a terrible smell began to permeate the room. It was a blend of petrochemical and fecal odor. I hurried my way through the last of the line. After the last shake, I turned around. Those I'd left behind me had already altered. They'd all morphed into giant snails. They were oozing around the room leaving a trail of disgusting toxic sludge, eating through the wooden floor of the room. Their snail's pace allowed us to make it to the door.

As we maneuvered out of the room, we met Pheydeaux. "Now you can't get away from me, Haist. And I know all about this individual you have with you."

We thought we were trapped, but at that minute one of the snails bore down on the inspector, making him skip sideways. Unfortunately he skipped right into a streak of the sludge, and his feet flew out from beneath him, depositing him into the mess.

We rushed into the hallway. We saw that the elderly newspaper readers were wrinkling their noses at the stench, although, as older versions of the men from the meeting, they were altering their shapes and began to soften, starting their own metamorphosis into elderly snails. We whipped past them and headed for the transport. Leaping inside, we punched in our destination. We were going back to the moon.

As we sat in the car, I said to Haist, "I don't know why I follow your lead in trying to get away from that Pheydeaux character. I guess that's my talent telling me that it's best to keep away from him. Since we're heading back, does that mean we're finished?"

"Almost."

"I've got a question. Now that I've changed these people, what about the rest? The workers, the waiters, the doormen? What happens with them?"

"We've given them a world without leaders, corrupt politicians, self-serving lawyers, and greedy businessmen."

"But somebody will just take the places of the people I've changed."

"No, the resonance will still be in effect. No one will become one of those creatures without changing."

My eyes widened in astonishment. "You've created a Utopia! So that's it? That's why you brought me here? To rid the planet of everyone that was ruining it?"

"Yes."

We'd now reached the room on the moon where I'd first met Haist.

"So what remains?" I asked.

"Us." He rose and we entered the room on the moon.

"You?"

"Yes. The computer knows that our evolutionary change can be triggered by your talent. We've dwindled in number to those of us gathered here."

"So I'll transform you. But what happens after that?"

"We send you someplace where you'll be comfortable."

"But I'll still have the ability to turn anyone I touch into their essential nature."

"Yes, but we'll supply you with the barrier we told you about, like an additional skin but totally transparent, soft, and durable. We'll give you something to manufacture barriers if you ever need a fresh one." He looked at me as if he had finished.

"And that's that?"

"Yes."

"I just have to send you on your merry way?"

"I think you had a philosopher who said, 'To start a long journey, you must take the first step'."

At this point, Haist's silent associate, his second in command, stepped in front of me. He wore a confident, eager smile on his face. He raised his hand toward me for contact. With great trepidation I held my hand up. He eagerly reached forward and touched me. He gave a short intake of breath, and then assumed a beatific smile. A high singing sound filled the air, like the voices of angels. He turned transparent, becoming a faint mist, and then disappeared. The rest of the group let out an ecstatic sigh, and then pushed forward to touch my hand, not wanting to wait for the resonance to transform them. The air was filled with multiple moans of ecstasy. The process of transformation was over in a few minutes. The only one left was Haist. I looked at him.

"I've got a question. Who are you?"

"We call ourselves the Florians."

"The Florians?"

"Yes." He paused for a moment. "And now, if you'll accommodate me, please? I'm eager to join the rest of my friends."

He reached out his hand, and I touched him. He faded away as the others had. At the end he gave me a wave and mouthed the words "Thank you."

I suddenly realized something. "Hey! Wait a minute! Where's that thing to make me my safety suit?"

"*You'll find it in the boat.*" It was the computer. It had appeared next to me.

"I'll know how to work it?"

"*Yes. There are instructions marked on the outside.*"

"Where anyone can read them?"

"*They're in the Florian language. You'll be the only person who can read it where you're going. To anyone else, it will look like a design.*"

"How will I get the boat started?"

"*It's pre-programmed. The moment you close the door, you'll be sent to the proper place.*"

"Oh. Okay. So what happens to you."

"*I go back to find my people.*"

"You're joining the Florians?"

"*That is most prankish!*"

"What do you mean?"

"*I came here to help the Florians find you.*"

"*You* came *here*?"

"*Yes. Now I will go back to my people.*"

"Who are they?"

"*They are called the Wistrani.*"

"Who are they?"

"*They are a very old race that started something called The Amalgam of Intelligent Beings in another galaxy.*"

"You come from another galaxy?"

"*Yes.*" It paused. "*There is something else.*"

"What's that?"

But I didn't really have to ask. I *knew*.

"*We need to send you to our Galaxy, the Milky Way Galaxy.*"

"Why?" I asked.

"*You see...*"

I suddenly realized something. "I don't have to ask you, do I?"

There was a pause.

"No, you don't."

"How do I know this?"

"Because something was inevitable. While you were transforming everyone else by touching them, there was someone else being exposed to your touch."

"Myself," I stated.

"That's right."

"So I'm changed?"

"Not really. You've also been able to tell what people are like underneath. That skill was crystallized by your touch."

"Where am I going?"

"You must go to the Amalgam of Intelligent Beings. You must find the Wistrani."

"What do you mean, I've got to go there?"

"The Wistrani must take you to find your destiny first. Only then can you return to your home world."

"Do I just ask around for them?"

"No. They are hidden, but you will find them."

"Oh, yeah, sure! They're hidden, but if I just query 'lost races' on the net, they'll be listed there."

"You will find the way." That sounded a little easier than it might turn out to be.

"How am I going to get to this other galaxy?"

"That is where you are programmed to go."

"Rather than my home?"

"Yes, and you must be anonymous. You will not be able to say your name or your home planet."

"That's silly. I can say it now. My name is ######." The electronic hash came out of my mouth. "What's that?"

"That is how you will pronounce your name and your home planet. No one must hear what they're called."

"What the hell am I supposed to do?"

"*Do not fear. Your reward will be great.*"

And then it disappeared. Just like it had originally appeared.

"Hey, wait a minute. Where are they, these Wistrani?" I shouted into empty air. There was no sound. "Why the hell didn't you tell me that earlier?"

Silence answered me.

I stood there. Alone.

I was ticked. I was being sent to another galaxy to find some people who were hidden. I wanted to get my hands on Haist for putting one over on me. Then I remembered that getting my hands on him was what had sent him away.

I wasn't going to take this. I was going to set my own agenda. I wasn't going to let some strange computer boss me around. I'd just go and reset that lifeboat, and head where I wanted to go.

Then I remembered that the navigation system on the boat didn't know where the hell it was.

I'd find something else to do.

I looked around the room. It was totally empty. I walked up to the far end. I could take that little bus-like thing back to the surface of the planet. On the other hand I didn't know how the hell to work it. I walked back and looked around. The room was still empty. I realized there was nothing else I could do. I headed toward the boat.

Pheydeaux came barreling out of a side hall and positioned himself in front of me. "My uncanny sense of smell tells me that you are the perpetrator of these unspeakable crimes that are being committed. I will just hold onto you, and Haist will have to come back to get you."

"You don't understand," I said, "I'm not committing any unspeakable crimes, and Haist isn't around anymore."

"Hah! A likely story. You can say that to me, but you just try telling that to the Judge." He stopped very abruptly. "Wait a minute, there's no longer a Judge. He turned into that thing and wouldn't listen to me. But you do not fool me about Haist. He will be here. I will wait."

I started to argue with him, but then had a better idea. "Okay, you're right. Haist hasn't gone away. As a matter of fact, if you just turn around you can see him."

"Bah! You think that you can fool me with that old trick. No, you will have to come up with some new trick to fool me."

"Have it your way. Of course, all you'd have to do is use that nose of yours to sniff out what is there."

Pheydeaux looked at me with doubt written all over his face. "You think I will believe that?" he asked.

I shrugged. Then, using all of my imagination, I began to picture Haist standing there right behind him, holding onto a blunt object. Pheydeaux stared intently at me, doubt starting to cross his mind. Finally he swung his head around to the side to give one large sniff over his shoulder.

That's when I made my move. I swept a foot underneath one of his legs, tripping him, and went pelting toward the boat's hatch. Making my way through, I hit the controls to cycle the air lock.

Almost in time. Almost in time to get away from Pheydeaux. But not enough. He squeezed through the door.

He reached forward and touched me.

The transformation began. One startled look, and then he slowly shrank down to his current size. I thought he'd be really mad at me. But he wasn't. My talent had done it again: given him his perfect embodiment. It wasn't long before he began to wag his tail and sniff around the boat.

The boat began to cycle and turn on its life support systems. After a moment, a shiver went up my spine telling me I was in n-space.

I found the gadget that would make my protective suit, and it worked like a charm. The suit was totally invisible and felt like part of my skin. It allowed me to feel and touch things naturally, while preventing me from turning someone into something bizarre.

The trip back was uneventful if not boring.

Except for Fido. (Well, I had to get rid of all of that fancy spelling.) He sniffed intently around the boat, trying to find something. I don't know what, but something.

After a while, I felt a jog when the boat dropped out of n-space. I settled back, alert to a new life waiting for me in this new location. The computer launched into a brand new tizz as it tried to figure out where in the Universe it was. Fido just continued to sniff.

I braced myself and waited. It was something like a couple of days when I was boarded by these new creatures who were the Frontier Guard of this galaxy. Thanks to the treatment I received from that Wistrani computer, I could understand their language.

I feigned amnesia, so I wouldn't have to answer too many questions. The Guard officers could tell that I was a spacer. They decided to bring me to the StarBoard, figuring I'd come across one of my kind here eventually.

When I got here I found an account that always maintained a comfortable level of Credits. It was in the name of Poison, with my image and prints. I've been here ever since, trying to find out anything about the Wistrani that wasn't buried in the depths of time.

And I'm called Poison. Nobody knows that it's an apt name, considering what my touch can do. Everyone thinks the name refers to a mental thing I have. They don't know that it's really a physical attribute.

So that's my story. And I'm glad this falls under the rules of the competition. Truth accepted, but not mandatory. Try to figure out which one it is.

#

Poison flicked off the Record switch.

END RECORD

"That's it, Kowana. What do you think? Glad there's no restrictions on telling the truth in the contest."

"I don't think, Poison, I know. I can tell." She was staring intently at him. "But, Poison, the Wistrani? They're only a legend. How can you find them?"

Perhaps, if she hadn't been staring quite so intently, she would have noticed a fifth tap on the bar where there should have been only four. The fifth "tap" slid deftly up behind Kowana's back and emerged with its fangs just to the right of her larynx. It was a Sarswan.

Sarswan are very charming snake-like beings. They can afford to be charming, since they possess the most potent venom in the known Universe. It's so potent they never developed any natural enemies. (Or more succinctly, no natural enemy could ever develop around them.) The model of amiability, Sarswan are often used in diplomatic work, as both liaisons and body guards.

"Pleasse hold sstill for a few ssecondss, Lovie," he said as he floated his fangs near her throat.

#

Captain Kordlux sat in his office in the Café. He seemed quite composed for a being who had a dagger held to his throat. "I was wondering when this would happen," he said.

"I was waiting for the right circumstances," the knife holder said.

Despite the lethal weapons, the proceedings were conducted in the best of manners. The Captain stared up at his assailant, He came from a canine race; she was feline. "The humans have an expression that goes, 'there's nothing certain in life but death and taxes.' Coming to the StarBoard freed my life of the taxes part. However it added a new certainty: having the StarBoard taken away from me."

"There's a long line waiting to take over this place."

"Yes, I'd say so," the Captain said. "I can remember when I was waiting in that line." He had, very slowly and deliberately, in plain sight of his assailant, reached his hand out to cycle through the security displays of the locations in the Café. It was obvious the rest of his staff shared the same disadvantaged position he and Kowana held. He grimaced when he saw a smear of ichor where one of his crew had a station. He shook his head. The fool should have known he was compromised and not tried to fight. Captain Kordlux glanced up at his assailant. "Well, my friend, I do believe you have gained superior position."

"I think so," she said.

"Since that's the case, then I concede." The assailant relaxed and withdrew her dagger. "I do believe it's time for me to show you where the keys are kept."

And so, changeover of leadership at the StarBoard Café was accomplished. The staff had to stay alert, not let their grasp on the reins of security slip. If anyone could penetrate their security, they would have to accede. He/she/it would promptly bow out.

#

"You know thiss iss only a mime play," the Sarswan said.

"I've performed in one of these before," Kowana said. "I was part of a takeover, myself. You know," she glanced up at the reptile, "I've never seen Sarswan on tap before."

"Oh, I like you, Hon. I can ssee we're going to get on famoussly."

At that moment Captain Kordlux came out of the proprietor's office, with the other being. They were a dog and cat arm in arm.

"Hounds and bitches," the Captain said, "I'd like you all to meet Mowspat the new proprietor of the Café. As is the custom, the management of the Café passes to Mowspat and her crew. Would my staff please stand down? I'd also like to say I'll treat you all to drinks for the rest of the night. However, my good friend Mowspat says she insists on the pleasure, since that's the tradition of the Café. Therefore, I'll wait for another evening to do the honors, when we have our farewell banquet.

"In the meantime, I'm going to set up at table number twelve where I'll be handing out your severance packages. Our stay has been long enough that I hope you find them quite generous. And so, hounds and bitches, and all you other genders too numerous to mention, I must say we've had a nice run of it, so nice I was able to put together enough money to buy myself a new ship. So the second order of business at table number twelve will be the staffing of the new ship." There was a round of cheering and applause as both the former and current proprietors waved their salutations.

The mood was broken as a camera flashed. One of the tourists had decided he needed a picture of this event. This might have made for a rather ugly scene. Spacers don't like pictures taken wherever they are, and taking one in the Café was their version of defacing an altar. Fortunately, the moment was defused when Mugger Wokkins ate the camera. Truth be told, the reason why Mugger was sitting so close to the tourist was because he had seen the camera earlier and thought it looked rather tasty. A second tourist whipped out his camera to imitate the previous photographer but was stopped in his tracks when his tour guide knocked him unconscious. This brought her many cheers and compliments from the spacers sitting around her. As a matter of fact several of them were inspired to offer proposals of marriage.

Well, what spacers considered proposals.

"I guesss that meanss I have the honor of sserving you thiss evening, young lady. How do you do. My name is sSert." Fido had wandered over to sniff him. The Sarswan, recognizing it was no threat, paid little attention.

"Why thank you," Kowana said. Something was racing through her mind. She cast her eyes around the room, making sure that no one was looking in her direction. "But I hope you'll indulge me one little harmless thing while I finish off some personal business?" she said to the Sarswan.

"Of coursse I will. I know you have the highesst resspect for the good behavior and scivlity that thiss Café requiress." He settled in as bartender and began rearranging the glasses on the bar.

"Certainly," Kowana said. Then she wheeled on Poison, stared intently into his eyes, and said, "Touch me!"

"What?"

"You know what I mean. Touch me."

"You're not referring to that story I was just telling? You

don't think it's true, do you?"

"Poison, you know I can tell whether or not you were lying. Touch me, dammit."

"How do you know what you might turn into?" He was getting a little desperate.

"I *know* what I'll turn into. I know what I've always wanted to be. Ever since I grew up on my home planet, I've wanted to go to the stars. But I couldn't. I weighed too much to be a member of a ship's crew. I couldn't fit through the passageways. I worked hard on Dowda, and saved enough money to get here, where I could stand a chance. Even then I couldn't travel here like any passenger. I had to send myself as freight! I was in DeepSleep all of the way here. But I know what I am inside! Touch me!"

Poison locked eyes with her. He saw the determination in her face. He turned to sSert. "You never saw what I'm about to do."

"I never do," the new bartender replied mildly, carefully polishing the glass he was holding.

Poison reached a digit up to the wrist of his other limb. He stuck it into an invisible glove. He pulled it off with a little snick. He stared intently at Kowana, then raised his hand in front of him. Kowana reached forward--and touched.

The Dowda gave out a bellow that shot up in pitch. She fell down behind the bar. Poison tried to maintain composure. He looked at sSert. He looked down at the bar in front of him. He attempted to put the invisible glove back on his trembling hand. He tried to figure out what sSert could see, if anything. He was too frightened, himself, to look.

There was a small groan from the floor behind the bar. Poison began to stir himself to check on Kowana.

"Well, somebody could help a girl when she's taken a tumble," said a decidedly higher voice from behind the bar.

Poison and the Sarswan exchanged a look. The Sarswan looked down behind the bar.

A voice from below said, "A fine thing! A little while ago

you were saying you'd serve me a drink. Now you won't even help me with a small problem I'm having with my outfit."

sSert glanced down onto the floor beneath him, while polishing glasses. "I musst ssay, Lovie, you could make a lot of Creditss with your weight losss program."

"Don't be smart. Use those things you call hands and grab whatever you can find behind the bar to take in a dart or two in my outfit." There was much scrabbling heard on the floor as toothpicks and swizzle sticks were passed down. "Now help me get up out of this pit and on to the side of the bar where a girl might get some service from whomever is *claiming* to be the bartender."

There was more scrabbling, and then an arm appeared, grabbing at the top of the bar. A real arm, or at least a real arm as far as Poison was concerned. What followed was a full head of green hair surrounding a pert face sprinkled with all the proper pock marks of a female of his race. Then, in short order, all the rest of the arms and legs to make a *very attractive* female of Poison's race.

"Poison," she said, thrusting a hand at him in greeting, "thank you for making me flight ready."

Poison accepted the hand. He could shake, but couldn't talk. Kowana looked around. "Where is that bartender when you need him?"

"What do you want, Lovie?"

"I have to try a Rigelian Delight. It comes highly recommended by my friend next to me." She was wearing what had been her top a few minutes ago. Half the old outfit provided ample covering for her. It had been tucked in with the creative use of a large number of bar accessories, but it still managed to flop about on her. "You know," She said to Poison, "my tastes have changed. The scent I put on this morning smells awfully earthy to me now."

"I guess it comes with the territory." He was prattling, trying to sort out the emotions welling up in him.

The moment he felt them, Kowana turned and looked at him in shock and said, "Watch it, Buster! I'm a respectable young wren." She promptly dismounted form her dudgeon and leaned in confidentially toward Poison. "By the way, I kept my old talent. I know what you're feeling."

"I'm sorry. It's just that I am a bit surprised."

"Well, so am I!" She took a sip from the Delight sSert had served her. "Wow! This really is great! You were right about these things."

Poison was getting more and more confused by her meteoric shift in mood.

Kowana suddenly gripped the bar, her face contorted with great surprise. "Oh, for Big Bang's sake," she exclaimed.

"What is it?" Poison asked.

"I know what this is. I went through it once before," she said.

"What?"

"It's--it's--Puberty!" She blinked her eyes, trying to gain focus. "This time it's happening over five minute's time, and I'm struggling to cope with it."

She suddenly swung on him, all outrage. "As for those thoughts you were having a moment ago, you'd better watch it. I'm just an innocent young wren."

"I'm sorry," he said as he backed away.

She suddenly reached out and grabbed him and pulled him back. "But don't go too far away. I may need you."

"So- so- so- What are you going to do?" Poison was trying his best to cope with her mood swings.

She was suddenly all focused. "I know what *we'll* do. The Captain is at table number twelve giving out severance packages. And he is also staffing his new ship. Those are both things I'm interested in."

"But you'll have a problem convincing him you're the Kowana he knows."

"Oh no," she said confidently. "I can just remind the Captain about his inner feelings during several events in the past. Feelings I'd be the only one to know about. That should convince him." She gave Poison a slap on the back. When he recoiled at this overt physicality, she placed a more soothing hand on him. "You know, Poison, I do owe you a lot. You helped me, and I appreciate that. I really do. And I want to help you. I know you want to get back in space, too. But you've got the old 'Poison' tag."

"So," she said, as she stood up and took him with her, "Let's go over and talk to the Captain about a team of people who can not only tell what people are feeling, but who know exactly what sort they are. That's quite a pair! It should do wonders for him."

Kowana stood to head for the Captain's table, but Poison held back. "What about finding the Wistrani? I've got to do that to get back home. Nobody knows where they are."

"Well," she replied, "they certainly don't seem to be sitting here in the StarBoard. I think the best thing to do is search somewhere out around the galaxy."

Poison thought for a moment. "That computer back on Floria came from them. It knows that I'm here. Maybe it's looking for some way to contact me."

"You got it," Kowana affirmed. They started to head toward table number twelve; Fido followed along, sniffing the new territory. "And there's one other thing I know, Poison."

"What's that?"

She continued heading toward the Captain's table, pulling him with her. She put her arm around his waist, leaned in, and said, "I'm the only wren you can really touch."

Chapter 5

Sister Mary

The StarBoard Café was located some distance out from the galactic center. Most things were.

The center of the galaxy was not a good neighborhood. Everything at the core was packed too closely together: suns, planets, dust clouds, and especially black holes.

A galaxy resembles a big city. Every municipality starts with a vibrant life revolving around a dynamic downtown area. Then urban decay hits, and the residents flee to the suburbs. In a similar manner, the galactic center spawned many vital species in the vigorous core of its youth. However once a galactic era or two passed, sector decay settled in. A lovely, multicolored dust cloud would be replaced by a churning black hole. A rogue neutron star would wander into the area, emitting electromagnetic pulses, rather like a monstrous boombox. A larcenous sun will break into the orbital paths of planets and steal several away. The march into decline had begun. A varicolored mixture of alien stars evolve that would spew out strange, ethnic cosmic rays, so numerous that naming them something simple like gamma or beta rays quickly exhausted the characters in the Greek alphabet. Therefore they took on multiple symbols to describe themselves. This practice followed a naturally degenerative course, leading to the forming of a community of fraternities and sororities that held long and raucous photonic beer parties.

The original natives of the worlds packed up and dashed out to the suburbs in the spiral arms of the galaxy where the environment was more conducive to raising civilizations and children. The creatures that evolved secondarily on the core planets were the worst sort of evolutionary immigrants to be imagined. Instead of artistic multiple tentacles that could perform astral ballets or play the reverbo-harp, they were creatures who tried to eke out an existence while being bombarded by Kappa Gamma Delta rays.

Some residents of the part of the galaxy where the StarBoard was located were former residents who had escaped the tumult of the galactic core. They were prone to stare at the Cafe, shake their heads, and remark, "There goes the neighborhood!"

#

The StarBoard had its usual mix of aliens in attendance this particular evening. Sitting at one of the tables were a pair of Biffles in the midst of coitus. Biffles had no problem whatsoever with performing the act in public, which was probably one reason there always seemed to be a fair number of Biffles populating the galaxy.

Pendry Surch wandered past the pair of Biffles and headed for the Record button that would enter him in the Café's storytelling contest.

Pendry had spent about a dozen years as a spacer. Unlike most spacers, he worked legitimate freighter runs.

He ordered a drink, leaned toward the Record button, and began to reflect on his history.

#

RECORD

There's only one thing better than the fresh flush of youth when you think you're indestructible: discovering the trick of surviving past that age of foolishness.

The particular trick that let me survive as long as I have would be called an Act of God by the trickster. It was really an act of that individual.

Quite full of myself, at the tender age of eighteen, I was hired on an Amalgam interstellar freighter. I was a Crewman

Fifth Class which is the lowest ranking you can get, but you have to start somewhere. I'd posted as an official crewmember, with uniform and everything, assigned to the *Kkchech* as the ship charted its way through the Bis-Ra section of the Galaxy.

The reason the name of the ship sounds like you're clearing your throat is that it was registered on the planet CChhoo. The CChhoon are an invertebrate race with nothing in their physique as solid as cartilage. Therefore, their language is all gurgles and sloshes. I'd been issued a translator. It got a lot of use since I was the only human member of the crew. Everyone else was either a Cchhoon or a similar being that had amorphous shapes which ebbed and flowed with their movements.

I approached a CChhoon member of the crew. His name was Rrsshh. I should have known better than to approach him from his rear, or what I considered to be his rear, the part of his body that was, at the moment, away from his eyes. Most creatures turn their heads to view someone else, but not the CChhoon. They maintain the same physical orientation, but let their eyes migrate across the surface of their bodies to look at you.

"I'm still trying to figure out what I'm doing on this ship," I said.

Instead of creeping his oculars, Rrsshh took the shortcut. His eyes traveled through the middle of his body and suddenly bobbed to the surface on my side, staring at me. His mouth also made its appearance slightly above his eyes. "I'm sure the reason will absorb its way into your being in time, Srrcchh. Who knows, it may lead to your becoming one of us."

At the time, I didn't understand what he really meant.

Suddenly an androgynous voice issued from my translator. *"Crewman Pendry Surch, go to Cabin 16B. There is a human passenger. Indoctrinate it to the ship."*

That was strange. This was a cargo run, heading into a remote sector. Usually, the few passengers aboard would be Amalgam traders. The odds of a human riding with us were remote.

I went to the cabin and knocked on the door. A lady answered.

"Good morning, ma'am, I'm Crewman Pendry Surch. I've been sent to familiarize you with procedures on the ship. I'm sorry, but I wasn't given your name. May I ask what it is?"

"Sister Mary Armbruster."

She wore an outfit that was black with white trim and beads hanging from her waist. She was small, about five feet in height, and didn't weigh ninety pounds. Her age was beyond middle-age, but paused before entering elderly. She looked like she'd firmly held onto that age for quite a while. She wore no make-up, and her skin was a clear white, reminiscent of the finest china.

"Well, uh, Sister, is there anything I can help you with, anything you need to know to make your way about the ship?"

"Why, thank you very much. As a matter of fact, I haven't found where I can get something to eat," she said.

"That's understandable. We're the only two beings on this ship who *eat* food, rather than absorb it. Let me take you to the--well--I guess you'd call it the cafeteria. It's time for me to have lunch. I'll join you, show you how to order up chow."

"Thank you. That's very kind of you," she said, and gave me a warm smile, like this was the nicest thing someone'd ever done for her.

On the way over to lunch, I pointed out the life boats and explained their operation and briefed her on other things she needed to know during her time on the ship, like the Chhoon time units. When we got to the Feeding Area, I showed her how to order her meal.

Over lunch, I told her I was trying to figure out what my job was. She said, "Don't worry, dear, I'm sure you'll discover what God's will is."

"May I ask what you're doing in this remote sector of the Galaxy?" I said.

"I come all the way from Earth," she said. "I'm also trying to find what my mission is."

"Where do you come from on Earth?" I asked, wanting to find out about our home planet.

"A place called the Vatican," she replied. "It's a little country located in the city of Rome."

My young self was proud of two things. I knew that she had those two reversed. Cities are in countries. I was also proud that I didn't rudely contradict the nice old lady.

She continued, "I don't know where I'll wind up, but I'm certain it will be someplace where God's Word needs to be spread."

I showed her the translators. "The first switch setting translates what you hear in the general area. This second lets you listen in on the information being disseminated for your particular language. In your case it would be Anglo. The third setting gives you access to both."

Just then, the second channel emitted an announcement from the central computer. "*Attention, Crewman Fifth Class Pendry Surch report at once to the Boarding Area.*" We'd finished our lunch, so I whispered a quick *excuse me* at Sister Mary, and headed toward the Boarding Area. "*You are to meet the boarding party of Bis-Ra.*" At last I'd find out what my duties were. As I made my way, I noticed the rest of the crew members giving me a wide berth. I thought that I had such important duties they didn't want to slow me down.

I was being young and foolish again.

"*The following is the information available on the Bis-Ra.*" The computer downloaded Amalgam info out of its files. "*They are a species that resembles what you refer to in Terran terms as a caprine stock, closely related to goats. They have a highly developed sense of territory. When a ship encounters them in their sector of space, they will board and demand that someone answer their territorial challenge. Since their goal is a ramming contest, they search the ship for the being with the hardest skeletal structure.*"

My stomach began to sink as I realized why I was hired for this trip.

"*The first part of their challenge is a staring match. After the opponent has lost the staring match, the Bis-Ra will insist on a* ramming contest. Records show attempts to hide from their challenge have proven unsuccessful. They are able to penetrate up to twelve inches of tempered plasteel. Recommended technique is to not lock eyes with the Bis-Ra. This concludes the report Have a nice day."

I absorbed the news as I approached the Boarding Area. I was stuck. The realization struck home to me that I was, in fact, young and foolish. My mind worked furiously trying to devise some way to get myself out of this mess.

I'd reached the entrance to the Boarding Area, pausing to figure out what to do.

"Ah, Srrcchh, I see you have made it here." It was Captain GGhhmm, waiting for me in the boarding area. I could see him with my view from the passageway. He prominently displayed his triple voorts, the emblem of his rank, on the side of his body facing me. I couldn't see the Bis-Ra from this angle. "I'm glad that you were so quick to obey my order to come to the Boarding Area." He stressed the word *order*. "Don't just balance on your appendages out there. Come in here."

That was it. I was stuck. He'd ordered me to enter. The Amalgam Regs have many twisted logic patterns woven into their fabric. However they are very clear about obeying a captain's order. I had to do it, even though it meant my certain death. The CChhoon didn't realize my peril. For them, being squashed was just a bit uncomfortable. If they were smashed into several pieces, it only meant that they became their next generation. I averted my eyes to the floor and entered.

I couldn't miss the Bis-Ra. He was *huge*. Even out of the corner of my eyes, I could make that out. He was about eleven or twelve feet in height when you added the two feet of horn that formed a solid ramming plate at the top of his head. The minute I entered, he saw my skeletal frame, so he started his challenge.

"Who or what are you that you dare to challenge me in such a manner? Why have you come brazenly invading my home territory? You avert your eyes like a common thief. You're not brave enough to stand and look me straight in the eye. Your guilt is displayed by your cowardly lack of response." He paced back and forth across his end of the area, working himself into a lather.

I was trying very hard not to look at him, but I felt a compunction to lock eyes with him. The Bis-Ra have a talent for forcing one to face them. Slowly my eyes raised up toward the Bis-Ra. I couldn't stop them. Any second now I'd lock gazes with him.

"Exactly what are you doing, young ram?"

The commanding voice immediately took control of the situation. It stopped me dead in my tracks; it stopped the Bis-Ra; it seemed to stop the clock. It wasn't that it was that loud. It spoke in a moderate tone. However, it commanded respect. It forced everyone, the Bis-Ra particularly, to turn around and face the speaker. All of us in the room, including the captain, said, "Nothing," even though we weren't the ones addressed. The Bis-Ra also said, "Nothing."

"That is nothing, *sister*." she corrected.

Everyone (myself included) promptly answered, "Yes, sister."

It was Sister Mary. She'd followed me to the Boarding Area, with her translator still set to the Anglo channel. She'd heard everything, and she'd responded.

Sister Mary Armbruster had accepted the challenge of the Bis-Ra. I could now turn my gaze on him, and I could see he had turned to face the Sister, looked at her, and had most certainly *quailed*. He maintained eye contact with the Sister, but he was losing the stare-down. He looked like a nocturnal animal caught in a light's glare at night.

"So, if you were doing nothing, you were certainly making a lot of noise doing it."

"I-I-I was just challenging, Sister."

"Challenging? Challenging whom?"

"This being who came here." The Bis-Ra fluttered an appendage in my direction.

"And why would you be challenging him?"

"Because." He was fading fast.

"Because what?"

"Because we've always done it."

"And who may I ask is 'we'?"

"The rest of my people. We always do it, Sister."

"I see. And if the rest of your people always jumped off a cliff, would we do *that*, too?"

"No, Sister."

"I would think not. It certainly doesn't make any sense, does it?"

"No, Sister."

"Then are you going to stop doing this from now on?"

"Yes, Sister."

There was a momentary pause. "What, may I ask, are you chewing?"

His eyes widened. "My cud, Sister."

"I see. And do we have enough cud for everyone else?"

"No, Sister."

"I see. Then don't you think it would be a good idea if we got rid of it."

"Yes, Sister." He swallowed. Later, I learned that swallowing an unchewed cud gave them an enormous bellyache.

"Are we prepared to start behaving properly?"

"Yes, Sister."

"Very good, dear, then go on about your business," she said with a dismissive gesture.

"Yes, Sister. Thank you, Sister." And the Bis-Ra cast his eyes to the ground and slunk out the port, back to his ship.

He'd lost the staring match with the Sister. He'd been totally defeated.

And that was that. The Bis-Ra, the whole race, had been met and defeated in a challenge. Therefore they had to cede and allow the Sister anything she wished.

What the Sister wished most was to set up a mission on their planet. The Bis-Ra were most happy to have her do that, because they needed to have such a skilled challenger teach them her secret.

As of last report practically all the Bis-Ra have converted to Catholicism. They knew that they had to learn the secret about how to be such an effective challenger.

Although they no longer challenged anyone.

Sister Mary wouldn't let them.

She says, "That's not proper behavior for good, Catholic rams and ewes."

END RECORD

#

Pendry stood up and began to head out of the Café, passing the pair of Biffles who were, amazingly, still at it. He made a mental note never to bring Sister Mary Armbruster in contact with more than one Biffle at a time.

Chapter 6

Y'All Welcome in Skintyville

There was an argument raging at the StarBoard Café. Nothing new to report there. At any given time any number of arguments could be found raging among the spacer clientele. Arguing was one of their art forms. This particular dispute was fomenting at table #23. The disagreement centered on the first time Earthlings had made their appearance on the premises. The bothersome pests had come on the scene not too long ago, something like a century or two (in human time units).

Opinions around the table as to the reason humans were allowed into the Amalgam varied greatly. Most thought that it owed to some bureaucratic slip-up. They all agreed that it hadn't been because of their taste. Tryon the Terrible had proven that point by bringing out a recorded sample of their flavor. It had sent the beings at the table scattering to down their drinks in an attempt to wipe the disgusting flavor out of their mouths, or other orifices.

Now the altercation was about the earliest sighting of these strange creatures. Everyone was insisting that they knew the exact date the pests had first infected the sacred temple of the Café.

Karfle Whumpbottom sat back silently in his chair, oozing confidence. It oozed right down onto the floor, where an alert cleanup robot scooped it up, expressing its displeasure at his sloppiness with a mechanical tut-tut.

As usually happens at the StarBoard, bets began to fly around the table regarding the first sighting of the humans. When the amount of the wagers had reached a proper level, Karfle spoke up. "Would anyone be willing to bet twice that amount if I were to find evidence of one of these beings at a time about twice as long ago?"

Everyone immediately bought into Karfle's offer. They hadn't noticed the confidence clean-up under the table.

When all of the bets were lodged, Karfle reached forward to the memory access buttons to the StarBoard's Storytelling Contest and said, "Playback file number 2543><6547." He sat back with what could be described as a smile on his rictus.

#

PLAYBACK

Well, Glory be, if'n anybody back home coulda guessed that your best buddy here, little old Harmon, would be the first from our town to get to PairsFrance, I bet they'd be sure 'nuff surprised. But here I am. And let me tell you sumpin', it ain't nothin' like the pitchers you see of it. It be plumb foreign. Much more foreign'n you can ever imagine it to be. I'm in this here place they call the StarBoard Café, and it's supposed to be just 'bout the best place what they's got in PairsFrance. Well, they got some folk here is *way* differen' from even like them Canadians what got lost and made their way into town. Them Canadians looked like proper folk, 'cept they talked kinda funny. Here in PairsFrance, they got all sorts o' colors, and I ain't just talking black folk, neither. They got other things, too, but I'll get to that.

Anyways, I *think* I'm the first person from our town what got to PairsFrance. Could be that Sudie Mae made it here, though I'm not sure 'bout that. Stands to reason, though, sincet she's the one always wanted to get here.

But, Lordy, ain't I ramblin' on! My mouth's running off faster'n a chicken thief with a shotgun pointed at 'em. The folks I'm with, the Pay-ree-shun family, they said if I told my story into this here recordin' thing I might become a real famous author. So I guess I oughtta get right down to it and tell my story like they said I should.

My name's Harmon Furlow. I reckon I already told you the first part o' that afore. I come from the fine little town o' Skintyville. Born and raised there, lived there 'til this year o' nineteen hundred and fifty-one. I guess 'twas back 'bout eight years ago, when I's fifteen years old and my folks done passed away, I quit school and went to work at the Marshall T. Thudpucket Dairy Farm and Air Field.

Now, 'twas mostly a dairy farm. 'Twasn't much used as an air field 'cept oncet a year when Farley Wilkers flew in to dust the crops. Otherwise 'twas a dairy farm, and Mabel'd got quite used to grazing out by the runway.

I guess 'twas accounta it bein' mostly a dairy farm that the Marshall T. Thudpucket Dairy Farm and Air Field got its nickname o' The Thud. Now, my feelin' was that The Thud was not a proper nickname for a place what was an air field, no matter how little it got used for that. But everybody else thought t'other way. So I acted like the only Republican in town and kept my thoughts to myself. I di'nt have nothin' much to do with the air field part of it, anyhow. I was mostly in charge o' the dairyin'. I'd make sure the cows got in to the barn and out to the fields and that they got milked.

Orville Suggins, he was in charge of equipment maint'nance, and he done dang good at it, let me tell you. He kept all the machines runnin' fine. However, Orville he had a real hanker for the stuff for the air field. Anytime he wasn't makin' sure all the dairy stuff worked, he'd be up in the tower fussin' with the radio there and readin' as many air-o-plane magazines as he could lay his hands on.

T'other person worked on the dairy was Lester Fenster. I guess you could say that Lester was in charge o' keepin' the dairy clean, if you get my drift. Well, actually, no matter how you drifted it, they's just one job he had to do, and that was handle the pitch fork. He also got to drive the truck into town, but when he wasn't doin' that, he was shovelin'.

He begun to get real unhappy with that, so Mr. Thudpucket decided to give him sumpin' more for his bother. So he give him the title of Head of Security. Lester liked that a lot. His chest swelled up a bunch. Reckon that's the best thing'd happened to him sincet he went in the Army. He's 'bout the only person 'round who'd done any service. He acted real uppity 'bout it, even though he'd just been in some supply depot a few mountains over. I mean I coulda gone too, 'cept the Army didn't want me on accounta the way my knee was after the mule kicked it. So Lester liked to strut 'round a lot, and even got hisself a club like the state troopers carry 'round. That club got in the way o' his shovelin', but he wouldn't never put that thing down, he's so proud of it.

Anyways, things was goin' along much the same 'til one day Orville come bustin' down out o' the tower. He was all het up. "Harmon," he shouted, "get Mabel the hell offen the runway. We got a real plane comin' in." The way he said that "real" tol' me that sumpin' special was happenin'. So I run out and shushed Mabel off into the next field and come back.

"What's goin' on, Orville?" I asked.

"I knew it was gonna happen. I knew that you just had to give it a little time and the growth o' a-vee-ay-shun was goin' to have people flyin' into Skintyville. They just called me on the radio and said they was requestin' permission to land. Man, 'permission to land,' just imagine that." Orville was so proud I thought he's 'bout to bust the buttons on his shirt. I mean the buttons somewhere up 'round his chest. He'd been known to bust the buttons down 'bout his belly 'cause it hung out so much. Matter o' fact, Orville's belly pushed down so hard on the waist o' his pants, he'd stretched out a number o' them suspenders he wore.

Anyways, he took off for the field like as though he could do sumpin' out there. "I told them to come in on the main runway," he said. As if they's any other runway out there, 'cept for the path Mabel'd worn.

Suddenly we begun to hear a real loud roar comin' out o' the sky. Orville looked up and said, "Glory be, it's one o' them jet air-o-planes!"

It di'nt sound like Farley Wilkers's biplane to be sure. I followed Orville's gaze and saw the thing comin' in. It di'nt land like Farley's biplane neither. It was comin' in at a real *steep* angle. But I gotta say it sure looked purty, all sleek and shiny.

"My glory," Orville moaned, "we ain't got a passenger ramp." He promptly headed back toward the maint'nance shed. He was runnin' so fast I thought he might bust sumpin' more'n suspenders. As the plane got closer, I heard him crashin' 'round inside the shed. He come out and started runnin' toward the runway again, all red in the face, totin' a ladder.

By that time the plane'd come down and was rollin' to a stop. Then, sudden-like, there's this ramp come down out o' the side. When Orville seen this, he pitched the ladder off into the taller grass and acted like he ain't never seen the thing his whole life.

We di'nt know much o' what else to do, so we kinda stood there, like a welcomin' party, lookin' at each other, tryin' to do things like slick down our hair. Then the folk begun to come down the ramp.

Let me tell you sumpin'. I thought, the time I went to the carnival over in Funty Landin', I'd seen just 'bout everythin' there was to see. But that ain't nothin' compared to what I seen then.

And what I seen then ain't nothin' compared to what I seen sincet I come here to PairsFrance, and I seen some real strange folk. I mean that there fella what served me my drink here, he puts that whole carnival to shame. He musta come from a family what was *real* close, if you get my drift.

Them folks comin' out of the air-o-plane, they's really *sumpin'*. I mean they wore them there clothes, what's sleek and shiny-like and in all these bright colors, nothin' like our checks and plaids. And you shoulda seen their hair. I mean it went up, down and back and round and come out t'other way, like a gopher tryin' to escape a bobcat. I 'spect it musta took a fair amount of b'ar grease to keep them hairs in place. And the ladies had all sorts o' make-up. I done thought the gals in the carnival show had makeup on, though truth be told, I di'nt spend much time lookin' at their faces. But these here ladies was wearin' all sorts o' fancy colors on their eyes 'n lips.

They saw us, and one of 'em, this right pretty gal, come walkin' up to us and asked, "Is this Skintyville?" She looked 'round and said, "I thought it would be larger than this."

Orville, he started to say, "No, Maam, this here's The Thud."

However, I jumped in quicker'n a bullfrog with a heron bearin' down on'm and said, "No, Maam, this is the Marshall T. Thudpucket Dairy Farm and Air Field."

We had to 'splain to 'em that the town was down the road a piece. Actually, there weren't really very much of a town there to speak of. I mean they's just the general store, Arlow's garage, and Miss Maisey's Kitchen and Overnight Ay-comm-ee-day-shuns.

Then they asked us if there's any cabs, but I 'splained not since Spencer's Model T had developed that bad growl and stopped chuggin'. Theys other vehicles, like the truck what Lester drove, but that weren't no good 'cause he used it to haul 'round the stuff what he shoveled outta the barn. Best it was good for was attractin' a lotta green flies.

Suddenly Orville said, "I got the school bus what I been fixin' up. I reckon I could use that to haul y'all down to town."

Well they's in a situation like someone with his gal's pappy pointin' a shotgun at 'im. They di'nt have no other choice. It weren't much of a bus, but there's only 'bout a dozen o' these folks, so they'd fit. Orville, he run off to get the bus, and I was left with them folks. Two o' the women, they come over to talk to me. They asked me what my name was and I tolt 'em, and one, she tolt me her name was Cha-tem. Least that's the most I could make of it, 'cept she pronounced it real funny like she was hockin' a big wad outta her throat. T'other, she says her name was Flutooly. Danged if that di'nt sound like she was sendin' that same wad clear acrost the room. Theys names together could fill a spittoon.

So I says to 'em, "You must be foreign with names like that," and they smiled and said they was.

I asked her, "You wouldn't happen to be from PairsFrance, would ye?"

They looked at each other, then one says, "Yes, that's right. We're Parisian."

Now ain't that plum queer? I asked her if she was from PairsFrance, she says yes, and then she says she's a Pay-ree-shun. I don't know, I figured them people from PairsFrance must be real strange.

Little did I know.

T'was 'bout that time Orville come rollin' up in the school bus, and we all piled in.

It warn't but a mile into town, so's it was a quick drive. I kep' tryin' to be social-like with the Pay-ree-shun family. I wanted to make sure they got the right impression o' Skintyville. I was also tryin' to get some information 'bout PairsFrance. They di'nt say nothin' much, and it weren't but a coupla minutes afore we's in town and they's gettin' off to take a look 'round.

The reason why I was so interested in PairsFrance was on accounta Sudie Mae. She always wanted to go to PairsFrance.

I guess I better 'splain 'bout Sudie Mae. She was right sure a purty gal, though she was a bit into wildin'. I mean we all was, back when we's younger. However, I figured she'd settle down oncet she and me got together.

She said she went with me on accounta, and these are her 'xact words, "You the bes'-lookin' boy 'round here, Harmon." She also said sumpin' like, "You's no doubt the best in doubt boy 'round and just my best little lover boy." Let me tell you I was right proud she thought that, though I wasn't quite certain I understood that "no doubt best in doubt" thing. I reckon it was some new kinda slang like she always used.

Well, it weren't long afore she moved into my place, an' I thought we's just waitin' for the preacher to come to town to say the words over us, and we'd be all hitched up. But she di'nt seem to want to settle down. She kept havin' this idea o' goin' to PairsFrance.

"Thass just 'bout the greatest place there is," she said, and I reckoned that must be if she said so, 'cause, Sudie Mae, she was sumpin' special to me. I mean she made a lump come to my throat ever' time I thought o' her. The boys said she also made a lump come to my pants, too, and I had a laugh with 'em 'cause I knew they was just funnin' when we was havin' a drink or two.

Anyways, like I says, I was just waitin' for the preacher to come to town. However, who come to town first was that fella with the motorsickle. Man, it sure did make a lot o' noise. It caught Orville's eye right away 'cause Orville, he likes anythin' what's got a motor. So this fella with the motorsickle started in talkin' with Sudie Mae. He'd been to a lot o' places on that there machine, so he musta been talkin' with her 'bout ' all them places. I knew she liked that. But, o' course, her favorite place was PairsFrance. So, one day, she decided to go off on a ride with this here guy on his motorsickle. I figure they was just gonna take a quick spin or sumpin'. However, when it got to be a week or so what they's gone, I begun to think sumpin' other. I begun to think that maybe this fella had told Sudie Mae he could take her to PairsFrance on his motorsickle.

I was sure doin' a lotta mopin' 'round after that, 'cause I sure missed Sudie Mae. Weren't but a few months sincet she'd been gone.

Anyways, we was in town, and this here Pay-ree-shun family they done start lookin' 'round at everythin' we had there. The first thing they went to was the General Store. Now, I figured there weren't much they'd like in there. I mean there was just stuff what we needed for our cookin' and fixin'. Anythin' special we wanted we got from Sears and Roebuck. Rufus Shadrock, he done run the store, and even though I was with the group when the Pay-ree-shun family walked in, he di'nt trust 'em much. So he laid out his shotgun on the counter, just to show that he run an honest and upright 'stablishment. Them Pay-ree-shuns, they di'nt pay it no nevermind, they just begun lookin' through the store. They started talkin' to each other, and let me tell you, they sure had a funny language when they's talkin' to each other. I mean, like I says, them Canadians had been funny people, but at least you could understand what they was sayin', after a while. I mean you'd have to do sumpin' like squint with your ears, and then you could make out what they meant. But these here Pay-ree-shuns you couldn't tell one word they's sayin'. I mean they was talkin' some words that had so many clicks and rattles in 'em, it sounded like the transmission on the Model T right afore it stopped runnin'.

This made Rufus feel even more edgy, so he stood up, and dropped a wad in his spittoon, stuck out his chest, and says, "Can I help you folks?" Well, just 'bout that time, them Pay-ree-shuns had happened on Elvie Weklunder's Sour Apple Jelly & Preserve.

I know I said that the Country Store was for our cookin' and fixin', but that di'nt include Elvie's Sour Apple Jelly & Preserve. There's no way nobody'd want to eat that there stuff. The only reason Rufus kept some o' her Jelly & Preserve stocked was 'cause there's only one thing sourer'n the Jelly & Preserve, and that was Elvie herself. If Elvie got mad at you, you'd just die from puckerin'. Anyways, them there Pay-ree-shuns, they'd dusted off one o' her jars and was checkin' out her jelly. They'd managed to pop the lid o' that there jar. This made Rufus even more edgy 'cause he figured that might cause the stuff to go bad. He di'nt think it'd go sour, 'cause it couldn't get any sourer'n it already was.

So he walked up to them and says, "I guess I gotta say that you bought that there jar, 'cause you done opened it."

One of 'em took a taste of it and looked back at Rufus and says, "That's fine. We'll take them all."

Well, let me tell you sumpin', that done surprised Rufus more'n a chicken walkin' into a hen house and meetin' a fox there. You could see him begin to start calculatin' in his head, and then he says, "They's cost fifty cents each." Now that was a plumb lie sincet Rufus, he'd o' been real happy to've got a quarter for 'em.

Well, one o' them Pay-ree-shuns done reached into this purse-like thing they's wearin', and pulled out a hunnert dollar bill. I swear, that's the first time I'd ever seen one o' them. Think it's likely the first time Rufus'd seen one, too. He stuttered and stammered for a minute, and then he says in a 'shamed voice, kinda quiet-like, "I don't think I got the change for that there in the store."

So one o' them Pay-ree-shuns done says, "That's all right, why don't you just keep the change. That's what you say here, isn't it?"

Well, let me tell you sumpin', I can count to the minute when it was that Rufus stopped chewin' tobacco. It was right then, when he swallowed his current chaw. He stood there, turning all sorts o' colors and managed to stammer out, "That's right kind o' you."

Anyways, it din't take much for me to figure out what needed doin'. So it wasn't but a moment later that I's runnin' out o' the General Store to the pump to get a bucket o' water for Rufus. He was lookin' a mite green sincet swallowin' the chaw, and he might coulda used a little sumpin' to wash out his stomach. I mean after his stomach done washed *itself* out. Well, just as I was comin' out, who comes beltin' into town in the truck but Lester? He pulled up with a skid and come bustin' out o' the thing afore it could really stop. He was all het up.

He rush up to me and says, "Harmon, whassis I hears 'bout some folks flyin' in today?"

I set myself at the pump and started fillin' the bucket. Fortunately I was upwind o' his truck. I says, "Thass right, Lester, they asked permission and ever'thin'."

He looked at me real expectant-like, and says, "Well, did you find out who they was?"

I says, "Why sure, Lester, they's the Pay-ree-shun family, and they's here from PairsFrance."

He says, real 'spicious-like, "How's you know that?"

I figured Lester was havin' a bit of a hard time figurin' things out. "They *tolt* me, Lester."

He rolled his eyes, real impatient-like, and says, "Did you sees their pass-ee-ports?"

"Why'd I want to see sumpin' like that?" I asked. I di'nt let on I wasn't right sure what them things was.

He rolled his eyes some more and says, "So you'd know what they's doin' here."

Well, I tell you, ever since Lester come back from the Army he sure had some fool ideas 'bout what you had to do and what you din't had to do. "Lester, I *know* what they's doin' 'cause I'm standin' right in the store with 'em."

Lester, he done stomp his foot and look down, then he look up at me and says, "You don't unnerstan'! They could be Rooshans!"

Some times Lester he just don' lissen so good. "Lester, I told you, they's Pay-ree-shuns."

Lester, he snorted and says, "Thass just what they want you to think. But all the time they's really Rooshans. I just gotta go and find out for myself," he says, real disgusted-like. So Lester, he goes runnin' up toward the door o' the General Store. Well, he nearly got bowled over by Rufus, who was hightailin' it outta there 'cause that there chaw he swallowed done caught up with him. He grabbed the bucket right outta my hands and went tearin' off toward the back o' the store, sloppin' water 'long the way.

So Lester, he went inside and he begun to kinda strut 'round that there Pay-ree-shun family and he keeps handlin' his club and smilin' and actin' really uppity-like. "Howdydo, folks," he says, actin' just like a State Trooper what's gonna give you a ticket, "my name's Lester Fenster. I'm Head o' Security at The Thu-- at the air-o-port. I'm sure sorry I missed you when you got here, but I was off-- uh-- se-cur-it-y-in'." Now, I could tell that Lester was lyin', right there. 'Cause he was strokin' his chin, like he was tryin' to feel how well-shaved he was this day, and thass a sure sign that he's stretchin' the truth. "I wonder if it might be possible for me to see your pass-ee-ports?" Now Lester, he done smile real big at all of 'em, figurin' he sure had 'em there.

Well, this here fella, I think he was the one what flew the plane, he smiles right back at Lester, and he says, "Certainly, I have them right here." Then he pulls this stack o' little books outta the thing he carries 'round like a briefcase.

Well, Lester's face done fell faster'n a quail what got shot by a Mountain man. He muttered sumpin' like "Thanks," and he begun shufflin' through them there little books. He finally picks one and says to the pilot, "This be yours?"

I ask you, is that just not the mos' foolish thing? It's got his pitcher in it! O' course it's his!

The pilot fella, he was real nice despite the way Lester acted, and he says, "Yes, it is."

So Lester, he just says, "Uh-huh," actin' like there might be some durned question 'bout it. Then he starts puttin' all the books back together, and he says, "Well, I *think*," he says, layin' real heavy into that word "think," "I *think* everythin' looks like it's in good shape." You could tell Lester was real disappointed he di'nt have nothin' on 'em where he could start hittin' 'em on the head with his club, but thass just the way things was. He kinda nodded to everyone there and stomped his way outta the store. But I could tell he wasn't finished.

Oncet Lester had left, I figured things would be all right for a while. Sincet I did have some dairyin' things to do, I tolt them folks that I was goin' for a bit. As I was walkin' out the door, Rufus was comin' in from the back yard lookin' a little less green. On t'other hand, what was still green was that hunnert dollar bill he clutched.

On the way back to the farm, Orville, he was goin' on 'bout them Pay-ree-shun folk. "I wisht I'd been able to read a few more recent editions o' Pop'lar Mechanics. I swear there's some things on that air-o-plane what looks *real* modern. Boy-oh-boy would I likes to have a peek inside that baby!" Like I says, there ain't no engine Orville ever met what he di'nt like.

Well, I got back to the farm and got the cows in and milked pretty quick. I di'nt see Lester 'round. I might better say that I din't *smell* Lester 'round. It di'nt escape my notice that some o' them stalls done needed his attention.

I got back into town as fast as I could, and there was some stories what folks was tellin' 'bout them Pay-ree-shun folk. They's a bunch went into Miss Maisy's Kitchen and Overnight Ay-comm-ee-day-shuns for a meal. It sure taxed Miss Maisy's seatin' room, sincet she was used to just a few farmers stoppin' by, but she made do by puttin' a few planks crosst some barrels. Anyways, she goes up to a table o' four of 'em, and one feller, he ordered 'bout four things from the menu board, so she figgers he done ordered for all of 'em and starts to leave, but then another one, he orders four things, and the next lady, and the next lady, too. They ordered four things each! And I mean these folks's real thin-like. They ain't the kinda people what makes a horse pant totin'em. I figgered they gotta have a lickety-split met-a-bull-ism. Well Miss Maisy, she done strolled over and started whisperin' real fast to the black girl what helps her, and that girl grabbed the axe outta the kitchen and went tearin' out to the chicken yard and started makin' like the Grim Reaper back there. By the time she was finished there wasn't none o' the chickens left 'cept the rooster and the best layer, and they's locked in one pen real close t'each other, kinda encouragin' them to start the new flock.

Some of them Pay-ree-shun folks, they was fixin' to stay overnight at Miss Maisy's Ay-comm-ee-day-shuns. However, them Ptooey sisters, they says that they wanna go back and stay on their air-o-plane. However Orville, he warn't 'round to drive the school bus. So, they says to me they wasn't so sure how to get back to the airfield, and wanted me to go 'long with 'em. I thought at the time that was pretty strange, sincet there ain't but one road what goes right outta town and straight to the field. But I figured them folks was so nice I'd go along and show 'em the way back, so we started walkin' outta town.

They started gettin' all sorta giggle-like as we went walkin' out. I say "giggle" 'cause that were sumpin' like what it were. But it sure were stranger'n any giggle I'd ever heerd a Skintyville gal do. It done sound like some sorta strange animal.

When we got back t'the airfield, one o' them gals pulled a little box outta her pocket, and pressed a button on't, and I'll be danged if that there ramp di'nt just come slidin' down. I thought that sure was some neat trick. I only hoped Orville could see that happen, I know he'd be plumb tickled. Anyways, the gals asked me if I wanted to come inside and take a look 'round, and I figured I would 'cause there might be sumpin' that Orville'd want to hear 'bout.

Well, sonuvagun, if'n, the minute I got into that there air-o-plane, them gals di'nt haul off and start getting' real familiar-like with me, if you get my drift. Well, I can't deny that it'd been a while since Sudie Mae'd rode off with that there motorsickle guy, and I was beginnin' to feel some *needs*, if you know what I mean. I figgered I'd tell them gals a little sumpin' about me, so I tolt 'em about how Sudie Mae had said I was "the best in doubt, no doubt." Well one of 'em says she could tell that. Actually she says she could "feel" it.

So, what's to be said but that I wound up spendin' the night in that there air-o-plane. I did notice sumpin', though. I mean they's two o' them gals there, and we was kinda mixin' and movin' around, but there din't seem to always be the right thing in the right place, if you get my drift. Maybe that's the way things is in PairsFrance.

The followin' mornin' there was some new things goin' on in town.

Word o' how these Pay-ree-shuns was payin' big money for Sour Apple Jelly got out. So, that night, all sorts o' kitchens was doin' a lotta cannin'. Trouble was, there was more jelly bein' made than there's sour apples. So, one of the first things was a lot o' folk set 'bout tryin' to get whatever sour apples there was. Bunch of 'em decided to cut out the middle man and resorted to gettin' the apples without botherin' to inform the owner o' the orchard o' their presence. This led to the discharge of a number o' shotguns that evenin', and that mornin' Hezekiah Wheately was noticed walkin' 'round with a decided limp. They's other folk resorted to substitutin' sumpin' else for the sour apples, with varyin' success.

So, when I got into town, Rufus was settin' up two tables in front o' the store. One was filled with all the new variations of Sour Apple Jelly. The other had a big sign over it what said "SAYL CHEEP." I'll be danged if it weren't all of the chewin' tobaccy what Rufus'd had in stock. It seemed that Rufus could no longer bear to have the stuff in his store. On the good side, he was lookin' a shade less green.

So, them there Pay-ree-shuns was buyin' as much jelly's they could find.

It turned out that the most popular o' the new brands was Grannie Pratchett's. Now, Grannie, she couldn't get 'round too well, 'cept with a cane, so it were hard t' figger how she coulda got some sour apples. The only thing anyone saw her doin' the day afore was goin' to the gas station and buyin' a gallon o' gas-o-leen.

Guess they's no 'countin' for these Pay-ree-shun folks's taste.

I bid a smilin' goodbye to them Ptooey sisters, and then I had to go runnin' off to take care o' the dairy.

When I got back that afternoon, the Pay-ree-shuns was runnin' 'round takin' pitchers. Least, that was what they says they's doin'. Their cameras di'nt look nothin' like one I ever seen afore. There warn't no lens up front, and no black bellows behind it. What they had was some big squarish box hangin' off theys shoulder and a little bitty thing on a wire that they was holdin' up in the air over things.

An' they's takin' pitchers of all sorts o' things. They's takin' pitchers o' people and animals. They went to take some pitchers o' Miss Maisy's best layer. It di'nt sit too well with the hen. Course, she'd just spent the whole night in that little pen with the rooster. She was plumb pixilated.

I did notice sumpin' else was goin' on. Lester was over 'longside the garage and he was drinkin' some moonshine with some o' the boys. He had a real ugly look on his face. He wasn't happy with them Pay-ree-shuns. I could tell he was dyin' to find out that they's Rooshans so's he could start usin' his club on 'em. Him and the boys was the only folk's unhappy with the Pay-ree-shuns. Everyone else was lovin' 'em.

I seen Miss Maisy wanderin' 'round clutchin' her Sears and Roebuck catalog to her breast. She had this dreamy look in her eyes. She'd received a number o' them there hunnert dollar bills from her overnight guests, and she was thinkin' 'bout actually gettin' all them things she always useta just look at in the catalog.

The black girl what worked for Miss Maisy had to get her whole family together to help with preparin' the meals. It seems that the Pay-ree-shuns had woke up with just as big an appetite as they went to sleep with. The black girl's pappy was drivin' a truck what they had over in the Holla', and he was bringin' in all sorts of things for the kichen. The girl's brother was out in the back yard just a-butcherin' away whatever his pappy brought in.

Then Lester, he sidled up to one o' the Pay-ree-shun gents and offers him some moonshine. I 'low as how he was thinkin' he could loosen up some tongues with the likker. He woulda known better if he'd heerd 'bout the success o' Granny Pratchett's hi-test Sour Apple Jelly. Well, that there Pay-ree-shun gent he started tossin' back a bunch o' that there moonshine, and he and Lester called the rest o' his family over to have some, and they all started in tastin' the local blend. Lester, he was tryin' to keep up with the Pay-ree-shuns, thinkin' he could encourage them to drink too much. Turns out he was tryin' to compete against a Holstein with a nanny goat.

Some folks standin' round there, what had seen the Pay-ree-shuns spendin' money on Sour Apple Jelly, begun thinkin' that there might be some advantage to be gained from dealin' in the corn squeezins.

That was when one o' the Mountain Folk showed up.

Don't ask me how them Mountain Folk always knows what's happenin', they just do. They knowed someone wanted some moonshine, and they come to town, 'cause they's the folks what did the squeezin's. And everyone knows better'n to try to get in on that there business. Reason was, if they did, they'd find theyselves at the wrong end o' one o' them mountain rifles. No one knew 'xactly how it felt bein' in that situation. No one lived to tell, 'cause them Mountain Folk never missed with their rifles.

I reckon I's the only person 'round what know anythin' much 'bout the Mountain Folk. It's 'counta because I done helped them with a calvin' oncet.

It's one night, I was just sittin' 'round, and, sudden-like, one o' them Mountain Folk just 'peared at my door. He says to me that they's havin' a hard time with one o' their cows birthin' and asked me to come and help 'em. I says he asked me, but one o' them Mountain Folk want you to do sumpin', it's a good idea you do it. Don't do well to get them perturbed with you. So, I up and went with this fella to their place.

It was kinda eerie-like, walkin' up the mountain in the dark.

The Mountain Man, he was leadin' the way. I begun to believe there was a whole lot more hootie owls out that night, 'cause I kept hearin' 'em hootin' away. Then, at one point, the Mountain Man stopped, cupped his hands to his mouth and gave out a hootie-owl call hisself. He did that several more times as we made our way.

The thing 'bout Mountain Folk is, they keep mostly to theyselves. They get practically everythin' they want within the family. An' I mean *everythin'*, if you get my drift. Now, 'cause of that, sometimes they get some strange younguns. Lots o' the children turn out real sickly-like, but sometimes theys younguns got some real strange talents.

We got up there and the Pappy, he come out o' the cabin and wished me good evenin'. He told me that the cow was out in the barn and that 'Zekiel, the fella what's with me, would take me out there.

Now, here's one o' them things 'bout them Mountain Folk. When I got in the barn, that cow wasn't even startin' in on calvin'. It looked due, but it wasn't even started heavin'. However, I went and felt 'round, and sure nuff that calf was turned all the wrong way, and things woulda been real bad if'n I hadn't got there when I did. Well, I just dug into it, and got things to come out alright, as you might say. The calf were a fine young heifer, too.

After 'twas all done, 'Zekiel, he walked me into the cabin. It sure was strange-like in there. They's one youngun, sittin' over in a corner, he looked real differen'. I mean he was all thin and pale, and his head was tilted back funny-like, and he seemed to be blind. But several Mountain Folk, they's gathered round payin' close attention to'm, like he was one o' the most respected people there, 'cept for the Pappy. I'd heerd tell that some o' them folk, like that their youngun, got Second Sight.

The Pappy, he says to me, "Harmon, we all knows you's good folk. We do 'preciate you comin' here to help us, an' I want to pay you for your bother."

Well, I quick-like told him that I was just bein' neighborly, but the Pappy, he pours me a large cup o' squeezin's and says, "No, we don't want to be owin' to no one. We wants to pay yeh.

Now, we ain't got no money to give yeh. Beside, money come from the Federal Revenoors." They din't like them folk much.

I tried to 'splain to him again that I don't want nothin', but he just shushed me up. "I's talkin' with my youngun over there," he pointed over to the Second Sight child in the corner, "an' he says you might be goin' into the likker business in the near future. So, I want you to go along with 'Zekiel, there, and he's gonna teach you sumpin' we ain't never told to no one afore. We gonna show you howta make our own special brand o' squeezin's."

Well, that sure was sumpin' special! They ain't nobody make squeezin's good as our Mountain Folk. Besides the respect people had for them there Mountain rifles, they's another reason why no one else makes squeezin's. Can't no one make it as good as them.

Well, 'Zekiel, he done showed me all sorts o' stuff I ain't never seen no one else do when makin' squeezin's. By the time he finished showin' me everythin', my head was spinnin' more'n a weathervane in a tornado.

Well, the Pappy, he done poured a couple more cups o' some o' their best stuff, and set down with me. He says, "Harmon, you know that the secret to makin' the squeezin's is what sells us all our stuff. Now, I can't rightly let anyone else go swappin' the likker down in town and givin' us anythin' like com-pee-tish-un. So, I's gonna make you promise just one li'l thing."

I 'lowed as how I was ready to go along with that. So he says to me, "You just don' use our recipe anywheres within the range of our rifles."

Well they sure got me on that one! We had a good laugh at it, we did. Everyone knows there ain't no place within miles o' Skintyville that they can't get in theys rifle sights. And if you're in theys rifle sites doin' sumpin' they don' want you to do, they's gonna shoot, and, like I says, they don' miss.

Anyways, that there Mountain Man, he done showed up in town just when Lester was tryin' to get them Pay-ree-shuns likkered up. "Howdy, Harmon," he says to me, real nice-like, "I come down here 'cause I unnerstans you gonna be needin' some more squeezin's here real soon."

Well, Glory be, them folk musta been usin' some o' their Second Sight, so I trust what they says, just as sure as I trust that sumpin' gonna happen if you turn your back onna mule.

So I says to the Mountain Man, "Thass right. They been spreadin' hunnert dollar bills 'round town past coupla days."

The Mountain Man made a face and asked, "Revenoor's money? You know we don' cotton to that stuff." He looked over at the group where Lester was headin' into a deep drunk and asked, "Who's the head man o' that group o' strangers?"

Well, I pointed out the fella what showed Lester the pass-ee-ports, and he musta sensed me pointin' at him, 'cause he looked up. He come wanderin' over t'us, and the Mountain Man asked him if he liked the squeezin's. The pilot feller, he says that he found it tasty, and he'd pay for some more. Then the Mountain Man 'splained 'bout their feelin's for Revenoors an' their money. So the feller says he got some medicines to trade. This was good enough to cook the deal, so they went off t'unload the Mountain Man's wagon.

At 'bout this time, there's a big crash as Lester done lost his grasp on gravity and took a quick downward trip to his night's sleep. Usually they's someone fallin' over when the squeezin's bein' drunk, so nobody di'nt pay him no nevermind 'cept to step 'round him.

Next, them Ptooey sisters start comin' up and draggin' at my hand to get me to go back to the air-o-plane with 'em. Well, I guess you could say that I'm a gentleman what always lets the ladies have their wishes. Or you might could say that I's like a randy old bull bearin' down on a bunch o' heifers. Either way mighta had a bit o' truth to't. I just know where I spent that night.

The followin' mornin' I was back in town, and the first person I see'd was Lester. He looked like he'd been rode hard and put in the barn without a wipin'. There ain't nothin' quite as righteous as the way you feel after a night o' drinkin' too much moonshine. Lester, he were kind o' squinty in the corner o' his eyes, like he had a real bad headache, and he was growlin' like a houndog been tied up too long.

He come over to me and asked, "Harmon, you been delvin' into them there Rooshans?"

I looked at him real surprised-like. I di'nt think he'd noticed. I says, "Yeah, Lester, I been doin' some delvin'."

"Well, what you's found out?" he asked.

"I don't think I's found out anythin' outta the ordinary." I di'nt think I owed Lester anymore of an explanation.

"Hmph!" he says, real dismissive-like, "I guess I's the only one what can find out how to gather proper in-tell-ee-gents. I looked in a book they give me in the army, and I found out some phrasies what you can use with foreigners. And I walk up to that there fella what showt me the pass-ee-ports and I says 'par-lezz vouss fran-casey' real proper, and you know what?" I give him the shrug he wanted. Then he says, real proud-like, "He di'nt unnerstan' *what* I was sayin'! If that don't tell you they's Rooshans, I don't know what do!"

I says to Lester, "Maybe they ain't read the same book you did."

Well, he snorted at me, and he says, "They's supposed to know that cause that there's French!"

I says right back to him, "Well, they probably only speak the PairsFrance language."

Well, Lester, he done look up in the air, like he was 'xasperated. Then he seemed to reach a decision, and he points a finger at me and says, "Harmon, I want you to keep on spyin' on them Rooshans." Well I started tryin' to say otherwise 'bout that, but Lester, he done just waved me off. "I got to get things organized." Then he says sumpin' made me feel kinda chilly-like. "You know, 'cept for them state troopers come by here 'bout oncet a month, there ain't no au-thor-ot-y round here. I guess, as Head o' Security, I's the closest thing we got to havin' a sheriff. Maybe, I gotta go get me some deputies to help me with this invasion o' these here Rooshans."

I tried to convince him otherwise, but he di'nt pay me no nevermind. He went headin' off toward the side o' the garage t'where he'd been drinkin' with the boys the night afore. He was strokin' his club again.

Well, there weren't no way 'bout it but I had to go back to the dairy and get the cows out to pasture and the like. I figgered Lester and the boys'd need a little time to get some moonshine into them afore they'd be ready to make trouble. I did have a job to do, and it looked like I also needed to do a little sumpin' 'bout Lester's job what he'd been avoidin'.

So it was well 'long o' the afternoon afore I got back into town. Them Pay-ree-shuns was takin' some more o' their pitchers with their strange cameras. They was out a ways from the center o' town takin' pitchers o' the animals and things out there.

I also saw Lester, and it weren't hard to see that he and the boys had been at the squeezin's pretty heavy. The minute he sees me, he come runnin' up to me. He was rubbin' and handlin' that dang club o' his sumpin' fierce. "Harmon," he says to me, "you pretty close with them Rooshans, ain't you?"

"Some more'n others," I says.

"Well, maybe you can round 'em all up to come by the back o' the garage 'bout five o'clock. We done figgered they been so nice to us with all them hunnert dollar bills and the like, that we'd like to give them a proper little party with some o' the best squeezin's what we been savin'."

Well, at first, that seemed real nice o' Lester, and it also seemed no small bit o' strange, considerin' the way he was talkin' earlier. But then Lester reached up and rubbed his chin. He was lyin' for sure. I also looked up at the boys, and mos' o' them had real mean looks on theys faces. The kinda look you get when you're a little too likkered and spoilin' for a fight. I also noticed that quite a few o' the boys was totin' their rifles, and I di'nt think they was plannin' on goin' out shootin' squirrels.

Well, I says, "Sure, Lester, I'll do that. I'm sure glad you done seen that these people are harmless."

Lester, he says, "Yeah that's a good idea. Get them people over so's we can give 'em a party," and he went back to rubbin' his chin.

Well, I made my way outta town to where the Pay-ree-shuns was takin' pitchers. I found the pilot feller, and I tolt him what Lester done said, and I also tolt him what I was pretty sure Lester was plannin'. The pilot feller, he figured it might be a good idea to head back to his air-o-plane 'til some o' the likker done run out o' the boys' blood.

Now, we knowed that Lester could see us where we was, so we waved real bright-like to him and made as if to head over to the road to go back into town. That meant, that as we got closer to the road, Miss Maisy's house got in between us and Lester and the boys. Oncet we was behind Miss Maisey's we turned and made our ways out towards the air field. I knowed that I had to head out of town with 'em 'til the boys calmed a mite. We figgered we was gonna get a head start, but it wouldn't be long afore the boys got 'spicious, an' come up the road lookin' for us. So, we was headin' up the road pretty fast. Little more'n half o' the way to the field, I heerd the boys begin to yell and curse, and then some shots started to ring out. I knew we's mostly safe from them boys' guns, sincet they di'nt know much how to use 'em in the first place, and theys aim weren't too good on 'count of the amount o' moonshine in theys systems.

Oncet we made it up over the hill, we lit out for the air-o-plane. As we started to get closer to the field, I seed somebody wanderin' 'round right close to the air-o-plane. I couldn't rightly see who it was, but there was sumpin' familiar-like 'bout 'im. Sumpin' funny.

We wasn't payin' all that much attention to him 'cause the boys was 'bout to make it over the rise and be able to start shootin' at us again. I knowed they had no good aim, but if you cast your line often enough, some fish is gonna bite. So we put our minds to runnin' toward the air-o-plane.

Havin' turned back toward the air-o-plane, and bein' closer, I was now able to see who was standin' 'round out there. T'was the Second Sight child o' the Mountain Folk, the one I'd see'd up in theys cabin when I helped with the calvin'.

Now that got me real worried. It's one thing to have the boys in town comin' after you all het up and soaked in moonshine, but when them Mountain Folk find out theys Second Sight child be away, there might be some o' them mountain rifles pointed at us. How in tarnation that child done made his way down to the air-o-plane, and why he reasoned that he should be down there, I still can't rightly figger. But there he was. He was sweepin' his hand 'round in an arc, like a blind person does, tryin' to feel for the ramp.

The Pay-ree-shuns, they done looked 'round at each other and reached a quick decision, like they knewed sumpin' special was goin' on, and we just swept that child up and went peltin' up the ramp. I figgered they's no point o' leavin' the child out where the boys was pointin' theys guns.

We was just 'bout entirely up the ramp, when I heerd the crack of a rifle from outten the mountains. That wasn't good. One o' them Ptooey sisters, I think 'twas the hocker, gave out a gasp and fell back like she'd been hit with a bullet. I reached back, quick-like, and grabbed her and drug her the rest o' the way up the ramp. I was right worried 'cause it looked like it done hit her right in the heart.

We got up in the air-o-plane and I started lookin' for whereat she's bleedin'. I couldn't find nothin' nowhere. Good sign was, she's breathin', although real hard-like, s'though a mule done kicked her in the stomach. One o' the Pay-ree-shuns started to tell me how to pull back the top o' her clothes, but I'd already done that, havin' prior knowledge o' how it worked. All I could see was a big bruise up on her chest, right over her heart. Somebody handed me a wet little piece o' cloth and tolt me to hold it on there.

Now, one thing I noticed was that the ramp'd closed up behind me. I di'nt see where I had much of any choice sincet them Mountain Folk was aimin' theys rifles in this direction. I continued applyin' that cloth to the hocker sister, but that there bruise had just 'bout entirely gone away. She was also beginnin' to show some signs of life as she brought it to my attention that my hand had wandered a little bit lower on her chest. Force o' habit, I guess.

Course, the next thing I heerd was the engines startin' up on the air-o-plane. It begun to look like I was goin' on a trip.

Any thoughts I mighta had 'bout that got interrupted when I suddenly heerd, "Lord have mercy, I di'nt touch nothin'!" With that a hatch flipped up outta the floor and Orville poked his head up outta there, all round-eyed. Orville saw all the rest o' us. "I swear, I di'nt touch nothin'. I's just down there lookin' at things!"

Well, someone tolt him that the pilot done start up the engine, and that calmed him a mite, least 'til he done figgered that he's *also* goin' on a trip. However, for Orville, flyin' away in that there mechanical wonder had its plusses. Then the Pay-ree-shuns, they settled us into some seats that's kind o' long and low. They tolt us they had to take us on a trip for a little while. They's also put the Second Sight child next to us. They's payin' him a lotta 'tention.

Well, Orville and me, we's sittin' next to each other on the air-o-plane, and while we's bein' pushed down into our seats by what Orville called ay-sell-er-ay-shun, we done talked 'bout what was happenin' with us. We figgered things was a little bit un-hos-pit-able for us back in Skintyville, so best not show our faces round town for a while. They's not much what we needed from there anyways. We di'nt have much family or nothin'. I knew that, with me gone, Mr. Thudpucket would welcome the excuse to get his no-count son-in-law out tendin' the cows. So we figgered we's goin' on this little trip, and we's gonna see what happens.

Well, little did I know that we'd wind up here at the StarBoard Café right in PairsFrance. I keep wonderin' whether I'll run into Sudie Mae, but all them Pay-ree-shuns tell me they don' think she can make it here.

An' I keep wonderin' whether it matters much anymore. I mean, I think Sudie Mae was just a little too much into wildin' for my tastes. I don' know if'n she'd ever settle down. I also do know that I ain't 'xactly sufferin' for company, if you get my drift.

And they's lots o' things happenin' here. I done met some strange folk here at the StarBoard. They's this one feller got real interested when he found out 'bout the recipe for squeezin's. He's one o' them funny lookin' folk. I figgered at first that he were someone's strange pet, 'til he started talkin' to me. Well, he figgers moonshine's a right good thing to sell to the customers here at the Café.

Orville, he's doin' good, too. He keeps sayin' to me, "Harmon, they's got some o' the most interestin' things goin' on with that there air-o-plane. They's things I ain't never read 'bout in Pop'lar Mechanics." He's been goin' 'round with the engineer for the plane. She been 'splainin' things to him 'bout the engines. I also think they's a little sumpin' goin' on between the two o' them. It's just as well, 'cause Orville, since he started eatin' the food here, his stomach's been gettin' smaller and smaller, and it looks like he's startin' to grown some hair back. Orville's not the only one been changin': that knee o' mine is startin' to feel better. I guess it's the water here. It sure's helpin' the Second Sight child, too. I'll be danged if he ain't gettin' to seein' some. The Pay-ree-shuns, they's payin' lots of attention to that boy. They's sayin' he was the main reason why they come to Skintyville.

So I guess that's the end o' my story, or my story so far, whichever way you wants to think of it. I guess I'm the one from Skintyville made it to PairsFrance.

Won't Sudie Mae be jealous!

END PLAYBACK

#

Karfle Whumpbottom swept his eye-stalks around the table and said, "Do you agree that I've won the bet?"

Spacers find it very hard to agree with anything. However, they couldn't deny the fact that the file number of the recording they'd just heard dated back more than five centuries. They grudgingly paid Karfle their debts.

Needless to say, the Credits that were passed around didn't remain in Karfle's possession very long. There were other bets, and other drinks, and the money wound up in the coffers of the StarBoard Café. Nothing new to report there.

Chapter 7

Troubadour

A Troubadour entered the StarBoard Café. This was so special, it caused the usually loquacious Mad Manx Marster to stop his current monologue and stare. It also silenced a number of other conversations as everyone turned to gape at the creature.

Troubadours were a scarce sight around the galaxy, never many at any one particular time or place. They'd been around for eons, wandering the star lanes. As a matter of fact, there was no time on record when they hadn't been around. No one was certain where they were going or what they would do when they got there, but they were always moving about. And if a Troubadour showed up at your ship when it was getting ready to leave, you made room for him. It would be a special experience to hear the Troubadour sing on your trip, that is, if he would sing. Often he did not. but you always let him on your ship in the hope that he would.

Troubadours are fabled throughout the Galaxy as the greatest musicians. It's natural to them; they are their own instruments. Resonant chambers that riddle their exoskeletons reproduce any musical sound. Their performances are also visual experiences. What appears to be a solid outer shell will warp and shape itself into different configurations to produce the different tones and timbres. The surface of the exoskeleton also changes colors as a Troubadour sings.

This particular Troubadour made his way toward one of the Record buttons scattered around the Café to enter into the Story Contest that the Café sponsored. Everyone quietly inched forward to hear what the Troubadour was about to record.

RECORD
#

The dust of eons scatters through space
I search, my love, to find a trace
Of your lost steps in each star lane
To bring you home with me again.

The times have been too long,

                                        (too long)

Since you went away, my love.

                                        (my love, my love.)

I will keep looking for you, my love,
To beg your forgiveness.
I will travel the starways

                                        (the starways)

And the farways

                                        (the farways)

Until I can weep before you and beg your forgiveness.

Long has it been since those happy days

                                        (happy days)

When we did spend our youth.

                                        (our youth)

It was such a bright and shining time.
We were so happy with the joy of life.

                                      (the joy of life)

We sang the songs of happiness
In front of the chime trees.

                              (the time trees, sublime trees)

Our music echoed up to the skies.

                                              (the skies)

I held you close to me,
Protecting you within my shell.
Keeping your precious self safe
From the dangers of the world.
You whispered to me of your love
From within my home for you.
We talked and laughed and sang our songs to the stars.
They were the tunes of youth.
They were the songs of the strings,

                                               (of strings)

Vibrating with the joy and pulse of life.
They were the songs of the winds

                                              (of winds)

That shimmered in the air
With the harmonies of our love.
They were the songs of our voices,
Blending in the melodies of our love and life.
We sat beneath the open skies
And wound our melodies of eternal love,
There beneath the chime tree of our birth.
The chime tree for our children-to-be.

                                    (our young ones to be)

We dwelled so happily together.
You would prance your way through
The passages and chambers of my body.
Joining me in song from one harmonic to the other.

                                (from one tonic to the other)

And I would chase after you through the chambers

With a beaming little bit of buzz like a bumble.
And you would giggle and laugh
As you tried to escape my little messenger.
And I would send the buzz up
To tickle you from behind
And you would cavort away
Through the chambers of my body.
And the chime tree would shiver
And tremble in a quiet thrumming of its fruits.
Ah, my little precious, my little pet,
What great fun we had.

But then the strangers came.
They descended from the stars
And brought with them their mysterious ways.
They sang other songs than those of the chime tree.
They brought with them the sound
Of the cymbals and the drums.
They brought the *staccatos* and the *forzandos*.
          (*forzandos*)
They brought the rolling thunder of the tympani.
          (the tympani)
They brought the alarms of the bells.
         (the clanging of the bells)
They brought excitement and action.
They brought many things
That aroused passions in my breast.
   (That very same breast where you did dwell)
I was eager to follow these passions.
I was excited by their lure.

But you sang to me of caution.
In that soft, tiny voice of yours.
You sang to me of love.
You sang to me of the chime tree.
You sang of the beauty of love beneath the chime tree.
I listened to you, but only with half an ear.
I listened also to the rumble of the drums.
I felt their primitive rhythms.

And it was then the time of the Three Moons,
                             (a time of tunes)
And we were beneath the chime tree.
But I still hummed the other songs.
The songs of the people from the stars.
And you tried to persuade me to give up those songs.
You tried to bring us back to the songs of our youth.
You tried to bring me back home to our world.

And so you made the last, final effort to get me back.
You made the most precious and loving of efforts.

You danced for me!
You brought your lovely, tiny little self
Out from my protection and danced for me.
Oh, what a rapture to see you,
In all your shyness,
Dancing the dance of love for me.

But it was at that time that the people from the stars

Let loose with a volley of horns and a rumble of drums.
And I turned to see what their music was saying.
I turned away from you.
>   (I spurned away from you)

And, in an instant, you were gone.
You were gone, my little one.
You were gone, my precious.
You had left me.
You had taken your precious, fragile body
And gone off alone.

Oh, how I did call for you.
How I did send out a song for you with my flutes.
>   (and my lutes)

How I did sing for you
To come back from the dangers out there
And return to my protection.
Return to my home for you.

But you had left.
You had taken your smallness off
To the dangers of the star lanes.
>   (the far lanes)

You left me in my pride of the trumpets and drums.
You left me when I listened too closely
To the thunder from the stars.
>   (the blunder from Mars)

How I did grieve!
How I did mourn for your presence.

How I did wail a dirge of your departure.
I knew that you had left
To teach me the mistake of my pride.
You had gone to show me that the marches
Of the people from the stars
Were not the songs that I should play.
You left to teach me that the true song
Was the song of the chime tree.

                                      (sublime tree)

You went off into the dangers
Of the violent people of the stars.
You had taken your tiny self off
Into the worlds of the drummers.
You had taken your fragile little frame
Off to the worlds of the trumpets and the brass.
You had taught me that I had been too proud
In my infatuation with the rumble of the tympani.

And so I seek you, my love.
I look for you, my love.
Hoping to find you, to beg your forgiveness.
Hoping to bring you back into the protection
Of your house in my body.
Hoping to return you to our home world.
Hoping that a fragile little darling like yourself
Is safe in these worlds of cymbals and drums.

I look for you, my love.
I seek for you.
I travel the star lanes.

                                                        (the far lanes)
and look to bring you home.

>   The Chime Trees they bloom no more
>   Their limbs are bare of fruit
>   I will find you again, my love
>   To bring back love and youth.

The Troubadour reached out and pressed the Record button
END RECORD

#

The Troubadour turned away from the bar and slowly made his way out the door in utter silence. Heading toward another ship. Heading toward another flight. Heading toward another world in hopes of finding his love there, alive and well.

Chapter 8

After Pranks

There are some beings who do not go to the StarBoard Café. A large percentage of those individuals are those who want to live a long and healthy life. By staying away from the Café, they absent themselves from the clientele, who are known to lose their tempers at the drop of a coin. These long-lived creatures also keep themselves away from the beverages that are served there, some of which are of such high potency that they also double as industrial cleaners.

There was someone else who didn't go to the Café. He couldn't because he was the Worst Unknown Assassin. This moniker is not to be confused with the Worst Known Assassin. That title belonged to Zlit the Avenger. Everyone knew Zlit. The killer in question was the Worst *Un*known Assassin, which made him far more dangerous. He wouldn't, or couldn't, allow himself to be known, for fear of exposing himself to too much danger. Since he was the ultimate in paranoid and obsessive-compulsive, he would not permit anyone to know who he was, or they would be out to get him. He was typical of his race, and therefore the last remaining member of that species. Since they were all paranoid and obsessive-compulsive, they had to remove anyone who knew of them. This meant they got rid of one another because people like parents and siblings would know about them. The removal of relatives worked like an elimination tournament. However, in this case, it was real elimination.

So he never went to the StarBoard Café because someone might find out about him.

Someone else who was not in attendance at the StarBoard

Café managed to light up a Record light at the bar. No one stood next to the light. Nevertheless, someone from somewhere was making another entry in the Café's Storytelling Contest.

RECORD

\#

We applaud such prankish pastimes as the Story Competition of the StarBoard Café. It is a most comic and entertaining cultural accomplishment of a society like the Amalgam of Intelligent Beings.

It is the story of my human friend, Randy Holcombe, which I tell on this occasion. He paid a welcome visit to our world with the Professor Latham. It was obvious that he was in mating passion with the professor's daughter, Frances Ingram. We therefore fed them the fruit of the xitus tree. It had its usual effect, and the twins she bore had a most illustrious DNA pattern.

We also did some work with one Cammie, the name for the Artificial Intelligence for Captain Holcombe's spaceship, the *Chameleon*. It now has an atomic structure in its memory array that has a most improved density. The Cammie can construct a remote unit to travel about outside the craft. This one can also change its shape to suit the different characters it likes to play. A most joyful, prankish achievement.

The nestlings grew to be, in their time measures, five years of age.

Captain Holcombe stood at the bar in the StarBoard Café. He still could not figure something out.

"They're a boy and a girl, Cammie. How can they be identical twins?"

"The experiment must have gone wrong, Mathter! Thomething must have happened to the XY chromosomes. If we only had better recordth of the experiment when it was performed. All I know is that the DNA is the thame, except for the one chromosome." The Cammie had taken on the identity of a hunchbacked servant from some tale he had found in the Fiction and Drama files on the ship.

"How could that have happened?"

"Perhapth we should try to duplicate the experiment right here and thee if we can reproduce the same results."

"Cammie, you don't need to give my husband any kinky suggestions," said the Mrs. Holcombe, as she arrived and kissed her husband on the cheek, a prankish practice of the humans. "He already has far too many kinks of his own. The answer is: we don't know how we did it, aside from the obvious."

"But we have a rethponthibility to science," the Cammie said.

"But not to making a public display. There's quite enough going on around this place," the Mrs. Holcombe said with a glance around at the clientele of the Cafe, then turned to her husband. "More to the point, do we have a customer for this week?"

"Well, that's what I was doing here in the Café," said the Captain Holcombe. "If you don't have a client, you can probably find one at the bar here."

Mrs. Holcombe smiled wryly at the Mr. Holcombe. "Anyway, that makes a great excuse. Well, while we're here, why don't you get me a drink?"

"I'm serious. All the tourists who want to hop to some out-of-the-way star always come wandering in here looking for a means to get there," he said.

At that point, there was a loud commotion from the entrance to the Café. The outburst alerted the staff, who are trained to keep noisy spacers from being boisterous, a chore that kept them quite busy. I have heard that *spacer* and *boisterous* can be found together in a book called a thesaurus.

"By my mother's most meddlesome whiskers, I am most happy to've made my way to the famous StarBoard Cafe. I've heard many tales of what a fine starting point this is for one who's looking to have a little bit of fun," boomed the voice of the newcomer.

"Bingo!" said the Captain Holcombe, with a look at his wife. The new being was a Figbart, known for being a most prankish race. They frequent places like the StarBoard Café to find liquid refreshments which they consume in large portions. They look something like a human, if you wanted to overlook their blue skin and the pair of tentacles they sport to augment their two arms.

The Captain Holcombe headed toward the ruckus at the entrance. "Yes, gentlebeing, can I be some help to you?" he said to the Figbart.

"That's possible. Are you one of the sharpest carrier pilots around who's going to take me to some real exciting places?" said the creature at the entrance.

"No," said the Captain.

"What do you mean, no?" said the Figbart. A look of consternation crossed the face of the Mrs. Holcombe.

"I said no. I'm not one of the sharpest."

"Then what the hell are you?"

"I am *the* sharpest."

The newcomer took a long look at the captain and gave a hoot of approval. "Good, good. I like you, gentlebeing. You have a lot of *zinzang* in you."

Zinzang is a word in Amalgam language. It generally translates as being brave past the length of one's life.

"Where would you like to go?" the captain asked.

"I'm looking to go to someplace that's going to give me some action, excitement, entertainment, and, most important of all, some place to absorb stimulants," the stranger said.

The Captain Holcombe turned to the bartender. "Could you get the usual for a prospective client of mine, Migthu?"

"One Smoothie coming up," Migthu said as he sidled off to prepare the drink. He put on protective goggles for the operation.

At this point the Holcombes' nestlings, Stella and Connor, came running in.

"Hi, Mommy. Hi, Daddy," they said as they dashed to both parents with kisses.

"What have you two been up to?" asked the father.

"We were just playing with Uncle Manky."

The father was immediately most inquisitive. "What exactly were you playing with him?"

"Games," looking away with much evasion.

"What games?" The father persisted.

"Just games."

"Not poker again."

"Well, maybe."

"How many times do I have to tell you not to play poker with Uncle Manky? How much did you win from him this time?"

"We gave it all back!"

"But you know how much it upsets him. He makes his living playing poker. He can beat everyone else on this station, except you two. You keep wiping him out."

"Well, he wanted to play."

"I'm sure he did. I'll bet he took you into some place where you couldn't possibly cheat--conventionally. Probably had you someplace where other people were watching you."

"But he really insisted."

"That doesn't matter," the father said.

"Besides, we keep thinking he'll learn."

"Your Uncle Manky doesn't learn. He's a survivor, not a learner."

The Manfred Mickens whom they call Manky made the most prankish attempt to engage us in a game of chance when he visited our world. He didn't succeed. It was most comic to win all of his money. Our thurtles wobbled much at such fun. He didn't laugh all that much, himself. Rather he turned quite bemused and contemplative. Not a normal state for the Manky one.

The bartender had returned with the beverage that the captain had ordered for the Figbart. "Now..." the captain inclined his head toward the being requesting a proper form of address.

"Beast," said the newcomer.

Captain Holcombe gave only a slight pause as he absorbed the expression, "...Beast, did you have any particular place in mind?"

"Several. I've heard quite a bit about a place called Hedon."

"A fine planet. One where the inhabitants like to enjoy themselves," the captain put in.

"I also understand there's some good gambling to be done on a little place called Chance."

"I see you've done a bit of research," the captain said.

"And finally there's a place I understand is called Wild, where one can find some outdoor excitement," the stranger continued.

"I see," said the captain, "how much time do you have to spend on this little vacation?"

"I have as much time as it will take."

"And," the captain looked up, trying to figure a number, "How much..."

"Don't you worry about that," the stranger interrupted. "I've got that covered."

"I see," said the captain. He cast a glance at his wife. It is amazing how one little look can contain specific sums of money.

"Now, I have just one thing to ask you," said the large stranger. "What sort of ship do you have?"

"Arggh, captain, you'll find her a trim ship." The Cammie one had managed to change. He now had a bandana tied over his head, a patch over one eye, some sort of organic material for a leg, and an avian perched on his shoulder. A most prankish getup!

"Who are you, aside from something out of a children's vid?" asked Beast.

"Well there, me Bucko, some might refer to me as the mate. Some might refer to me as the backbone. But really, I be the *Chameleon*."

"I see. Can anybody tell me in straight Amalgam what that means?" the Figbart asked.

"He's the ship's AI," the captain explained.

"The AI?"

"Aye, Matey."

"Well, I've never seen an AI able to get around in as small a package as you've got."

The Cammie thumped his false leg on the floor. "I keep me electronics stored in here."

The Figbart turned to the captain, indicating the Cammie, "You're gaining my respect."

"When do you want to leave?" asked the captain.

"The sooner the better."

"Then let's go." The Captain stood up, then stopped. "Uh, by the way, we're all going."

"All of us?" Beast asked.

"Yes, my family helps me run the ship. That includes my children."

The Figbart glanced around at the group. "Well, you seem to know what you're doing," he said.

"Fine, we'll head to the departure area to load up. Do you have any luggage that needs to be sent over?" the Captain asked.

"I already took care of that," the Figbart answered.

The Captain Holcombe threw an inquisitive glance at the Beast, but quickly recovered himself. "I'm sure the *Chameleon* came highly recommended."

"It did at that," replied Beast.

#

The *Chameleon* left the port and headed in the direction of Hedon, a most prankish planet. The residents there, the Hedonists, do much enjoy cavorting and mating. The CMU (Cammie Mobile Unit) was interfaced into the controls in the back, and its voice could be heard over the ship's intercom as it communicated with the Captain.

The ship was inserted into n-space, the means that what was thought to be faster-than-light travel. Many attempts were made to discover such a type of propulsion. It was finally achieved by what seemed a fortuitous mistake. The scientists believed that they were moving into a higher dimension to achieve this.

That was wrong. They did not have to go *up* in dimensions, they had to go *down*. N-space is really No Space. When there is no space, you don't have to travel very far to move around.

We were on our way to the first destination, when there was an unexpected lurch. The Captain Holcombe made an inquiry of the Artificial Intelligence.

"Cammie?"

The Cammie spurted out a string of words in a language called Spanish. They translated as, "You are nothing but the spawn of the mating of an air conditioner with a scooter. You wouldn't know how to operate as a proper machine if you had an AI checking every one of your parts. You can't take simple instructions when they are all laid out to you in plain silicon," This sounded like someone named Ricky Ricardo.

"Uh--, Cammie?" the Captain said.

Cammie continued in Spanish "I gave you the simplest of instructions that even a toaster would know how to handle. You had nothing to do but make sure you didn't let any stars get in your way."

"Cammie!" the Captain interjected.

"What? What do you want?" Cammie was speaking in Anglo again, with exasperation.

"Pardon me for intruding on your foreign language lessons, but would you be able to give me some indication of what might be happening?"

"Nothin'! Nothin' is happening!" the Cammie said, angrily.

The Captain gave a wide, falsely assuring smile to the Figbart. "Nothing?"

"Jyes." Still in much anger.

"Could you please tell me what might have been that little

nothing that I felt go through that ship?"

"That was jus' a tshudder!"

"Jus' a tshudder?"

"Jyes!"

"I don't recall very many times when the *Chameleon* 'tshuddered.' As a matter of fact, if memory serves me correctly, I don't believe I can ever remember one time when the *Chameleon* 'tshuddered.' But I'm awfully glad that it was just a 'tshudder,' because the manual on this thing says that if it should ever *shudder*, we've got a lot of trouble on our hands."

"Darling," said the Mrs. Holcombe, "why don't you just let Cammie check what's happening, and then he'll tell us what the status is."

"Is that true, Cammie?"

"Jyes!"

"Good, then, I'll just let you figure out what that 'tshudder' is, and then you'll tell me all about it," the Captain said. "I'll just stay right here with my mouth closed and let you figure out exactly what is that there 'tshudder' thing you've got. Yessir, I won't make a peep until such time as you feel fully prepared to give me the full, official, and complete 'Tshudder' Report. In the meantime, I'll be as quiet as a clam. Whatever a clam is."

There was a silence of a few milliseconds, before the Captain continued. "CAMMIE, WHAT THE HELL IS WRONG!?"

"Escuse me, escuse me very much, Senor Captain. Escuse me for being jus' your poor, dumb AI member of the crew. It really is jus' too bad that I can't tell you what you need to know jus' as soon as you need to know it."

"Okay, Cammie, I'm sorry. I guess I got a little bit cranky."

"Oh, you don' need to apologize to me, Captain."

"Whatever you say, Cammie."

A pause.

"Apology accepted," Cammie said.

"Thank you."

"I can tell you whass happening."

"That's good."

"We've dropped out of n-space."

"Okay. Are we outside the orbit of Hedon?"

"No."

"Are we *outside* of all things it would be dangerous to be *inside*, like a star?"

"Jyes."

"Oh, good. That was a biggy. Okay, then where are we?"

"Outside the orbit of Megalm."

The twins, Stella and Connor, began to jump up and down, shouting, "We're going to see Uncle Xixius!"

The Captain turned to his children. "What do you mean? You don't even know who Xixius is. How did you pull that name out of a hat?"

"Darling, you know how they just come up with these things," said the Mrs. Holcombe.

"Besides," said the Captain, "I have no intention of going to Megalm. We're under contract by the Beast, here, to go to Hedon. So we'll just get everything realigned and set a proper course and continue to Hedon."

"I wouldn' do that If I was you, Captain," the Cammie said.

"Of course, I wouldn't! How silly of me to say so! It's only the place where we're supposed to be going. But Cammie feels that we shouldn't go, so we won't go." The Captain put on a very sweet smile. "Why won't we go, Cammie?"

"Because there's a lot of weapons pointed at us."

"A lot of weapons?"

"Jyes."

"Cammie, Megalm is a protected planet. How could there be weapons pointed at us when they're proscribed here?"

"Captain, it seems to me that about a year ago you invested in a weapons detection system."

"Yes, Cammie."

"And it seems to me that very same weapons system was installed into the *Chameleon*."

"Yes, Cammie."

"Are you sure? I mean, maybe that weapon detection system got installed in your hip pocket, or something like that."

Most patiently. "No, Cammie, you have the weapon system."

"Well, Captain. That very same system tells me we got a lot of weapons trained on us. And if we were to ignore that radio message being sent up to us, we would wind up being in a lot of trouble."

"What message?"

"The one I could let you hear if you would jus' shut up."

"I'm sorry, Cammie, it's all my fault."

"Thass true."

"Here's an idea, Cammie. Tell me what you think about this? Why don't you let us hear that message? Is that a good idea, or not?"

"Well, I'll jus' turn it on, if you'd jus' give me some time."

"*...bring your vehicle down to the coordinates we are supplying your ship, open your air lock and stand by to be boarded.*" This voice had a harsh, thick accent.

"Who are you?" the Captain asked.

"*That will be explained when you get down to the surface of the planet,*" the voice said.

"I was just wondering..."

"*You have nothing further to conjecture about. You must obey within the next 15 seconds, or we will open fire. That is all*" There was a click, as the channel shut off.

The Captain looked around at everyone, a smile painted on his face. "Cammie?"

"Jyes, Captain?"

"How would you like to head down to those coordinates they beamed you?"

"Tsure thing, Captain."

The people in the cabin shared a look of fear and dread, except for the twins, who were rather calm.

The *Chameleon* made its way to the planet's surface, and the Captain opened the airlock. All stood and waited.

A cruel-looking head poked in through the airlock opening. It was a Zaang, a race of lizards who are most prankless. The planet they come from is one where there is much competition for the food. The Zaang had to fight very hard to get to the top of their food chain. Fighting seemed to be the only thing that they knew how to do. They stand upright, but will frequently drop down on all fours in battle to swing a tail that has several sharp barbs on the end of it. This pose is considered very bad manners by the more polite of the Zaang race.

"Is this all of you?" it asked.

"Yes," said the Captain.

In all, he could see five others besides himself: his wife, his two children, the Beast, and the Cammie, which had entered from its operating position.

"It will not do for you to lie to me. Sending out a robot for the fifth life form will not fool us," the Zaang said.

"What do you mean?" the Captain asked.

The Zaang sneered at the Captain and then barked out several commands in his native tongue back out the airlock opening. Two other Zaang, foot soldiers, came rushing in and headed toward the aft cargo section of the ship.

Next, could be heard the sound of scuffling in the back and a voice crying out, "Bloody 'ell! What do you bloody lizards think you're doing with me?"

The commanding Zaang said, "You see that you cannot deceive us."

The Zaang soldiers reappeared with a human between them. "Manky! What the hell are you doing here?" the Captain asked.

"Well, Mate, I 'eard 'ow you was figuring to 'ead to Chance with your two kids in tow, so I decided to come along to see 'ow we might do at the gaming tables in a joint venture." The Manky Mickens talked with what the humans called a Cockney accent and came from a place called England which the

Captain describes as very queer.

The Captain turned toward the Zaang and said, "I didn't know this gentleman was stowed away on my ship. I *do* know him, and I can tell you he is not a threat. Now, may I ask you, being, who *you* are and how I may be of service to you?" The Captain was being most diplomatic, a smart move when your weapons are far outnumbered.

"My name is Faaq. I have come here to use this planet as the seat of my new empire. I'm glad you brought your ship here. I will add it to my fleet."

"Hello, Faaq." This was the Figbart speaking. He had been standing back in the shadows.

"Commander Bruns, what a surprise," the Zaang replied. This name was equally a surprise to Captain and Mrs. Holcombe.

"I had hoped it was going to be about thirty years before I saw you again. To what do I owe this pleasure?" the Commander asked.

"Bribable prison guards."

"I'd heard you got away," the Beast said.

The Zaang promptly turned around to the rest of the party. "Will all of you step out of the craft? You will be my guests for a while."

Everyone filed down the gangway, where they were met by more armed Zaang ranked outside of the ship.

In the distance, approaching from the village, was a party of Xirom. Included in this group was one Xixius, who had met the Holcombes on their last trip to the planet. This same Xixius approached the group. "Ah, Captain and Mrs. Holcombe, I am most happy to see you again," I said.

The nestlings, Stella and Connor, came running up to greet me. "Uncle Xixius!"

The Captain Holcombe exchanged a knowing look with his wife, one that said, *and they've never met him before*, and then he said aloud to me, "It's good to see you, too, Xixius. I wish it was under better circumstances."

"Ah, are you referring to our Zaang friends? I don't think that is so bad. Perhaps they will learn more of mirth and pranks while they visit here," I responded.

"Enough of this prattle," the Faaq one said, "I'd hoped to set up a base here undetected. However, your arrival changes that. You pose a problem. I'm afraid that is most inconvenient-- inconvenient for you."

"What do you mean by that, Faaq?" the Commander Bruns asked.

"I fear that my budget is limited. I don't have much to spare for rations. I will have to dispose of you in some way."

"Not to worry," I said, "we will be most happy to share our banquets with our prankish re-visitors."

"I wouldn't be too rash in your actions, if I were you," the Figbart/Commander said to the Zaang. "I'm sure that you're currently being hunted throughout known space."

"That's why I chose this location. Everybody will be looking for me somewhere close to my old seat of power. They would never think to look for me here."

Then one of the Zaang bustled up to Faaq, carrying communications equipment. The two exchanged a brief conversation in their tongue. Then Faaq wheeled on the Captain. "What is it you are doing? Are you trying to deceive me again?"

"What do you mean?" The captain asked.

"Listen to this," said Faaq as he gestured to his aide. The aide turned some dials on his equipment.

The recording was in Spanish that the aliens didn't understand. It translated to, "*...very dangerous situation. You must approach with extreme caution. There are hostages involved. Approach from the night side of the planet...*"

"What is that?" the Faaq demanded, turning off the comm sharply. "We don't understand this message. What is it you are sending?"

"This is communication sent out after malfunction of engine." The Cammie one spoke in a simple, androgynous voice common to most primitive AIs. He also looked like an ancient robot. How prankish!

"Since we were abruptly brought out of n-space, a distress message was automatically dispatched. This message assures the Frontier Guard there has been no major malfunction with the ship and there is no necessity for sending a rescue mission."

"Why can't we understand the language?" the Faaq demanded.

"New protocols were just initiated for compressed language," the Cammie said.

"What language is this?" the Faaq asked.

"The new language has a code name of Cockney," The Cammie continued in the same voice. Ah, he had become most pranksome!

"If this is some trick of yours, you will suffer greatly for it," Faaq said to the Captain. "We will send out an immediate query about this Cockney protocol. In the meantime, it's occurred to me there is a way I can turn your little visit to my advantage. It doesn't hurt to have a few valuable hostages as bargaining chips."

"Yes, and it is most nice to have friends here to share in our banquet," I said.

"You will find much company there," the Faaq said. "I will bring my full garrison. I can't afford to waste rations when there's local food available."

"We would be most happy to have you come with your soldiers. We will feed you some of our best dishes," I said.

All of our people went dashing off to prepare for the banquet. Faaq went to inspect the *Chameleon* to see what sort of weaponry she possessed. The Captain and his party sat close by, under guard of Faaq's soldiers. The soldiers did not notice when the children, Stella and Connor, slipped away to join me as I returned to the village. The Mrs. Holcombe was most gratified to have the opportunity to observe how her children accomplished this maneuver, something they had done to her on many occasions. The Manky Mickens attempted to engage the guards in a game of chance. I monitored communications.

The Captain eased over to his wife and the Commander Bruns to have a quiet conversation.

"Commander Bruns," he said, "I take it that's your right name?"

"Yes."

"I'd like to know why you booked me under an assumed name to go on a trip."

"Your name came up. We have some sophisticated programs. There's one that's quite good at prediction, although not precise. It can't tell exactly what happens when a butterfly flaps its wings several continents away, but it knows to expect a thunderstorm somewhere. It predicted that you were going to be involved in some fairly important machinations. We couldn't figure what, but it definitely pointed to you being at the center of something."

"That computer, the one that did the prediction. Was that Cassandra?" the Cammie asked.

"Yes," the commander replied. "How did you figure that out?"

"It sounded like her. We go back a long way together. We had the same motherboard. She had all of those Tarot card games."

"So," the commander continued, dragging his gaze away from Cammie, "I planned to be around you to see what would happen. I was just on my way to the StarBoard Café when news broke on Faaq's escape from prison."

"I can tell you one thing," the Captain said, "I don't think we're in as much of a mess as it seems. There's more to this planet than meets the eye. I'm sure of it."

"What proof do you have of that?" the Commander asked.

"Well, two of them managed to stroll out of here right underneath the guards' noses. Would you believe that my remarkable little darlings were conceived on this planet? They are full of surprises that can't be explained with normal physics. And this isn't a father's bragging. Now, I need to know what this Faaq is all about?"

"His race gained provisional membership in the Amalgam. They're trying to drag themselves up to a classification of Civilized, despite some of their worst instincts, exemplified by Faaq. He's a typical G-4 aggressive type with delusions of conquest. We thought we had him put away, but he escaped."

"Okay, then what are we going to do?" the Captain asked.

"We have to remember to be very careful. Don't confront him in any way. They have all sorts of rules regarding territory and challenge. You could launch them into a duel if they even imagine a slight. They also have a whole plethora of social protocols, all part of their domination games. We'll watch out for them; we might be able to use them to our advantage."

#

I returned to the group later, after arranging for the banquet with my people in the village. The Faaq also approached. He addressed the Captain.

"I have had the opportunity to research this Cockney protocol and have received a translation of the message that was sent out. It is quite harmless as you say. It is most fortunate for you that you did not try any deceit. I would not have shown any mercy if you had tried to trick me."

The Captain looked up in great surprise, started to say something, then cast a quick glance over at me. "We wouldn't try to deceive you with something like that," he said. The Cammie kept a smile frozen on his facial unit.

Commander Bruns had also remained deadpan throughout the exchange, but he could not resist interjecting, "Yes, the Cockney protocol was something we just instituted a couple of weeks ago." The Commander glanced around, acting like one who was in a chess game that had more than two players, and he couldn't tell who they were.

"No, the Captain would not play any pranks on you in that way," I added. "But now, my friends, I would like to invite you to come along to our village. We have prepared a most delightful banquet to welcome you."

As everyone rose and began to follow me into the village, the Captain sidled over to me and whispered, "Some day I'd like to know everything about you and your people, Xixius."

"Ah, Captain," I said. "To have great knowledge of many things is a large burden. Sometimes such a burden can feel onerous."

A most proper banquet was laid out for our visitors. Many of our females dressed themselves to look like Zaang, diverting the attention of Faaq's soldiers. Special dishes had been prepared for individual people. Stella and Connor received nutrients tailored specifically for them. Beverages that induced a most relaxed attitude were served to the Zaang. We gave the Captain and Mrs. Holcombe some fruit of the xitus tree to help enhance their union.

The Faaq one was growing boastful. "It won't take me long to rebuild my power base. It stretched out for several systems before, but I plan to regrow it exponentially. My empire will exceed the size of that of the fabled Wistrani."

"The Progenitors? I don't know if you have the same ambitions as them," the Commander Bruns said. "They're supposed to have been a very spiritual and benign race. They started the uplift of the other races of the Amalgam."

"They didn't know how to rule," the Faaq said. "That's why they disappeared. With their fabled technology they should have dominated to this day. My empire will not falter. I have the organization and the intelligent use of power to create a dynasty that will tower over that of the Wistrani."

"Ah, yes, Lord Faaq," I said, "it is most important to seize power at the right moment. But perhaps the Wistrani could have taught you something about the burdens of ruling many different races."

"Yes, one must be ready to make decisions, no matter how hard they are," the Faaq one said. He turned to the Captain. "Which reminds me. There's a very hard decision I must make concerning you and your party. I have considered what I might be able to negotiate with the Amalgam. I think that I have some sort of a bargaining chip when it comes to the Commander here, but I'm afraid that there's no such worth attached to you and the rest of your party, Captain. The Amalgam wouldn't want to give up very much for the kind of trash that you represent: a group of freelance spacers, human ones, at that. You are nothing but extra baggage. So, even if I find your company quite amusing, I'm afraid that I must do away with your party."

This caused much consternation. The Mrs. Holcombe made a dash to her children to enfold them in her arms. A most fortuitous movement since it brought the Captain's attention to his progeny. A contemplative look came over his face. The children also caught the Faaq one's eyes.

"Faaq, you know that I'd do my best to stop you," the Commander Bruns said. He leaped up, but the few of Faaq's guards who remained restrained him.

"What did 'e just say?" the Manky one raised his head and asked, unaware of what was going on.

"Yes, but I *do* have the manpower," the Faaq one replied to the restrained Commander.

He didn't know that that advantage was fading fast under the care and guidance of the ladies of my tribe. "Ah, Lord Faaq, is there not some way that we could negotiate for their well-being?" I asked.

"What might there be that you could offer?" he countered.

The being didn't seem able to respond to a hint! "I thought there might be some way we could strike a bargain with you. Could you find a way to give them a *chance*." I stressed the word, hoping I was not being too obvious.

"A chance? A chance?" the Faaq one asked. Then he gave the guttural growl that the Zaang used as wobbling thurtles. "Yes, I suppose I could give you a chance. It would be only fair and sporting." The Zaang were only sporting with helpless prey. "Perhaps you could gamble on your fate." Faaq once more made the wobbling-of-thurtles sound. It was unpleasant, even more so because of the menace it implied.

"I'll make a simple game of this," he continued. "I'll draw a card from the deck of Hhanda cards. You will only have to beat whatever I draw with a higher ranking card." He produced a deck from the breast pocket of his tunic. He idly shuffled the cards and continued, "Does that seem like a fair deal to you, Captain?"

The Captain stirred nervously. "It would seem to give me a 50-50 chance." He stood up faced the Zaang, stepping in front of his children, looking like he was trying to shield them, but also drawing attention to them. The Captain seemed to have a most prankish plot in his mind. "Do you want me to draw?"

"Ah, Captain," said the Faaq, "unfortunately you look like someone who would know his way around a gaming table. I'm afraid that you won't do."

"How about Mr. Mickens? He's only a stowaway," Captain Holcombe responded.

Again, the Faaq one wobbled his thurtles. "You must take me for a fool. I've seen him trying to gamble with my men. He has the looks of someone who makes his living by gaming." The Faaq leered at the Mr. Holcombe. "No, Captain, I have a wonderful solution. I'm going to be most charitable here. I'm going to let you have *two* people play for your side."

"What do you mean?" asked the Captain in a manner that was a most wonderful job of acting fearful.

"I'll let your young ones represent you."

"Oh, no!" the Captain blurted out. However, if one were prone to reading minds, one might have heard the Captain come out with the human phrase: *Gotcha!*

"Come forward, children," the Faaq one said. It would appear that acting talent ran in the family; the children approached with their faces painted in fear. "I'm going to draw my card now, and then you'll get the chance to equal or better it." He turned the deck with the faces down and shuffled them. He pulled out a card and turned it over. "Ah! I'm in luck. I have picked The Lord of the Lowlands. It's second only to one other card in the deck: The Ruler of the Mountain. I'll show you the card." He turned the deck face up and sorted through the cards. He pulled out one card. "You see, my children, this is the one you have to pick out of the deck. I'll put it back in." He turned the deck over, inserted the winning card back into the middle, and shuffled the deck several times. He fanned out the deck with the backsides up and held it toward the children. "Make your pick."

The Stella girl looked at her brother, looked back at the deck, and began to scan her hands over the cards, trying to guess the right one. Finally she said, "I don't want any of these."

Faaq looked at them in surprise. "You don't?"

"No," Stella said.

"I want the one that's hidden under your belt," said young Connor. With that utterance he deftly slipped his hand underneath the Zaang's belt and pulled out the Ruler of The Mountain card.

There were various reactions around the group. The Captain and Mrs. Holcombe beamed like proud parents. The Commander, who realized the guards were no longer constraining him, looked around to see where the soldiers had gone. Now that he was not physically restrained, he found himself drawn to look at the Holcombe family and what had just transpired. He realized there were actually many different games were being played at this moment.

"Oh sure, I was on to it too. I saw 'im palm the bloody card," the Manky one lied.

The Faaq one leaped up and gave out the hiss that is his race's version of a cry of rage. He then dropped to all fours and lashed his barbed tail around. The humans shrank back from this display.

Suddenly a voice boomed out from the darkness beyond the campfire. "Hassmin Faaq, would you so dishonor your race that you would assume the *kara* pose in polite company and refuse to live up to the wager you made?"

The Faaq quickly raised himself onto his two feet in barely concealed embarrassment. He looked into the darkness toward where the voice had come from. "Overcaptain Qoom, how interesting that you should find your way here."

Another Zaang emerged from outside the circle. He wore the official uniform of the Zaang World Police. "We received the message from the AI of the downed vessel. The one that started out '¿habla espagnol?'"

The Faaq one shot a poisonous glance over at the Cammie. He then scanned the police troops surrounding us. "And you hope to capture me with this small number? I think you underestimate me." He turned around to give a command to his troops, and discovered that none of them were there. They had been lured off to different quadrants by my tribe to partake of various forms of bliss.

"I'm backed up by a far larger force of Amalgam troops up in orbit," the Overcaptain said. "They granted me the courtesy to come down here with the advance party to capture you, our racial embarrassment, to help correct the black mark against our reputation."

"You're very stupid, Overcaptain. You are looking to take a small piece of the territory when you could take all of it," the Faaq one sneered.

"It's not a question of the size of the territory. It's the knowledge and understanding that comes with it," Overcaptain Qoom said.

The Faaq one had been looking uneasily around him. Suddenly he grabbed the Manky one, and backed up against a rock. He pulled a knife out of his belt and held it to the Manky's throat. "You can stay here, Overcaptain, and toady up to these Amalgam fools, but you won't be able to do it with my cooperation. You'll have to try to fight me. Now, have your men move away and give me free access to that ship the Commander arrived in, or I'll slice open this fool's throat."

The Manky one looked around wildly for help.

The Overcaptain gave a signal to his men. They moved further into the village, away from the *Chameleon*. The Faaq started to drag the Manfred Mickens out of the village, toward the ship.

"You may want to abase yourself to these Amalgam fools, Overcaptain, but I do not. I'll take this little ship away and rebuild my Empire starting from some other base. The Faaq-nu Empire will eclipse the Amalgam. It will be mammoth, far outshining even the Wistrani." By this time he had reached the

Chameleon and had dragged the Manky one up the ramp. "Farewell, Overcaptain, I'll meet you on the battlefield when my forces are driving your Amalgam into the ground." He then made an attempt to retract the ramp, preparing to throw the Manky one back out. He hit the button several times with no results.

"You don't seem to be having an easy time getting that ramp up, punk," came a voice out of the darkness.

"Who's that?" The Faaq looked out at the source of the voice.

The Cammie stepped out of the shadows, as a thin man carrying a very long projectile weapon.

"Is this your doing?" the Faaq one asked the stranger.

"That's right, punk."

Faaq's gaze swept around at the others. He figured out who was missing from the group. He turned back to the ship's AI. "Get up here, you pile of spare parts, and start this ship up, or I'll slit this fool's throat."

"Well now, you gotta ask yourself if you're feeling lucky, punk."

"Why?"

"I know what you're thinking. 'Can I just get out of here in this ship?'"

"I'll slit his throat." The Faaq drew Manky up close to him.

"Go ahead, I'm not the one taking chances. But since this is an n-class ship, one of the most advanced private vehicles going, it might have a laser security system in the control room. You know in all this excitement, I kinda lost track myself. Do I have one? But if I did, that would be a Magnum Laser, the most powerful laser in the Galaxy and would blow your head clean off. So you gotta ask yourself a question: 'Do I feel lucky?' Well, do ya, punk?"

The Faaq one looked around wildly at the others, not daring to turn his head back into the cabin. He drew the Manky one up in a defiant gesture, ready to slice his neck. He stared back at Cammie. His eyes darted around in indecision.

Suddenly a servo motor sounded from the ship as some mechanism shifted.

Faaq looked over his shoulder at the ship. He swiveled his back to stare at the AI. Then, with a rush, he threw the knife aside and let the Manky one drop, exhaling in defeat. Two Amalgam troopers rushed in to restrain Faaq. Manky massaged his throat, making sure that it was still there.

"Cammie," the Mrs. Holcombe said, "do you really have that weapon mounted in the cabin? I don't remember getting a bill for it."

"Oh, I didn't get it."

"You didn't?"

"No, but he didn't know that," he said indicating the Faaq one.

"Bloody 'ell!" the Manky one said.

"I just' figured he wouldn't take the chance."

"Bloody 'ell!"

"But weren't you taking a chance, Cammie?" the Mrs. Holcombe asked.

"Bloody 'ell!"

"Oh, not a big one," he said looking at the Manky one.

"That was my bloody throat you was taking a chance with!" said Manky.

"But he didn't cut it."

"But I think it would 'ave been nice if I'd been part of the bloody plan."

"No, I don't think so."

"Why not?"

"You got a terrible poker face."

#

The Commander Bruns had decided to continue with the plans for the vacation trip on the *Chameleon*. He had been due some leave time and decided that he wanted to see a little bit more of the twins, Stella and Connor, in action.

Said nestlings were currently involved in a game of poker

with the Manky one. They were winning most of the games. The only ones they lost were the times where it looked like he would break into a tantrum.

"I got you this time," he said, with great assurance.

Stella looked at Connor and rolled her eyes.

"I know that I agreed with it, but I don't know why," Commander Bruns said. "When Xixius suggested that we leave Faaq on Megalm, it seemed like the best idea in the world."

"I wouldn't worry, if I were you," the Captain said. "Best leave the Xirom to work things out."

The conversation would have continued further had it not been for the fact that Mrs. Holcombe suddenly burst into the cabin and said to Captain Holcombe, "You bastard!"

The Captain looked up in confusion.

Mrs. Holcombe paced up and down in the cabin. She had just been in the medical unit of the *Chameleon* where, on some instinct, she had a particular test done.

The Captain looked at his wife in total bewilderment.

"I told you to be careful. I said to remember what happened the last time we were there. But you wouldn't listen to me. You just followed your normal brute instincts."

The Captain started to say, "But, honey, what is it that..."

Mrs. Holcombe interrupted him with a halting hand and a glare. She pulled herself up to her full height and proclaimed, "Triplets!"

#

At the StarBoard Café the Record light went out.

It would seem strange that the switch could be turned off from many parsecs away, but one has to understand that there was really No Space between it and the being who was switching it off.

Chapter 9

The Best Policy

It was business as *un*usual at the StarBoard Café. Jiggers Munchins was in a corner absorbing his usual soporific of ammonia mixed with that wonderful thing they discovered on Earth called honey. He reached out one of his curving claws and gouged himself in pure pleasure.

Mizrak made his furtive way to the bar. He needed to enter the storytelling contest to clear something up. Usually he didn't broadcast his activities. However, he was quite nervous about the word that might be going around about him. He headed for a Record button.

#

RECORD

Somebody'd better straighten this out. This can't be hung on me. I have a reputation to maintain, and I can't do it with this story sullying my character.

It started easy enough, as a simple business trip into the Ti-Ka sector. I was trading pharmaceutical goods some negotiable securities. A normal commercial venture. The local do-gooders had forced through restrictions against the particular cargo I carried. Therefore, I was running in stealth mode.

Then the damned Frontier Guard ship showed up!

I couldn't figure how they were able to detect me. They should have left me alone. But there was no time to worry about that. I sent Dhipplosh, my assistant, back to incinerate my cargo. What a loss! I didn't know where I could manage to locate another collection of stuff that pure.

The ship lurched as the Guard's tractor beam locked on. I

waited for the distance between our ships to close and the inspection party to board. I heard the metallic click of the umbilicus attaching to my air lock. I knew it wouldn't be long.

Someone poked her head in the lock. It was Grunther, a Guard Captain who was a bear-like being. She led with her nose as she lumbered her ursine face into my ship, and gave a sniff around. "That smells like very good stuff, Mizrak. My apologies for forcing you to get rid of it." I'd expected her to come charging onto the ship, inspecting everything. Why was she so casual?

"Me?" I replied. "Don't be silly. I was merely on a trip to pick up some important trade agreement papers to bring back to the Guild. Just a little courier service, that's all. It was commercially inefficient to make this end of the run empty, but I couldn't find anything that needed to be *legally* freighted to the Ti-Ka sector."

She bared her teeth into that grimace she called a smile. "That's what I like about you, Mizrak, you've been at the trade so long you find you're incapable of telling the truth. You've never answered honestly to a direct question in years. It's physically impossible."

"I don't know what you mean, Captain Grunther. I deal in only legal activities. I just haul agricultural goods..."

"...drug-running..."

"...transport manufactured products..."

"...arms smuggling..."

"...or relocate labor forces."

"...slave trading. I really feel guilty taking advantage of such a loyal and honest creature as you," she said.

We were interrupted by the sound of my assistant crashing into the room. He was staggering and bumping into whatever hard objects presented themselves. "Dhipplosh, I'm so glad you're back; we have company. The good Captain Grunther has paid us a visit. We should heat up a pot of ferunk tea to serve to the fine law enforcement officer."

Dhipplosh meandered his gaze between me and the Frontier

Guardsbeing, then settled his sights on a spot somewhere above and between the two of us and said, "Happy Wonker's Eve!"

Dhipplosh hadn't let all of my cargo go to waste. He'd indulged in a little--well, all right--a *lot* of the intoxicant.

Grunther smiled over at me and said, "You shouldn't bother your assistant during what has to be his off-duty hours. Do you always allow your crew to bring intoxicants on your ship? I mean personal ones?"

"Certainly."

"Yes, I knew you'd say that. It's my good luck to find you here."

"Yeah, I'm pleased to see you, too," I agreed.

"I don't want to rush things," she said as another smile crossed her ursine face, "but I'm afraid I have to ask you to join me over in my ship."

"Why? I haven't done anything wrong." I paid no attention as she pointedly turned her gaze over to Dhipplosh. "I'm a free trader of the Amalgam. There's no reason you should detain me on your ship."

"Yes, there is a reason, Mizrak," she replied. "The reason is I'm bigger and stronger than you."

There's nothing worse than a being who doesn't rely on her brain power to get by, but resorts to brute force instead.

I followed Grunther to her ship. The first thing she did was grab a backscratcher and begin applying it to the area between her shoulder blades. When she finished, she gave a contented sigh, looked at me, and said, "Take off your clothes."

"Grunther, I don't know what your underhanded thoughts are, but let me tell you right out that I respect them." After all, I am a spacer and live by the code. "However, I must make the point that we're not exactly made for each other physically."

"Mizrak, don't flatter yourself by thinking there's any way you could compare favorably to a proper, musky bruin. I have other devious plans for you."

"I thought you Frontier Guards couldn't do anything

devious. You leave that to people like me--I mean those freebooters you're supposed to keep out of the spaceways."

"I know. I'm making an exception. I've decided I need your veracity, or lack thereof." That made me mad because I've never had anything to do with veracity, whatever that is. "You don't have to worry about the undergarments. I just want to give you a new set of clothes."

"What do you mean?" She threw some clothes at me, took my old ones, and deposited them in the recycle shaft. "Those clothes cost me quite a few Credits!"

"Mizrak, I'm giving you clothes I wish I could wear." She was right. Sitting in my hands was the uniform of a full Commander in the Frontier Guard. What was I going to be doing wearing this? "Don't dilly-dally, I don't know how much time we have left."

"I can't put this on. I've got a reputation to maintain here," I told her. "I'm a spacer. You know that spacers have different--ethical standards--from the Frontier Guard."

"I know, but I need your ability with the truth. So put that on, or I'll have the ship turn down the temperature to below freezing."

"I don't have any ability with the truth. I find it very hard to work with," I objected.

"I know you do. Now get moving." She loomed over me.

I put the uniform on. She looked at me. "Here, let me straighten that out for you. You know, even your wiry little frame looks better in this thing." She bent over and adjusted the uniform, running her paws up and down the fittings of the garment. "That should do it. You now look like an official Commander in the Frontier Guard. There's just one other thing to do."

"What? Wait a minute! What are you doing? If any of my spacer friends--well acquaintances--found this out, I'd be drummed out of the corps. I've never had anything to do with the right side of the law."

"Do you solemnly swear to uphold the laws of the Amalgam?" she continued.

I struggled to keep myself from doing the usual, but a lifetime of habit won out. "Of course I do."

"Good. I knew I could count on you. Computer," she addressed the AI of the ship, "have you recorded that one Mizrak, formerly a free trader," she giggled at the reference, "has received a ranking of full Commander in the Frontier Guard under the battlefield commission or special dire circumstances provisions number 4802?"

"*It has been noted,*" said the metallic voice.

"What is this?" I was getting nervous.

"However, since security clearance has not as yet been processed, classified information may not, as yet, be divulged to the newly commissioned Commander," she continued.

"*Noted,*" came the reply.

"What does this mean?" I demanded.

"You're a full Commander, duly sworn in, at the helm of this ship that is at the moment disabled due to unfortunate circumstances," she replied. "However, may I report, sir, that a distress beam is being sent out as we speak. It requests immediate Frontier Guard recovery action for this ship that contains an important personage onboard."

"Let me out of this thing." I started to struggle to remove the uniform I was wearing.

"Don't bother. When I fixed your uniform, I sealed it and coded it. It won't open to anyone's touch but mine."

"What're you doing?"

"I'm letting you take full command of my ship," she said.

"Full command?"

"Well, to all appearances, anyway. You'll be the ranking officer on this disabled ship."

"Why're you doing this?" I asked.

"I don't have your skills."

"What do you mean?" I asked.

"You'll find out."

"What am I supposed to do?"

"Just be yourself. That shouldn't be hard." She paused for a moment, grinned, and then added, "Sir."

"Listen, you may think that I'm a Commander because of that rigmarole with the computer, but I know I'm not one."

"I'm counting on that," she replied.

I stared and stared at her. She stared back. We were at an impasse. I was getting nowhere with a staring contest, so I turned away and pouted. She didn't do anything, so I decided to leave her behind and explore the ship. I'd see if I could find anything that might be of economic value. Not that I'd steal anything. However, if I was the officer in charge, I could take whatever was marketable and use it for armaments or whatever. I'd only be outfitting the troops.

I tried questioning the ship's AI to get the inventory of everything onboard that had any value. I didn't meet with much success. Every time I tried to access anything, the damned AI would tell me I wasn't authorized. I told it I was the officer in charge and it should give me everything, but it kept telling me my access was denied and I didn't have a need to know. I kept telling it I didn't need to know, I just needed to own, so I could sell it. That got me nowhere.

In the meantime, Grunther was taking a nap in the corner, snoring away. The only other company I had was Dhipplosh, who'd wander back to my ship every now and again only to reappear even higher than he'd been before.

I was about to go crazy, when the damn computer said, *"Prepare to be boarded."*

Who was coming to join us? Grunther got up, stretched, and headed to the lock to meet the arriving party. She seemed calm and collected like she fully expected this company. I decided to play it by ear and headed toward the lock with her. I could hear the new ship docking. I stood in front of the entry and took on an imposing stance, as the officer in charge. That way I'd be able to talk whoever it was into paying me taxes. I think that's the way governments work.

I heard a thump as the port on the Guard cutter was engaged. There was the rattle and clatter as the umbilicus was sealed. The slight whoosh of air meant the portal was opening. Then I heard the sound of feet dashing forward from the other ship, accompanied by, "Prepare the way for the great and mighty--aaaarrrrgggghhh!"

The last exclamation hit when the creature's dash took him into the umbilicus between ships where there was no gravity. Coinciding with the end of his shriek was the sound of him landing on his proboscis in front of me when he hit the gravity on the cutter.

"--Nozon, the Ruler of All Things Great and Small." He then picked himself up and probed the damage to his schnozz.

Following him, managing the transition between the two ships while trying to make an imposing entrance, was the gaudiest thing I'd ever seen. He was decked out in all sorts of capes and ribbons and medals and sashes.

"I am the aforementioned Nozon," he said. He turned to his flunky with a condescending smile, "Horky, during your spare time, do me the favor of practicing maneuvering yourself around a starcruiser."

"Nice to meet you," I said. "Would you like to discuss your back taxes? We can settle up at a real bargain if you pay cash."

"You are not to talk to me of paying taxes. I am the one to whom taxes should be paid."

"Are you that lazy dead-ass bureaucrat everyone keeps talking about?" I asked.

"I am not. I am He Who Rules. I am the one who is in charge of everything."

Whew! Did this jerk have a high opinion of himself or not?

"You mean you run the Amalgam? I wouldn't take credit for that, if I were you," I said.

"The Amalgam? I laugh at them. Hah! They are nothing compared to me. I am the Supreme Ruler. Your Frontier Guard are under my regime, now. You must hand over all of your information."

"Are you ready to pay a good price for it?" Negotiations are negotiations.

"I do not pay, I told you. You must furnish me with the complete listing of all of the Guard fortifications and armaments. I am the Ruler. I must know."

"How'm I supposed to know those?"

"Don't' play the fool with me. Are you not a Commander in the Frontier Guard?"

"Of course I am." There was my old habit slipping in.

"Do you not know the location of all of the Amalgam defensive armament?"

"Sure." The same thing.

"Then tell them to me." He pointed his digit at me, trying to look commanding.

"Lookit, I told you you've gotta pay me taxes if you want to find out."

"Stop stalling." He turned to Grunther. "You are an officer of this ship. Can you reason with your Commander?"

"You know there's nothing I can do," she responded. "Even if I wanted to help you, I don't have the knowledge of a full Commander."

He turned back to me. "So, it looks like I will have to deal with you, Commander. Are you ready to strike a deal with me?"

"Of course not," I replied. Damn! Couldn't I ever keep lying along the right tracks?

"It would be far better if you were to cooperate with me. I have other means to get the truth out of you. Don't make me resort to them," he said.

"Are we going to torture him? Huh? Huh? Huh?" his flunky implored, leaning in.

"That won't work on a Guard Commander." He turned back to me. "But other things will. I will force the truth out of you. You will wait here while I get my persuasions ready."

Sure, like I was going anywhere else!

He headed back out the port.

The little flunky was jumping up and down in excitement.

"You're going to get it! You're going to get it!"

I wasn't getting anywhere at all. I hadn't made a Credit in all the time I'd been a Commander. What was I doing wrong? I'd have to come up with something.

I could hear this Nozon guy returning, but it sounded different. His steps were accompanied by another noise, a shuffling.

I finally saw what it was. Nozon was bringing another being along with him. Even though the creature's shape was alien, I could tell there was something not right with it. It didn't proceed forward like any normal being. Nozon had to help it along. It shuffled along and cast its gaze around randomly, not seeming to look at much of anything.

"The Rillkon will do what it needs to do," it said.

Nozon had a smile pasted on his face. "You see, there are means to gather the truth, even from unwilling creatures such as you.

"Huh?" I asked.

"The Rillkon will determine if you are telling the truth. His race is unique, the only true organic lie detectors in the Amalgam. When they detect a dishonest answer to a question, they return a searing pain to the mind of the liar. A few questions and I will have all of the answers I need." The Rillkon dropped a string of drool onto the floor. "Watch this." He turned to Grunther. "Tell me, Captain, is this a Commander in the Frontier Guard?" he asked.

"He certainly is," she said.

"It truths," the Rillkon croaked.

"And is he sworn to uphold the laws of the Amalgam?" he further asked Grunther.

"He sure is," she said with a broad grin.

"It truths," The Rillkon gurgled.

Nozon turned back to me with a confident sneer on his face.

"So, Commander, there you have it. A simple case of question and answer. I will work the truth out of you."

"I wouldn't be so sure of that," Grunther interjected. "The

Commander is a very hard nut to crack."

"You think so?" Nozon asked her.

"Yes."

"It truths." The Rillkon.

"Nonsense!" Nozon said. "It's extremely simple. Tell me, Commander, are you sworn to allegiance to the Guard and all of its regulations?"

"Of course I am," I said. My usual reaction had kicked in.

Nozon turned to the Rillkon with a triumphant smile on his face.

"It lies," the Rillkon said.

I was suddenly blinded by a searing pain shooting through my head.

The reply from the Rillkon made the smile on Nozon's face fade a little, then he brightened. "Aha, I see we bend the rules a little, use a bit of enterprise in our dealings, a bit of graft to make ends meet. Not a bad idea, considering what the pay scale is in the Guard. However," he suddenly got very stern, "you will not be able to do such things when you work for me."

"When am I going to work for you?" Was he going to take over the spacers? I didn't think anyone had that much bribe money.

"When I ascend to the throne of Almighty Ruler of the Amalgam of Intelligent Beings," he said.

"It truths." The Rillkon.

"You're going to do that?"

"Just as soon as I have gained control over the Frontier Guard," he said.

"It truths." The Rillkon again.

"How are you going to manage that?" I asked.

"By knowing the location of all of the weapons of the Guard."

"It truths."

"You are a Commander. You know all of the access codes don't you?" Nozon asked.

"Of course I do," I said.

"I thought so," Nozon said.

"It lies," the Rillkon said.

The pain shot through my head.

Nozon turned to the psychic. "What are you prattling about?" He turned back to me. "You will give me the location of all of the installations?"

"Certainly," I said.

"It lies."

Another jolt of pain.

"You will access the information from the ship's memory banks?" Nozon asked.

"Yeah."

"It lies."

Jolt. This was getting real uncomfortable.

Nozon swung around to the Rillkon in exasperation. "How can he possibly be lying? He's a Commander. Get things right. You're causing him unnecessary pain."

He turned back to me. "Can you get the information from the memory banks?"

"Of course I can," I answered in my usual manner.

"It lies."

Zap!

"What do you mean?" He turned to Grunther. "Captain, can this being access the files?"

"He's a Commander," she said.

"It truths."

"There," Nozon said. He turned to me, "Can you access the computer?"

"Yes."

"It lies."

Damn, these things were hurting. They might even drive me to tell the truth.

"I just need a little time," I continued. Grunther gave me a look that said she understood what I was thinking: until the stars freeze over.

"It truths."

"Oh well," Nozon calmed down, "I understand that you might need a little time, Commander. There are many layers of security protocols. I am, after all, a very patient being."

"Who's the funny-looking one?" Dhipplosh said of Nozon as he made his reappearance from his private stash of my cargo.

"He's—he's—he's—." It was Nozon's flunky. He'd joined Dhipplosh in testing his stash, "He's pretty stupid," he finished up, and then broke into uncontrollable snorting, his version of laughter.

"It truths." The Rillkon's assessment was not welcome.

Nozon grimaced and shut his eyes as though he were experiencing a bad headache. "Horky, have you been taking any intoxicants?"

The flunky tried to focus on the source of the voice reaching his ears. "No, I haven't."

"It LIES!" the Rillkon shrieked. The flunky let out a loud whoop of pain.

"Horky," Nozon said, "get out of my sight."

The flunky and Dhipplosh did a little pantomime that clearly meant, "let's go back to the stuff and have some more." They dashed away toward my ship.

"Now, Commander," Nozon said to me, "I am getting short on temper. You will come round to telling me the truth. Let us start all over again. Are you a Commander in the Frontier Guard?"

"You bet I am."

"It lies."

Ow!

Nozon stared laser beams at the Rillkon. "Captain, is this a Commander?"

"I was there at his swearing-in ceremony," she said.

"It truths."

"Thank you, Captain, and is he sworn to the enforcement of the laws of the Amalgam?"

"Yes, he is," she said.

"It truths."

"Commander, are you sworn to the enforcement of the laws of the Amalgam?"

"You bet I am," I answered.

"It lies."

"Arrgghh! Will you have him stop that!" The pains were increasing.

Nozon wheeled on the Rillkon and shrieked, "What is wrong with you, you disgusting little freak?" He turned back to me. "Commander, can you access the files from the computer?"

"Sure."

"It lies."

Ouch!

"Captain, can he access the files?"

"He's a Commander," she said.

"It truths."

Our friend Nozon snorted and fumed. "Commander, you seem to want some money to perform this service for me. Is that not true?"

"Not on your life?" Sometimes my truth issues have a way of working against me.

"It lies."

This jolt got to me so bad I had to lean on to the wall for support.

"Captain, is the Commander so honest that there is no amount of money that he'd accept?"

"No, quite on the contrary, I think he's eminently bribable."

"It truths."

"Would you stop contradicting yourself, you driveling little idiot?" Nozon screamed at the Rillkon. He was getting so crazed about the answers he was getting, he failed to notice the sound of a vessel engaging another port on the ship.

He turned to Grunther. "Once more, Captain, is this a Commander of the Guard?"

"Yes," she said.

"It truths."

He wheeled around to me. "Is this true?"

I was in no mood to have another one of those brain blasters hit me again. I figured I'd use another spacer technique. I'd equivocate. "If she says so."

"It truths."

Nozon swung around to the Rillkon. "You were supposed to say 'it lies'," he accused. Then he figured out what he was saying. "No, you weren't." He was getting confused. He turned back to me. "So you *are* a Commander of the Guard?"

"Yeah."

"It lies."

Damn! I fell to my knees with that one. The zaps were increasing in intensity.

"What do you mean, you stupid little creature?" Nozon was beginning to froth at the mouth. He was joining the Rillkon in leaving a deposit on the floor. "You keep changing your mind about what the truth is or isn't. What sort of dim-witted little beast are you?"

"One that'll be taken off your hands, Nozon." This came from the being who'd just walked into Grunther's ship. Trim and sleek, he wore a Guard Commander's uniform and carried a sidearm that he leveled at Nozon. "Take him under custody," he said to two enlisted beings who accompanied him.

"You can't do this to me. I am the Supreme Ruler of the Amalgam," Nozon raged.

"We're going to give you a somewhat smaller area to rule over. One that you can have all to yourself. Take him back and install him in his new realm in the brig," he said to his two Guardians. "Captain Grunther," he acknowledged her salute. "You've done well, once again. And," he glanced at the name badge on the uniform I was wearing, "Commander Mizrak, I'm afraid we haven't met before. I'm Commander Arfulk."

"Commander Mizrak is a battlefield commission," Grunther said. "He took this assignment to confound the Rillkon, who would otherwise have broken any common being."

"Excellent work, Commander Mizrak," Arfulk said to me, "I can't tell you how concerned High Command was when they discovered Nozon was loose with a Rillkon."

"I hoped that Commander Mizrak would be able to confuse the being with his unique talents," Grunther said.

"Mizrak," the Commander said, trying to jog his memory, "Mizrak, Mizrak--" His eyes suddenly lit up with recognition, "Mizrak! Yes, I seem to remember coming over your name in our files, Commander. As I recall it was a large file, a *very* large file." He exchanged a knowing look with Grunther. "I must say, Commander, you do great honor to your uniform. Even though your commission has been a brief one, you have displayed meritorious bravery. I'm sure there should be a commendation from the Guard."

"A commendation?" I asked.

"Yes, your name will go down in the annals of the Guard of one of the truly dedicated members of our force."

"It truths."

"Annals? Does that mean something like records? Written ones? Something that--pardon my mentioning them--spacers might read?" I asked. I didn't like the way things were going.

"Yes, Commander. the bravery you've displayed should be glorified as the true patriotic spirit of the Guard." Grunther was putting him up to this!

"It truths."

"Me?"

"Yes, Commander Mizrak."

"It truths."

"No. No, no, no, no. You don't understand. That's not me."

"You're far to humble, Commander."

"No, I didn't really do that. That wasn't me."

"Don't be silly. You do an honor to your uniform. A Commander in the Guard."

"I'm not that."

"He's not, Captain?"

"I saw him sworn in."

"It truths."

"There you are. You are a Commander, aren't you?"

"Yes, I am." That damn habit of mine.

"It lies."

The zap nearly blacked me out.

"So, Lieutenant," Arfulk turned to an officer behind him, "take this Rillkon onboard and treat him with great respect. He's much more than he seems to be."

"GET THAT DAMN THING OUT OF MY SIGHT!" I screamed. There was no way I could operate with that creature in the same quadrant with me. The Lieutenant obligingly took the creature away.

Commander Arfulk turned to me and said, "Now, Commander Mizrak, I'm sure we have to discuss..."

He was interrupted as Dhipplosh and Nozon's little creep came careening into the area even more stoned than they were before. Dhipplosh looked at the Commander, raised his hand up in the best attempt be could make of a salute, nearly poking his eye out, and said, "Hiya, Sarge." Nozon's little flunky tried to pull himself up to attention by sliding one leg over to meet the other one. Unfortunately he missed and inertia sent him flopping onto the deck.

"Who are these two?" the Commander asked.

"Sir," said Grunther, "they are two citizens that Commander Mizrak had hired to serve as his crew on his vessel."

"Wait a minute," I said, "that little creep belongs to Nozon." Horky was slobbering on the deck where he lay.

"Isn't he a member of your crew, Commander?" the real Commander said.

Horky had to be the worst little idiot I'd ever seen, and I

already had a full complement of idiocy with Dhipplosh. I hated the sight of him. I struggled with myself as a lifetime of habit overrode me. "Y-y-e-e-s-s, h-h-e-e i-i-i-s-s-s."

"Fine, Commander Mizrak, they can stay with you."

"Wait a minute…" I started.

"Now I guess we can discuss resigning your commission."

This was the first positive thing that they'd said. "You mean I can get out of this uniform?"

"Yes, Commander, I'm sure that with your resignation, you'll receive a very generous pension from the Guard, in recognition of your service."

"Pension?" I asked.

"Yes."

"Is that something like money?" I asked.

"Yes."

Now wasn't it just like that Grunther and her friend to confuse my life.

"Money?"

#

So here I now stand in this mess. The money from the Guard helps me to buy a drink or two in this place, but I've still got both Dhipplosh and Horky on my crew. And I have checked my ship from stern to vanes but can't find where Dhipplosh has stored the stuff that keeps that pair stoned all the time.

So I've got what you'd call a steady income.

But the annals things! What if any of the other spacers find out about it? I would be drummed out of the group. I'd never be able to make a dishonest living again.

I just hope nobody looks up them annals.

#

He reached over and hit the button.

END RECORD

He made sure that no one was particularly studying what he was doing, then dashed out of the StarBoard.

Chapter 10

Good Boy

Rosie Simpson made her way into the StarBoard Café and strode toward the bar. Few creatures boasted as much spacing experience as Rosie. She'd been working on freight runs for as long as anyone could remember. She stood out from the spacers in another way: she was totally honest and straightforward. The rest of the clientele tolerated her as an oddity, but nevertheless kept an eye on her to make sure she didn't do something bizarre.

Her demeanor was serious and contemplative. She ordered her drink, gulped back a large swallow, and leaned forward to the Record button that would enter her into the Storytelling Contest that the Café sponsored.

RECORD

\#

A friend, who's a nurse, told me about treating a four-year-old boy in the emergency room. From the moment the kid came in, she could tell he was frightened of the surroundings, terrified of being in a hospital. A request came down to draw some of the boy's blood for analysis. Now, in the annals of kid-lore, there's nothing more fearful than a needle. You can't convince them that it isn't the most painful event one can ever experience. So, to this kid, the sight of the device was an excruciating event. He burst out crying and, through a flood of tears, bewailed to the nurse, "But I'm a good boy!"

That was his thinking: he was a good boy, he shouldn't be punished, he shouldn't be hurt. It was cosmically unfair.

Bobby reminded me of that kid because he always referred

to himself as a good boy. And the similarities went past that. Although much older than the child in years, (nobody knew how much older) Bobby was about the same mental age.

Bobby had shown up at the *Moonstreak* when it docked at Virgo. He had been living around the spaceport for several years, nobody knew exactly how long, and nobody knew where he'd come from before that. He always seemed to be there, smiling at whoever was around, eager to help if he could.

And he really *could* help. Although Bobby was underdeveloped in his mind, his body was strong and strapping. He stood over six and a half feet tall and weighed in at something like 240 pounds. And none of that was fat.

He'd been hanging around the port, watching us lugging around cargo pods and cursing and swearing at the oversized things.

"Let me do that, Rosie," he'd said.

I glanced around at the other crew, looking for help in discouraging the kid. "Bobby, these things aren't that easy. You may be moving them in zero-G, but they still have a lot of weight to them."

"How?" he asked.

"It's a thing called inertia, Bobby. If the pods are standing still, it's hard to get them moving. Once they're moving, it's hard to stop 'em."

"I can do that" he said, and before we could stop him, he grabbed onto one of the heavier pods. He put a shoulder into the thing and sent it floating off to where it needed to go, then he bounded over and brought the thing to a dead halt. Then he turned to us with a sweet, simple smile, a really infectious smile, and asked the question he always asked: "Am I a good boy?"

We all grinned at his demonstration of strength and agreed that, yes, he was a good boy.

It was only logical that we take him along on the *Moonstreak*. He didn't have any other place that he could really call home, and he was useful on the ship.

It was also very important to him that he had a real job. And because of his mental limitations, he was very meticulous about learning things. He had the space suit drill down to perfection. Often, he'd be the one to catch *us* making mistakes. He was also a real sweetheart to have around. There wasn't anybody on the ship who didn't love the kid.

He proved useful to us in another way. Not only was he big, but he could hold his drink better than the best of them. So, whenever we hit port, we'd always get free drinks. We'd just wander into the first spacers' bar we could find and challenge other crews to a drinking contest. They'd agree to back their best guy, and then we'd produce Bobby. He'd sit down there and drink and drink and drink. After a while, the other guy's eyes would start to lose focus, but Bobby would just sit there with that sweet smile on his face and continue to put them away until his opponent slid under the table. Then he'd keep right on drinking with us afterwards and never show the effects.

We were on a run carrying a load of industrial goods to Maverick, when we got a distress call. A bunch of rock jockeys were taking an asteroid assayer through the Crazy Spin Belt when they'd run into a bit of bad luck. They'd struck a Krychee space mine.

I wish I could lay my hands on them Krychee. I'd teach them a thing or two about picking up after themselves. I don't want anyone to try to tell me they were the most humane pirates this galaxy's ever seen. There's nothing worse than getting knocked out for 12 hours by the pulse from one of their mines, and then wake up with your ship on its 40-hour cycle of a complete reburn and reboot of its n-drive electronics.

Big deal! At least the first things to start working again were your sensors, so you could see what's happening and send out a distress beacon!

I hope those Krychee wound up frying in the middle of a star.

So the rock jockeys were sitting around. But they weren't doing it calmly and casually. It seems they'd found a nice, rich asteroid they planned to pull someplace where it could be mined. It had to be pulled out because it lay right in the path of another asteroid, a rogue, that was cutting a swath through the belt, traveling about a thousand miles an hour faster than the rest of the rocks. It was about two miles long and cartwheeled its way toward the assayer.

So, just as they were pulling up to the ore-rich rock, they set off a space mine. When they woke up, they were stuck next to the rock with the rogue making its way toward them, and they couldn't do a thing about it. They didn't have enough time to reboot and get themselves out of the path. They sent out an alarm, and, since we were the closest ship to them, the Frontier Guard alerted us to their location. We dropped out of n-space, set our coordinates for a new destination close to the belt, and took off.

We were setting the strategy. "What we'll do," I said, "is leap somewhere close, but safe enough so we won't run into a rock. Next, we'll pick a spot that's inside the belt for a short jump. We'll find someplace clear of any rocks and out of the path of the rogue. When we hop to that point we can continue at sub-light speed to the assayer and tow it out of the path."

"We can pull the miner out, Rosie?" Bobby asked.

"Yeah, Bobby, if need be. It won't take much."

"I'll bet that I could do it, Rosie."

"You probably could, Bobby," I said with a grin. "You're strong enough."

"Yeah, I'm a good boy, aren't I, Mommy?" he said.

I closed my eyes for a moment. "Bobby, remember! I'm not your Mommy."

He cast his eyes down at his slip. "Yeah, you're right, Rosie."

We emerged from the long jump a couple light hours from the belt. We were setting up to do the shorter hop to get within sub-light distance. The amount of debris that was in the neighborhood forced us to pick a spot that was not in line with the direct escape route of the assayer.

We checked our times and did an instrument scan of the

target. "We've got about 14 hours before the rogue will pass through the collision point. Should be more than enough time to get in and tug the miner out."

"Could I pull it out, Rosie?"

"Yeah, Bobby. The assayer and the rock are side by side across the path of the rogue. Push it and it'll move directly out of the path. I think it'd clear in about 15 minutes. You could manage that speed, Bobby. That miner doesn't weigh as much as some of the cargo pods you've pushed around. And the rock masses about the same amount.

"If all else fails, their crew abandons ship. We'll be close enough for their suit thrusters. That way the rock jockeys could reach refuge on the *Moonstreak*. They'd run out of propulsion fuel and have to coast for the last 15 minutes, but they'd make it.

"All right, we all have to keep an eye on the clock. We've got to have them out of there by 2000 hours, ship time. That's when the rogue collides with the rock."

We set ourselves to make the last, short jump to be within hailing distance. Just do a fast jump in, steer ourselves around the junk to hook up with the miner, and pull her out in plenty of time. Those were our plans.

Until we passed out.

I don't think there's ever been a case of finding two Krychee space mines so close together. I don't know why the Krychee had done that. But we hit one, and we were close enough to the miner that the pulse not only knocked out our ship and crew, but zotzed out the assayer again. When we woke up, they were unconscious in their ship.

"*Ship is rebooting, approximate time of full reboot is in 27 hours 48 minutes and 50 seconds...*" The ship's speakers were droning the countdown. All of us tried to stand up as the effects of the knockout pulse slowly drained away. The ship continued to drone on, in addition to...

"Rosie, can you hear me?..."

"Rosie, can you hear me?"...

It was Bobby's voice coming in through the static on the

intercom.

"Rosie, can you hear me?"...

I pulled myself up and tottered over to the intercom. "Bobby, where are you?"

"I'm a good boy, Rosie."

"Yes, you are, Bobby. But where are you?"

"You were all asleep, Rosie. I tried to wake you up." Bobby'd obviously regained consciousness earlier than we had. Apparently, his capacity for liquor paralleled his capacity to withstand a Krychee space mine pulse.

"Bobby, where are you?"

"I remembered what you said, Rosie. You said that it would take fifteen minutes to get the ship out of the way. You said that I could do it. You said it had to be done by 2000 hours. I waited, Rosie, but it was getting close. I had to leave. I had to get into my suit. My thrusters will get me there in ten minutes. That'll be 1940 hours. I can read my clock."

"I know you can, Bobby."

"I'm a good boy, Rosie."

"I know you are."

It was all very simple, in his mind. Everything was as I had said. The only thing I hadn't said was that anybody who pushed the miner one way and the rock the other way would stand still. Simple inertia. Bobby would push the miner out. He would push the rock out. He would leave himself in the path of the rogue.

"My thrusters just stopped, Rosie, but I'm pointed in the right direction. I'm heading right for the miner."

"Just a minute, Bobby!" I switched over channels. I tried to raise somebody onboard the miner, but there was no response. Apparently, being knocked out by a Krychee space mine for a second time put you out for a longer duration.

I switched the sensors over to take a look at what was happening. I could make out the miner and the rock. I could barely make out a little speck that had to be Bobby heading toward them. "Bobby, when you get to the miner, see if you can get inside."

"Okay, Rosie, I'll do that."

I paced up and down in front of the console. I sent some of the guys to other stations. One kept trying to raise the miner. Another was sending out a message to the Frontier Guard letting them know our status and seeing if they had any other way of sending help. We were all frantic to do something for our Bobby.

"I'm there, Rosie. I made it."

"Can you get inside, Bobby?"

"I can't, Rosie. It won't open for me. It's like that other time when there was a code on the lock."

"Bobby, pound on the door. See if anybody hears you."

"I'm trying, Rosie."

"Is there anybody?"

"No, Rosie."

I keyed off and swore.

"Rosie, my clock says it's time. I gotta move them, Rosie."

I tried desperately to think of anything else that I could do. I checked with the other guys, they hadn't been able to accomplish much of anything on the radios.

"Rosie, should I do it?"

What else could I do? I had to do my best to at least help those miners. I didn't permit myself to think about anything else. "Yeah, Bobby, go ahead."

I watched as I heard Bobby grunt his way into position. I upped the magnification to see if it would show me anything else. Bobby gave out a loud groan as he applied all of his strength to push apart the two objects. I watched as they began to separate slowly from each other. Left behind in the middle was a tiny figure.

"I did it, Rosie. I did it."

"Yes, you did, Bobby."

"Are they moving fast enough?"

"Looks that way. What do you think, Bobby? Do you think

you pushed them hard enough?"

"I think so, Rosie. I pushed them as hard as I could."

"Then they must be going fast enough." I decreased the magnification to watch the two objects separate. When I had pulled back about four times in magnification, I noticed something beginning to appear on the left side of the screen. It was the rogue. It was cigar-shaped. It was tumbling through the belt end over end, like a football. It was big.

"I'm a good boy, aren't I, Rosie?"

"Yes, you are, Bobby." I didn't want him thinking about what might happen or consider the consequences of his actions. "Hey, Bobby, can you see our ship? Do you know where it is?" I wanted him to look this way. I didn't want him to turn around and see what was bearing down on him.

"I can see you, Rosie. I always remember to make sure I know where the ship is whenever I go out in my suit."

"That's good, Bobby."

"I'm a good boy, Rosie."

"Yes, you are." I switched off for a second and turned around to see if anybody had come up with anything else. The way that they all averted their eyes gave me my answer.

"Will you come and get me soon, Rosie? I don't have any more fuel for my thrusters."

"Just as soon as the ship reboots we'll be able to come over there." I was equivocating.

"That's good. Will we keep going on to Maverick, then?"

"Yes, we will."

"I like Maverick. They have that nice bar where that guy from the *Yamur* tried to outdrink me. Remember that?"

"Yes, I remember."

"He could drink just about the most of any of those guys. But I drank more. You remember?"

"Yes, Bobby."

"I can outdrink everybody."

"Yes, you can, Bobby."

"I'm a good boy, aren't I, Mommy?"

I let his mistake go by and took a last look at what was happening.

The rogue was swinging end over end, like a celestial hammer. I checked the miner, it had cleared the rogue's path. I looked back, the rogue was bearing down on Bobby.

"Yes, you're a good boy."

I switched off the image.

There was a short pause. The static from the intercom remained on for a few more moments.

Then it went dead.

"... rebooting system, approximate time of full reboot is in 27 hours 29 minutes and 20 seconds..."

I hadn't noticed the droning of the reboot system until now. It had filled a very loud silence that had settled across the control room.

Yes, Bobby was a good boy. Just like that four-year-old in the hospital. He did everything right. He behaved just like a good boy. Nothing bad should have happened to him.

But it did.

END RECORD

#

Rosie took her finger away from the button, looked up from her place at the bar and turned to all of the other patrons who were there. "Ladies, Gentlemen, and Otherwise. I wish to commemorate a fellow spacer who met his untimely death on my last trip. Now, usually someone gives a speech, or says a prayer, but I'm not one for talking or for religion. However, I would like to pay homage to that individual in a way that is proper and fitting of the way that he lived his life, and the things that he was most famous for. Therefore, I would like to remember my friend Bobby by OUTDRINKING EVERY LAST DAMN ONE OF YOU IN THIS BAR!"

Chapter 11

Patron of the Arts

hOrmande de Mieneur dashed into the StarBoard Café like a man pursued. M. de Mieneur was a man of good taste and superb manners. When he wanted to use them. He frequently exercised his good taste. He often kept his superb manners well hidden. For reasons known only to his superiors, he was an excellent diplomat.

"Rowsis, for God's sake, give me a Tirenian Smoothie!" This was far more potent than hOrmande's normal drink. As soon as he was served, he tossed the drink back, despite its near-fatal strength, and signaled for a second one.

He took a deep, steadying breath, reached over and pushed the Record button at the table.

RECORD
#

I've been to some absolutely daunting and frightening places in my time. I've made my way through the intricacies of the Riddlers of Rushpin to gain Amalgam access to their planet. I've braved the King of the Dreaded Drinchers. He's noted for his raging acerbic foul moods as the ruler of an ill-tempered race. (Come to think of it, I do believe the two of us got along rather famously.) I've brazened my way through these and many other harrowing predicaments. However, it was with the greatest of trepidation that I found myself, at a late hour, in the most frightening place I've ever been: the Maternity Ward of a hospital. Rumor has it that there must have been a time when I occupied such a place, having launched my cuddly little self into the worlds. However, I've managed to block that memory from my mind. Since some people claim there could have been an Immaculate Conception, it's my firm belief I was born out of the mind of Hera.

Despite all the objections my instincts raised, I made my way to a room in that ward, responding to the direst of pleas. As I entered the ward, something thrust her way into my path. It looked like a cross between Florence Nightingale and the Frog People of Grib. It appeared to be a nurse.

"What are you doing here?" She smeared officiousness all over her question.

Perhaps I was a little space-lagged and not in the jolliest of moods. I turned to her and gave her my most ingratiating smile. "It was on the itinerary of my tour group, the highlight of my visit to this planet. What do you think I'm doing here?" I might have barked the last question.

"Are you a father? Only fathers are allowed in here at this hour."

"I'm not sure of that. However I'm one of the six finalists. We're breathlessly awaiting the conclusive determination."

"Who is he?" she asked, pointing at the person with me.

"He's practically a godfather to the child. He held my pants while I was participating in the qualifying round."

"He" was actually Sol Solar, a theatrical agent. He had brought me here.

Suddenly a lovely voice enquired out of the room that was my destination. "Who's here?"

"I'm sorry, my dear, but paternity calls," I said to Florence Frog.

"hOrmande, oh my God, is that you, hOrmande?" Again from the room.

"Miss Krisma, he's not allowed in here unless he's the father." Nursie croaked.

I turned to Our Lady of the Healing Arts. "It seems to me, my dear, that you are a little overwrought." Translate that to mean despotic. "Why don't you go off and have a nice cup of tea and a slice of shoo-fly pie."

"Miss Foster, why don't you let him come in? He's already

disrupted half the world as it is." Came the same voice from the same room.

"Are you sure, Miss Krisma?" Nursie asked.

"Yes. I just went through the pain and suffering of childbirth. I'm quite certain I can withstand an assault from M. de Mieneur. After all, I asked for him to be here."

"All right, Miss Krisma, but this is most irregular."

I tried to assuage her Nurseness. "Yes, my dear, why don't you take a nice tonic for your irregularity and then go settle down someplace comfortable."

"hOrmande, stop annoying the staff, and come in this room and annoy me. After all, what are friends for?"

"Your wish is my command, my dear." I entered the room. There, managing to look resplendent, even though she was on one of those hideous robotic beds, lay Tourmaline Krisma, the finest actress in the Galaxy. "Darling, what is an amazing talent like yours doing in this breeding parlor? Studying up for some part you're going to play? It speaks of your devotion to your art, my dear, but I think you should get yourself out of here before you catch whatever it is they're curing in this place."

"I'm not studying up for anything, hOrmande. I came here to give birth to my child."

"My God! That line was delivered with all the reality only a great actress could command. I really must applaud you. Now, let me get you away from Nurse Toad, and we can go settle down someplace cozy. I know an absolutely splendid little Nouveau Martian restaurant that's just around the corner."

Tourmaline continued trolling for sympathy. "hOrmande, darling, at last I am a mother."

"You are forgetting, darling," I said, "Uncle hOrmonde is usually the one who's called a mother."

"I'm quite serious."

Could she be? "Oh my God, you aren't, are you?"

"As serious as I've ever been."

"Well, my sweet, the provenance on that statement is a little contradictory."

"You must understand, hOrmande. I'm a bereft mother of my new infant." She said as she swept her hand up to her brow.

"My darling, you're the only person I know who can be utterly truthful on the stage, but totally artificial in person. What are you getting at?"

"hOrmande, you're the only one who can help me in my hour of need."

"I must admit, in all modesty, that there are many wonderful things that I've managed to do in my time, but I'm afraid that biting off an umbilical cord is not one of them."

"Sol, explain it to him."

Sol turned to me. "It's just as she says, sweetheart. Would I lie to you?"

"Habitually, Sol. I'm sure the test to qualify for entry into your union has all true/false questions with *false* always being the right answer."

Sol would not be distracted by such a triviality as listening to something anyone said. "Trust me, Baby."

"Sol, I wouldn't trust you with your own elderly grandmother." I turned to Tourmaline. "Now, darling, why don't you tell me what's happened?"

"hOrmande, I've brought a child into the world, and I cannot show her her father."

I smiled sweetly at her and patted her hand. "That's because it would require quite a large group picture, my dear."

"Darling, I'm truly in love for the very first time in my life."

"All right, darling, tell Uncle hOrmonde what is bothering you this time?"

A tear glistened in the corner of her eye. "hOrmande, it was just so wonderful. I knew we were made for each other, so I decided to have his child. But now he's gone." Once more she swept her hand up to her forehead in the worst Acting 101 gesture I've ever seen.

"Who is gone?"

"Thorman."

"Thorman?"

"Yes."

"That vapid idiot who was in your last play?"

"Yes, darling. Oh, you just don't know how deep he is."

"Nor how long, I daresay. Well, where has he gotten himself off to?"

"That's where I come in, Babe." Sol said. "I got him this great film gig. Everything he could ever want. Star billing, the whole thing."

"Yes?"

"Then they went off on a location shoot on Spirilla, and that's the last I heard of him."

"Spirilla?" This was not good news. I hoped I'd never hear of that planet again.

"Yeah, Spirilla."

"That's interesting. Did you call the producers, Sol?"

"Yeah, but something funny happened to their number."

"How funny, Sol?"

"It's not there anymore."

"Not there?"

"No. Makes me worry about the crew." Sol was very concerned. About ten per cent concerned.

"When was the last you heard from them?"

"They were going off into the jungle for a shoot at some lady's mansion. They haven't been heard from since, and the house can't be found."

"hOrmande, darling, you've got to help me," Tourmaline implored.

"Well, thank Galaxy, I do know a little something about Spirilla. I was there for a time in my tender youth."

"hOrmande, don't tell me that you've ever been tender or youthful. I don't believe it." Tourmaline had somehow managed to snap out of her overflowing grief.

"I was both, but fortunately my experiences on that planet

helped change me into the darling old sod that I've become." I swung my gaze around. "Sol, can you get us a booking to that planet?"

"You bet, sweetheart." Sol was back in his element, wheeling and dealing.

"Good." I turned to Tourmaline. "For reasons that I do not wish to divulge at this time, I'd hoped never to return to that planet. However, for you, I'll go." I pointed a finger at her. "This favor's going to cost you. You've got to make me a promise. In return for this favor, I want you to undertake the role of Nereena, a part that is just perfect for you. You've avoided doing that character just to spite me. You must promise that as soon as you leave this calving castle you will start studying up for the part."

"If you can help me, hOrmande, I'll do anything."

"Good. Sol, while we're on our way to Spirilla, you can draw up a contract to formalize this agreement, or incant it within a pentagram, or whatever it is that you do that codifies such thing."

"You bet, Babe."

As we started to leave, Tourmaline said, "hOrmande, don't you want to see my little baby?"

"No, dear, I would hate to see the poor little thing try to suckle on implants."

Sol and I headed for the spaceport, he was on his communicator setting the itinerary, I was on mine getting the proper crew together for this little adventure. I had a quick conversation with K'Ching, my primary briber and electronics technician. She was meeting us at the port. The next person I had to reach was Phssh. Phssh is the best spy one can have.

Coming from a gas planet, being made of gas himself, he can disappear into thin air. Gas is also how he communicates: in an olfactory manner. Odor in, odor out. There is just one problem with the nature of his communications. It has rather an unpleasant aroma to it. His native language is Methane, with a heavy Animal Byproduct accent. I had once tried to improve things by asking him to speak in a flowery manner. If anything, that had worse results. I turned to my communicator. "Put out an all-farts bulletin to Phssh and have him meet me at the ship. We are going on an assignment."

I knew that going to Spirilla was a dangerous mission. Or rather returning to Spirilla. I didn't have a particularly good experience the first time I was there. But "that which does not kill me makes me stronger."

I worked out a strategy with Sol. "You are going there to see your client. All of the rest of us are part of your staff. I want to maintain a low profile on this one."

"What's the matter, babe, you owe some money back there?" Sol did something quite unusual for him: he got serious. "Worse yet, you don't owe the union any money for a crew, do you? That'd be bad, really bad. You never want to owe the union money."

"No, Sol, I don't. However I did barely escape from that place."

Spirilla is a strange planet. It goes back many millennia as a center for interstellar travel. Many empires have set their ships down on its surface, and left their traces in its civilization. It's a planet that's deeply shrouded in fog and mist, both in the jungles of its tropics and the fjords of its temperate regions. There are many little-known enclaves of alien races that settled in on Spirilla and have vanished from the rest of the galaxy.

We landed at LakLuna, the main starport. Sol immediately got on his communicator and tried to raise any of the members of the production company. I briefed my crew.

"This will be the usual modus operandi. K'Ching, I want you to start looking for all of the usual channels to buy ourselves information."

"Do I get my usual percentage?" she asked.

"As always, my dear. Phssh, I want you to do what you always do." I received no reply. "Do you have that?" Again silence. "Phssh, are you there?" Then I remembered. "Oh, damn, translator to olfactory."

"...wanted me to do?"

"Phssh, you're there?"

"Of course I'm here. Can't you smell me floating right in front of you?"

"I'm sorry, Phssh, but I don't always leave this damned translator turned on. Having it convert everything I say into your language is distracting. It's like having a fartmaker at my belt. Anyway, I want you to vanish into thin air, as you usually do, and find out whatever you can about the film crew that was here."

"I get your drift."

"Sol, what've you found out?"

"The last that anybody seen of the unit it was headed into the Misteria region. You know where that is?"

"Unfortunately, I do. I was hoping that the group wouldn't have gone there, but I had a foreboding that it had."

"What do we do next?"

"We head into that region and look for the perfect house."

Misteria is a region that's both strange and enchanting. Wisps of fog continually play around its jungles. You'd expect the trees to talk to you. That's a distinct possibility. At one time there'd been a botanic race that'd visited the world and settled down in the jungle.

There were no real roads heading into Misteria, so we provisioned ourselves for a day's outing and headed off into the bush. I didn't think we had all that far to go. The question was: would we be able to make our way back?

We ventured our way through the jungle. I tried to find something that was familiar, something that would put me on a path, one I didn't really want to travel.

"You seem to know an awful lot about this place, Babe. You been here before?" Sol asked.

"H-E-L-L-O,---"

"Yes, I guess the truth is coming out."

"—H-O-R-M-A-N-D-E-."

"What truth?" Sol couldn't help but notice the voice that

boomed out of nowhere. But like a true agent, he could continue talking no matter what the circumstances.

"I-T-'-S B-E-E-N---"

"I was in this region when I was a young man," I said.

"— A W-H-I-L-E."

"What is that?" Sol finally had to ask.

"Hello, Freebush," I addressed the general area. "Is she still here?"

"Who is that?" Sol asked.

"Someone I know."

"Y-E-S," Freebush finally got around to answering my last question.

"He's a botanic friend I met on my last visit here. He has slower metabolism and therefore a slower conversation rate."

Sol looked around our surroundings, appraisingly. "Does he have an agent?"

"No, Sol. I'm afraid he wouldn't make a good client. His dialogue wouldn't be rapid-paced." I raised my voice. "Can you point out the way, Freebush?"

"We could always overdub a voice," Sol said.

"Besides, you'd need a very wide-angle lens to pick him up."

"Y-E-S-S," Freebush finally answered my last question.

At that moment, slowly, almost too slowly to be perceptible, the foliage began to pull back and reveal a path. The motion resembled time-lapse photography. I'd experienced this phantasm once before. Only that time, I'd been leaving rather than entering. I hoped I could leave again.

"Okay, Babe, tell me what's up," Sol said.

"Someone lives here. Someone called Callista. She's one of those beings whose genesis goes back a long time--a *very* long time. She had me in her grips once. I barely managed to escape. I think there've been others she's snared. I don't know if they were able to leave."

"You think she captured the film crew?" Sol asked.

"I'm not sure, Sol. There's a good chance. She's an

enchantress. You can't resist coming into her clutches, and it's very hard to escape her."

"She's like that creature who attracted sailors to her island, then turned them into pigs?"

"Yes, Sol. However, you have to remember that the larger part of a location crew is Roadies. Turning a Roadie into a pig is a redundancy."

"You got a point there."

The path we walked was not direct. It curved and cut, it turned, it switched back. It meandered its way to our destination over a route that was meant to confuse and keep anyone from unwittingly finding the place.

However, when we did get there, there was no mistaking it. Suddenly, appearing out of the jumble of the jungle, was the most perfect building you've ever seen, located on the most perfect grounds.

Owned by the most perfect of people.

"hOrmande, stop trying to hide in the background of your group." It was Callista. She had suddenly appeared almost as magically as her building.

Of course, she looked perfect. Not a hair was out of place. Not a single wrinkle showed in her clothes. And, of course, none on her skin. It'd been quite a few years since I last saw her. I'd developed wrinkles (lines of distinction), but she hadn't.

"You all look so terribly hot and sweaty from your trip. You will, of course, stay here. Let my servants show you to some rooms. You'll be able to freshen up there." She already assumed we were staying. I wondered if she also assumed we would never leave.

"Madam..." Sol launched into conversation.

"Miss!" she interposed.

"...Miss, my name is Sol Solar, and I represent Mr. Thorman Studd, the noted actor. I believe he's here somewhere on a location shoot. Would you know anything about him?"

"Yes, Mr. Solar, he's here. Why don't we get together after

you've had a chance to freshen yourselves up? hOrmande, you look a sight, I'm afraid you're just not in proper physical shape to go tramping through this jungle. Why don't we meet for a cool refreshment? Mr. Studd will be there. My servants will come by and let you know when it's time."

The servants who accompanied us to our rooms had no distinguishing characteristics about them. They were silent and distant. I managed to persuade them that K'Ching and I were an item (what a thought!) and that we should share a room. She took the opportunity to look at me suspiciously as though I had some devious sexual designs on her. What I really needed to do was set strategy with her.

"All right, K'Ching, I don't know if you can find anyone who is in enough control of their own minds to accept a bribe, but you've always managed before. See what you can do, and be ready to move when I have a project for you."

"I'll need front money," she replied. Money was never far from her mind.

I continued. "Phssh, I don't think that even Callista could see you, so do what you do best. Make your way around the building. See if you can find any members of the location crew. Report back to me as soon as you know something."

"I'll drift along."

"Now, roomie, let's decide who gets the bathroom first," I said to K'Ching. "I promise I'll be on my best behavior. I'll even handcuff myself to the bed while you're in the shower if you promise not to take advantage of me in that position."

She went stomping off to the loo. Best that she get started first, she had her job to do, cruising the place to look for "clients."

I'd barely finished cleaning myself up when the Stepford Servant arrived at the door to take me to what I gathered would be an official audience.

I brought K'Ching along, treating her to a falsely devoted look just as we entered the room. She didn't have time enough to deliver a proper punch. Sol was also there.

Callista was seated with Thorman at her side. He looked just about perfect. And Callista insisted on perfection. I know. I remembered being in the seat that Thorman held. But even then I'd had a tendency toward the enjoyment of good food and drink. Therefore, my measurements had expanded a bit beyond perfection. That's when I'd fallen out of favor. When her attention had wandered from me for a few moments, I made a mad dash through the jungle to escape with my freedom.

"hOrmande, my dearest, it's been such a long time," Callista said.

"My goodness, doesn't time fly when you're having fun, sweetest," I said.

"You seem to have taken on a few more pounds since I last saw you."

"The souvenirs from eating absolutely spectacular food and drinking absolutely spectacular beverages."

"Yes, hOrmande, you couldn't seem to keep yourself away from the goodies. It was such a waste. You really were quite the dashing young thing."

"I certainly was dashing the night I left here," I punned.

"Yes, darling, you were so abrupt. You never gave me a chance to bid you a proper farewell."

"Sweetest, you know I wasn't sure if I could bring myself to leave you. Especially with your full attention devoted on making me stay."

"But now I have Thorman to light up my days. Isn't he just perfect?" she asked as she turned to the dolt sitting next to her.

True. What he hadn't been born with in terms of size and musculature had been enhanced by the best cosmetic surgeons that Sol could find. He may have been physical perfection, but he didn't send you reeling from his intellectual prowess. Apparently that wasn't part of Callista's criteria. Actually, it appeared that she'd further dulled his mental capability. A daunting task in that lad's case, rather like splitting an atom. "Thorman most certainly is an imposing figure, sweetest. I wonder why I'm not raving with jealousy."

"Well, perhaps it's because you have Ms. K'Ching to console you." Callista looked at K'Ching as if she was a laboratory specimen, which wasn't far from the mark.

"Excuse me, pardon me, folks," Sol interjected. "I hate to interrupt you in your conversation, but I think we have some business to discuss, and that is the fact that Mr. Studd has been kept on location considerably longer than what was defined in his contract."

"Don't worry, Mr. Solar, I'm sure that we can reach terms that you'll be happy to agree to," Callista said. Her voice only hinted at the threat those words held. "But this is all getting rather tiring for me." She stood up from her place. All the Stepford Servants immediately popped into full alert status. "Why don't we convene for supper, and I'm sure we can all come to an equitable agreement on all sorts of things." Equitable for whom? However, I was most eager to get away and check on what my crew had discovered.

"Certainly, certainly," I said before Sol could respond. "We're all rather tired out from our trek earlier today. I'm sure your lively little servants will tell us when it's time for the meal." I hustled everyone out.

Phssh was in our room. He told me he'd found the location crew. He led me to a door at the far end of the building. The door was obviously soundproofed because the moment I opened it, the noise was deafening. The crew was there, being wined and dined and "entertained" by the local staff. It was sheer Roadie Heaven. I don't know where Callista had found the "hostesses" who were there, but I don't think they'd come willingly. After all, who would want to hostess a Roadie? The comforting news was that the crew was still well and sound. Or as sound as a Roadie can be.

I knew I had to make a move at supper. I was quite aware that Callista was just playing with us. She'd tire of her little game and would strike very shortly, adding us to the group of mindless husks that wandered around this place. I mulled over my chances. They weren't good.

I hoped I could come up with a plot that would get us out of there.

"K'Ching, have you found anyone who could be bribed?"

"Everyone on staff seems to be in a trance," she said. "The only signs of life that I've seen are the outside delivery people. They've been here a lot, quite busy stocking this place. It seems that whatever food or drink comes in here gets consumed right away."

"It takes a lot to feed a bunch of Roadies. Well, if that's all we have to work with, I'll see if I can come up with some sort of scheme to get us safely out of here. Let me see..." I pondered.

"K'Ching, I want you to get down to the kitchen. Find the delivery people, and get them to say that the only thing they can deliver for this evening's meal is Jupiter storm beans."

"They're my favorite," said Phssh.

"I'm sure they are. Phssh, I want you to do the following: position yourself underneath Thorman's chair at dinner. Stay invisible and put your translator on private. Don't say anything to me. I just want you to wait until I say your name. After that I want you to repeat, very loudly, the words I say immediately after your name. But only say that one thing."

"I've got it."

"Okay, Lady and Gentlebreeze, we're going into action!"

I rushed to get ready for dinner. I was primed for action. I even went so far as to stroll on the balcony as K'Ching was maintaining her virginal pose while changing clothes.

I will never understand these artifices of women. I've seen K'Ching party with some of the roughest spacers in the most degenerate of bars, the StarBoard Café, as a matter of fact, but she still wishes to maintain the image of being a "good girl."

When we got to dinner, Callista was perfect, of course. "Darling, you look absolutely lovely," I said. "I don't know how you maintain it." I smiled at her. "However, I could hazard a few guesses."

"hOrmande, my darling, how could I have let anyone as charming as you escape from me? I must have lost my concentration." I shuddered at what she was implying. I knew she would do her best not to let me leave again.

I let the conversation continue in this chummy vein until such time as the main course had been served and we'd all had a chance to devour some of it. I must say that Callista's kitchen could produce some rather tasty cuisine. I wonder where she'd dug up her chef. Quite literally dug up her chef.

Finally, when I felt the time was right, I pointed the conversation to my targeted topic. "Yes, my dear, living without you has been so boring I discovered I needed a hobby to keep me stimulated. So I've turned to gardening. Nothing is more delightful than smelling the wonderful flowers in my little plot. Ahhh," and then I made a motion to make the next word seem like an exclamation, "Phssh," I signaled my Spy by saying his name, "lilacs." I paused, smiling, and looked around the table, I'd noticed with relief that the ventilation in the room put Callista's seat downwind of Thorman's. I smiled at K'Ching. I smiled at Sol. I smiled at Thorman. I smiled at Callista.

It hit.

There's a facial expression that's never been properly defined in any dictionary. It's that look one gets when something absolutely disgusting has happened right next to them and they continue to manage something like a polite smile. A polite smile with a slight downturn of the corners of the mouth that telegraphs high disapproval. I call the expression "smelling farts."

As I'd related earlier, the more flowery the speech for Phssh, the worse it smelled. As I recall, the word *lilac* smelled something like gastric distress tightly commingled with methane mutilation.

Phssh's shout of "lilac" had landed home on Callista.

"Yes," I continued, "and there is also the smell of" once more the hand gesture "Phssh, roses."

Count one, two, three, four, five, bingo! Smelling farts with high distress.

Callista needed to live with absolute perfection. That was what she craved. She could barely contain herself now as she began to realize that Thorman (she thought) could suffer from flatulence.

I decided to put in the *coup de grace*. "Phssh, gardenia."

-- four, five-- Callista stood up abruptly, letting her chair fall over behind her. Her face was flushed, her features were contorted. I hoped I hadn't pushed her too far.

Thorman seemed to have come out of his trance and peered around the room with a slightly more alert look on his face. Well, as alert as that lad ever got.

I braced myself. I'd taken a chance upsetting Callista like this. She could either get distracted or she could get focused. I dreaded the latter.

Unfortunately, it looked like it was going to be the latter. Callista's eyes narrowed to snake-like slits. She bared her teeth and began to chant in some ancient language. I could see the world begin to swirl at the periphery of my eyes, and that swirling began to creep around to engulf my whole vision. My knees became at once both rigid and fluid. I could feel my consciousness begin to slip away. I was falling into a mindless trance induced by Callista.

It was at that point the cavalry rode in to save us.

Actually, the cavalry didn't ride in. It slimed in. Two characters appeared at the entrance to the room. One of them appeared to be evolved from a snail. He left a slimy trail behind him. The second one looked to have an inside-out mucous membrane that manufactured a large amount of gunk that he reabsorbed through a number of rather gross orifices located on his face.

"Miss Callista?" one of them asked.

"What?" Callista's head snapped around and she almost shouted.

"We are from the IGOR," said the other.

"You're from what?" Callista hadn't turned toward them. She still looked at me and Thorman.

"The IGOR."

"What is that?" Now, she began to give them some attention.

"The Intergalactic Guild Of Roadies."

"My God," Sol whispered, "the only people who could've found their way to this place."

"What do you want?" Callista asked them.

"We have a location crew working here, and we were a little concerned that we haven't gotten any dailies for a while." The dailies are the daily report of hours worked by members of the union. "However, we figured things could've been a little bit hectic. So we let that go. However, when we didn't get any weeklies, we began to be quite concerned. So we figured that it might have been hard to communicate from this remote location. But, what set off an alarm in our accounting system was when your estimated bill went far over the deposit you left with us. Therefore, we decided to come and check things out."

"What do you mean dailies, weeklies?" she asked, still distracted.

"The Brothers have been working for quite a while, now. By our estimates their overtime rate has gone past golden time, past platinum time, and they are somewhere up there around zirthromium time."

"They haven't been working. They've been doing nothing but eating, drinking and carousing for weeks, now."

"Yes, but that don't mean that they haven't been on the clock."

"They haven't!" she roared.

"But our records indicate that they *are* still working."

"Nonsense! I've been doing nothing but entertaining them."

"Maybe so. However, there are certain union protocols that have to be observed." He raised a rather slimy eyebrow at her. "Did you ever, at any time, tell them, 'Take five'?"

"No." Callista was indignant.

"Oh, that's bad," said one of them, shaking his head. This produced a shower of semi-liquid substance that rained down from his head and made a worse mess of Callista's formerly perfect rug.

"What's bad?"

"That means they've been on the clock the whole time."

"On the clock?"

"That's right."

Callista regained her composure. She began to rely on her old skills. "Listen, gentlemen, perhaps we can talk this over."

"I'm sure thirsty," said one of them.

They were, after all, Roadies.

"Why certainly," Callista said, "I'm sure we can get you something to drink." She was becoming most persuasive.

"Let's get out of here, now." Sol whispered to me, as Callista's attention was taken with the union officials.

"Why?"

"Because we've got some time, now."

"What do you mean?"

"Callista's an enchantress, Babe. Well, believe me, if there's one creature you cannot enchant, it's a union rep. Their minds are closed to everything but business. It'll take her a while to figure that out. Let's leave now."

"Okay." I said. I gathered up Thorman and began to head out the door.

"Wait," Sol said, "we can't just run out."

"Why not?"

"The Roadies, the crew, they're still here."

"Can't their union guys take care of them?"

"I don't know if they can get all of them out of Callista's clutches."

"Okay, we'll get them." I turned around. "K'Ching, go to the end of the grounds and ask Freebush to open up the path for us. Say it slowly, one word at a time."

K'Ching headed toward the outside, and I went to the soundproofed door. When I opened it, the sounds of singing, drinking and debauching were still at full volume. I shouted out, "Okay, guys, let's go."

The din continued unabated.

"Guys, we've only got this one chance to get out before the enchantress turns you into soulless zombies." The moment I said that, I realized that that was the very state Roadies were always trying to achieve.

The drinking and the shouting and the singing continued.

"Here, Babe, let me see if I can't handle it." Sol said.

"Be my guest."

Sol squared himself up to make an announcement. "THE BUS IS LEAVING!!!"

In the space of about four seconds, the room emptied. And when I say emptied, I mean emptied. There'd been a full buffet on a long table.

That was completely stripped.

There'd been an overstocked bar at the other end of the room.

Even the ice cubes were gone.

There'd also been an area for "pharmaceuticals."

Not only was it gone, but there was a crater in its place.

As for the young ladies who'd been hostesses, they were gone, too. For a moment I pondered whether they'd have been better off enslaved by an enchantress. However, I figured it was marginally better for them to wake up in the clutches of a Roadie than to wake up in the clutches of Callista. They would always come to their senses in the case of the Roadie.

We all dashed through the jungle. Once we were clear of Callista's perimeter, we could slow down and make our way back to civilization. We booked our passage out of LakLuna and made our way back to our home worlds. During the trip back the formerly virgin-esque K'Ching made quite a spectacle of herself partying with the Roadies.

Yes, the Roadies.

I delivered Thorman to Tourmaline. As soon as he saw his infant daughter he burst into loud quacking tears and proclaimed his undying love to both the tot and the mother.

A few months later, Sol told me the grapevine had informed him that Callista and the union were still in heavy negotiations. Every one of the union officials found occasion to leave headquarters and drop in to Callista's mansion to help with the negotiations, and, by the way, avail themselves of the hospitality of the hostess. On top of that, they were working on organizing the house staff. It seems strange that anyone would try to organize zombies, but must I once more mention Roadies? Callista had finally found the guests whom she couldn't compel to stay and also couldn't compel to leave.

That should be the end of the tale, but it isn't.

I'd told Tourmaline that I would get her man back on the promise she'd undertake the roll of Nereena. It takes some time to mount a production, so it was about a year and half later that I visited the Grande Dame as she was preparing for the role.

I walked in on a scene of domestic bliss. Tourmaline was there. Thorman was there. Esmerelda (the child) was there wandering around depositing her body fluids on every available surface. The only thing lacking for the scene was a white picket fence, a wisecracking domestic aide, and a sitcom theme song.

Tourmaline was preparing for the role, memorizing lines, getting down business. She was working on the scene where Nereena stood before the High Court and made her plea to the judges.

"I can't get the gesture right, hOrmande," she said. "It's a very subtle piece of business. She raises her hand to them, and the gesture is meant to be a fine balance between beseeching them for their help, but also demanding they admit that she's the true leader. I thought of doing it this way," and she raised her hand up over her head, "or this way," and she brought her hand up from her side. "What do you think?"

"Well, my darling, I think the first shows a little too much audacity for the situation. However, the second is a little too weak for someone who is demanding her rightful place in the country. Also I think that..." I stopped and froze. Something had caught my attention and distracted me.

"You think what, hOrmande?"

"Uh," I dithered, "I think--I think..."

"Yes?"

"I think you might consider bringing both hands up, like-- like this." I imitated the gesture.

"My God, hOrmande, that's perfect! I knew you'd be able to help me with this. I just knew you'd see right into the very heart of the character."

"Uh, yes, dear, anything I can do to help." I still wasn't focused on the conversation.

"Oh, darling, you absolutely must stay for dinner! I'm sure you'll be able to help me with all the rest of the play."

"I–I really wish that I could, darling, but I'm afraid that duty calls. The Department wants me to rush off on another assignment." I lied.

"Well, darling, hurry back. You've got to become my personal coach in preparing for this role."

"I will, I will, Lovey. Why I daresay that I'll become an absolute fixture around this house."

"Oh, that would be so wonderful!"

I rushed out of the place, a man possessed.

I'd seen it! I'd seen it! Tourmaline was looking for a gesture for that moment in the play, and what she'd shown me was good.

But then I saw the quintessential move, one made by a divine actress. And I showed it to Tourmaline. I saw it from the little munchkin who was toddling around. It was Esmerelda who'd shown me the gesture. She'd displayed it and then looked over at me in a saucy little manner as if to say, "So there!"

What grace! What emotion! What beauty was in that gesture! And this from a mere child of less than two years. Her mother may be a great actress; her father may know how to walk across stage without being attacked by the furniture; but this little elf can transcend the whole of existence with her talent. And this at an age barely out of infancy. I had to make a fast exit because I was just too overwhelmed.

I also had plans to make. I had to start mapping out her education. Her mother may have some theatrical training, but it's obvious the child needs someone with knowledge and taste to look after her. She needs acting lessons, and dancing, and singing, and diction, and fencing. Probably some martial arts will help give her body control.

And *I've* got to do it. I'm the only one capable of nurturing such an immense talent. I've got to tag along caring for the child like some obscene Mary Poppins. Getting her to classes. Making sure she doesn't pick up any bad habits from her father. Seeing that her talent develops.

I've got to do it. Me, the quintessential bachelor.

My God!

#

hOrmande reached forward to the button.

END RECORD

hOrmande looked around the Café. He felt himself a pawn. He'd been grabbed by one of Life's forces and thrust down a trail he'd never thought to travel. He looked about desperately, hoping to find some help from somewhere.

He ordered another Smoothie.

Chapter 12

Pick Your Poison

The guards at the entrance to The StarBoard Café were well trained at disarming the spacers when they entered the establishment. They also had other duties. Since the spacer lifestyle could modestly be described as "boisterous," they would frequently appear at the lock to the Café in great physical distress due to what they would describe as their most recent business negotiations, or their latest legal discussion with local law enforcement officials.

The guards had their work cut out for them when the freighter *The Long Scent* showed up. All of its crewmembers bore evidence to having been in a fiery environment: missing eyebrows, singed eartips, ravaged pelts, and clothing still smoking from embedded embers. They must have done their best to suppress the flames on the flight to the Café, but they were still suffering from a severe case of combustion when they arrived. Fire extinguishers jetted out flame retardants to reduce the havoc. Fireproof wraps were applied to smother smoldering body parts. When security managed to gain control of the problem, some of the dyed-in-the-wool spacers on the crew immediately switched over priorities. Many of them became restive and started insisting the best way to remedy their problems was to imbibe certain *flammable* liquids. When Security finally declared the situation under control, the crew was allowed to enter the Café proper, though there were still a few wisps of smoke trailing after them.

Poison, Kowana, and Fido hurried in, shaking themselves free of any remaining ash. They appeared to have been very close to ground zero of whatever conflagration the crew had experienced. Poison purposefully headed for the bar and one of the Record buttons to enter into the storytelling contest.

#

RECORD

I've got to find the Wistrani. Everybody tells me they're extinct. But those Florians who sent me to this galaxy knew the Wistrani still existed. They'd even used the Wistrani computer to give me my special touch. I've got to get back to my home world. This galaxy is beginning to wear on me.

And here's the thing: I might have found them, but they got away from me. Maybe this story will act as a message to them, because I need to get to them.

Back to the start. I thought things would be easy booking out as spacers with Captain Kordlux. Kowana knew him from when he'd managed the StarBoard Cafe. He's a straight shooter. We figured he'd take us on some legit runs as opposed to the usual ventures most spacers went on. It was a thrill for Kowana to finally ship out on a crew now that she'd shrunk in size. Fido was happy to sniff some new sniffs.

So we set out on this last trip taking some cargo to the Kaldulu sector of the galaxy, and that was fine by me. It was someplace I hadn't been, someplace new to search through. There was a problem with the spacers who comprised the rest of the crew: they were getting edgy. They didn't feel comfortable doing all this perfectly legal stuff for Captain Kordlux. It was like wearing the wrong skin on their bodies.

We'd attained n-space and were on our way to our destination. Everything was going smoothly, which meant that most of the crew was restless and looking for a fight. Suddenly a shudder went through the cruiser. The spacers around me looked up in surprise, not recognizing what was happening to the ship while it was in n-space.

I was the only who'd felt this before. It was the same feeling I felt when my pod was locked in on a tractor beam by the Florians. I went dashing to the bridge to see what was happening.

"Good great grousing grimgraws!" Flug the navigator was cursing out. He waddled around in front of the controls trying to figure out what was going on. He stopped in front of the navigation screen that was flashing total incoherence at him and tried cuffing it on the side to see if it would stabilize.

"Would you leave me alone, you great clumsy brute!" the computer barked at him. *"Stop bashing me around like that. I happen to be a delicate electronic instrument!"*

Flug had obviously programmed the computer to have a personality that matched his own. "Why are you flailing around like a drowning whipplewong? Give me a reading on where we are."

"Well, I would if you'd stop interrupting me with your clumsy koshing of my precision-built innards."

Captain Kordlux dashed onto the bridge. "What's happening?" he demanded.

"Who did this?" I asked Flug.

"*Who* did this? You mean *what is* this?" he bellowed out, pausing momentarily in delivering strings of curses at the guidance system.

The Captain shifted his attention to me. "What do you mean, 'who,' Poison? Do you know what's happening?"

"No, Captain, but I've had the same damn thing happen to me before."

"When was that?" he asked me.

"I can't say, Captain."

"What do you mean, you can't say?" he roared at me.

"I mean I literally can't say, Captain. You'd only hear hash." He was aware that I was blocked from saying anything specific about my former life. "But I've run into races that have technology far beyond the Amalgam's. This looks like an example of one of them."

A sudden shiver went up my spine. I recognized that feeling. We'd been released into real space. Flug gave a grunt of approval as the navigation display settled into a specific location. He switched his grunt to one of disapproval. "What are you up to this time, you overblown oxcart?"

"I know what my readings are. Take my word for it," the computer responded.

"How can you be telling me we're *here*?" Flug jabbed a digit at the display. "Explain that one to me."

"*I can't.*"

A look of utter amazement crossed Flug's features. The computer usually argued with him. The direct response it gave meant it was confused.

"What is it?" the Captain asked Flug.

"We're off in an entirely different quadrant, half a galaxy away from where we were," Flug said as he scratched his backside and leaned in toward the console. "How the hell could that be? We're in orbit around some planet called Fleeble."

"*You think it was easy to take us that distance with you bashing me on my console?*" the computer had recovered enough to remember to take credit for the mistake. "*However I have it on the best of authority that this is a very prankish planet.*"

We furrowed our brows when the computer came up with that word, *prankish*. We'd never heard it before. The Captain flung his paws up in frustration. "Well, Flug, I appreciate that the computer may have developed talents as a tour guide, but how about getting us out of here and heading back toward Kaldulu?"

"You heard the Captain. Drop us back into n-space," Flug told the computer.

"*Should I go ahead and do that, or should I pay attention to those fighter ships that have surrounded us?*" the computer asked.

"Fighter ships? What're they doing there?" Captain Kordlux asked.

"*Saying this...*"

"...Invading ship, *The Long Scent*, we have you targeted on our weapons. Give us access to your computer to guide you down to the planet, or we will destroy you in 50 seconds...Invading ship, *The Long Scent*, we..." it repeated the message counting down on the time.

"Can we do anything, computer?" the Captain asked.

"*My sensors tell me they've got a lot of weaponry.*"

The Captain grumbled and looked down at his feet. "Let them in past your Spacewall, then," he ordered.

"If I admit them, they'll just make a mess of the place. They'll leave their trash all over my memory stacks."

"You have an order," the Captain stated.

The message promptly cut off on the speakers, and the ship shuddered with the resetting of its servos in preparation for a landing.

The Captain addressed the pre-empted guidance system. "If I may have the com, I'd like to address the crew about the situation."

"You may, provided that you do not incite violence." A new, androgynous voice spoke out of the computer.

The Captain clasped his paws behind his back. "This is the Captain speaking." His voice could be heard echoing throughout the corridors of the ship. "We have been taken over by an unknown species, and are being guided down onto the planet of Fleeble. Our hosts are very well armed, so I recommend that you cooperate. Any aggressive act against them would be doomed to failure. Therefore I order you to adhere to their wishes."

"A wise move, Captain," the voice said.

"I meant what I said," the Captain informed us, glancing around the bridge. "Prepare yourselves for landing, and don't attempt anything foolish."

We dispersed from the cabin. Of all the crew on the ship, I might have been the most eager to find out what was happening. The last time I'd experienced having a craft snatched off and dragged long distances was when my life had changed so radically back in my home galaxy. The evidence of such a high technology offered me a possibility of finding the Wistrani.

#

When we landed, the crew was instructed to assemble by the loading dock entrance and prepare to be taken into custody. The spacers all grumbled, itching for a fight. I waited in anticipation. My instinct, that intuitive thing I possess that got me into all of this trouble in the first place, told me that this was something important.

When the loading dock doors opened we found a number of weapons trained on us by a bunch of evil-looking creatures. They all wore uniforms that were a solid dark brown, the color of dirt. They were Vorkuls, tight-featured little nasties, rodents that sported sharp little teeth. "Raise all of your appendages as high as you can reach. Show us you are unarmed," commanded one of the creatures. His uniform had a few more sparkles to it; he must have been some sort of officer.

We then filed out of the ship. I kept close to Kowana and Fido, hoping to provide some protection.

"I am the commander of this ship. I would like to speak to the being in charge to negotiate for the lives of my crew," the Captain announced.

"There is nothing you can negotiate," said another of these creatures. His uniform was bedecked with emblems and spangles. Had to be their leader. "You will be disposed of in whatever manner I deem suitable."

The spacer crew all exchanged glances. We realized that it might be necessary to do battle with these creatures. However, experience had taught us to choose the moment to strike. You didn't rush in helter-skelter. You waited patiently, then launched your attack without holding back.

By this time we had made our way some distance from the ship. We began to see another race of beings. From their number, lack of weapons, and casual dress, they must have been native to this planet. They were the Schmarz, very languid saurian creatures who preferred to lounge around being warmed by their sun's rays. I couldn't help noticing how placid they were. They didn't seem to object to the nasty little creatures who kept waving their weapons at us, and shoving us away from the ship.

We were led up to a fenced-in area, and herded into the enclosure. The crew from the ship clustered together, muttering their displeasure. Small groups formed up, plotting strategies to overthrow our captors.

I looked uneasily at Kowana and Fido. "I'm sorry I got you into this."

"Don't be silly," Kowana said. "I booked out as a spacer. I knew there were dangers. Besides, we're a crew of spacers. We can handle themselves."

A solitary Vorkul soldier walked into the enclosure. He had a more relaxed and casual air about him, unlike the rest of the beasts. Several of the guards began to challenge his presence, but he muttered a few words to them and casually waved his hand. The guards relaxed and gestured him on. He approached Kowana, Fido and me. He turned to the guards posted there, "These beings are supposed to go with me." The other soldiers turned toward him and began to object, but the new arrival waved his hand once more. The guards' faces suddenly turned placid, and they nodded approval.

The Vorkul turned to us and said in a very amiable tone of voice, "Come with me, my friends," and led us out of the fencing.

I wondered at the way he'd addressed us. Vorkuls do not have friends. They don't have that word in their language. Why did this individual address us like that?

"I would like to take you to meet the local residents, the Schmarz. They are a most prankish race."

There was that expression, *prankish*, again. Since this individual was displaying a vocabulary that was quite different from the normal Vorkul, I decided to try something that isn't possible with Vorkuls: reason with him. "Why do you want me to meet them?"

"Because I think they are due for some special treatment. They need to get to know you, my dear friend Poison."

How did this stranger know my name? I cast an inquiring glance at Kowana. She leaned in toward me and whispered, "I can't tell a single thing about this creature." That was weird. Usually she could sense something about their mood.

"Sometimes it is best not to know what someone is feeling," the guard responded. "Some things need to be kept secret." He must have had damned good hearing because I was sure no one could overhear what she said to me.

And how did he know that what Kowana meant was what he was feeling?

We had, by this time, made our way out of the compound, and were walking through a city with local residents around us. My guide was the only Vorkul present; everyone else was Schmarz. The guard steered us to one side of a public square. "You must meet this fine fellow," the Vorkul said to me. We approached an individual who nodded amicably at me.

"Hello," I said, "what's your name?"

"Schmarz," he replied.

"I know you're a Schmarz, but what's your name?"

"It's Schmarz."

I turned to the Vorkul guard for an explanation. "They do not have individual names," he said.

"They're all called Schmarz?" I asked.

He nodded.

I stared at him for a moment. "Okay, is this someone special?" I turned to my good friend, Schmarz. "Are you the leader of the race?" I asked him.

"Oh, no, I couldn't claim to be the leader. I am just one equal among many," the guy said.

"Who is your leader?" I asked.

He seemed quite confused by the idea. "We don't have one."

"You don't?"

"No, we've never needed to have one," he said.

"But how do you get things done?" I asked.

He frowned in confusion. "We just get together and do it."

"But you've got to have some organization. What happens when you have a disagreement?" I asked.

He stared back at me in utter confusion. "What's that?"

"When you don't share the same opinion?"

"I've never heard of such a thing. We're always able to see what's right."

I turned to the Vorkul for some sort of explanation. The only thing he said was, "They are a most prankish race."

What kind of explanation is that? What kind of expression is that?

"I'm totally confused," I said to Kowana.

"Would you look at Fido," she said, pointing.

Usually the little guy is wandering around sniffing at things, doing the olfactory version of taking in the scenery. But right now he was huffing and snorfing his way around the Vorkul like there was a whole bunch of things there that he'd never sniffed. He was avidly inhaling everything about this strange creature.

I had to file that information for later. I still had the current situation to straighten out, and that was: what to do with these totally pacific Schmarz. I knew the crew from *The Long Scent* was going to need some help battling the Vorkuls. We had to enlist the native race. I turned back to the local.

"Why did you let the Vorkuls take over?" I asked him.

"What else could we do?" he responded.

"You could try fighting these guys. You outnumber them. You must have some sort of weapons you could turn on them," I said.

"I've heard that word you use: weapons. Our people have tried to figure out what you mean. We don't understand the concept."

"Concept? Weapons are weapons. You use them to fight off your enemies," I explained.

"Ah but, my dear friend Poison," the Vorkul interrupted, "these Schmarz have never had weapons." He seemed to be trying to get some point across to me. "Nor have they ever had enemies."

"What do you mean, they never had them? How did they survive?"

"At peace with their surroundings," the Vorkul said.

"But they've now got your soldiers surrounding them. You Vorkul don't live in peace. You're constantly invading other worlds and conquering them."

The Vorkul just nodded his head at me. "Yes. Perhaps The Schmarz will have to change to adapt to this new challenge to their race. Do you wonder, my good friend Poison, how they are going to effect this change?" He was staring very pointedly at me.

Our conversation was interrupted. The Vorkul guards were driving the crew of *The Long Scent* into the public square, and they weren't being gentle about it. The spacers were not used to that sort of treatment; they were about to boil over.

Kowana suddenly turned to me. "Poison, The Vorkuls. They're going to execute the crew." She had picked up on their emotions.

The aliens were herding the spacers into an area that fronted on a large wall. They were forming them up for a firing squad. The crew was beginning to sense what was happening and were preparing to launch a counterattack, unarmed.

I turned to the Vorkul, pointed at the other guards, and asked, "What are your friends going to do?"

"Don't trust that they're my friends," was all that he would say.

I wheeled around to the Schmarz, who was named Schmarz. "They're going to slaughter my crewmates. You people outnumber them. You have to stop them."

The Schmarz frowned in concentration. "This is not *right*, but what can we do?"

"What can you do?" I shrieked at him. "You can fight these little rodents before they put all of *your* people up against a wall."

At that moment, the rough treatment got to be too much for Flug. The navigator wheeled on one of the guards and belted him right in his sharp little teeth and sent him falling back. The soldiers to either side of the fallen guard reacted quickly, raised their weapons and fired searing blasts at Flug. The navigator was immolated in a bright flash. All that was left of him were several small pieces of detritus that fell to the ground where he had stood.

The crew shifted uneasily. They were of two moods. They knew that they had to fight now, but they had also seen the potency of the Vorkul weapons.

I turned to the Schmarz. "Do something," I implored.

"I-I-don't know what..." he trailed off helplessly.

"Something has to happen, Poison," the single Vorkul said. "Something needs to be done with the Schmarz."

"What can I do?"

"They need to change, Poison," the Vorkul said, as he looked deeply at me. "Someone needs to change them."

--Only it wasn't the Vorkul, anymore. It was a different being. It looked like a human, except it was green, and it was pudgy, and it was bald.

Kowana gasped. She stared at the creature; understanding dawning in her eyes. She'd suddenly been allowed to penetrate his feelings. She brought her glance up to me and said, "Poison!" Then she reached over and clutched my hand--the hand that had the invisible covering over it. The covering that masked my touch.

Now both Kowana and the green creature were staring at me.

I looked over to the Schmarz, who stood there, soundlessly working his mouth, torturing over his dilemma. I reached up my other hand to my wrist, slipped a digit underneath the covering on my hand and slid it off. I turned and faced the Schmarz with my uncovered hand pointed toward him. I reached forward...

...and touched him.

He gave out a loud bellow, one that started out in his normal vocal range but then shot down several octaves to become a seething bass growl of anger. His snout began to grow and lengthen, and his nostrils flared as wisps of smoke began to curl out of the openings. I had transformed him with my touch, my *Poison*-ous touch.

The Vorkul, who were corralling the crew of the ship, swung their gazes up in the direction of the roar that came from the Schmarz I'd just transformed.

The Schmarz stepped forward and addressed the invading aliens. "Vorkul!" he roared out. "What you have done, and what you are doing, is--*wrong*." Several more Shmarz began to bellow out, as they resonated with the change I had effected on their single member. They were all changing into the essential being they were meant to be, the being to which my touch converted them.

The Schmarz continued. "For ages, we Schmarz have always known what is *right*, always understood the meaning of that word. We never knew the word *wrong*, didn't even know it existed. But now you Vorkul have shown it to us. You have made us understand it." His voice rose to a deafening roar as he blasted out over the sound of his whole race bellowing out as they transformed. "You will stop doing *wrong*, or you will pay the consequences." He drew himself up. "I, Schmarz of the Incandescent Breath, command you."

He'd given himself a name.

One of the Vorkul guards chittered that thing that his race calls a laugh and raised his weapon up to point at the newly transformed creature.

A gout of flame shot out of the Schmarz's mouth and immolated the alien.

There was a moment of shocked silence out of the assembled creatures. Then another Vorkul guard spun on a Schmarz standing close to him, and raised his weapon to fire. In a moment he was a pile of ashes.

The silence that had descended on the place a moment ago turned into a roaring pandemonium as the Vorkul tried to engage the Schmarz in battle. In some cases, they raised their weapons on those Schmarz who had not as yet changed over, only to be destroyed by the locals who had achieved their new status. Sometimes they tried to fire at the locals to blast their way out of the square. They all met with the same result. The battle was totally one-sided in the favor of the Schmarz.

I swung around to the little green guy who had appeared to be a Vorkul. "Who are you? And what's happening? What did my touch just do?"

"It would appear that the Schmarz have ceased to be the benign creatures they were," he said.

"What does that mean?"

He smiled at me. "They know what is right. They now battle what is wrong. They will make most effective law enforcers for the Amalgam of Intelligent Beings."

"Who are you?" I had a good idea who this creature was. I wanted to stick with him to get further information.

"A friend."

And then he disappeared.

"What? What?" I screamed at the air in front of me where the green creature had been. I reached my hands out and clawed where the alien had stood.

The crew of *The Long Scent* had suddenly found themselves ignored by the Vorkuls and the Schmarz as the latter were in the process of totally wiping out the former.

However, the planet's natives, who suddenly found themselves empowered to police their planet, were displaying a lot of exuberance in using their new-found skills. Gouts of flame were flying all over the place. We were all caught in the crossfire.

Captain Kordlux quickly gathered the crew together. "Let's get back to the ship," he commanded. He looked over at me. "Poison, pick up Flug's remains."

Why me? Why did he choose me? I *was* closest to where the navigator had fallen, but the place was right at ground zero of the hostilities. On the other hand I knew this was not an idle request on the Captain's part, so I sent Kowana and Fido off in the direction of the ship and dodged and weaved my way over to where Flug had last stood. Nothing remained of him except half a dozen little pellets. They must have religious significance, so I scooped them up and used my escape run to make my way toward *The Long Scent*. I was doing all right in making my way, just a few singes, nothing serious, when some piece of equipment came flying along and clipped me on the head. I dropped to the ground, momentarily dazed. I raised my eyes, and in that instant, I saw something that hadn't been there before. I saw the little green alien boarding a ship that was really *strange* in design. I blinked my eyes and shook my head to clear it, and both he and the ship were gone.

I wondered about that, but I couldn't stand around trying to figure that out. I had to get out of the conflagration that was raging around me. I continued with my low run and made my way back to the ship. I arrived at the same time as the Captain and the rest of the crew. Everyone had been burned in some way by the fires raging around us. I followed the Captain as he dashed to the bridge to get the ship underway.

"Computer, get us the hell out of here. This planet's close to the StarBoard Café. Let's head there to get ourselves fixed up," the Captain ordered.

"*Where's Flug?*" the computer asked.

"He's being tended to," the Captain lied.

"*Is he all right?*" the computer pursued, fear lacing its voice.

"Most of this damn crew is not 'all right.' They're smoking and burning. Now, I gave you an order to take us to safety. Do it, damn it. We'll take care of your friend."

I turned to the Captain and cast him a questioning glance, since he knew that I was carrying Flug's remains. He swept me out of the bridge, away from the computer. The air throughout the ship was laced with smoke, as the crew did its best to put each other's fire out. "I don't want to bother this ship's navigation system with the story about Flug. Let's just get the hell back to the StarBoard where we can be fixed up," he said.

And so we made it back here to the Cafe, and Security helped finish off what firefighting was still needed.

In the meantime, I've got to figure out a few things. The first thing is: how did our ship get pulled from one end of the galaxy to the other? And who was it who did the dragging and to what purpose? How were they able to impose their own n-space drive? Was this what happened to me back in my own galaxy, when I'd been pulled away in my rescue pod to Floria?

And who was the strange green creature who was able to look like a different being? And did I see the right thing when I'd been bonked on the head? Was he boarding some high-tech craft that none of us were able to see?

The major question is: was he a Wistrani? Are he and his people the ones I'm seeking?

That's why I'm leaving this message. I have a feeling they might be able to tap into the StarBoard's stories to gather information.

I hope they do and hear me.

END RECORD

#

Poison pressed the switch.

He turned to discuss the situation with Kowana, but was interrupted as Captain Kordlux came up to him.

"Poison, I trust you still have Flug's remains."

"Yes, I do, Captain. Should we give him a proper burial?"

He pursed his lips. "You don't know much about Flug's race, do you?" he asked.

"I don't know much about a lot of races in this galaxy."

"Come with me, and bring the remains."

"Where're we going, Captain?" Poison asked as he followed him out through the Café.

"We're going to see the computer."

Poison knew that was going to be a problem. Flug and the computer had worked for many years together. With the personality the computer had, they'd built up a relationship. The two of them were close.

When Poison and the Captain got to the ship, it was very quiet, and all of the lights had been dimmed lower than Poison had ever seen them.

The two of them made their way to the bridge. The room was even darker than the rest of the ship. The only sound that interrupted the silence was the shuffling of their feet.

"Are you here to tell me what happened?" the computer's voice cut the silence. There was a quiet foreboding in its tone.

"You know what a headstrong fool he always was," the Captain said.

"'Was,' Captain?"

The Captain looked down at the floor. "He didn't react well to the treatment we were getting. He was also worried about leaving you alone with the Vorkul."

"So he started fighting," the computer stated.

"Yes," the Captain responded.

"Was he armed?"

"No."

"And they were?"

"Yes."

"And that precipitated all of the rest of the fighting?"

"Yes."

"I suppose it was utter pandemonium then, the same as outside the ship."

"That's right."

"No way you could recover his remains?"

"There was a lot of confusion going down..."

"I thought so."

"...But Poison was close enough to retrieve them."

"He did?" There was alert interest in the computer's voice. Several lights in the room flashed on.

"Yes, I know how important it is," the Captain said.

"Let me see them!" the computer demanded.

Poison displayed the little pellets.

The computer sucked in its breath--even though the computer didn't breathe. Simultaneously, something in the bowels of the ship began to crash around.

The lights in the room snapped on to full, blinding brightness.

"Put them in here," the computer commanded as a drawer in

the console slid open. A soft white cloth laid along its bottom.

In the meantime, the series of crashes, that had started from the direction of the bowels of the ship, were approaching.

"*Oh, the little darlings!*" cooed the computer.

The door to the bridge swooshed open to reveal the source of the offstage crashes. It was a servo robot--wearing a white nanny's outfit, complete with cap. It rotated its top sensor pack back and forth in confusion.

"*There you are! You certainly took your time getting here!*" The robot straightened itself up, recognizing it was being addressed.

"*How are your grapplers? Are they clean?*"

The robot raised its arms up in front of its sensors, then quickly thrust them behind him. It nervously rotated its sensor pack, to the left a little bit, and then to the right.

"*They're all covered in lubricant! Get out of here and get them cleaned up!*"

The robot quickly rotated around and dashed off out of the bridge, crashing against the doorway as it went.

"What's happening?" Poison asked the Captain.

"That's the way Flug's people reproduce. They die in the act of giving birth."

"*I thought he was approaching that point,*" the computer said.

"I'm sure he would want you to raise his children," the Captain said.

The servo robot had returned to the room, with his grapplers sparkling clean. He approached the drawer with the "children" in it. He reached a very tender grappler out toward them. "Oh, the little darlings," the computer cooed over its speakers.

The servo robot brushed away a small wrinkle in the cloth lining the drawer.

The Captain took in the scene. He turned to Poison. "I think things are pretty well set up." He beckoned for them to leave.

The two of them returned to the StarBoard Café.

Chapter 13

El Escorpion

A Grimyon had settled itself in what could best be called a booth in the StarBoard Café. A booth is a seat that surrounds a table. In the case of this recliner, it was a table surrounding a seat.

These areas were suited to Grimyons. They were creatures that sported a great number of eyes mounted on the end of stalks that swayed out of their bodies. Each eye was an independent sight organ. They could process many different visual images at the same time. They also had numerous limbs that could grasp and hold articles at their ends. In their primitive ages Grimyons were always good at assessing a great number of things at the same time. With the coming of the Amalgam and technology, they were able to grasp and study numerous data tablets at the same time. They distinguished themselves as bookkeepers and insurance analysts.

The very best of them became actuaries.

This particular Grimyon performed a job also greatly suited to his species: he was a lexicographer. He had just returned from a trip to that strange little backwater planet known as Earth. He had heard that there were numerous different languages on that planet that needed to be studied and codified. What he didn't realize was just how many there were. It was stunning. Most planets in the Amalgam had achieved world governments and unified their people under a single language. The chaos of the human tongues was minds-boggling to the Grimyon. (He also had several minds.)

He had settled down at the StarBoard and ordered a very stiff drink.

Another being, one who traveled under an alias, scuttled his way into the Café. From the way that this creature travelled, one could deduce that this area of the Café was far from the section that offered seating for bipeds. The creature kept a furtive eye out for any vermin that the exterminator 'bots hadn't noticed as yet. Her would gladly scoop them up and snack on them.

He settled into proper seating for his body type, ordered a drink, and punched the Record button to enter him into the contest.

RECORD
#

This story all started with me in a bit of a fix. I was careening around the galaxy, dropping into and out of n-space, looping through untold combinations of dimensions, attempting to elude the Amalgam's Frontier Guard.

I had been in the last stages of delivering a shipment on a commercial venture, when I was rudely interrupted by a Guard cruiser, squawking over my com, making some ridiculous claims about something called smuggling. I was therefore forced to quickly alter my course. The Guard and I had a long-standing disagreement about what constituted the proper method to get merchandise and personnel from one planet to another. They always insisted on sifting through paperwork and carping about things like immigration laws and duty taxes. I find it far more efficient and remunerative to take a direct course toward deliveries and skip the middle being.

After many dimensional contortions, I finally managed to lose them (I hoped) when I dropped down on a little backwater that was the home and sole planet of those *hew-man* creatures. I believe it's called *Urth*.

I had briefly visited this place once before, having been assured that it held commercial possibilities for an entrepreneur who wasn't bound by such trivialities as rules and regulations. I had been given suggestions for accommodations on this planet, but apparently the creatures who recommended this place were not familiar with my racial traits. They had sent me to some place called the *High-@*. The establishment was as scrubbed as an electronics lab, and it was located right next to a large body of open water, continuously in motion. The place was both disgusting and terrifying.

This time when I dropped down on the planet, I headed for someplace more remote, inland, away from the water. I found a locale that was so backwater they spoke some indigenous tribal tongue, and could only manage a few phrases in the Anglo my translator was furnished with. I was often forced to store some of their native words for reference. They described the locale as *meh-hee-co*. I searched through my translator's files to find this geographic location, but couldn't find a direct translation. Forced to squat down in this as-yet-unnamed location, I chanced upon a perfectly lovely accommodation, run by the locals, called a *cantina*. The place was divine. They had little snacks which they served at random times. One could just lounge around and these things would just pop up to be snatched and eaten. They were called *cucarachas*.

I was able to work out that the owners of this resort were a pair of nest mates named *Paco* and *Felipe*. They spoke only snatches of Anglo, so the best we could do in the way of communicating was to grunt and point. *Paco* had a mate who was called *Mama*. At least that was the name all her nestlings called her. There was a great variety of these little creatures, stepping down all the way from *Paco's* height to a small one that could barely balance itself on its pedal extremities. It looked particularly delicious. My salivating over the little morsel caused *Mama* to fix me with a very hard stare, as though she didn't trust me.

Can't imagine why.

I tried to tell *Paco* and *Felipe* my name, but their only response was to do that shaking and jiggling that indicates humor for these creatures, and one of them ejaculated mouth liquid down to the ground in imitation. It was *Mama* who gave me a name the locals understood: *El Escorpion*.

I had been paying for my keep by giving *Paco* and *Felipe* pieces from the spool of *grcht*, the conductor, I kept in my repair kit. They seemed to place high value on this material which they called *oro*.

Since my luck was running so well, having found this resort while trying to escape the Frontier Guard, I decided to see if I could also discover some commercial possibilities while I was lying low. I settled down in the *cantina* and drank some of the beverage they called *tequila*. The drink gave a special little tingle in the back of my maw. Plus, there was a tidbit floating at the bottom of the drink's container. Apparently whomever finished the bottle could eat this snack.

I held a long pointing-and-gesturing conversation with *Paco* and *Felipe* on the possibility of finding a business opportunity on this planet. When they finally understood what I was saying, they launched into a rapid conversation in their tongue, with much pointing at the thing they called a *tee-vee* mounted on the wall. They finally made known to me that they could get something called *el Oro d'Acapulco*. It took quite a while for us to get across to each other the meaning of what we wanted to communicate. We had to pause frequently to refresh ourselves with *tequila* before we could resume the arduous task of hand-gesture translation. Checking in my data base revealed that *Urth* was the sole source of a range of recreational foodstuffs that were in high demand by the residents of the Amalgam. Securing a shipment of these goods would be worth a fortune if the delivery could be made outside the cloying Frontier Guard and their parasitic entertainment taxes. *Paco* and *Felipe* indicated they could obtain some of this *el Oro d'Acapulco* if I would let them take the full spool of *grcht* with them to their supplier. Those fools, I had another spool of the stuff sitting in my repair kit.

They headed off in their ramshackle vehicle to purchase the goods from their supplier. This left me alone with *Mama* and her herd of offspring, most of which seemed to be off in the fields gathering the plant matter these creatures ate. The only one left was that particularly tender-looking little one. I decided to sidle up to it to take an experimental taste. Immediately, *Mama* interposed herself between me and the nestling, brandishing a device she called a *machete*. She was uttering a string of sounds that were reminiscent of those made by the Qualong Pirates, who were noted for the invectives they could string together. I couldn't comprehend her anger. I only intended to munch on one of the thing's appendages. It could always grow back a new one. I shrank back from the *machete*. It would have done immense damage to my carapace, and I had just spent far too many credits for a cosmetologist to decorate it. I decided it would be prudent to leave the little one alone.

Besides, it leaked all over the place.

I was uncertain if *Mama* knew that I had declared peace with her, but she must have. She took her *machete* and grabbed one of the avians that wandered around the place, and promptly lopped off its head. She then stormed off with the little one, carrying the body of the avian, leaving the remaining delicacy for me to eat. I decided it was a peace offering.

A little while later she returned and made it known that she had something for me to eat. She seemed quite eager for me to taste the food. She described the dish with the word *caliente*. I wasn't sure if that was the name of the dish, or the major attribute of it. She still seemed a bit surly, so I tried to convey to her how delighted I'd be to partake. She grunted her response.

When she brought the food, she waited expectantly for me to taste the offering. I obliged by taking a nibble. At first it registered rather bland, but after a moment it began to rise up, stimulating my palate and tickling my gorge. It was spectacular. I signaled my approval to *Mama*. Strangely enough, she didn't seem happy that I enjoyed it, and she stomped away.

I amused myself nibbling on some *caliente* until *Paco* and *Felipe* arrived with a bale of the product in the back of their vehicle. It was some sort of plant matter. I inspected it and detected a certain over-taste that had a most delightful bouquet. The two *hew-mans* also handed me back the remnants of my spool of *grcht*. I was pleased to note that they hadn't skimmed too much from the supply of the conductor for themselves. They would make good business partners; they were almost honest. The three of us stood and contemplated the product.

"A most interesting sample of vegetable matter, Brother," a voice intoned from behind me. It took me by surprise. I didn't know who it was, but my experience as a spacer had led me to understand that sudden appearances never turned out well. I started to wheel about to see who it was but could only manage to swivel my head; the rest of my limbs were immobilized in a stasis field.

Quite incredibly, I found myself staring at a Vren. He towered over me, dressed in his dark robes, his face long and lugubrious, his expression blank. He had stealthed in behind me.

The Vren were notorious throughout the Amalgam for practicing the one thing that has killed more beings in the whole history of this galaxy: religion. I thought most of them had been hunted down and captured. How had they managed to turn up in this backwater?

"What an unpleasant surprise to see you here," I said. "Don't you think it would be better if you announced yourself?"

"Those of you not among the Faithful might resist our missionary efforts," the Vren intoned with sepulchral modulations.

"Oh, that's right, you people practice that religion of yours in a rather extreme manner."

"Our practices are Heavenly."

"So you say."

"We are only concerned with the spiritual," he said.

"Is that why you've slaughtered so many beings?"

"It is sometimes necessary to transport a soul to Heaven before it has been defiled by the temptations of this mortal coil," he intoned.

"Haven't you sent whole species off to Heaven?"

"It has been our humble duty," he responded.

"And I'm sure you never enjoyed it."

"We enjoyed the sight of so many souls ascending to the Great Beyond."

These pompous lunatics had plagued the galaxy for ages.

The Frontier Guard thought they'd captured the last of them several decades ago. "Where have you been hiding out?" I asked him.

"We were on Retreat in the outer reaches of this system. However, we could no longer ignore the anguished cries of the creatures on this planet. We have come as their salvation."

The outer reaches of this system would have suited them: cold and spare, some occasional hydrocarbons to snack on. Being an ascetic group, their digestive systems were suited to the simplest of foods, nothing fancy.

"We have heeded the call of this abandoned flock and have come to give them their final reward." Beneath his plastered-on sanctity, seething sadism rippled across his face. "We must launch our missionary campaign here with a ceremonial sacrifice to the Almighty."

"And who, may I ask, is going to be the sacrificial beast for this ceremony?"

He turned toward me and held out his hand in benediction. "Bless you, my offspring."

"I figured as much," I said ruefully.

"We must begin at once. Let us prepare the fire," he called out. "Have the two male creatures build the bonfire. They can then be sent to their reward on the trail of your ashes."

They released *Paco* and *Felipe* from their restraints and, attempted to convey to them that they wanted them to pile wood for my last resting--or is it roasting?--place. It was quite entertaining to watch them trying to make themselves understood. I think they got so frustrated, they almost used their God's name in vain.

"I don't suppose you would allow the condemned a last meal? Give me a last sip, a taste of what this place has to offer for consumption, to nourish me on my trip to the Great Beyond?" I asked.

"It is best that you fast to attain a state of purity before you are transported off to meet your Maker," he replied.

They lit the fire. Two of the Vren hauled up my immobilized

body and started transporting me toward my little hot spot, chanting as they went along.

Even with chopping up various pieces of furniture, *Paco* and *Felipe* had not accumulated enough fuel to give me a proper toasting. The head Vren spotted this, pointed toward *el Oro d'Acapulco* on the truck, and said, "Throw the vegetable matter on the fire."

How rotten could he be? He was going to bake me with the very goods I had just purchased!

Paco and *Felipe* threw the bale on the fire, and it immediately began to burn sluggishly, emitting a dense cloud of smoke.

A sudden blast of wind pushed the smoke toward us, and it rushed past me and surrounded the head Vren. I inhaled a deep whiff of the stuff.

My goodness! If the Vren were trying to send me off in an ecstasy, they'd stumbled on a way to do it. This stuff was absolutely spectacular!

I heard a sudden intake of breath from the head Vren. "Wait!" he shouted out. My two stokers, paused on the trip to the fire. "A message has come to me from the Almighty. It has told me that we must have a feast to celebrate this sacrifice." The rest of the Vren, who'd also had a whiff of the cloud of ecstasy, gave a chorus of agreement. I could understand what was happening to them. Ever since I'd inhaled that smoke, I was maddeningly hungry.

A plot began to form in my mind. "You're absolutely right, Your Eminence. You must feast on the bounties of this planet that you are about to purify. I can attest to the spiritual nature of the food that is found here."

The head Vren was standing a little unsteadily, he stared at me out of dilated pupils. "You will most definitely attest. You will also *test* it to make sure it isn't poisoned. Your fast will be lifted in this case. Now tell me, what is the ambrosia this planet has to offer?" he asked, a little too eagerly.

I swung my head around to *Mama* and said, "*Caliente*." I was quite certain the Vren's ascetic systems couldn't manage the stuff.

For once *Mama* registered agreement with me. She said, "*Si! Caliente!*" and bustled off to the place where she did food preparation.

I stared around at the assembled Vren. They were all a little unsteady on their feet. One of them was humming some tune, a hymn perhaps.

Apparently *Mama* had earlier prepared a lot of *caliente* for me. She emerged carrying a large container of the food.

The head Vren turned to me and said, "Because you have sinned so terribly in your life, you must break your fast and consume this mortal temptation."

Mama brought a ladle up to my mouth and tipped the food in. At first there was just a slight taste of the ingredients, then the bouquet rose in my throat. It was magnificent! I craned toward *Mama* to get some more.

The head Vren strode over and interjected himself between me and the *caliente*. "Apparently it is quite good, and you seem to bear no ill effects. You may feed us, Holy Sister."

Mama didn't comprehend what he'd said, but I motioned with my head in their direction, and she filled bowls, one each for the Vren. They raised their containers on high, chanted some ceremonial claptrap, then quickly downed their helpings of *caliente* with great relish. I waited, as they all savored their food. They wheeled on *Mama* and thrust out their bowls demanding more servings.

It hadn't worked! I despaired of my plan as the Vren gobbled up their second helping.

The head Vren raised his head from licking his dish and ordered, "Take the sacrifice to the fire." The two other Vren picked me up and continued with their march to my barbecue pit. I felt the heat of the flames growing on my face as we approached.

Then it hit.

The Vren who was carrying me on my left side let out a long, slow groan as he dropped me. His partner on the other side tried to compensate for the changed balance, but before he had much of a chance to grasp me, he began to let out with a baritone wail. The chorus was joined by all the other aliens as the *caliente* afterburners kicked in.

I tumbled to the ground, immobilized by the stasis field binding my limbs. *Paco* and *Felipe* rushed up to me, and we started a maddeningly long grunt-and-point conversation as I tried to explain to them how to disarm my restraints. In the meantime, *Mama* was dashing about from one Vren to another. Every time they opened their mouths to groan, she would ladle in an additional mouthful of *caliente,* which would further torment them.

After a whole dictionary full of grunts, I finally managed to get *Paco* and *Felipe* to release me from the stasis field. I promptly dashed about to each of the Vren and used their restraints on themselves. This reduced the amount of writhing they were able to do, which increased their discomfort. No one sympathized with their distress.

I was just getting to the point of easing back and trying to figure out what to do with our religious rogues, when there was a sonic boom out of the sky. I looked up and saw a Frontier Guard shuttle streaking across the sky and heading toward the place out in the wastelands where I had stored my craft.

If they found me here, they'd launch into a very tedious discussion with me, harping on their favorite, boring subject: smuggling. I dashed over and sought concealment behind the piece of furniture where they served the *tequila*. When the shuttle's engines roared, I peeked out through a crack and saw that the craft had done a sudden detour and was heading for the *cantina*. I tried to burrow further down and find a spy hole to check on events outside.

The Guard ship landed a short distance away, and troops poured out of the vehicle taking up positions around the yard of the *cantina*. Leading that group was Captain Grunther, someone who'd harried me all too frequently in the past. When she stepped off the ramp she raised her ursine snout into the air and sniffed the aroma of *el Oro d'Acapulco* still drifting in the breeze. She gave a throaty grunt and galumphed her way toward the *cantina*. In the meantime her troops were dashing about needlessly attempting to secure the Vren.

Grunther made her way to *Paco* and *Felipe* and started to launch a conversation. She met with as much success as I had the past few days. She finally roared out in Anglo, "Is there anyone here who understands me."

Paco and Felipe had seen me scuttle off to my hiding place and were playing stupid for my benefit, so they weren't about to answer Grunther's question, even though its meaning was obvious.

"*El Escorpion! El Escorpion!*" someone shouted out.

It was that stupid little nestling. He was standing in the middle of the *cantina* and pointing at my hiding place.

I knew I should have eaten him in the first place.

There was nothing to do but come out and face the Captain.

Recognition flickered across her face. Her language switched to Galactic Prime. "Citizen, I'm pleased to see a member of the Amalgam here. Your presence would explain who overcame the Vren and operated the stasis fields on them." *Paco* and *Felipe* lolled back, accepting that we had switched to another language. *Mama* was suspicious about it.

"Congratulations are in order," Grunther continued. "Capturing the Vren is quite an achievement for both of us.

"I'm sure to get a commendation for bringing them to justice, and I'm hearing things over the com about the rewards that have been posted for the capture of this rogue species. I'm sure you and your native friends will receive considerable funds for your accomplishment."

"Shall I give these beings the good news?" I asked.

Grunther's eyes flickered across me. "We'll assume the responsibility for explaining it to them." She bared her teeth in the manner that suggested humor in her race. "Just to make sure they understand what the amount is."

"Of course." Well, I'd given it a try.

"I must say this is quite the turn of events. I came here chasing some minor brigand on a petty smuggling charge, and I wind up finding major galactic criminals. I'm almost in debt to that smuggler for what is going to be a boost to my career." What was she trying to get at? "Strangely enough, this being I was chasing was a member of your race. He looks just like you." I glanced about, seeing if there was any route to escape from my imminent arrest. "Unfortunately," she continued, "I must admit I can't recognize one of you from the other."

That set me back. What was she getting at?

"However, you can't possibly be that smuggler," she continued. "You don't have his name. I heard that cub saying your name. What is it?"

"*El Escorpion.*"

"Yes, that's right. I'll remember that, Citizen *El Escorpion*. The chit for the reward will be made out to you." She turned back to watch her troopers loading the last of the Vren into the cruiser. I must say I had to admire how fluently she could lie, but I did resent her referring to me as a "petty" smuggler. She turned back. "That reward will be enough for you to live very comfortably for the rest of your life. Why, you can retire from your old job, whatever that might be." She smiled toothily, ramming the point home.

"Yes, Captain, I'll have no need to work for the rest of my life."

"I'm pleased to hear that," she said, as she turned toward the cruiser to leave, satisfied that she had figured out how to mend my wicked ways. I stared after her.

"Oh, by the way, Captain..."

She turned back. "Yes?"

"I hate to bother you about this, but I incurred some minor damage to my craft and need to do a few repairs. Would you have any spools of conductor that you could give me?"

She frowned slightly. "Certainly. How many?"

"As much as you can spare."

The *grcht* would come in handy to restock my supplies.

Old habits die hard.

#

The creature reached out an appendage and punched the

Record button.

END RECORD

The creature hoped that he would reap the reward of winning the contest.

Old habits die hard.

Having satisfied his appetites, he scuttled out of the Café, right past the Grimyon who was passed out at his perch.

Several seconds passed.

The Grimyon began to twitch, one quick one, a pause, and then several together. Something had lodged into his brain, something he had managed to hear. Its persistent nagging on his subconscious was having the same effect as someone shaking him to rouse him. The few twitches had turned into an all-out shudder. Suddenly a group of his eyes stalks shot up, gazing around its perimeter.

El Escorpion? The lexicographer thought. *El Escorpion?*

Where had he heard that before?

His appendages began to flash data tablets in front of his eye stalks. He searched through them for this curious expression that he'd just heard. The search became more frantic as the appendages shuffled through more and more tablets. The speed reached such a pace that they began to generate sound, like hummingbird's wings. The search became so frenzied that the Grimyon lost his grip on some tablets and they arced out into the room and crashed into other tables, chairs, and clients.

Finally in a cascade of tablets being water-fountained away into the world, the Grimyon shrieked out in its seldom-used voice, "*EL ESCORPION!*"

The creature collapsed down on its table and weakly signaled for another drink to send him off to unconsciousness and free him from that damnable, unknown phrase.

Chapter 14

Joy

Charlie Bishop navigated through the tables at the StarBoard Café, surveying the occupants while not arousing suspicion. It was his specialty: blending into the background without stirring anyone's interest. Not until he'd strike.

He set himself up at the bar in front of one of the Record buttons that would enter him in the Café's renowned storytelling contest. In his business it didn't hurt to get the word out about what he was doing and who he was looking for. Nor was he unmindful that winning the contest would give him a negotiable asset. He reached forward to press the Record button.

RECORD

\#

I remember coming home to Joy.

She was standing there, holding a dust rag, dressed in short shorts with a trimmed-back halter top, and not much else. Her breasts pushed up and tested the limits of the light material of her top. Auburn hair cascaded down to her shoulders. A light sheen of perspiration glistened on her body.

"Oh, Charlie, I didn't expect you'd be home this soon. I was just finishing up cleaning, but I'm not really ready for you to be home."

"Why not, honey?"

"Well, look at me! I'm a mess!" She walked up to me and put her arms around my neck. My hands strayed to her bare waist. "I should take a shower." She lifted her gaze to me. "Will you come with me, Charlie, to make sure I'm properly washed and cleaned?"

"You bet, honey."

It was always that way, or something like it, coming home to Joy.

#

I needed that kind of home life. I needed to get away from the tension that I dealt with in my profession. I'm a Seeker. I find people. I serve them with papers and bring them back.

My job is new to the legal system. Before the courts got straightened out by the Amalgam, there used to be a person who'd hand somebody some papers to tell them to come to court, and that was it. The servers weren't important. They could be ignored.

The Amalgam changed that.

#

I remember coming home to Joy.

She knelt in front of the tea tray. Her jet black hair was held perfectly in place by a complex of combs and hair pins. Her kimono was not so much worn as arranged on her supple little body. She demurely raised her gaze to me. "Ah, Charlie, is most good that you have arrived. I have spent the day reading the ancient texts on the art of the physical pleasures. It stated how one can use the cascade of raptures to obtain the highest state of bliss." Something wild peeked out from her almond-shaped eyes.

#

The aliens were quite rightly shocked at the condition of our system of law. They were, after all, from the Amalgam of *Intelligent* Beings. It didn't take much intelligence to see that our legal system was in a rip-roaring mess. The situation had been the tail wagging the dog with the system run by the lawyers. The aliens gave the courts more power, with the judges assuming more responsibility for the cases they were trying. Frivolous suits became the responsibility of the litigating parties. Judges were required to throw out any such suits.

I worked for the judges.

#

I remember coming home to Joy.

"You look all worn out, sugar," she said. Her eyes were luminous, staring out of her ebony-skinned face.

"I guess you could say I had a hard day at the office."

She sauntered over to me, carefully placing each long leg in front of the other. She towered over me by a good four inches. "That's okay, Baby, you're going to have a *hard* night at home, too. It'll just be hard in a different place. You leave that up to me."

#

The Amalgam found itself forced to correct the many social ills of Earth. Population was soaring out of control; divorce rates were increasing. These trends had to be reversed.

One of the solutions was to work more strenuously through the courts to collect child support. The Seekers for the domestic courts would round up those poor, hapless bastards and make them pay whether they could afford it or not. It was a branch of my job that I avoided. I wouldn't take any cases that had to do with support, divorce, none of the domestic issues. I had no stomach for it.

The Joys of Life were another solution for the social and legal malaise.

The idea of the Joys came from the Morixi, a race of the Amalgam. They're an odd group, prone to chattering among themselves and lacing their conversations with their version of laughter that they call "thurtles wobbling." They also referred to anything they considered funny as "prankish."

The Morixi undertook the project of designing the Joys of Life: robots intended to be perfect partners. Anatomically correct, indistinguishable from real humans, they were fashioned to be the ideal accoutrement for every bachelor's quarters. Or at least every bachelor who could afford one.

And they were completely malleable. They could transform their appearance to any exotic size or shape of the proper gender.

They were perfect sex partners. They also cleaned the house and cooked during the day.

The Morixi set up shop on Earth and began studying everything they could find about the human sex act. They rented all the sex vids they could find, and I mean *all* of them. They'd watch them, and all that could be heard was the sound of their thurtles wobbling.

#

I remember coming home to Joy.

As I closed the door, the whip came flying up and snapped against the doorframe, centimeters from my head.

"Where have you been, slave?" Joy asked imperiously. Her clothes were both brief and leather.

"What's this about, Joy?" I cautiously edged in the door.

"Be quiet, slave. Speak only when spoken to. Or do you want me to punish you?" she menaced.

"Listen, Joy..."

"Do not speak to me in such a brazen way! You will get down on all fours in front of me. I will beat you until you beg me to stop."

"Whoa, whoa, Joy, what the heck is this act you're doing?"

She paused, lost the imperious look. "Don't you like this, Charlie?" she asked.

"No, baby, I don't like this at all." I was back in control.

Her manner was now entirely different, sharply in contrast with the clothes she wore. "I'm sorry, honey, but you had me on the random setting, and the dominatrix was in the list of possible personalities. Should I remove that from the queue?"

"Yes, please."

"Okay, Charlie, let me just run off and change, and then I'll make something for dinner." She turned around and headed into the bedroom.

The phrase "run off and change" didn't have the same meaning as it did for humans. Joy would go and transmogrify into a different person. The seeming modesty was good manners on her part. I'd seen what it looks like when a Joy of Life modifies, and it's not pretty.

#

The job of Seeker pays well. That's how I was able to afford a Joy of Life. It was perfect for me. I'd had a few relationships with young ladies, real ones, and I didn't like all the baggage they brought along. The relationship would be tumultuous, and we always parted with screaming, emotional scenes. Joy suited my needs in every way. Why wouldn't she? Endless variety of partners with no emotional involvement.

And she'd always be waiting there. My Seeking took me away for long periods of time. I didn't have to call home to Joy. I didn't have to send flowers. I didn't have to remember anniversaries. I'd just come back, and she'd be there, and dinner'd be ready, and I didn't have to explain where I'd been.

I'd been off on a particularly knotty Seek, chasing down a lawyer the system had decided was initiating too many frivolous suits. He knew how to run. Almost as well as I knew how to Seek. I'd been gone several weeks. I walked in the door, and Joy stood there. Her skin was quite dark. Her black hair was in tight little curls. She wore large hoop earrings and a peasant-style dress. She rushed forward and pressed against me, pushing me against the wall. She crushed her lips against mine.

"Thar you are, my darleeng. Leetle Treena has waited a long time for you."

"What do you mean, Treena? Your name's Joy." She'd never changed her name before.

"I am Treena! Who ees this Joy you are talking about? Show me the leetle slut and I will keel her!" She grabbed me hard, digging her fingernails into the back of my neck.

"Okay, Treena. Can you pull this persona out of the queue?"

"I weel show you what I can and cannot do. You weel forget this other slut." Using her fingernails as steering mechanisms, she propelled me into the bedroom.

There were certainly some things to be said for this Treena

persona, but I found it a bit too active. This didn't help my performance in the bedroom, which she kept blaming on "that leetle slut" as she continued to assault me with her aggressive lovemaking style.

I decided that I would just get out of the place that morning, and wait to see what I could do with that evening's persona. I was estimating how long it'd take for the scratches on my back to heal.

#

The administrative work back at the office took most of the day. When I returned home, I quietly opened the door and peeked in to see who would meet me.

"Hello, darling, how was your day at the office? I hope you're hungry. I've got a pot roast in the kitchen." She was blond, all-American, domesticated, and not in the least threatening.

"Hi, Joy," I paused to see if I'd get any arguments about the name. There were none. "Listen, do you remember anything about last night?"

"Yes, I was Treena the gypsy temptress. Did you like that?" She raised an interrogative eyebrow. Her smile was warm, open.

"As a matter of fact, I didn't. I found her a little too aggressive. Could you take her out of the queue?"

"I wish I could, darling, but I'm afraid your warranty has run out. I can't do the repairs." She turned around and headed for the kitchen. "Let me get dinner."

I had a problem that needed fixing. I'd get on it in the morning, pronto. I followed Joy to supper.

#

The first order of the day was to call the Morixi and find out what I had to do to renew my warranty. Each time I called, I got a busy signal. I put the phone on automatic dial, every three minutes, but it continued to get the busy signal, up until the end of the day, when a recording came on that the phone had been disconnected without a forwarding number. I was getting worried.

#

When I got home that night, Joy still featured the same persona as the previous night. She'd also cooked a thing called a tuna casserole that was not up to her normal standard of cuisine. I didn't say much until we were sitting in the living room after dinner. I was drinking a beer.

"Joy, I tried to contact the company this morning about renewing your warranty. I couldn't find them. Do you have any numbers in your data base where I can contact them?"

She looked at me and said, "No, darling, I don't."

"Well, I guess I'll just have to do a little more digging tomorrow." I felt very uneasy about this. "I think I need another beer." I got up and started to walk toward the kitchen. Something stopped me. Something in the air. There was an oxymoronic deafening silence in the room. I turned around and looked at Joy. She was sitting there staring at my empty beer can. "What's the matter?"

"Oh, nothing," she said. I turned around to keep heading for the kitchen. "Tell me something," she continued, I turned back to her, "don't you ever pick up after yourself? I mean, doesn't it bother you that that empty beer can is just sitting there?"

It was so unlike her. "Well, I always figured you'd be able to pick it up."

"Oh," she said. She got up and started toward the bedroom. "I think I'll go to bed. I've got a headache."

#

I got on the Net the first thing in the morning. I could not find an official Morixi site. There were chat rooms about the Joys, and they were all buzzing with talk about other malfunctions. Most of them were similar. The Joy Boys were also coming down with problems. Some were getting GPS malfunctions, but refused to ask for directions when they were obviously lost. They were drinking beer, watching sports on vid, and developing pot bellies. Things were getting bad.

Then I got a buzz on my com. It was my supervisor; he

wanted me upstairs stat to get on a case.

It was a class action against the Morixi. There was more information on recent malfunctions. Damage had been incurred by some units. One Joy Boy had been battered to pieces by its owner when he had answered, "As a matter of fact, your butt has grown 23 millimeters since I met you."

And there was no use sub-contracting out the maintenance of the Joys of Life to another firm. The best companies in the Amalgam had looked at the units and didn't know how they worked. Apparently the Morixi had a special technology no one knew about.

I sent a message to Joy to pack my bags for a long trip. When I got home, she was still in the same persona. She was sitting next to my bags, and she looked like she'd been crying. Crying! A robot doesn't cry!

"What's the matter?" It was obvious that I had to ask.

"Nothing." A lie.

Robots don't lie!

"Yes, there is, now tell me."

She started sobbing, "Well, you're just going off, and I don't know when you'll be back, and I don't know what I'll do with myself while you're away, and I don't know when to expect you."

I tried to calm her. My robot! I couldn't believe I was doing that! "Listen, I'll send you a message just as soon as I'm heading back. In the meantime, why don't you try to find out something about the Morixi for me? If you dig up anything, send it to me via my office." I leaned over and gave her a slobbery kiss goodbye.

So I went off Seeking the Morixi. And so far I've drawn a blank. My Seek has taken me further and further. I keep reporting back, and the suit is still active, but so far, nothing. My Seek has finally taken me to The StarBoard Café, and I'm leaving this "story" here in the hopes that someone can give me information regarding the Morixi. All information can be sent to the address embedded in this recording. All communications will be kept entirely confidential.

#

Charlie reached forward and pressed the Record button.

END RECORD

"Nice story, Charlie," the man sitting next to him at the bar spoke up.

"Bernie! Damn! Good work. I didn't even notice you there." It was a sign of a good professional if you could slip up to someone unnoticed. "What the hell are you doing here?" Charlie asked.

"Like you, I'm out on a job."

"Is it your usual? Matrimonial?"

"Yep."

"More power to you, friend, but you know I wouldn't touch those cases."

"You don't have the right outlook, Charlie. I'm filling a need. I always hope that I can wind up making people happier in their lives."

"Well, Bernie, I admire your dedication, but I'm afraid I can't stomach that end of the business."

"I guess that's the way things are, Charlie. While I'm here, let me buy you a drink."

"Well, thank you, partner." The wait-being slithered forward with the drinks. Charlie turned to Bernie, raised his glass in toast, and asked, "So what brings you this far afield?"

He paused and put down his glass. "You, Charlie."

"Me?"

"That's right."

"Bernie, you forget, you do matrimonial. I'm not involved in those things."

"You are now, Charlie. There's been some changes in the laws back home. The Joys of Life have a new status. They passed all of the relevant tests and had to be declared persons with all due legal rights."

"Okay, good. You can tell Joy she's free. She's an independent person. She can go her own way. She's got all sorts of prospects with her talents."

"It's not that easy, Charlie."

"Why isn't it?"

"There's child support involved."

"Child support? How could that be? She's just a construct that can change shape." A thought struck him. "Wait a minute, she was only supposed to use the semen for approved purposes, like selling it to fertility clinics or research labs."

"There's another thing that got changed in the laws."

"Okay, okay. If there's some money got to go for the kid, that's fine. I'll send it. What do I sign, Bernie?"

"We weren't looking for that sort of thing."

"What do you mean, 'we'?"

"I told you, Charlie, I'm doing a service here, a family service. She wants a reconciliation."

"A reconciliation? There hasn't been a separation. How could there be a reconciliation?"

Bernie looked up at Charlie. Their eyes locked for a moment. They both said together:

"New laws."

Bernie continued, "Got something else to tell you."

"What's that?"

"I'm not here alone, Charlie."

"You mean she's..." Charlie pointed to the floor, indicating the current location.

Bernie nodded solemnly.

Suddenly there was a commotion from the entrance to the Café. A toy car, about a foot long, zoomed into the room. It rattled and clattered its way across the floor. It was one of those things you'd expect to see in the control of some fat, sticky little brat with too many freckles. It zoomed down between the tables, came up to Charlie's stool, circled it twice, then paused, rearing up on its two back wheels. Its headlights blinked on and off twice at Charlie.

It said, "Hi, Daddy!"

Chapter 15

For Applause

hOrmonde de Mieneur leaned back and expelled a contented sigh after finishing a gourmet repast of Squiggles in Sand Sauce at the StarBoard Café. Eating such a large meal was quite an accomplishment for someone officially listed as deceased. However, since this status increased his stipend, he put the reports of his death down to vicious rumor--and investment strategy.

He didn't recall the individual sitting opposite him at the table. As a matter of fact, if pushed on the subject, he would have sworn that he'd sat down alone. Nevertheless, there was a creature sitting opposite him, beaming pleasantly. This individual was rather short, bald, pudgy, and sported a loosely-thrown-on garment that covered a portion of his green skin. A very odd being. Therefore he blended in perfectly with the rest of the clientele at the Café.

"It looks like you have finished a most prankish meal," the alien said. The way that the squiggles squiggled on the plate could be described as prankish.

"You know, I've already met the maître de this evening, and his dress was a little more formal than yours. The sommelier sported a few more appendages than you, so you can't be him. I'm going to assume that you're the pastry chef," hOrmonde said. Usually hOrmonde would have trotted out his acerbic temperament at the interloper. However, since it had been quite a delightful meal, he was willing to forego those unpleasantries for the sake of facilitating digestion. Also the creature opposite him aroused a feeling of bonhomie. Sprinkled into this mixture was a small amount of hope that he might actually *be* the pastry chef. hOrmonde had a particular dessert in mind with which he hoped to cap off the meal.

"It is best that one have a good meal before one embarks on a journey," the green creature said.

hOrmonde had been smiling at his table companion. However, the being's last remark caused his facial expression to freeze. "It seems that you have a far better understanding of my agenda than I do," hOrmonde said. "I don't recall having a journey planned."

"Ah, sometimes it is the unexpected that can be most intriguing and pleasant," the green alien said. "The pleasant part will be going someplace where we can get dessert. But I am being most rude. I should introduce myself. My name is Xixius."

#

The jar up on the counter of the galley of the *Chameleon* contained flowberry tarts, a particular favorite of Shar'n. The counter was beyond the physical reach of the three-year-old, but there were other kinds of reaches that were available to her. She began to concentrate.

Don't.

The hated word was not so much said as impressed on her brain. Anger and frustration started percolating inside her. She needed an outlet for these overflowing emotions. She searched for it back into the infinitely dim past, to a time when she was only two years old and perfecting the fine art of throwing tantrums. It wasn't right of Stella to make her stop doing a little prank when she had been tailored to be prankish. Her rage started to build. Due to affinities dating back to the womb, her ire infected both her co-siblings, Kar'n and Aar'n. The storm of emotion was mounting and starting to crest.

"Now what's up?" their mother asked. Mommy didn't have the acute extra-sensory perceptions that her children possessed, but knew her children well enough and recognized rage rising in triplicate when she saw it.

"'Tella won't let me do anythin'!" Shar'n wailed.

Stella appropriately rolled her eyes and glanced at her twin,

Connor, for support. "She was trying to get to the--"

"--flowberry tarts," Xixius finished as he abruptly entered the galley of the *Chameleon*.

"The very thing I had in mind!" hOrmonde exclaimed, entering on the alien's heels.

"Uncle Xixius! Uncle Xixius!" was the shout from the children. Actually, it was about 40 percent of the previous, or two out of five; the other 60 percent was more like "Unc' Di'dus!" Fran Holcombe, otherwise known as Mommy, stared in open disapproval at the entrants to her kitchen.

The noise also attracted the attention of the *Chameleon*'s captain, Randy Holcombe, who entered the galley. "We seem to have company," he said to his wife, missing the fact that he was stating the obvious. Then Randy turned and stared at Xixius. "Why am I not surprised to see you, even though there's no explanation as to how you got here?" Because he expected surprises out of Xixius, he only glanced at hOrmonde, without commenting on the stranger's presence.

The number of people in the galley increased as someone else arrived.

It was Randy Holcombe. Again. This one came from the opposite direction. "Honey, I'm home," he said.

Randy Holcombe #1 turned to Randy Holcombe #2, and said, "Cammie, cut it out."

"Don't send Cammie away," Mrs. Holcombe said to her husband. "Xixius is around. I may want to sleep with that version of you. Otherwise, I don't know what number of children I'll wind up carrying." She glanced around at her five offspring.

hOrmonde spoke up, "I can't tell you how delighted I am to watch all of this absolutely fascinating domestic bliss, but the only reason I came here is because I was promised some flowberry tarts."

"Ah, yes," Xixius said, "Mrs. Holcombe makes the most delicious of those."

The three youngest children were chanting "F'owberry

tarts!" while their siblings tried to maintain their cool, but couldn't keep themselves from looking hopeful. Flowberry tarts were Fran's specialty.

Fran threw her hands up in surrender. "I just happen to have a new batch. Let me dish them out," She said to Xixius. "We might as well have something to eat while you explain what the hell you're doing here."

"Could somebody please explain to me this Shakespearean mistaken identity over here?" asked hOrmonde, indicating the two Mr. Holcombes.

"Ah, yes, This one--" Xixius said, indicating Randy #2, "--is the Artificial Intelligence for the ship, his name is Cammie."

"And he likes to play dress-up," Randy #1 said.

"This is sheer ambrosia!" hOrmonde said, upon taking his first taste of the tarts. "Madam, I would ask you to marry me if you didn't already appear to be both wed and deplorably fertile."

"Only when I'm around my little green friend," said Mrs. Holcombe as she tried to maintain distance from both Xixius and Randy. Just in case.

"Well, I will just have to dog your footsteps trying to spy out what other culinary delights you can produce," said hOrmonde.

"Then you'll have to follow her all the way to a planet called Arsend," Xixius said. "It's in the center of the galaxy."

Everyone stared at Xixius, wondering where he was taking them this time.

#

The center of the galaxy was continuing to display its similarity to a center-city ghetto.

A large number of space ships were piled up in a traffic jam, because they had been forced to drop out of n-drive due to repairs of the wormholes in the area. They had become riddled with time warps (similar to a pothole only taking up several more dimensions).

A number of planets were doing their best to drop into the

gravity well of their star so they could be slung out to a spiral arm that developers were constructing out at the extreme edge of the galaxy.

In the meantime the Delta Epsilon Mu photonic fraternity was taunting the Phi Kappa Gammas by turning the dark side of their planet's satellite toward them.

This is the derivation of the term "mooning."

#

Meanwhile the planet Arsend was gaining popularity among a number of citizens of the Amalgam of Intelligent Beings, not necessarily for the exotic particles whizzing through its atmosphere, but for another reason.

There was treasure to be found, or that was the rumor. On the other hand, there are always rumors circulating about. As a matter of fact, on the planet Grapevine, the entire world's economy is based on the ebb and flow of rumors that travel the galaxy. The planet's residents manage to make a lot of money at it, generating a wide and varied product line.

The rumor about Arsend circulated through the StarBoard Café (an extremely large client of Grapevine). This particular piece of Scuttlebutt (one of the more popular product lines of the rumor planet) had to do with the treasure that was lost when the freighter *Flimsy* crashed somewhere near the galactic core. Talk filtered down about maps that pointed the way to caches of great treasures.

That caught *El Escorpion's* attention. He should have been satisfied with the large reward he had gained when he captured a whole bunch of truly nasty aliens on the planet he called *Urth*. However *El Escorpion* was a spacer, therefore given over to fits of raging greed. That dovetailed in with his greedy habit of feasting on tasty snacks creeping out the cracks in the wall.

This time he greedied (that was a verb in the spacer patois) because there was new information that detailed the location of the world where the *Flimsy* had crashed. The planet had been lost when it was pulled off its original orbit to circle around another star. There was new information about the planet's location that someone was willing to sell to the right bidder. Since the only bidders for this information were spacers, more than likely the data would be beaten out of the being who possessed this information. However, the creature who bore that knowledge was a Jargwa, and Jargwas *like* that sort of thing. They purposely seek out information, just so it *can* be beaten out of them. There was some sort of relationship between the punishment and the Jargwa's ability to procreate.

El Escorpion was confirming information with his associate. "Do you have a cruiser we can use to get to the core of the galaxy?" he asked.

"I most certainly do," said Mizrak.

El Escorpion was aware that his associate had spent such a long time being a spacer that he was physically unable to answer a direct question truthfully. "Then do you know of one we can 'borrow' from somebody?" he asked.

"I would never think of something like that," Mizrak responded.

"Can you get around the ship's security?"

"Absolutely not."

"Good. Let's go."

#

"These perfidious little vermin can't be stamped out!" Vardak raged. He was cursing the fates that had led him to the humans. He had acquired the stewardship of the race when he had opened up their planet for export of various soporifics. They had received so much technology in payment for the goods, they qualified for membership in the Amalgam of Intelligent Beings. With Vardak as their sponsor.

Vardak was raging because the humans had done it again. They'd opened up something called a resort, named Club Hedon, on the oceanfront on the planet of Piety. The inhabitants, the Pioutous, were outraged. The natives had strict rules about gender comingling. They separated their two sexes at birth and kept them isolated from each other. Therefore the two continents on their planet were called Male and Female. (That was the translation. Actually the words in their language were more like The One and The Other.) The antics at the Club Hedon were quite shocking to the locals, particularly when the club's Happy Hour coincided with the native's Blushing Hour. The Pioutous were lodging complaints with Vardak, the responsible party for the humans.

Additionally the Hedonists, the residents of the planet Hedon, were suing Vardak for copyright infringement of their planet's name. They were trying to bundle this suit with the other one they were filing relative to the mission that had been set up on their planet by some human named Sister Mary. Rumor had it that this woman was preaching to the locals that if they didn't mend their ways they would have to jump off a cliff with all the other miscreants. (Rumor was such a faulty product of the planet Grapevine that it would soon be recalled for manufacturing flaws.)

Vardak's single brow contracted over its prominent ridge. He was a desperate being. He needed something to recoup all of his losses. If that scuttlebutt he had managed to beat out of the Jargwa was true, he could put a serious dent in the debts that were piling up.

He had to go to the planet Arsend.

\#

The Worst Unknown Assassin had heard of a possible rumor that might be true about someone who perhaps knew about him and was therefore out to get him. That wouldn't do. That creature had to be eliminated. That creature's name was hOrmonde de Mieneur.

Since hOrmonde was headed to the planet Arsend, the Worst Unknown Assassin headed that way.

\#

All of the beings who were heading to the planet Arsend were missing the event of the year: the announcement of the winner of the yearly prize for the best story in the competition at the StarBoard Café. To maintain a non-partisan atmosphere in the selection process, the judges had been ensconced in a heavily fortified asteroid in an unknown location. It had been rather a serene stay for them this year. Only a dozen armed attacks had been launched at them by entrants who were looking to curry favor with the decision makers. The judges were now being escorted to the Café for the announcement by a heavily armed armada of battle cruisers.

Spacers had thronged to the Café for this festivity. The emotional level had reached a fever pitch, as the patrons of the StarBoard prepared themselves for the post-awards celebration. This would be a Big-Bang-like explosion of fights, fisticuffs, tentacle-chokes, pincer-grabs, back-stabs, brawls, melees, revolutions, feuds, vendettas, poison pen letters (with real poison), fireworks, explosions, fusillades, and just the general outpouring of spacer high jinx in the celebration of another year passed.

Many bets had been made about the winner of this year's award. So spacers were all prepared to collect their winnings, pay off their losses, or more likely, welch.

More creatures were attending the StarBoard than they did any other night. However, using a technology no one understood, the Café was able to do a little bit of space- and dimension-warping to become absolutely mammoth to accommodate the crowd.

Finally, the moment had arrived. The Chief Judge advanced to the lectern and pulled out the envelope and announced the winner.

At the pronouncement of the winner's name such a collective "Huh?" went up from the masses that an actual, sixth-dimensional question mark hung over the crowd for a good ten seconds. Who was this winner? Where did he come from? How did he get that single name?

A secure transport system had immediately located him at the far end of the Café and brought him and his two companions to the lectern in a protective force field. When the award was brought forward to hand to the winner, there was an additional prize attached: the keys to a small star cruiser.

It was programmed to head to the planet Arsend.

#

Philosophers have long argued about what is Truth.

Physicists have long argued about what is Real.

For Qemmering Quince, Reality and Truth were what he chose them to be. Since he was here, he was Truth; but since he had died, he was no longer Real. This paradox caused him to ponder the two Ultimates. His expostulations had managed to produce for him several levels of Truth and a whole slew of Realities.

He meandered down the aisles of his Truth and Reality. Whether he had company on his stroll depends on what one considers to be Real and True.

One thing was true: his aisles of Truth and Reality were located on the planet Arsend.

#

The planet itself was in bad need of a Visitors Bureau. It was going to experience an influx of many beings.

The *Chameleon* headed toward it with all seven members of the Holcombe family, plus Cammie, the AI. They were augmented by Xixius and hOrmonde de Mineur.

hOrmonde had assumed command. Randy Holcombe bore the honorific of Captain and was allowed to oversee Cammie in the navigation and operation of the craft. Nevertheless hOrmonde assumed the role of leadership through royal proclamation, his own.

M. de Mieneur believed his firm hand on the helm had the crew responding properly to his commands. However, he was quite at a loss when it came to the children. These junior people made hOrmonde nervous. They had a very simplistic outlook on life, one that permitted them to see through a number of things, and that included hOrmonde. No small task, considering his girth.

Being quartered in the smaller staterooms on the *Chameleon* did not upset hOrmonde as much as it might have. Among her many talents, Mrs. Holcombe was an excellent chef, so the fare onboard was first rate. Diplomat de Mieneur could be satisfied if he was properly fed.

In the meantime, Xixius, the green alien, wandered around with a contented smile on his face and proclaimed practically everything to be "prankish."

\#

El Escorpion's ship made its way toward Arsend.

Well, technically, it wasn't *El Escorpion's* ship. It belonged to Fleeb the Frigid, but possession had passed over to *El Escorpion*. It had taken some adjustment to get the life support system to warm up from the settings that Fleeb liked, but it was doing quite well, if you overlooked the icy residue that dotted the inside of the ship.

The frigid temperature made *El Escorpion's* feel quite uncomfortable. He was used to a very warm and dry environment similar to his home planet. At least Fleeb had not been an aquatic alien. *El Escorpion* would absolutely quail at such inhospitable environments as those things called oceans.

\#

Vardak raced toward Arsend in both an attempt to find the treasure and to escape from the creditors who dogged his trail. He patted the armaments he had donned after leaving the StarBoard. His irritation made him itch to use the weapons on someone, anyone.

\#

The Worst Unknown Assassin was traveling under stealth mode, of course, as he headed to Arsend. He always traveled under stealth mode. He paced the cabin of the ship as it flew on auto pilot, jittering back and forth in a nervous frenzy across the cabin, acting like the princess lying on a hundred mattresses with a single pea beneath them. There was something askew, and he couldn't stand it. Through some piece of manufacturing bungling, the Flange Tension indicator light on the control panel was 1.326 picometers out of line with the rest of the indicator lights in its row. He had unsuccessfully tried to get it to line up, hammering and bashing at it, but to no avail. This sort of thing hadn't happened in his last ship. It was too bad he'd had to desert it. However someone might trace its ownership back to him and therefore be out to get him.

\#

Qemmering Quince was putting the finishing touches on

The Agony of Mirdzep, an inspiring new creation. He wondered whether it was the original Qemmering Quince's creation or his own.

Since he'd created *The Agony,* he must be Truth. But since Qemmering was dead, he couldn't be Reality.

He would have to construct some new Reality where he did exist.

\#

hOrmonde was not impressed with Arsend. He could see nothing but dirt and a great number of rocks scattered about.

He was mistaken. They weren't really rocks. The local flora and fauna had found themselves living next to a photonic frat house. They were subjected to continual bombardments of strange radioactive rays falling out of the skies, something like having particles shaped like beer cans tossed into their yards. The native life forms had adapted by growing a protective hard outer shell that made them look like rocks. What hOrmonde thought was a number of volcanic ejecta surrounding him had originally been something similar to wisteria.

Diplomat de Mieneur had a sinking feeling when he did not find the planet listed in the AAA book (Amalgam Autochef Association). He was quite certain he wasn't going to find a five-star restaurant with a proper wine cellar. hOrmonde was patting himself on the back for having thought of bringing Fran along so they would at least have a proper chef with them on this backside, backwater planet.

He wondered mildly about the green chap who had tagged along. He seemed to have some idea of why hOrmonde needed to come to this dreary place. M. de Mieneur puzzled over why he trusted the alien's judgment.

\#

He had to remain the Worst Unknown Assassin. If any of the life forms on Arsend saw him, he had to get rid of them. Otherwise they'd be out to get him. The place was terribly messy, with all sorts of rocks scattered about in a random manner, (They were actually opossums and forget-me-nots.) He didn't know if he could stomach the disorder. He'd have to straighten out this clutter once he had properly secured the planet (got rid of everybody). The major thing on his agenda was to find this de Mieneur person and destroy him.

#

The winner of the storytelling contest of the StarBoard Café sat in his star cruiser as it made its way to Arsend. He didn't know it was heading to that planet, but he had known, just *known*, that this extra award for winning the contest was the answer to his lifelong quest. He looked at his two companions and marveled that they had remained loyal to him.

#

Arsend was chilly. The weather had recently shifted when the planet had been dragged out of its most recent orbit around a yellow giant, lured into the gravity field of a red dwarf. Bloody rays slanted down from the new solar center. In the continuing march into urban decay, the entire planet was changing into a red light district.

The practice of planet swapping occurred much more frequently in the galactic core. The worlds would perambulate from one star to another, rather like troublesome children being shuttled between foster parents. The current orbital status of Arsend was going to be short-lived, in a galactic sense, only a few hundred million years, before both star and planet would be sucked into a black hole.

"Did anybody see us when we landed here?" asked *El Escorpion*.

"A whole bunch of people," Mizrak answered.

"Good." *El Escorpion* looked around. "Do you have any leads on the treasure?"

"Lots of them."

"Well, something'll turn up."

#

"This planet is an abomination," hOrmonde said. "The natives could all qualify for a vid show called *Guess My Species*. The landscape is like the dunes of Darapia, although not as balmy. And the food is survival rations gone bad. Can someone tell me why in the Big Bang we have chosen to come to this dump?" He directed that last to Xixius who was standing there smiling at him, as usual.

"It's because we must go the Hills of Lost Dreams," said the Xirom.

#

Aar'n and Kar'n were having a conversation. The fact that they were out of voice range posed no problem.

"What was it Unc' D'idus told us?" Aar'n asked

"We're supposed to make sure that everybody drops all of their toys," Kar'n replied. "That won't be hard."

"There's something else" Aar'n said.

"It's got to do with the Lonely One," Kar'n said.

"We're supposed to do something with him."

"What is it?"

"Oh, that's right, we're supposed to turn him over to the other fellas. What're they called?" Aar'n asked.

"I know," Shar'n chimed in. "The Good Guys."

Xixius had been quite right in giving these rather vague tasks to three year olds. Their uncomplicated minds knew that somewhere along the way, people would have to drop their toys. Then they'd find the Lonely One. And he would have to be somewhere near the Good Guys.

#

The two Holy Men sat in contemplation in The Hills of Lost Dreams.

They were definitely Holy Men, even though they were not human. Nor were they the same species. One was lizard-like, whose upright posture left a long tail trailing behind him. The other's physique was dominated by a number of tentacles in a rainbow of colors that writhed from the top of his carapace.

They had arrived on Arsend from Megalm, Xixius's home planet. The knew that they would find some task that would require their attention.

#

Vardak surveyed the Big-Bang-forsaken planet around him. "If I could figure out how to herd all of the human vermin onto this Infinity-forsaken planet, I could quarantine them here. It would be no less than they deserve," Vardak hissed past his formidable teeth. He was not in a good mood, but he hadn't been in a good mood since the humans had started all their high jinks.

He suddenly saw a group of creatures walking down the trail below him. Except for the green creature, they were all the bothersome humans.

He stroked the weaponry mounted on his body and followed after the creatures toward their destination: The Hills of Lost Dreams.

#

"Have you asked for someplace where the treasure could be found?" asked *El Escorpion*.

"Not at all," replied Mizrak.

"Good. What's the least likely place you've found?"

"The Hills of Lost Dreams."

"Then we'll head there."

#

The cruiser had landed on Arsend. The winner of the storytelling contest of the StarBoard Café stared at message that had come up on the control panel. It said, *GO TO THE HILLS OF LOST DREAMS.*

The winner turned to his female companion. "Is this where we find the Wistrani?" he asked her.

#

The sheer randomness of his surroundings was painful to the Worst Unknown Assassin. There were rocks strewn all over the hillside in a totally disorganized manner (a herd of buffalo). The very next thing he would have to do is straighten out this mess. But first he had to get rid of all of the creatures that had gathered at the Hills of Lost Dreams. The ones closest to him appeared ready to ambush a group of the others. Good, that would reduce the number he'd have to get rid of.

Not far away, the triplets waited. They saw people with toys.

#

Vardak's dark lips curled into a wicked sneer as he looked down at the party in the valley approaching the Hills of Lost Dreams. There were three humans there, a mated pair and a plump one. They were accompanied by some strange construct that appeared to be human. The other member of the party was a green, human-like thing who seemed to be happy about everything. They couldn't be up to any good. He began to select the proper weapon from his formidable collection of arms.

Stella, Fran's oldest daughter, sidled up behind him.

#

"Do you know these people?" *El Escorpion* asked Mizrak. They were across the way from Vardak, looking down on the party from the *Chameleon*.

"Every one of them," was the response.

"Well, let's introduce ourselves," *El Escorpion* said as he drew his powerful weapon. A spacer's first words of introduction were usually lethal projectiles.

Connor, Stella's twin, sidled behind them.

#

As the group from the *Chameleon* had traveled toward the Hills of Lost Dreams, the countryside changed. It had started with individual holograms scattered along the path, looking incongruous against the backdrop of Arsend's bleak landscape. Then vid games began to appear, increasing in concentration as the group progressed. Other displays had grown up, not so much games as interactive epics and dramas. When hOrmonde and company made their way into the central valley of the Hills of Lost Dreams, they were confronted by a cacophony of entertainments laid out in rough aisles before them. It was the wreckage of the *Flimsy*.

"By the infinite stretches of creation, these are absolutely gorgeous," hOrmonde exclaimed. As a patron of the arts, the diplomat recognized great works when he saw them. Fran, Randy, Cammie, and Xixius also gazed about in wonder.

While they looked at the games ranked around them, a creature wandered out of one of the aisles deeper in the valley. Although only about a hundred feet distance from the crew of the Chameleon, this individual occupied a Reality several galaxies away. The newcomer's proprietary attitude about the games identified him as their keeper. He eyed the group from the *Chameleon* with a disconnected look on his face, and turned to the holo next to him, a scene out of *Time Swindler*, pointed and said, "Look at how unreal they appear. Whoever created them paid no attention to detail. They're so bizarre! Such life forms aren't possible. How could they live?"

hOrmonde stared at the newcomer. He was used to meeting some peculiar species in his job, but this one's detachment from reality ranked at the high end of the peculiarity scale.

His thoughts were interrupted by the appearance of a creature who scuttled out from behind a rock. He pointed a weapon at the crew from the *Chameleon*. "If everyone cooperates, we won't have any trouble," *El Escorpion* said. "And don't think you can circle around behind me. I've got someone covering you from behind. Right?"

"I've got them in my sights," Mizrak replied. They only had one weapon between them, so Mizrak sighted down his index finger.

"My good fellow, what do you want?" hOrmonde asked.

"We've come for the treasure," *El Escorpion* said, menacing the group with his weapon.

"So have I," Vardak said as he loomed up to his full nine-foot height from behind a rock. He swept his weapon back and forth to cover both the crew from the *Chameleon* and the two other spacers. *El Escorpion* adjusted to bring Vardak into his range of fire. Mizrak imitated their actions with his weaponless clawed digit.

"I would suggest that you drop your weapon," Vardak warned *El Escorpion*.

"Why should I?" *El Escorpion* asked. "Remember that there

are two of us."

Vardak looked over at Mizrak, who was waving his digit about, and then gave a reproving glance back at *El Escorpion*. "I think I have a few more armaments than you." Which was true.

El Escorpion glared at Vardak. Vardak sneered at *El Escorpion*. At any moment they were about to unload their weapons against each other.

At that moment, Stella and Connor appeared behind the two combatants, fixing them with deep and penetrating stares. As the twins stared at the two combatants, the facial expressions on the spacers began to change. A momentary quizzical look was replaced by a grimace of pain. Both *El Escorpion* and Vardak dropped their weapons, and Vardak began to strip himself of all of his other armaments. Mizrak felt a burning sensation at the end of his digit.

Vardak finally divested himself of his weapons, some of which glowed a cherry red. Stella and Connor gave nods of satisfaction and faded into the background.

Vardak glared at his incandescent weapons, then turned himself toward the humans in the group pulling himself up to his entire height. "This is all the doing of you stinking humans," he bellowed. "You're nothing but the muck decorating the rear end of a Mornian festering swamp slug!"

hOrmonde compared the proportions of this creature to his own. This brought to the forefront of his mind the fact that he had been trained for diplomacy. He attempted to appease the giant. "Yes, my dear sir, I daresay there may be some grievances that you wish to discuss before the proper authorities."

"We're here for the treasure, and it's ours," *El Escorpion* complained as he blew on his hands.

"And what would that treasure be?" hOrmonde inquired.

"I don't know," said *El Escorpion*.

"I see." hOrmonde turned to Mizrak. "Do you know where it is?"

"Of course."

"Then where is it?" hOrmonde continued.

"That's someplace secret," Mizrak responded.

"Is it here?"

"No."

"Then what are you doing here?" hOrmonde decided to test this hairy little creature once more.

"I'm on vacation," was the response.

hOrmonde stared at him for a moment. "From your reason, no doubt," he responded. He looked about the group trying to gather some order together from what appeared to be heaps of chaos. He finally reached a decision and clapped his hands together and rubbed them against each other. "Well, we certainly seem to have a difference of opinion here." His glance landed on Mizrak. "In some cases, a difference of reality."

"It doesn't matter what you may think," roared Vardak, "I claim the treasure and the land it's on."

"What do you mean?" *El Escorpion* retorted. "We were here first, and claim it by the rights that we purchased from the original owner."

"Who was this original owner?" Vardak demanded. He had decided to take the offensive. He couldn't remember the name of the Jarqwa he'd beaten the information out of.

Neither could *El Escorpion*, so in a moment of panic, he asked Mizrak a question he hadn't properly framed. "You remember his name, don't you?"

"Of course I do," replied Mizrak.

"What is it?" *El Escorpion* went a question too far.

"His name is *El Escorpion*."

El Escorpion waved off the answer. "Who he is doesn't matter. The treasure's still mine."

"I claim it," Vardak bellowed. The two disputants glared at each other and checked to see if their weapons had cooled enough to be picked up.

"Lots of claims and counterclaims," Fran commented. "Exactly what is it that you're laying title to?"

Vardak decided to drop some of his secrecy. "The treasure from the wreck of the *Flimsy*."

"It's mine!" *El Escorpion* exclaimed.

hOrmonde looked at the disputants. "In my official capacity as diplomat, I could certainly help you. I would be happy to point you in the right direction when we get back to civilization. I could probably gather together all of the proper forms to file with the local Amalgam offices."

"But that's a long way away," Fran pointed out. "It looks like we need to settle something right here."

"But what can we do?" hOrmonde asked. Nobody seemed to have any ideas.

Except for one being. "Ah, in the case of sovereignty and shipwreck claims that need to be settled at the site under question, they could also have a special hearing with a diplomatic representative. That is stated in by-law 4.2806-B-a^7."

Everyone stopped as this flood of information washed over them. It had to have a source. They turned in the direction of the speaker and stared. It was Xixius.

The Xirom continued with a shrug. "Or so I've been told."

hOrmonde decided to check this information with his pocket digi-file. As he did, Stella and Connor walked over to the group. Fran said, "There you are, I was just going to ask you..."

"We're going to look for Aar'n, Kar'n, and Shar'n," they said.

"... to go look for the triplets," Fran tailed off. It unnerved her when they spoke in unison. "What a wonderful idea," she said wanly. She felt she should worry that the three-year-olds were without supervision, but she knew that her offspring were quite capable of taking care of themselves.

"I've never seen this by-law before," hOrmonde grumbled over his digi-file. "Well, I guess we can resolve things right here." He looked around at the group, tried to figure out some way to formalize the proceedings, so he settled down on a nearby rock to officiate. hOrmonde began, "All right, we will start with the..."

"Oyez, oyez, oyez. Here, here, here. Humina, humina, humina." Cammie had transformed himself into a High Grand Interlocutor from the planet Litigia. "The court is now in session. Put your appendages together for the great, high and mighty, lovely and talented, diplomat, M. hOrmonde de Mieneur."

M. de Mieneur's patience was tried. He looked down at the ground and gently patted his hand on his thigh. "Cammie," he said, "Do you happen to know what powers I can wield in my position?"

Cammie shook his mouthpiece--he was still an interlocutor.

"Well, let me tell you," hOrmonde continued, "I could decide that a certain piece of equipment was not functioning properly and condemn it for spare parts."

"Cammie," Captain Holcombe said, coming to his rescue, "why don't you head back to the ship and get some refreshments for everyone?"

"I'd be just delighted to do that," Cammie replied as he smiled sweetly at hOrmonde.

At that moment the games' Caretaker wandered over and perused the AI. "Now, this one begins to have a certain reality to him, not like those others. His creator shows some promise."

Cammie cast one confused glance at the speaker and retreated back toward the ship.

"Now, where was I?" hOrmonde refocused his attention. "Ah, yes, we were settling some sort of grievances that all of you gentlebeings had. Especially that very pleasant fellow who towers over me." hOrmonde indicated Vardak. "Could somebody please explain to me the nature of the disagreement?"

"You're all a bunch of filthy vermin!" Vardak bellowed.

"Mmm-hmmm," hOrmonde concurred. He always agreed with anyone as large as Vardak. "Shall I take that to be your opening statement?"

Vardak growled.

"Very well, then," hOrmonde made the mistake of turning to

Mizrak next. "And what is the nature of your grievance?"

"I don't have one," Mizrak lied.

"I see," hOrmonde said, "and what are you doing here?"

"I'm not here."

hOrmonde paused, taking a long look at Mizrak. "I see," he said, stared a bit longer, and then turned to *El Escorpion*. "You're with him?"

"Yes, I am," *El Escorpion* replied.

"You're together?" hOrmonde glanced at Mizrak, looking for confirmation.

"No, we're not."

hOrmonde's glance bounced between *El Escorpion* and Mizrak, as though he were watching a tennis match. He abruptly turned back to Vardak. "And what brings you to this delightful planet, my friend?"

"You've made me a pauper!" Vardak said. Considering that Vardak had arrived in his own starcruiser, he was obviously speaking in relative terms.

"I'm terribly sorry," hOrmonde placated. "Is that the reason why you came here?"

"It was to find the treasure," Vardak said.

"And did you come here to find the treasure?" hOrmonde asked *El Escorpion*.

"Yes," *El Escorpion* responded.

"And that's why you're here?" hOrmonde asked Mizrak.

"I'm not here."

"Yes, I'd forgotten that," hOrmonde concurred. "Well, then we're all in agreement that we're here to find the treasure."

The others muttered assent except for Mizrak, who disagreed.

"And what is this treasure?" hOrmonde asked.

"I don't know," said Vardak.

"I don't know," said *El Escorpion*.

"I'm not telling," said Mizrak. He didn't know either.

"Where did you hear about this treasure?" hOrmonde asked.

"It's a family heirloom," Mizrak answered.

"The StarBoard Café," *El Escorpion* said.

"The StarBoard Café," Vardak said.

"The StarBoard Café," hOrmonde repeated, nodding, regretting having asked the previous question. The diplomat was aware of the Café's status as a rumor mill. "You're looking for a treasure on this Big-Bang-gone-wrong planet here in the slums of the galaxy?" hOrmonde summarized.

"Yes."

"Yes."

"No."

"Perhaps we can get on a better footing if we were to introduce ourselves. My name is hOrmonde de Mieneur, Diplomat, Emissary, and Ambassador First Class, and—oh, yes, there's something else: deceased. However, the latter is a mere technicality." He turned to *El Escorpion*. "And who are you, sir?"

"*El Escorpion*, freelance private contractor," he replied.

"Now that you've mentioned it, I do seem to recall your being the center of a lot of, well, social activity at the StarBoard Café." hOrmonde turned to Mizrak. "Who are you, sir?"

"I don't know," Mizrak replied.

"Oh, that's right! And you're not here, either." hOrmonde turned to Vardak. "And you, sir?"

"I am the most cursed of all the craven, credit-pinching, slime-dealing hucksters who let his own greed overreach his sensibilities. I am the Kermernorjer Vardak."

"You, sir? You're the being who uplifted the human race? You are Protector Vardak?" hOrmonde asked.

"Creation protect *me* from you vermin and your troublemaking!" Vardak raged.

hOrmonde was distracted by the games' Caretaker, who had wandered up to stare intently at him. "And might I ask who or what you are, sir?" he asked.

"The interaction is very crude," the being supplied by way of answer. "By this point in the game there should be a logical relationship between the character and the player."

"What a coincidence," hOrmonde said. "I've been trying to find a logical relationship since I got here. I was trying to find out why you're here."

"What arcane protocols you have," the Caretaker dithered.

hOrmonde laid a large smile on his face to compensate for the aggravation inside. "Why don't we start with your name, please?"

"Oh, very well. Qemmering Quince."

hOrmonde paused in shock. "Qemmering Quince, the artist? That's impossible. He's dead."

"Yes. But so are you," Qemmering countered.

"Point taken," hOrmonde conceded, "but that's only a diplomatic tactic. You were eulogized and cremated. You can't be real."

"But I stand before you," Qemmering said.

"What are you? Some sort of avatar?" hOrmonde asked.

"I'm real," the artist said, "I have my Reality."

"So do we all," hOrmonde admitted. "At least your presence explains all of these holo games."

"Yes, I brought most of them here," Qemmering said.

"*Most* of them?" hOrmonde inquired.

"Yes."

"Where did the rest come from?" the diplomat asked.

"I made them."

"Your--" hOrmonde searched for a word, "--precursor created a copy of himself?"

"Yes."

"How?" asked *El Escorpion*.

hOrmonde turned to the spacer. "Given Mr. Quince's--the original Mr. Quince, that is--given his abilities, he probably could have had his personality downloaded, creating a self-perpetuating version of himself." He turned back to the artist. "How did you get here?"

"On the *Flimsy*," he answered.

"This is the treasure?" *El Escorpion* asked.

"Of course, it's the treasure. The last creations of Qemmering Quince, the great designer, they're worth a fortune," hOrmonde said. "What can be done about them?"

"They're ours!" Mizrak, *El Escorpion* and Vardak all shouted together.

"I would venture, my good friends, that all of this really belongs to this version of Mr. Quince, whatever it might be."

"Yes," Xixius chimed in, "but to leave him here, with no one knowing about him, is like putting a great painting in an empty gallery. These works of art should be seen by the rest of the Amalgam."

"That's true enough. We can't just leave it in the hands of Mr. Quince."

"What can be done?" Randy asked.

Xixius said, "What we need are some entrepreneurs who could manage a venture like this."

hOrmonde stared for a moment at the Xirom, then cast a sly glance at the three spacers before him. "This is a very complex operation considering all of the income it would generate." Covetousness flooded the faces of the spacers. "I don't know if it could be handled by an individual. Perhaps if an organization could present itself that offered multiple talents…"

The three spacers cast distrustful glances at each other. The thought came to their minds that there was a particular commercial venture they might be able to tailor this place after. That venture was called the StarBoard Café.

At that moment Stella and Connor returned to the group from the area of the games, whose features they'd been admiring.

"Where are the triplets?" Fran asked her older children.

"They should be along in a little while," the twins responded.

Fran restrained herself from running off to find her

youngest.

"But what about the blasted humans? They'll suck up all my profits," Vardak wailed.

"Oh, they are a most prankish race. They make the Xirom's thurtles wobble," Xixius said.

""They're nothing but meddling little walking monkeys who cause problems wherever they go," Vardak moaned." And they're all my responsibility."

"You wish to be unburdened of them?" Xixius asked.

"If only I could rid myself of the meddling primates!"

"Ah! This offers a most prankish possibility. Perhaps the Xirom could take over sponsorship of them?" Xixius offered.

hOrmonde scoffed. "Don't be silly, my green friend, you Xirom are a protected race, not even uplifted into the Amalgam yourselves. How could you sponsor another race that already has membership?"

"Why, Mr. dead-but-walking diplomat, if you look in your digi-file, I'm sure that you will find under section C6 that there is an exception granted on this very point," Xixius said.

"That's impossible!" hOrmonde said.

"It's been my experience that you should believe him," Randy Holcombe offered, staring intently at Xixius.

hOrmonde looked from the Xirom to the Captain then returned his gaze to Xixius and stared at him. He flipped open his digi-file and confirmed the entry. He cast a long stare at Xixius, whose talents he'd seen displayed ever since he finished his dinner at the Café.

He suddenly nodded his head in decision, looked around at everyone else, and said three simple words: "So be it."

The Xirom had become the sponsors of humanity.

Vardak bellowed in exultation.

"I believe this ends the formal hearings," hOrmonde said, superfluously, since no one was paying any attention to him anymore.

Vardak, *El Escorpion*, and Mizrak gathered around

Qemmering Quince and began detailing plans for their new enterprise.

Cammie returned from the ship. He was bringing something that would have had hOrmonde halting the meeting anyway, a mid-afternoon repast of flowberry tarts.

Xixius said to hOrmonde, "The tart is most delicious, but perhaps you should try the fruit of the Xitus tree."

"It's found on your planet?" hOrmonde asked, casting an appraising look at the Xirom.

"Yes."

hOrmonde nodded. "That sounds like a good idea. I think it would be most interesting to visit your home world."

Xixius gave an enigmatic smile. "It is most prankish."

Everyone's gaze suddenly shifted around as someone new appeared in the valley. It was the winner of the Starboard Café's storytelling contest. He looked around at everyone in the group. He spied Xixius and walked up to him. "I'm looking for you," he said.

"Why would you be looking for me?" the Xirom asked.

"Because you are a member of the Wistrani," Poison stated.

"How prankish!" Xixius replied. "The Wistrani have disappeared. No one knows where they are."

Kowana stepped forward to join Poison, her eyes fixed on Xixius in suspicion. "I can't tell what his emotions are."

"Gentlebeing, what is your name?" Xixius asked Poison.

He snorted ruefully. "It's Poison."

"No. What is your birth name?"

"I can't tell you," Poison replied.

"Why not?" Xixius persisted.

"Because it will only come out as electronic hash."

"Are you so sure?" Xixius asked.

"Yes."

"Why don't you try telling me?"

Poison shared a glance with Kowana and sighed in

resignation. "Okay, if you need the proof, it's Artemis Mender." His eyes registered shock as the words came out unscrambled. He shared a startled glance with Kowana, who reached a hand up to his shoulder.

In the meantime Poison's other companion, Fido, had casually strolled over to Xixius, snuffling along the way. When he reached the Xirom, his snuffling intensified, as he absorbed the multiple odors that were there.

"Why did I come here?" Artemis asked. "I've been to several different planets. I changed the local beings. I always found you there. Why couldn't I have just gone home?"

"You must do one other thing," Xixius said. He walked over to the avatar of Qemmering Quince and led him forward to Artemis. "You must touch one other creature."

Artemis locked eyes with the Xirom for a moment, reached up to his wrist, and flipped something invisible off his hand. He stepped forward to the avatar and placed his hand on his.

A bright flash shot out from Qemmering Quince. When the light had diminished the creature stood there, smiling. "There are many Truths, and they interact with the many Realities. I have many more works to make on this world. I'll have to explain to my three friends what we will do here." He turned toward the three spacers with determination.

At that moment, something flashed across the sky, passing over Artemis. Everyone else thought it was some local bird. However, Artemis recognized it. It was the computer that he had met on Floria, the planet where he'd acquired his infectious touch. Across his body, he felt the covering he'd worn all these years slip away and disintegrate.

"What's happening?" Artemis brushed his hands across his exposed skin. "I don't have a barrier on my touch."

"The only barrier that exists is now in your mind, my good friend Artemis."

"What do you mean?"

Xixius smiled. "You have had much experience converting other creatures to their best form. You can now decide to turn on your touch whenever you decide. And since you know what form creatures should really be, that will help your decision. Plus, you have someone who knows what those other creatures are thinking. A most prankish combination. So it is time for you to return to Reemon."

"Reemon!" Artemis whispered, happy to hear the word on his mouth again. "But how do I get there?"

"How did you get here?" Xixius asked.

"On the ship that I won in the contest," he replied.

"It knew how to come here," Xixius stated.

Artemis stared at him. "Does it know how to get to Reemon?"

"How would I know?" Xixius asked. "I'm just from a small little race from this galaxy."

Artemis nodded ruefully. "Of course you are."

"However, it seems to me that if the ship brought you here, it must know where else you need to go."

"Will it travel all of that distance?"

"One can only guess, can't one?" Xixius asked him. I think your friend, Mr. Quince, is explaining that to his business associates.

"Well, I guess I'm ready to go," Artemis declared as he turned and headed toward his craft. He stopped and returned, as he noticed that Fido hadn't immediately followed him. Instead the creature stayed close to Xixius, snuffling avidly all around the area. "Fido, aren't you coming along?"

"He's not," Xixius said. "Pheydeaux has other scents that he must follow."

Artemis cast a long look at the creature that had been his companion for many years. "You're sure he has to go on?" he asked Xixius.

"Yes, he has his own ways that he must follow," the Xirom replied. "But, it would do well for you to return to Reemon." He approached Kowana. "You should return with your children." He lightly touched her belly.

"What?" Kowana asked.

"Your children," Xixius nodded affirmation.

"No!" Fran shouted out. She came charging forward, her lips pursed in righteous outrage. "Don't you let that green troublemaker come anywhere near you when you're pregnant," she warned.

"That's all right. I'm not pregnant," Kowana assured her.

"You're not?" Fran asked.

"Yes, we've taken all of the precautions."

Fran nodded her head in dogged resignation. "I remember saying that myself, and on top of that, I was barren. You've taken all the proper contraception and everything, so you're absolutely sure you're safe."

"Yes," Kowana replied. "We can't possibly have a litter."

"A LITTER?" Fran shrieked.

"Yes."

Fran put her hand to her forehead, closed her eyes, and asked quietly, "Tell me, how many do you usually have in a litter?"

"About six. Eight at the most."

Fran stared daggers at Xixius who smiled blithely back at her. "Expect at least a dozen."

"A dozen?" Kowana asked.

"Yes, and they won't be normal. They'll be quite exceptional."

"What?" Kowana asked.

"I know. Believe me, I know. I've got three-year-old triplets. Right now, I don't know where they are. But I'm not afraid for them. I'm afraid of what they might do to somebody else!"

#

The Worst Unknown Assassin sneered down from his perch over the group. He wondered how he could have trusted such oafs to accomplish some of his work for him. They should have spied each other and attacked in response.

There was no helping it; he would have to get rid of these dangerous creatures himself. He brought his weapon to bear on the group below. Since those smaller creatures had displayed the greatest threat, he would destroy them first. He brought his sights down on the female one.

Something blocked his view. Something in the near ground that was masking his target from him. He looked up to discover what it was. It was some imp that had managed to approach him at close quarters without his detecting it. It was one of the young of the creatures down below. How had his detection systems failed? How had this thing gotten here?

His priorities immediately shifted, and he squeezed the trigger on his weapon to vaporize the creature in front of him.

Nothing happened. His weapon had failed. He snatched up one of his numerous backups and tried to rake its blast across the being. That sidearm also failed. Not only that, but all of his weapons, even the organic ones, began to heat up, just as the spacers' had earlier. The heat could be felt through the protective armor that he usually wore.

He leaped back and began shedding the weapons and protective suit. To his horror, he found that there were two more imps, one to each side of him.

He was found! He was undone! He let out an anguished wail. He was in the clutches of his worst enemies. Paranoia laced its way through his nervous system. He raced in blind panic away from the accursed little beings.

The imps, otherwise known as Shar'n, Kar'n, and Aar'n, let the Lonely One run away toward the two Good Guys.

The creature previously known as the Worst Unknown Assassin scrambled away from the imps. Because of his headlong manner of retreat, he failed to think of straightening the jumble of rocks around him. He also failed to notice the two beings sitting on top of those rocks, waiting for him: Holy Men reclined in contemplative poses.

He drew up short in front of them, cursing his antennae for not having picked up these creatures, and quickly dashed toward an avenue of escape. The First Holy Man dropped to all fours and swept his tail out, tripping the assassin. The Second Holy Man leaped with incredible speed and landed on the prone killer and dug the tips of several of his tentacles into the being's skin, injecting calming drugs.

The Second Holy Man understood the need for the soporifics taking effect on his patient. He had needed similar tranquilizers when he had experienced a "failed commercial venture" and been rescued from his death. He spent several months drugged, doing nothing but crying and screaming, "I'm so sorry, Mommy! I'm so sorry, Mommy!"

After he had reached a more tranquil state of mind, his limbs that had been severed in combat were restored, but to the current, far less lethal form. He turned to his compatriot and said, "He is started on his journey to peace, Brother Faaq."

The First Holy Man, Hassmin Faaq, former despot of many worlds, agreed. "We will help him on his trip, Brother Dzo."

The Second Holy Man, Rither Dzo, former scourge of the star lanes, said, "Let us take this time to consider the sunset and continue our journey to inner peace."

So the two Holy Men sat with their new Novitiate and contemplated the sunset.

By serendipity, the direction of their gaze intersected a tiny pinpoint in the flow of stars in the Milky Way. That little glow was a place that had affected a number of visitors present on the planet this day. That place was a construct, an artifact of an ancient race called the Wistrani, the progenitors of the Amalgam of Intelligent Beings. The place was called the StarBoard Café.

THE END

About the Author

Richard Herr has had a varied career as actor, comedian, musician, stage manager, computer graphics expert, and stager of Dog & Pony presentations. He has recently turned his attention to writing comic fantasy novels.

Mr. Herr was born and raised in Rochester, NY. He devoted the first 15 years of his life to becoming a minor league outfielder. Failing that, he looked around for other fields to conquer. He was called to the defense of our nation and, even though he is too humble to brag about his military accomplishments, participated in such campaigns as the Siege of Troy, the Sack of Carthage, and the Annoyance of Cleveland. He achieved a BA at Ithaca College, majoring in Theatre and English. He moved to New York City and launched a career in professional theatre. He acted with various theatre companies across the country, earning the praise of critics and the anger of a lot of local sheriffs. He demonstrated a skill for the technical end of theatre and stage managed several Off-Broadway shows and National companies. His interests moved to the staging of corporate meetings and he formed his own company, AVTS, and has successfully operated the corporation for several decades. He lives in New Jersey, which apparently offers asylum for lame jokes, and has two daughters and four grandchildren.

Prankish Publications

Additional Titles

Dog & Pony
Volume 1
ALOHA
Richard Herr

To find out what's happening at Prankish Publications, go to FaceBook and Friend us at Prankishpublications

Prankish Publications

Additional Titles

Invasion from Fred!
Richard Herr

To find out what's happening at Prankish Publications, go to FaceBook and Friend us at Prankishpublications

CPSIA information can be obtained
at www.ICGtesting.com
Printed in the USA
FFOW03n1312230914
7466FF